No Child of Mine

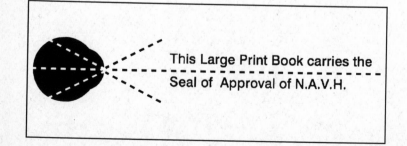

This Large Print Book carries the
Seal of Approval of N.A.V.H.

No Child of Mine

Kelly Irvin

THORNDIKE PRESS
A part of Gale, Cengage Learning

GALE
CENGAGE Learning·

Detroit • New York • San Francisco • New Haven, Conn • Waterville, Maine • London

GALE
CENGAGE Learning®

The publisher bears no responsibility for the quality of information provided through author or third-party websites and does not have any control over, nor assume any responsibility for, information contained in these sites. Providing these sites should not be construed as an endorsement or approval by the publisher of these organizations or of the positions they may take on various issues.
Thorndike Press® Large Print Christian Mystery.
The text of this Large Print edition is unabridged.
Other aspects of the book may vary from the original edition.
Set in 16 pt. Plantin.

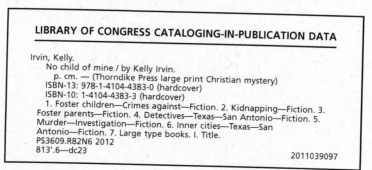

LIBRARY OF CONGRESS CATALOGING-IN-PUBLICATION DATA

Irvin, Kelly.
  No child of mine / by Kelly Irvin.
    p. cm. — (Thorndike Press large print Christian mystery)
  ISBN-13: 978-1-4104-4383-0 (hardcover)
  ISBN-10: 1-4104-4383-3 (hardcover)
  1. Foster children—Crimes against—Fiction. 2. Kidnapping—Fiction. 3. Foster parents—Fiction. 4. Detectives—Texas—San Antonio—Fiction. 5. Murder—Investigation—Fiction. 6. Inner cities—Texas—San Antonio—Fiction. 7. Large type books. I. Title.
  PS3609.R82N6 2012
  813'.6—dc23   2011039097

Published in 2012 by arrangement with Tekno Books.

Printed in Mexico
1 2 3 4 5 6 7 16 15 14 13 12

To Larry Lyne, Jr.
May the deer be plentiful
and the fish always biting.
You were gone too soon,
but never forgotten.

ACKNOWLEDGMENTS

Sometimes the most important thing you can give a friend or loved one is encouragement. My heartfelt thanks go out to a cheering section that started long before the publication of my first novel and has continued ever since. Thanks to my parents Larry and Janice Lyne, parents-in-law Stan and Mary Irvin (especially Mary who peddled my book like a pro). Thanks to Kay Gittinger for personally buying more books than she knew what to do with and convincing others to do the same. Thanks to Eileen Key and the Alamo City Christian Writers for their continuous support through the ups and downs on the road to publication. As always, a special long distance hug to critique partners and friends who make me laugh daily even when I really would rather scream or cry: Peg Brantley, Susan Lohrer, and Angela Mills. It has to be a God thing. How else could four writers spread out from

Canada to Colorado to Texas to Georgia become so close? Thank you for being there. Finally, thanks to my husband Tim and children Erin and Nicholas for putting up with me. You're the best. Love you guys.

CHAPTER ONE

Benny Garza tore down the gravel road like a bunch of gangbangers were chasing him.

He was used to that.

If Mom could see him now, she'd laugh. Always forgetting stuff. Stupid.

As he ran, he bit into the rolled-up tortilla and fajita in his hand, chewed, and tried not to choke. A hawk soaring over the trees caught his gaze. In San Antonio, he never saw stuff like that. He'd like to soar, too. High and far away.

His shoe hit something hard. Benny stumbled, arms flapping like a chicken trying to fly, and fell smack in the middle of the dirt. The taco flew. His nose scraped gravel, and he bit his lip. "Oh, man!"

He rolled into a sitting position, gasping from the sting. He clapped his hands to his face and rocked back and forth, working through the pain. He was used to that, too.

Dirt smeared the white church shirt and

black pants Mr. Daniel had bought him special for the wedding. He tried to brush it off. The stain darkened and spread. "Oh, no, no!"

That's what he got for rushing to get his jeans and tennies from the Jeep. That's what he got for being in a hurry to have fun at the party. Like Mom always said, everything came with a price.

Mr. Daniel might get mad. Sure, he never got real mad like Mom. He didn't yell or hit. He just looked sad, and his voice got soft. Benny's stomach would feel funny then, like he might puke. He didn't want Mr. Daniel to be mad at him. Ever.

Maybe he could ask Marco to show him how to use the washing machine. Maybe he could wash the clothes before Mr. Daniel saw them. Benny struggled to his feet, fighting tears. Eight-year-olds were too old to cry. That's what Mom said. He trudged to Mr. Daniel's Jeep and grabbed his clothes from the back seat.

He turned to shove the door shut. A giant man loomed over him, blocking the sun. He had a big smile plastered across his face. "Hey, buddy."

Benny jerked back. The clothes fell to the ground. "Who're you?" He started to squat and pick up his stuff. Something about the man's face made him stop.

He crossed his arms and tried to look tough. "If you want the wedding party, it's up by the house."

The guy took one step forward. "You don't remember me?"

Benny took one step back. The guy had a flat nose with a scar across it and blue eyes in a brown face. That face would stick in your mind. "I don't think so, sir." Mr. Daniel had taught him to say that. "Sir" and "Ma'am" were how you were supposed to talk to old people.

"Sir?" The guy laughed, a pig snort. His face crinkled up in a messy grin. One front tooth had a gold cap on it. "I'm a friend of *tu mama*. She told me to come get you."

That couldn't be right. "My mom's in prison."

The man wiped sweat from his forehead with the back of one hand. His fingernails had black stuff under them. That hand balled up in a fist would leave bruises. "Didn't Daniel Martinez tell you she was getting out?"

Benny took another step back and hit hard metal. He was wedged against the Jeep door. "No. He says she don't get out for a long time, like two or three years."

"Your friend is lying."

11

Anger swirled around in Benny's stomach. Followed by bigger waves of uncertainty. He wanted to hurl. That was the thing about grownups. He could never be sure with them. "No. Mr. Daniel, he don't lie." He sniffed hard. "He takes care of me."

"Maybe he don't want your mama to have you back."

That would be nice. It might make him bad, but Benny didn't want his mom back. He liked not having to worry about her being drunk and smacking him around. But Mr. Daniel had always been straight with him. Mom would get out of jail someday, and he would live with her again. "If she's out, how come she didn't come get me herself?"

"She's afraid of Martinez. She says he has a gun and he'll use it to keep her from getting you back."

Mr. Daniel did have a gun. Benny watched him lock it in a gun safe every day when he came home from work. "Mr. Daniel wouldn't hurt nobody. He told me she would be coming back sometime. He knows she's my mom. He says that's the law."

"I'm telling you, she's waiting for you at my place. Bought you a new video game and everything."

Mom never bought him a video game.

12

She'd never bought him anything.

Benny ducked his head and bulldozed forward. The man grabbed him and swung his body around. A thick arm choked Benny around the waist like a too tight belt. A sweaty palm covered his mouth, its nasty, sweet smell filling his nose.

He kicked and twisted, but his feet didn't touch the ground anymore. The man hauled him to a beat-up car the color of butterscotch pudding parked behind a monster SUV. The trunk lid popped up. "No! No!" Benny screamed, but the sounds were muffled against the man's big palm. Benny threw his arms back. His hand connected with skin and teeth. The man's grip loosened. He cussed in Benny's ear.

Benny kicked harder. The heel of his church shoe connected with a leg. More cuss words. He jammed his hand in a pocket, searching for something, anything that would help. His fingers closed around a handful of marbles. The marbles Mr. Daniel had let him pick out at the store last week. He let two drop.

The man tossed him into the trunk. "Scream and I'll kill you right now." His hand mashed Benny's mouth and nose. "You understand? I don't need you alive to make this work. *¿Entiendes?*"

Benny nodded. The hand pressed harder. It squashed his nose until he couldn't contain the whimper of pain. "Please, sir, *señor, por favor . . .*"

"Shut up!" The man used his teeth to rip a piece of tape from a huge gray roll. He slapped it over Benny's mouth. His lips were mashed together, trapping the air in his chest. His wrists were next, the tape so tight he thought his bones might break.

The man's wide, bloodshot eyes stared as he ripped off more tape and wrapped it around Benny's ankles. His breath coming in noisy blasts. The smell made Benny want to throw up. It mixed with the odor of oil and gas. He tried to cough and strangled on his own gagging. Shudders shook his body.

The man straightened, slapped his hand on the trunk lid, and grinned. "Enjoy the ride, *m'ijo.*"

The trunk lid slammed shut.

CHAPTER TWO

Shielding her eyes from the sun with one hand, Deborah Smith fanned herself with a wedding program. For early October, the air felt warm and humid, but still it was a beautiful day for a wedding. She gave up, tossed her gum in the trash, and snagged a plastic cup of foamy punch from the buffet table set up in the massive field that passed as her partner's front yard. Her throat ached for something stronger.

Deborah sipped the punch and concentrated on the cool, sweet wetness. Perfect. No need for anything else. Not even a cigarette. She'd just keep telling herself that.

She turned her back on the tables laden with food and studied Ray and his new wife, Susana. He had one arm draped around her shoulders. A grin lit up his face. The two stood on the front porch of his stone house, surrounded by well-wishers who'd crowded them since they'd arrived at the ranch in a rented Cadillac courtesy of one of Susana's many uncles.

A shot of tequila. Just enough to take the edge off. One cigarette. Deborah turned and snatched a raw carrot from a vegetable tray. She chomped on it and chewed. *God, help me overcome my weaknesses, please!* One day, one hour, one minute at a time. Her parched throat ached with a thirst punch could never quench.

"Detective Smith! Where's *Tío* Daniel? Have you seen him?" Marco Acosta, Susana's son, barreled toward her. "I need *Tío.*"

Deborah held her cup high and grabbed his arm with her other hand. "Whoa! Slow down, kiddo. What's the problem?"

The boy plowed to a stop just short of toppling a table. "I can't find Benny. He's gone!"

"Well, I saw your uncle . . ." Deborah scanned the crowd. The object of her scrutiny stood talking to his wife. The tense set of his shoulders and the way he held his head said things were not going well with Nicole. As usual. His gaze caught Deborah's. She jerked her head. He backed away from Nicole. His wife threw her hands in the air. He turned his back on her.

Deborah tried to focus on the boy in front of her. His dark curls were damp with sweat, and his agitation showed in the red spots that darkened his brown cheeks. He danced around her like a nervous puppy about to make a puddle on the carpet.

She couldn't help herself. Her gaze slid back to Daniel. She watched him stride across the yard. He had a runner's body. Stop it. Married man. Not happily married, but married nonetheless. Daniel gave new meaning to the phrase *until death do us part.* He'd been fighting a divorce forever. He reminded Deborah of a moth flying too close to the candle, getting its wings singed over and over.

"What's up?" His attempt at a smile didn't reach his coffee-colored eyes. "Is my *sobrino* giving you a hard time?"

"Is everything all right with your wife?" Deborah shoved her hair behind an ear and ducked her head. "Sorry, it's none of my business."

"Don't worry about it. Nothing's changed. I just thought that since she came today, we were . . ." His voice trailed off. "Anyway, what's going on, Marco?"

Marco squatted and retied a tattered sneaker. "Benny forgot his clothes in your car, so he went to get them." He sounded miffed at his foster cousin's behavior. "He never came back. I waited like fifteen minutes or an hour."

Daniel winked at Deborah, his expression lighter. "Knowing Benny, he's out there trying to pet a skunk."

"No. No." Marco popped up like a kid who'd had one too many juice boxes. "I went to look for him. The door to your car is open. His clothes are on the ground, but he isn't there."

"I'm sure he's fine, but maybe we should go track him down." Deborah stuck the carrot stick in her cup and tossed it in the trash can. A quick search would give her something to do until she'd been at the reception long enough to leave graciously. "I'm not doing anything else."

"That's your fault —"

A hand touched her back. She whirled. "Hey! No touching!"

"It's just me." Alex Luna stepped back, both hands in the air. "I didn't mean to startle you. I was just saying if you hadn't turned me down, you would've had a date for this shindig. With plenty of sparkling conversation."

"I don't date police officers, especially ones I work with." The excuse came easy. The truth was Alex's occupation had nothing to do with her reluctance. The thought that she might somehow have to reciprocate

18

his obvious interest made her heart ditch its regular routine. She stuck two more pieces of gum in her mouth. "Let's find Benny so Marco can stop worrying."

"Benny's missing?" Alex, ever the cop, practically stood at attention. "How long?"

"We gotta find him." Marco waved toward the road. "Come on, this way! Hurry!"

Alex moved to Deborah's side. "A search party. Now that's my idea of a party game. Perfect for a law enforcement theme."

"I doubt it'll take all four of us." Deborah quickened her step so she was even with Daniel and Marco. Alex kept pace with her, not taking the hint. His nearness made her feel off balance. It seemed as if the only way she could deal with men was professionally or drunk. Sober and in social situations, she hadn't a clue.

She was thirty-one. Damaged goods. Too old to be healed. She would never have a normal relationship with a man. The thought churned inside her.

Just one drink.

Daniel studied the line of vehicles that stretched about a mile along the dirt road that led to Ray's house. He'd parked the Cherokee nearly halfway to the highway, to give the vast bevy of older aunts and uncles *y sus familias* closer access to the house. The back passenger-side door stood open a crack. Benny's clothes and tennis shoes lay scattered on the ground.

It didn't mean a thing. Benny might have seen a raccoon or an armadillo and run after it without giving the open door or his errand a second thought. Animals he'd never seen in the city fascinated him.

On the road, just before the vehicle, footprints marred a patch of dirt. Flies buzzed around a piece of fajita meat and a half-eaten tortilla.

Benny had an insatiable appetite.

Daniel rubbed his temple, trying to assuage a headache that had shadowed him for two days. He glanced at Deborah and Alex. Their expressions mirrored his concern. "Benny! Benny, where are you?"

No answer.

Maybe he'd fallen and gotten his clothes dirty. He'd be afraid that Daniel would get mad. Had he run away rather than face Daniel? Surely not. He tried never to show Benny anger. The child shut down at the first sign of it.

Daniel studied the tall grass and straggly live oaks that lined the road. "Benny, come on. You're going to miss the cake!"

No answer.

"See. He's not here." Marco plucked at Daniel's sleeve. "Where'd he go?"

Daniel squatted next to him. "He has to be around here somewhere. He couldn't sleep last night, with all the excitement. Maybe he lay down somewhere and zonked out."

Marco frowned. "Ray said we could feed the horses carrots after we changed. He wouldn't sleep before that."

"He was very tired." Daniel tried to keep his tone light. Marco was right. The horses fascinated Benny. He'd never seen a real one before coming to stay with Daniel. "Deborah, why don't you and Alex take a look around the barn and the outbuildings? Marco and I'll walk toward the highway, see if Benny took off after a possum or something."

For a second Deborah looked as if she might object, but then she shrugged and started in the direction of the barn. Daniel didn't try to fathom the grin on Alex's face as he strode after her.

"Let's go!" Marco started toward the long line of cars.

"First I want to look around here." Daniel opened the hatch and tugged forward a large toolbox. Sweat formed above his dress shirt collar. Nausea built to a crescendo.

21

He'd been fighting the flu that had been going around at the federal building for three days, but he couldn't miss Susana's wedding. "Benny! Benny, where are you? Answer me. Come on, buddy, you're not in trouble."

Still nothing. Marco shifted from one foot to the other. "He's not here, *Tío.* I told you, I called him already. He didn't answer."

"He might've been sleeping and not heard you." He turned his back on Marco and grabbed a pair of gloves from the toolbox that served as his evidence kit. He slapped them on, snapping the fingers.

As an investigator for the U.S. Attorney's Office, Daniel was trained to work worst-case scenarios. Bad stuff happened to people all the time. He never kidded himself that it couldn't or wouldn't happen to the people he loved.

With missing people, every second counted. This could be a case of a messy little boy leaving his stuff all over the ground and running off to play. Or simply running away. Daniel had seen no signs of that coming. Benny had actually seemed happy today, acting like a normal kid.

The other alternative gnawed at him. Somebody had snatched Benny. If it were the latter, this was a crime scene. Technically, it belonged to the Bexar County Sheriff's Office, but he could have a quick look around.

Knowing Marco was watching him, Daniel kept his expression neutral. Using a flashlight, he examined the front seat. Nothing. No apparent blood.

He examined the clothes on the ground. Marco immediately knelt next to him. Again, nothing that appeared to be blood. Together, they studied the grass and the stunted bushes. The road itself was hard as concrete. Even in the fall, San Antonio heat baked the earth every afternoon.

He stared at the cars. Only one spot stood open in the line. A wet patch of oil represented the only obvious sign a car had been parked there. Someone had gone home before the party had started. He studied the ground inch by inch. Something shiny and round caught his gaze.

"That's a marble." Marco dropped to his knees. "Oh, man, his marbles, *Tío*."

He reached for them. Daniel grabbed his arm. "No, *m'ijito,* let me."

Using a pen, he tapped them into a small paper bag and sealed the top. For some reason Daniel couldn't understand, Benny loved those old-fashioned marbles. He had a little bag of them when Daniel had picked him up from the Child Protective Services facility after his mother's arrest. The only plaything he'd brought with him. Recently, Daniel had bought him more to add to his collection. "These could've been out there for days. They don't have to be Benny's."

His face doubtful, Marco touched the dirt where the marbles had rested. Daniel's voice sounded tepid in his own ears. His immediate family — now Ray's family, too — included at least a dozen kids who'd traipsed all over the ranch in the weeks leading up to today's wedding festivities. "Let's walk down the road. If we don't find him in five minutes, we'll call Ray, *Tío* Samuel, and the others."

Marco, straightened, the doubt replaced with excitement. "For a search party?"

"Yeah, a search party." No way someone would snatch a kid in broad daylight at a wedding reception where half the guests were in law enforcement.

No way.

"Why don't you like me?"

Deborah looked up to find Alex staring at her, his head tilted, the expression on his plain face puzzled. He slipped from behind a huge tractor tire in the back of a shed and crowded her. Flecks of gold stood out in his

24

amber eyes under a dark fringe of thick eyelashes.

She forced herself to study the crunchy hay underfoot. "What are you talking about? If you have a cigarette on you right now, I might even love you." Snapping her gum, she examined a stack of empty crates against the opposite wall. "Benny, Benny, come on, kiddo, wherever you are, come out now."

"Sorry. I gave up smoking about a year ago. Do I have a disease or something?" If she hadn't known better, Deborah would've said he sounded hurt. When she'd still been drinking, they'd seen each other plenty at parties. He never lacked a date. "I'm not buying the cop excuse. Why won't you go out with me? Did I do something to offend you?"

"I don't even know you."

"Yes, you do." Alex touched her arm for a split second and then let his hand drop. "I heard you got on the wagon. I'm rooting for you."

A chill revved up her arm. She swallowed against sudden nausea. As a homicide detective and Ray's friend, Alex knew all the gory details about what had happened in the past five months. The car dealership bust and Ray almost getting killed in a four-vehicle pileup. Her attempt to get her life straight, once and for all. "Thanks. One day at a time."

His full lips pursed, he squinted at her. "We could all use a little clean living."

"You want to search for Benny or dissect my drinking problem?" Something about the way he stared at her bothered her. Like he sought an answer to an unspoken question.

"Look for Benny." His response was quick, his tone reassuring. "I just wanted you to know that if you ever wanted someone to hang with, no strings attached, I'm available. It doesn't have to be a date. I promise I won't bite."

A grin flitted across his face, disappeared. "Let's take a look at that last shed out there and then go find Daniel and Marco. They've probably rounded up Benny and headed back to the reception."

Relief coursed through her, feeling strangely like dry heaves. Soon she could leave and escape all these churning emotions. "You're right. Let's go."

The closest liquor store was in Helotes.

She needed to call Omar. Her AA sponsor would shake her out of this funk.

Never mind that Alex stood next to her and he'd offered.

Fighting the tall grass, she rushed toward

an even older shed with a padlock on the door that had rusted deep red-brown with age. No way Benny had gotten in there. Deborah scanned the horizon. No little boy. She glanced at her watch. Alex was right. They should meet up with Daniel. He'd probably already found Benny, given him a good lecture about wandering off, and gone back for wedding cake.

Her heels sank into some loose clods of dirt.

A skeletal arm stuck up through the dirt. A small, bony hand waved at her.

She jerked back a step. Too late.

She stood on the edge of a shallow grave. "Alex!"

He moved closer. His gaze followed her pointing finger. The sick look that slid across his features told her when he understood.

"A body?" He knelt next to the patch of uneven ground. "A skeleton!"

CHAPTER THREE

Daniel shifted from one foot to the other. He shaded his eyes from the sun beginning to drop toward the western horizon. He wanted to interrupt, but Bexar County Sheriff's Detective Nash Cooper could only do so much at one time. The location of Ray's ranch in the county made Benny's disappearance the sheriff's business. Irritation, like an annoying mosquito, buzzed in Daniel's ears. All these police officers here for the wedding reception and not one of them had jurisdiction. Cooper insisted on quizzing Ray about a skeleton that had probably been on the property for years. With Benny missing. Maybe hurt or dead. The living should be the priority. *If* Benny were still living. "Detective —"

Cooper held up a hand. "Be with you in a minute, Mr. Martinez." His eyes were kind, but his tone firm. He turned back to Ray.

"So how long have you owned this property?"

"About five years, I guess." Ray's gaze strayed to the medical examiner's investigator, Tito Sanchez, who bent over the skeletal remains.

"And you've never worked the land?"

"I just have the vegetable garden and the xeriscape up by the house. I'm not much of a farmer —"

"What are you trying to get at, Detective?" Ray's neighbor Maddy Stover broke in. She stood next to Alex, her hands on her hips. "What exactly are you insinuating? I've lived next door to Raymond for five years. If he says he's never worked this piece of his property, then he hasn't."

"M, will you hush, please? Coop's just doing his job." Ray's face flushed red.

Detective Cooper's patient facade didn't change. "I understand your concern, Mrs. Stover, and I apologize for any inconvenience." He glanced at the notebook in his hand. "Who'd you buy the property from, Ray?"

"It was an estate sale. The owner died, and his son in California sold it to me. A family leased the property when I purchased it. They had first option but declined and moved out a couple of weeks before I took possession."

"You have paperwork on all that?"

"Sure — up at the house."

"I'd like to see it later, if you don't mind." Cooper turned back to the makeshift grave.

"Detective." Daniel gritted his teeth. "Please."

Cooper faced Daniel. "Look, Mr. Martinez, we've got every available body, including your family, out there looking for your foster son. By dark they'll have been through every nook and cranny of this property. For right now, I need to focus on these remains."

Daniel stuck a hand on the rough bark of a juniper. "Right."

Cooper knelt next to Sanchez, who brushed dirt from bones with a light touch. "An animal dug it up?"

"I imagine you're right about that." Sanchez held up a set of pink barrettes for a few seconds before dropping them into a bag. "Rain, wind, time gradually uncovered it until some animal got hold of her."

Ray looked like he might be sick. "It's a little girl who's been here the whole time I've lived on the ranch?"

"The length of the sternum, the shape of the pelvis, and the size of the skull support the fact that this was a female child," Sanchez said. "As far as the timeline, you're going to have to be patient."

Most of the small skeleton lay exposed. Daniel leaned on the tree and crossed his arms, fighting the desire to hit something. A natural sense of decency made him want to cover the remains as he would a body. Tattered, faded cloth draped the bones. Blue denim with overall buckles and a faded shirt that might have been red once. A little girl out here all alone. No marker. No visitors. As if she had no one who missed her or cared she was gone. "You can't give us any idea how long she's been out here?"

"Eventually, yes." Sanchez continued to brush dirt from bones with a short, precise stroke.

Cooper leaned in closer. "Any signs of how she died?"

"The back of her skull was crushed with a blunt object. We'll know more when we get her back to the lab." Sanchez dropped the brush into a container next to his feet and rose.

"She was hit with something?"

"Or she fell and hit the back of her head. Like I said, we'll know more after we get her back to my place."

"Daniel!"

He looked back. His brother Samuel strode toward him, Daniel's pulse jerked, and a wave of apprehension drowned him. He straightened, ready to move. "Anything?"

"No, sorry, nothing yet."

Daniel sank against the tree again. "He's not here anymore."

Cooper looked up from wiping his hands on a white handkerchief. "What makes you say that?"

Daniel tugged the sack from his pocket and held it open so Cooper could see the contents. "I bought Benny some marbles last week. I found these on the road."

"So he dropped them."

"You don't understand. No one ever gave this kid anything." Daniel's voice sounded thick in his own ears. He swallowed, trying to corral his emotions. "Benny wouldn't part with them unless he was desperate. He wanted us to find them. A car left before we got out there. There was one space open in the entire line. Someone was parked there and left — right where I found these."

"Easy, Danny, give the guy a chance. Detective Cooper is just getting started." Samuel shook hands with Cooper and introduced himself. "We've just come back from scouring the perimeter. No sign of Benny."

Cooper shoved his Stetson back on his

forehead. "I appreciate your help. Obviously we're stretched a little thin here. Mr. Martinez — Daniel, did you get the photo of the boy?"

Daniel handed over the snapshot, trying not to look at Benny's broad grin. He'd just made a game-winning catch. His curly brown hair was a mess, and his face was dirty, but he looked ecstatic.

"You say he's eight? Kinda small for his age, isn't he?"

"Yeah, he's a little undersized. I imagine from being malnourished." Daniel tried not to sound defensive. "He eats like a horse, but he can't seem to get caught up."

He gazed at the tree line in the distance for a few seconds. "Look, Detective Cooper, if y'all don't move fast on this, Benny could end up in a grave just like this one."

Cooper opened his mouth, but before he could speak Phoebe's high-pitched voice carried over the expanse between the main house and the shed. Daniel turned to see his daughter dart across the field, her long, thin legs pumping.

"Dad!" Panting, she stumbled through the knot of people to Daniel. "Dad, Aunt Susana says come quick. A guy's on the phone — he says he has Benny."

CHAPTER FOUR

Daniel sprinted to the house, weaving through wedding guests who danced out of his way, their mouths open in wide Os of surprise. The pounding sound behind him said the others followed. A cluster of relatives on the porch stood frozen, punch glasses in their hands, their gazes pinned to him as Daniel climbed the steps two at a time.

"It's him," Susana met Daniel at the door. She thrust the phone at him. "Whoever he is, he says he has Benny."

"Who is this?" Daniel gasped into the receiver. "What do you want with Benny?"

"Daniel Martinez?"

"Yes. What have you done with Benny?"

"Benny's gonna help me out with a little project of mine." A south side cadence rang in the caller's voice. "Benny has connections."

"What project? What connections? He's

34

eight. He can't help you with anything."
Daniel tilted the receiver away from his ear
so Samuel could hear.

"Sure, he can. Benny may only be eight,
but he's experienced." The man laughed, a
cackling sound that sent a chill through
Daniel. "Very experienced. His mama made
sure of it. I bet Benny hasn't shared all his
skills with you."

"His mother? How do you know Shawna?"
Daniel glanced at Samuel who nodded and
mouthed *get him to talk.* "What does this
have to do with her?"

"We were business associates."

Drug dealer and/or gangbanger. The
punch Daniel drank earlier burned the back
of his throat. "She's in jail. Kidnapping
Benny won't change that."

"She's got something I want. Me and her
have visited a few times in that nice prison.
She won't give me what's mine. So, now,
I've got something that belongs to her."

"Let me talk to Benny."

The guy chuckled, an eerie, disembodied
sound that lingered over the line. "Sure."

Quiet reigned for a second, and then the
sound of the receiver banging against something reverberated. Finally, Daniel heard a
whisper. "Mr. Daniel?"

"Benny, are you all right — did he hurt

you?" The pressure of Samuel's hand on his arm kept Daniel upright. "Do you know where you are?"

"I wanna come home. Can you come get me? Please." The boy's voice was tight, but steady. "Please."

"Benny, where —"

Muffled noises and the other voice was back. "He's right here with me, snug as a bug."

The man uttered a soft laugh that made the words sound dirty.

"You hurt him, and I'll —"

"You'll what? You want the kid back? Shut up and listen."

Daniel's fingers ached. He tried to loosen his hold on the receiver. "Talk to me. Just don't hurt him."

"I'm in sales. Before Miss Shawna went off to jail, she was holding some product for me. Now she's forgotten that product ain't hers. I got that product from my employer. He wants to be reimbursed. Now I'm in a fix. You make her tell you where my product is. You get it for me. We can do a little business. Know what I'm saying, *ese?*"

Anger coursed through Daniel. This was about drugs. A little boy sucked back into his mother's world even after she'd been found guilty and incarcerated for her illegal

36

activities. "You want to exchange drugs for Benny?"

"I never said it was no drugs."

The image of Shawna Garza glaring at him across the courtroom assailed Daniel. "What makes you think Shawna Garza will cooperate with me? It was my tip that ended up putting her in jail."

"That's your problem, ain't it? It's true Shawna baby ain't too happy with you. She knows you turned her into CPS. She knows you tipped off the narcotics guys. You better be real nice to her from now on."

"So I get Shawna to tell me where the dr — the product is and you return Benny?"

"Not exactly. Today's Saturday. You deliver the product to me Monday morning. I'll call you with details. If you don't want to fish the body of a dead kid out of the river, you better get busy."

"What —" The connection died before he could finish the question. What time? Where? He sank onto the couch and dropped the phone on the coffee table.

"You did good, *hermano*." Samuel sat down next to him. "You kept him talking. We know quite a bit."

"*Tío* Daniel, are you gonna get him back?" Marco broke away from his Aunt Piper's hold and lunged across the room. "When is he coming home?"

Daniel wrapped his arms around the boy in a tight hug, letting him bury his head in his shirt. "We will. Soon." He felt a shudder go through Marco's body. He held the boy away from him in a firm grip. "Look at me. We'll get him back. I promise."

Marco took a swipe at his face with the sleeve of his T-shirt. "I know you will, *Tío*, you and *Tío* Samuel are the best!"

"Marco, let's go get your uncle some water." Susana headed toward the door. Daniel knew she wanted to spare her son the gory details of the call that would now be dissected in infinitesimal detail by the officers in the room. "Come on, I need your help."

Marco heaved a sigh and followed his mother.

Detective Cooper eased into a chair, removed his Stetson, and laid it on the coffee table that separated them. "I take it drugs are involved?"

Daniel nodded and ran through what the kidnapper had said.

His gaze steely, Cooper contemplated his steepled fingers for a second. "Can you get the narcotics people involved who were in on Shawna Garza's prosecution?"

"I'll handle that." Samuel was a homicide

sergeant with years of experience and connections. He would run this show even if Cooper believed he was in charge.

Daniel studied the hardwood floor under his feet. "The guy sounded like a pervert."

"He was pulling your chain." Deborah sat down in the rocking chair next to Cooper's. "He wants you to be scared."

"He's got me right where he wants me." Daniel leaned back and sucked in air through the steady pounding like a hammer striking his temples. "I don't know if Shawna Garza will cooperate with us, even to get Benny back. Like the guy said, she doesn't like me much."

"With her child's life at stake, surely she'll want to do whatever she can."

Deborah didn't know Shawna. Daniel did. "I went to see her about a month ago."

Samuel's shaggy eyebrows cocked. "Why?"

"To try to get her to give up her parental rights so I can adopt Benny."

The screen door slammed.

His wife marched through the door from the foyer, their children trailing behind her. Nicole stared at Daniel, the jut of her jaw telling him she'd heard his statement. Phoebe bit her bottom lip as if trying not to cry, and Christopher had the usual studied indifference on his face. Before Nicole could say anything, Daniel went on. "I told Shawna I wanted to adopt Benny. She laughed in my face. She never took care of Benny when she had him, but he's still her son. Why make me — ?"

"Figures." Phoebe whirled and flounced down the hallway.

Christopher's gaze slid around the room and then came back to Daniel. "I don't get it. We get to stay with you every other weekend. Benny will live with you all the time? No fair."

"I want us all to live —"

"Now's not the time," Nicole interrupted. She glanced around the room. "We'll discuss it later — in private."

The room was quiet for a second. Daniel stared at Nicole, willing her to understand. She stared back. He dropped his gaze. She was right. Now was not the time. Later, he'd make her understand. Make the kids understand. Right now, Benny had to come first.

"Has Benny been to see her?" Samuel broke the silence.

"Several times. He didn't want to go."

"How'd he seem afterward?" Susana was always the counselor. She stood in the doorway, carrying a tray with coffee and bottled water on it. Marco grabbed a bottle, trotted over to Daniel, and handed it to him. He patted Daniel's back with his free hand.

"Thanks." His throat tightened at Marco's attempt to comfort him. "He seemed quiet. Obedient. Like he was scared I'd send him back to her permanently."

"He knows you can't do that, right?"

"He knows." Daniel drank from the bottle, trying to swallow his panic. "But he also has learned to never depend on an adult to tell him the truth. He's had so many promises broken, believed so many lies, he's never sure if he can trust anybody."

"What do you think the guy meant about Benny having special skills?"

"I've always suspected Shawna used him in her business. Maybe as a runner. Had him making deliveries on his bike. She did a lot of sales to kids, punks on the street."

"Maybe Shawna is in on it, and she's looking to punish you," Deborah said.

"Possibly. We need to connect the dots between the kidnapper and Shawna Garza," Samuel agreed. "We have to get in to see her. We also need to contact the CPS worker who handles Benny's case. Let's get moving."

"Shawna had gang connections, didn't she?" Joaquin Santos pushed away from the stone fireplace mantel, his sleeping son in his arms. "I can run with that connection. Get me some names, and we can go rattle some cages."

Daniel felt the vise around his throat ease a little. He had the best possible combination on his side — family, friends, and law enforcement. His brother-in-law served on a multi-agency gang taskforce. With Joaquin, Deborah, Ray, Samuel, and Alex, it was a formidable team. The kidnapper had no idea how formidable. "She never admitted to a gang affiliation, but she had to have connections to run her business in that area. It's Latin Kings territory."

"The kidnapping happened in the county. Sheriff's office has first dibs," Ray pointed out. "Coop, what do you want to do?"

Cooper stood. "I'll discuss forming a task-force with my boss. We're shorthanded and your support makes sense. But the BCSO takes the lead. I'll go see Shawna Garza as soon as possible. Most likely she can tell us who this guy is, where he hangs. We can snatch him before Monday."

"If he thought she would do that, he'd never have grabbed Benny," Daniel objected. "He knows her. For some reason, she won't give him up."

"Yeah, but he visited her. There'll be

records of who her visitors were," Ray said. "We need to get —"

"You nothing. Maddy's driving you to the hotel and tomorrow morning you're flying out on your honeymoon," Daniel interrupted. "Did you forget? This is your wedding day."

"We can't leave." Susana planted feet clad in the red cowboy boots she'd worn under her wedding dress. "Not until we get Benny back."

Ray wrapped both arms around his bride. "Susana's right. You think we could enjoy a honeymoon knowing you're back here trying to save Benny's life? Besides, we have skeletal remains in our backyard that Coop seems to think I might have buried. He won't let me skip town right now."

Silence filled the room.

They'd acknowledged that Benny might not come out of this alive.

Marco leaned his head against Daniel's shoulder and sobbed.

"Fine." Daniel hugged Marco. "But you and Susana go to the hotel tonight. You stay in your honeymoon suite. I'm not letting this guy take your wedding night away from you. We'll stay here with Marco as planned."

"No problem." Ray spoke first. "Sounds like a good plan."

"Sergeant Martinez, why don't you make the announcement to your friends and family out there that we'll be interviewing them all?" Detective Cooper slapped his hat on his head. "We'll try not to inconvenience them any longer than necessary."

Samuel moved toward the door. "*Mis primos* won't mind staying at all. There's still plenty of food. We planned to have the band play all evening anyway."

"We can use the dining room and kitchen for interviews — keep the living room as a base of operations," Ray added. "I'll let the catering people know."

Everyone began to disperse. Daniel realized he was about to be sick. He swallowed hard. No good. "I'm right behind you guys — I'll be right there."

He turned and dashed down the hallway to the guest bathroom.

Punch and water were the only things in his stomach. He was rinsing his mouth, furious with himself, when someone tapped on the door.

"Daniel!"

Nicole. Daniel toweled his face and stared at the mirror. He'd faced down plenty of bad guys over the years. Yet, he hesitated to open the door to his own wife. "Yeah."

"Are you all right?"

He opened the door. "I'm fine."

"We need to talk." She frowned. Her hand flittered up as if to touch his face, then dropped. "You look . . . sick. Is it just Benny or —"

"What do you mean, just Benny? Benny is very important —"

"I didn't mean that. Are you . . . physically sick?"

"I'm fine."

"I've been married to you for sixteen years. I know when you're sick." She planted two long, slim fingers on his forehead. He shivered at her touch. "I thought so. You're burning up. You have a fever."

A kind of relief surged through him. If he were sick, he didn't have to be so embarrassed. "It's nothing."

"You need to lie down. I'll get you some Tylenol and make you some soup."

"No. I'm not lying down. Not with Benny out there." Daniel stopped. "And since when do you care if I'm sick? You kicked me out of my own house a year ago."

Nicole's creamy complexion stained red. "I'm trying to help you, Daniel. But that's your problem. You never want help. Least of all from me."

She turned to go. Daniel grabbed her

wrist. She glanced back, her breathing ragged.

"No soup, but I'll take the Tylenol."

She jerked her arm free. Their gazes battled. "We need to talk. Soon."

"Soon. I have to find Benny first." He headed toward the door.

"Where are you going?"

"To get my gun."

CHAPTER FIVE

"Please don't put the tape back on my mouth. Please." Benny cringed. The man loomed over him. Benny wasn't a crybaby. "I won't scream. I promise."

The man stared at Benny like he couldn't decide. "You hungry?"

Benny nodded. He was scared, but he was always hungry.

The man scratched his ear and then moved on to his armpit. He didn't seem to know what he wanted to do. Benny snuck a peek around the room. Old furniture, trash, newspapers, and the smell of cigarettes. It reminded him of home — his home, not the place he'd been staying with Mr. Daniel. Benny concentrated on remembering Mr. Daniel's voice on the other end of the line. Mr. Daniel would come for him.

His hands had gone numb from the tape. Still, he felt better than when he was in the trunk. It smelled like mold in there. And his head kept smacking against something hard and sharp every time the car hit a bump. They'd driven a long time, but the sun was still up when the guy pulled him from the trunk and so bright he'd squeezed his eyes shut again. He had been so afraid, even more afraid than when his mom had been drunk and mad.

Mr. Daniel had sounded afraid, too. Mr. Daniel was never scared. He was like a cop, but without the uniform. Benny had seen his gun. He had wanted to ask about it, maybe get to hold it, but Mr. Daniel always put it away in a safe first thing when he came home every night.

Benny wished he had a gun now. His mom had one. Sometimes she let him hold it. Once she'd let him put the bullets in it. Then she'd held it to his head and told him he'd better do a real good job washing the dishes. She'd laughed like she'd made a funny joke.

The man had a gun stuck in the waistband of his jeans.

Without any warning, the man picked Benny up, hauled him into the kitchen, and dropped him on a chair. "You sit there like a good boy. Don't make no noise, and I won't have to stick you back in the closet."

Benny nodded. The man pulled a package

of wieners from the refrigerator. "You like hotdogs, boy?"

Benny nodded again.

"Me, too. We gonna have us some wieners. I even got some buns. And some mustard. Gotta have mustard, right?" The man dumped the hot dogs on a paper plate and stuck them in the microwave.

Benny's mouth felt too dry to talk. The man would have to take the tape from his hands so he could eat. Maybe then he'd have a chance. Maybe he could run away. Run where? Where was he? He looked around. The kitchen seemed small. Everything looked old. The floor had scratches on it. Dirty dishes and newspapers covered the table.

Through a window over the sink, Benny saw tree branches blowing in the wind. The kitchen was in the back of the house. Shouldn't there be a back door? He couldn't tell from where he sat.

The microwave dinged and Benny jumped.

The man didn't seem to notice. "You want ketchup?"

"Yes, sir."

"So, son, tell me, you miss *tu mama?*"

Benny squirmed in the chair. "Sometimes."

"You been to see her."

"Yes, sir." Every time, he'd lain awake the night before, tossing and turning.

"When?"

"It's been a while." He'd told Mr. Daniel he didn't want to go anymore, but Mr. Daniel said his mom needed to see him. Still, the visits hadn't been so close after that.

"What you two talk about?"

"She asked me about school and about where I was living, how I liked it." It had been hard for him to talk to her in that big room with all those other moms talking to their kids. The noise hurt his ears. A baby cried, and a little kid screamed when they made him leave his mommy. The guard kept staring at him like he thought Benny would try to bust his mom out. The place had smelled like baby throw-up and poop.

The man turned from the stove and drilled Benny with a look. "She don't talk business?"

"Business?"

"You know about business. You helped *tu mama,* didn't you?"

"A little, I guess. I rode my bike and dropped stuff off for her when her car broke down and we didn't have no money to fix it."

"Dropped off stuff. You mean the crack, right?"

"It wasn't crack."

"Don't play dumb, boy. It was drugs and you know it." The man dropped a hotdog on a bun and threw it on a paper plate. He slapped the plate in front of Benny and a second later, added a can of grape soda. Then he pulled a long knife from a wooden block on the counter and leaned over Benny with a weird little smile on his face. He waved the knife around in the air, then ran his finger along the edge. He chuckled.

He slid the blade between Benny's wrists and the tape. "Sharp, ain't it?"

Benny tore his gaze from the man's face and focused on the blade. *Don't move. Don't move.* He felt the cool metal slide along his skin. A sob burbled up in his throat.

The man cut the tape with a jerk. "Ain't got no chips. Have to make do."

"That's okay." Benny swallowed another hiccupping sob and sank against the chair. He grabbed the hotdog, his mouth watering. He froze. His hands were black with dirt and grease. Mr. Daniel always made Benny wash his hands before he ate, even if they didn't look dirty. The man wasn't going to let him wash up, and he was awful hungry.

51

His gaze dropped from his hands to the black, oily patches on his pants. Something from the trunk of the car had stained his church pants. One of the knees had a rip in it. Mr. Daniel would have to buy a new pair. Pants cost a lot of money.

When Mr. Daniel found Benny, he might send him back. A sob rumbled up inside Benny. *Stop it.* He wasn't a baby. He bit into the hotdog. It was still cold in the middle. A chunk stuck in his throat. What did the man mean, drugs? Mom said they were presents. They always gave him money to give to Mom. She said they were giving the presents to someone else, paying her to buy the presents for them. She called it being their personal shopper. It made him feel bad. His mom never shopped for him. She never gave him presents.

The man plopped into the chair across the table. "You know, when this is over, maybe we'll go fishing."

Benny didn't know what to say, so he nodded and kept chewing. When it was over, would he still be with this man? It wouldn't be over then, would it?

"Yeah, I never had no daddy neither, when I was a kid. I always wanted a daddy to take me fishing." The man took a long swig from a brown beer bottle. He burped and wiped his mouth with the back of his hand. "You like fishing, boy?"

"Yeah." The hotdog wouldn't go down. It stayed in his throat, gagging him. He liked fishing with Mr. Ray and Marco at the ranch. He wanted to go home. Go fishing.

"Me, too. I used to pretend I was fishing with my daddy. My mama would never say who he was, though. Musta been an okay dude. Had me, right?" The man cackled. "Yeah, I like to fish. Played some ball, too. You play basketball?"

The man didn't look mean anymore. He looked like a regular guy, talking about basketball. Benny loved basketball. Marco liked it best, so he tried to teach Benny all the moves. The lay-ups and teardrops and stuff like that. Benny didn't play as well as his buddy, but he tried. "Yeah, I play."

"I played in high school. At South San. Had some college scouts look at me. Junior college in the Valley. Places like that. Busted my knee. After that, school sucked, so I quit. Better things to do. Make money. Lotsa money."

If he made a lot of money, why did he live in this house? Benny knew better than to ask that question out loud. He'd learned the hard way from being around his mom. Things didn't always make sense, but it was best not to ask why.

"Don't turn up your nose at me, boy." The man's face switched to the mean look again. "Yeah, I got into the dope. But so did you. You know you been delivering crack for *tu mama* ever since she got you that bike at the sheriff's repo auction, right?"

Benny chewed and tried to swallow. He couldn't answer so he shrugged.

"Play dumb, boy. That's okay. You just like me. Just like me. You won't be running to the cops or trying to get away 'cause you just like me."

Benny wanted to say no. He wanted to yell, but he was too scared. He wasn't like the man. He didn't know he'd done something bad. His mom never told him. The cops would understand that. Fear boiled up inside him. Maybe not. Maybe they'd put him in jail like his mom.

He tried not to cry, but tears formed. He dashed his hand across his face. He wasn't scared. He wasn't bad. He was good. Mr. Daniel said so. He wanted to yell at the man, tell him Mr. Daniel said so. The man had a gun. Benny stayed quiet.

"You don't know who I am, do you, boy?"

"No, sir."

A big smile creased the man's face.

"I'm your daddy."

Daniel threw his suit in the backseat of the Jeep. Changing into jeans and a T-shirt made him feel a little better — not much, but at least the tie wasn't strangling him. He adjusted his shoulder holster. Right or wrong, the weapon made him feel better, too. He slammed the Jeep door and started back toward Ray's house. They had a ton of interviews to do. Maybe someone had seen something or heard something that would help them find Benny.

"Dad!"

Daniel jerked to a stop at the sight of Phoebe picking her way on bare feet through the rocks and weeds on the road. His fourteen-year-old still wore the sleek dress she'd told him made her look grownup enough to date — a notion he'd quickly nixed — but she'd ditched the hose and heels.

"What are you doing out here, *m'ija?* Your mom will be looking for you."

Phoebe balanced on one foot and picked at a pebble stuck to the other. "I'm sure she'll show up any minute, yelling about something." She leaned against the Jeep, her face morose. "Dad, I have to tell you something."

He hesitated, aware of the clock banging in his head. He needed to get back to the house and the interviews, but he couldn't remember the last time he had exchanged more than a dozen words with Phoebe. He'd never been around for the important stuff. If he was ever going to make it right, things had to change. Just a few seconds, a minute, to let her know she counted. "You don't have a date, do you?"

"No." A tiny grin scampered across her face — so like Nicole's — and disappeared. "But I'm working on it. No, it's about Mom — and you."

"Try not to be so hard on your mom. You know she loves you, just like I do. She's going through a hard time, and it makes her mad." They all were — because of him. "She has a reason to be mad. I ignored her. I ignored you guys. I had my priorities all messed up. Now I'm paying for it."

"No, Chris and I are paying for it. And Mom won't even try to work it out. She's —"

"Wives have a right to expect their husbands to be around, to spend time with them, to do stuff together." Daniel couldn't let her criticize Nicole anymore. She was too young to understand how complicated a relationship could be. "That's not an unreasonable expectation."

"Kids, too."

Daniel didn't know if it were a question or a statement. "Children, too. Are you mad at me because I didn't spend more time with you?"

"You came to my volleyball games. You helped me with my science fair project. You took me camping for my Girl Scout badge."

It was almost as if she were making a list. Daniel had a feeling it wasn't the first time. "You know I love you, right?"

"Yeah." The emotion had seeped out of her voice, leaving it small.

"Even if I spend time with Benny. Even if Benny is living with me right now, and you're not."

She started to cry. Daniel pulled her into his arms. "It's okay, sweetie, it will get better —"

"What's going on? Why's she crying?" The metal in Nicole's tone as she sauntered toward them on heels that added two inches to her height told Daniel she had a theory all ready. And it involved blaming him.

"We were just talking." Phoebe slipped away from Daniel, wiping at the tears with the tips of her fingers.

"About what?"

"Nothing, Mom, nothing." Phoebe whirled and plowed past her mother. "Just forget it, okay?"

Daniel met his wife's gaze and waited for the explosion.

None came. "What was that all about?" She flipped her dark hair away from her face, her tone soft but still accusatory. "What did she tell you?"

Daniel shook his head. "Nothing. Look, I'm sorry I didn't tell you about Benny and my plan to adopt him."

She halted a few feet from him, hands on the curve of her hips, her face flushed with the late afternoon heat. "You know I like Benny."

She'd given Daniel boxes of clothes Christopher had outgrown, offered advice when Benny had come down with the flu, and invited him to family birthday parties. "I assumed you did."

"I can't believe you're talking about adopting a little boy when we're in the middle of a divorce."

"You may be in the middle of getting a divorce, but I'm not."

They battled with their gazes for several seconds.

"Don't you think Benny's been through enough without dropping him into a family that's disintegrating?" Nicole's voice quivered. "Think about it, Danny. Think about how little time you spent with Phoebe and Christopher when they were smaller. Always on the road or involved in investigations that went on for weeks, not coming home night after night. And now, they're old enough to know they were cheated. They resent it. Benny will, too — eventually."

She was right. So very right. All the plays he'd missed and dance recitals and basketball games. Things he could never get back. "I'd like a chance to make up for that. Just let me come home." Emotion rolled over him in a wave. He cleared his throat. "I could spend more time with them if you would let me come home. And they like Benny. They play with him. They want us to all live together again, be a family. You're the one who won't let us do that."

"Somehow everything is always my fault. Even now you can't take responsibility for any of this, can you?" She stalked away.

"Yes, I can. I do." He charged after her. Before he could grab her arm, she whirled around and faced him. He reached out. She stepped back. He let his hand drop. "Give me a chance. I'll do better."

"I don't think so." Tears gleamed in the corners of her hazel eyes. "I'm not sure you

59

truly are capable of doing better. You're too driven. You're the guy who can never give up and never give in. The guy living in his big brother's shadow. You'll always have something to prove."

"Can we talk about this with Pastor Wilson on Monday?" She might as well have stabbed him and gotten it over. The counseling sessions with the pastor had been painful, but never this raw. "Benny's life is on the line right now."

"Why didn't you give me the divorce when I asked for it?" The trembling in her voice deepened. "I don't enjoy hurting you like this."

"I can't divorce you because I love you."

"Or is it because you don't believe in divorce? You're staying in this marriage to make God happy, even if we're both miserable."

"I thought we both believed our vows were a covenant."

"And I hated living the way we were living enough to ask God to forgive me and let me go."

Daniel had to ask the question. "So you don't love me anymore?"

Tears ran down her cheeks. "Yes, I love you. I just can't be married to you."

The faint sounds of *Tejano* music wafted

on the humid air, reminding Daniel of the reception. It had begun as a celebration of a new beginning. The space between Nicole and him measured no more than ten inches. *I love you, too.* He took a deliberate step forward, bent his head, ignoring her startled expression, and kissed her.

Her hands came up and touched his face. She kissed him back, even as small, wet sobs escaped. He let his hands caress her hair for a second. He forced himself to back away from her. If he didn't stop now, he wouldn't be able to. He didn't want her to regret this kiss. *Please God, don't let her regret it.*

The same physical bond that had held them together for sixteen years remained as strong as ever. He could feel it, and he knew she could, too.

She jerked away. "I'm seeing someone else."

"What?" All the emotion of the previous seconds collapsed under the weight of the sucker punch. He tried to grasp her meaning. She couldn't be saying this. It wasn't possible. "What are you trying to tell me?"

"I've met someone else. I've been trying to find a way to tell you."

"Before . . . when we —"

"No. No!" She ran the words together in her haste to explain. "It happened after you moved out. I wanted to tell you, but I couldn't figure out how. He's a good man. A Christian."

"Then he knows you'll always be married to me."

"Joshua understands vows, but he's been through a divorce, so he also understands how marriages can come apart at the seams." Her chin lifted, and her voice got stronger. "He urged me to keep going to the counseling sessions with Pastor Wilson. He's been waiting to see how they went. Yesterday I told him I didn't think he needed to wait anymore."

"You're going to marriage counseling because your boyfriend said you should?" Daniel's hands balled in fists. How could he have been so stupid? "I have to find Benny."

He started walking away.

"Danny!"

He heard her stumble, but he didn't look back. He didn't have time to look back anymore — Benny needed him. His wife obviously didn't.

CHAPTER SIX

Ignoring Nicole's footsteps behind him, Daniel stuck his phone in his pocket and strode toward the group of officers clustered in the gathering dusk near Ray's front porch. Benny's caseworker wasn't very happy with him, but she was on her way out to the ranch. Whatever information she had regarding Shawna Garza, her family, her relationships, Joanna Thigpen would bring it. Given her high caseload, it probably wouldn't be much, but it would be better than nothing. Samuel glanced up at him. His brother's gaze probed. His frown deepened. "Everything all right?"

"Everything's fine. What do you have?" Daniel squeezed between Ray and Joaquin, ignoring the staccato of Nicole's high heels on the front steps.

"Are you sure?" The screen door slammed. Samuel's gaze flickered from Daniel to the porch. "I don't want anything else spoiling

Susana's wedding day — or upsetting *Mama*."

Daniel turned toward Cooper, giving his brother his back. Samuel always wanted to control everything — and this wasn't something he could fix. The band started on a Toby Keith tune with lots of steel guitar and drums. They'd taken Samuel's instructions to entertain the guests seriously. Even though the guests were hardly in the mood to celebrate now. Most of them were sitting in lawn chairs in Ray's front yard, their faces long. It couldn't be helped. "What's going on?"

"One of my guys found a couple of fresh cigarette butts on the ground about ten yards from the Cherokee." Cooper wiped his wrinkled cheeks with his handkerchief. All his years showed on his face at the moment. "Looks like the kidnapper waited out there in those trees and watched for his opportunity."

"Pretty gutsy to make a move with so many people around." Samuel smoothed his moustache. "Broad daylight and no way to know if Benny would come out that way."

"Desperation?" Alex speculated. "Benny lives with a law enforcement officer. Snatching a kid out of his living room would be tough."

"He had to have been watching us, waiting to make his move. Somehow he knew we'd be here today." Fury revved up Daniel's pulse. "He's been stalking us."

"Could be. Maybe the mother knows something." Cooper stuck the handkerchief in his back pocket and adjusted his hat. "We'll work her as soon as we can get in to see her."

"I called the prison. They'll get you in tomorrow morning." Samuel glanced at Daniel. "You should be in on that interview. You know her. They're putting together a record of her visitors for us. You'll be able to pick it up when you see her."

"Works for me. Daniel and I'll take a ride in the morning." Cooper studied the ground for a few seconds, then raised his gaze to Ray. "I need you to stand down on the other case until we know how long the little girl's body's been here and what the COD is."

"You calling me a suspect?" Ray looked half amused.

"I'm not calling you anything — yet. I'm just saying I have to do this by the book." Cooper adjusted his hat again. "No one gets special treatment — not even a homicide detective. I'm asking you to understand that and put up with it until I round up a real suspect."

"I've lived here for five years. I'll eat my hat if that skeleton has been out there less than that."

"We'll see," Cooper said. "I'm just asking you to sit tight and bear with me. The forensic anthropologist will make that determination. We need a COD, identification, and particularly, how long she's been dead. That will take time."

Daniel's hands balled into fists again. He tried to shake them out. Couldn't. His stomach lurched. Cooper looked blurry around the edges. "In the meantime, a kid who's very alive has been kidnapped."

"I know that. We've already started with the guests. Maybe somebody saw the guy. Saw his vehicle." Cooper's gruff voice softened. "Have you contacted CPS?"

"Benny's caseworker, Joanna Thigpen, is on her way out here. She's very concerned, of course, but I doubt there's a whole lot she can tell us. She's got thirty-five, forty other cases. Benny's a drop in the bucket for her."

"Let me know when she gets here. Right now we've got more interviews to do." Cooper didn't drop his gaze this time. "Except for you."

"Why?" The guy was nuts if he thought Daniel would stand around and watch him work. "I do witness interviews all the time."

"Not when it's your kid. I need objective officers doing this. I wouldn't even let your buddies here help if I weren't so short-handed. Besides, you look like you're about to drop in your tracks."

"He's right, Daniel," Samuel intervened. "You're weaving all over the place. I heard you're running a fever. The way you look right now, you'd probably scare them to death. Go rest in Ray's guest bedroom. That's an order."

"You're not my boss." Daniel's stomach rocked. "I want in on the interviews."

"Thirty minutes, Daniel." Samuel had that big brother look in his eye. "You have to get that fever down or you're no good to any of us. Go or I'll call the women."

Hardball. If Samuel got the women involved in this, they'd have Daniel slurping *caldo* chained to his bed with them hovering over him for the next three days. "Fifteen minutes and I talk to Mrs. Thigpen."

"Twenty and you get the interview with the caseworker."

Feeling like a kid who'd been sent to his room, Daniel stomped into the house. The hallway to Ray's guest bedroom seemed interminably long. The pain reliever Nicole had given him earlier wasn't doing a thing

67

for his headache. The silence closed around him in a suffocating blanket. He laid his Glock on the nightstand and eased his head onto the pillow.

He wouldn't sleep. He'd close his eyes long enough to make Samuel happy. Daniel was forty-three years old, and his brother still thought he was in charge of the family. Nicole had been very close to the mark when she said he was the little brother always fighting to prove himself. Growing up in the shadow of a guy like Samuel, who seemed larger than life in everything he did, hadn't been easy. When their father died, Samuel had stepped into his role without missing a beat. If the responsibility ever got to him, he never let his siblings see it.

Daniel fought fatigue that numbed him to the bone. He needed to get back out there, find Benny. This was one battle he planned to lead. Samuel could follow.

The long cement walkway in front of the apartment was dark. Daniel shivered in a frigid wind that sliced through his heavy coat. Benny wore shorts and a T-shirt, no shoes or socks. His body shook as he told Daniel that the man he was looking for wasn't home. He jabbered about peanut butter and jelly sandwiches and how the guy liked those PBJs. Daniel knelt next to him, taking in the bruises on his arms and legs, his emaciated body, the dirt on his face and the nose that needed to be wiped. He dropped quarters into the child's outstretched hand, telling him to call if he ever needed help.

An explosion of sound ripped the balcony, causing it to sway. Benny's hands flew up into the air. His feet lifted from the ground. The coins were falling, falling, spinning, the light bouncing off them in a crazy pattern on the wall behind them. Blood splashed everywhere. Frantic, Daniel fought to staunch it with his hands, but there was so much. So much pouring out, all around him.

Benny's eyes widened with fear and pain. Daniel scrambled to reach him, but the boy fell away from him, crimson spreading across the white T-shirt covering his thin chest. "No, no, Benny, no," he screamed as he tried to get to him. The walkway was slippery with blood. Benny's blood. Daniel was falling. "Benny, Benny!"

"Daniel, wake up! It's just a dream. Come on, wake up. It's a nightmare."

Hands shook Daniel. He jerked up, struggling, reaching for the nightstand and his weapon. "What, what?"

"Easy, it's just a dream."

"Nikki?" He pulled her to him. She felt different. Thinner. His eyelids popped up. "Nicole?" Not Nicole. Deborah. Confused, he pushed back and stared at her face. Her long, blond hair hung across her cheeks, but he could see emotions at war on her face.

"You were having a bad dream." Her voice was soft, strained. "I was just trying to wake you up."

"Daniel?"

He looked past Deborah. Now, there was Nicole. Standing in the doorway. Looking at him. Looking at them. She laughed, a brittle sound of disbelief. She slapped her hand against the doorframe and turned to go.

"Nicole. Wait."

He pushed Deborah back even as she pulled away.

Nicole stopped.

"I just came to tell you Benny's case-worker is here." Deborah glanced at Nicole, her cheeks stained red. "Samuel said you wanted to talk to her."

"Yeah. Yeah." Daniel rubbed his eyes, trying to get them completely open. His wife stood there frozen, like a deer trying to decide if the hunter could really see her. "I'll be out in a minute, Deborah. Could you tell Mrs. Thigpen?"

She squeezed past Nicole and disappeared down the hall.

Nicole moved. Leaving. Right behind Deborah.

"Nikki, don't walk away. She's telling the truth. I was asleep." The awful truth twisted in his gut. It didn't matter that Nicole was seeing someone else. She was his wife, and he still loved her. He couldn't let her go without a fight. "Stay and talk to me. Please."

"I'm leaving, and I'm taking the kids with me." Icicles hung from the words, but her eyes snapped at him with brilliant, white-hot electricity. "What you do is your business."

"What I do is *our* business because we're married. This other guy is just your way of getting my attention." Phoebe had been trying to tell him, and he'd instinctively cut her off. Postponed the inevitable.

"Joshua isn't some guy on the side. He's an attorney from the office. A very nice corporate attorney. He's divorced. He has two daughters." She might have been reading from one of those dating service profiles. Finding the perfect date. "He likes to golf

71

and sail, and he attends the church I've been attending since we separated."

"If he's so perfect, why did you come today?"

"To tell you. I tried at the last counseling session but you were so upset by the time it was over, I couldn't do it. Now it's not hard at all." She pivoted and flounced down the hall.

"Deborah's a friend." Vertigo spun the room around him. He stumbled after her. She was almost to the front door. "Nikki." He grabbed her arm and jerked her around. "I don't care about that guy. I don't care about anything else. Just you and the kids. If you want to be mad, be mad, but don't give up on us. We have an appointment Monday with Pastor Wilson. Please be there."

Tears had left tracks in her makeup. Her nose was running and her skin blotchy. She still looked beautiful to him. He tried to wipe the tears away, but her hand caught his fingers. "It's too late, Daniel."

Not Danny. Daniel. "I'll be waiting for you in Pastor Wilson's office."

She didn't nod. "Come on, kids, it's time to go home."

For the first time, Daniel became fully aware of Phoebe and Christopher on the couch, Marco between them. His sister-in-law sat cross-legged on the floor with his sister Lily, a stack of papers between them. Susana stood in the doorway that led to the kitchen. She had a telephone in one hand and an address book in the other. They all seemed frozen in their spots, an audience electrified by the performance of two.

"I want to stay here until they find Benny and bring him home." Christopher's knuckles were white around the glass he held with both hands.

"Christopher. Move." Nicole grabbed her purse from the coffee table without looking at Susana, Lily, or Piper. The trio of Martinez women would make even the bravest soul tremble in her high heels. Nicole showed no fear. "Now!"

Christopher smacked the glass on the coffee table and made a beeline for Daniel. "Can't I stay here, Pops?" He burrowed against Daniel's shirt. "I want to be here when you get Benny back."

He encircled the twelve-year-old with his arms and let the optimism in his son's face soak through his aching body. "Squirt, I know you do, but right now, it's best that you go with your mom. It's been a long day, and it's gonna be a longer night."

He let go and caught his chin with one

finger, forcing Christopher to look up at him. "I love you, kiddo. Call me before you go to sleep, okay?"

Christopher nodded. His eyes looked suspiciously bright. He didn't cry in public anymore, but Daniel could see the tears pooling. "Go on, it's gonna be fine."

Christopher turned and let the screen door slam behind him. Daniel turned to Phoebe. The surly look on her face and the tense way she held her shoulders told him she wouldn't be as easily convinced. "I'm older," she began before Daniel could. "I don't need as much sleep. I can help my aunts make coffee and serve it. I can be useful."

Daniel glanced at Nicole. A miniscule shake of the head gave him his answer. "Honey, it's sweet of you to offer, but your mom needs you at home."

"No, she doesn't." Phoebe threw her mother a hostile glance. "I'm sure she'll have plenty of company."

Nicole propelled her toward the door. "Your dad has work to do. He'll call you later."

The screen door slammed again.

"Are you all right?" Susana asked from behind him. He couldn't turn around, couldn't let her see the emotions that buffeted him. He felt her hand touch the tense spot between his shoulder blades and start rubbing.

"Yeah." He fought for a calm façade. "I blew it."

"Is that why Deborah charged out of here looking like a pack of pit bulls was chasing her?"

Daniel swiped at his eyes with both hands, still trying to get the sleep from them. "Yeah. I have to find Benny's caseworker. Could you look around for Deborah, make sure she's okay? She was in the wrong place at the wrong time."

"Sure." Susana's tone made him glance back as he pushed through the door. She said something to Piper that he couldn't catch. Of all his family members, Susana was the most outspoken critic of Nicole.

And Deborah wasn't one of Piper's favorite people either since she'd unintentionally come between Piper and Samuel a few months earlier. Why did everything have to be so complicated? He shut the screen door, careful not to let it bang.

Joanna Thigpen sat on the porch swing a few feet from the open door, scribbling furiously in a notebook. It was obvious from the expression on her face that she'd heard the heated exchange between Nicole and Daniel.

His chances for adopting Benny slipped away with every word she wrote.

CHAPTER SEVEN

Daniel walked across the porch, intent on formulating the questions that would tell him how much Joanna Thigpen knew about Benny's background and family. Anything the caseworker might have gleaned from her interviews with Benny's mother might be the key to unlocking the kidnapper's identity.

Joanna Thigpen hoisted her huge body from the porch swing, stood, and held out a hand. She was built like a Dallas Cowboys linebacker. His dealings with her had always been cordial. Even Benny had warmed up to her eventually. The Tootsie Pops she kept in a huge leather purse helped. From the frown on her face, she obviously wasn't in Tootsie Pop mode. Daniel forced a smile and shook her hand. "Thank you for coming. I know your weekends are short as it is."

"One of my kids has been kidnapped, Mr.

Martinez." She sat in the swing with a thump. "It was your duty to notify me immediately. Now, tell me what happened."

Daniel pulled up Ray's favorite rocking chair and ran through the day's events. The frown on her face deepened. She occasionally made a *tut-tut* sound. When he stopped talking, the silence filled with what seemed like disappointment — her disappointment in him. The porch light popped on, startling him. The harsh light bathed the yard and created shadows that wavered in front of him. He studied the slats in the porch floor, feeling like a child in the principal's office.

When Mrs. Thigpen finally spoke, she sounded tired. "I would be remiss if I didn't tell you this doesn't look good. It doesn't look good at all."

"Believe me, I know this is an awful situation." Her accusatory tone raked Daniel's already raw nerves. "Surely you don't think there was some way I could have foreseen that some psycho from Shawna Garza's past would snatch Benny in broad daylight at a wedding reception?"

"How old is this nephew who discovered Benny missing?"

"Marco's nine."

"When he came to tell you he couldn't find Benjamin, how long had it been since you'd seen him?"

Daniel didn't need an interrogation. He'd already flagellated himself with the hindsight of a parent who'd lost a child. "Thirty minutes, at the most. He'd just been in the wedding."

"So what was he doing?"

"Changing his clothes, only the clothes were in the car so he went to get them."

She shook her head so hard, the folds of her triple chin wiggled. "Do you always let him wander about the countryside by himself?"

The disapproval in her eyes just kept getting deeper until Daniel felt he would drown in guilt.

"Benny is a very mature eight-year-old boy. He's been navigating on his own for a long time."

"That's one of the reasons Benjamin went into foster care; so that someone can take better care of him." Mrs. Thigpen looked almost triumphant over making this point. "Foster parents are held to a higher standard."

Daniel had heard horror stories about those high standards. "Surely you're not blaming me for something a criminal did."

"No, Mr. Martinez, I just want you to understand the questions my superiors will ask. The things they'll think about if you decide to seek permanent custody."

Daniel's heart beat did a painful hiccup. "Is there a possibility the request won't be granted?"

"Are you and your wife divorcing?"

Her gaze bore into him, challenging him to tell the truth. "She wants to, I don't. But that's not —"

"You were allowed temporary custody of Benny under rather unusual circumstances, Mr. Martinez. Permanent custody is another ball of wax." Mrs. Thigpen's voice softened almost imperceptibly. "If you can't provide a stable home life, the chances aren't good. It's my understanding that Shawna Garza is a model prisoner. She's been taking parenting classes and working on her GED. She may even get an early release for good behavior."

"The kidnapper says she has a stash of drugs that belongs to him. She refuses to return it because she wants access to it when she gets out. Does that sound like a person who has been rehabilitated?"

"I'll wait to hear what Ms. Garza has to say about the alleged stash of drugs. You're talking about a kidnapper's version of the story."

"Right." They were both quiet for several

seconds.

"So, say Benny goes home with her when this is all over." Daniel couldn't let it go without a fight. "What's to keep her from mistreating him all over again? It's a terrible roller coaster ride for a kid to be on."

"That's why we monitor these situations." He marveled she could say that with a straight face. San Antonio was famous for its overworked, underpaid Child Protective Services staff. Children routinely fell through the cracks of the system. Babies died days after CPS visits, beaten to death with a vacuum hose or drowned in bathtubs and smothered in plastic bags. The thought of Benny back in a cockroach-infested apartment with a woman who went though men the way some women went through shoes made his skin crawl.

"With varying success." He managed to keep his tone neutral.

"Without a doubt." Her sigh had a brittle sound. "Without a doubt."

First they had to get Benny back. Then Daniel would fight this battle. One thing at a time. "You've done background checks on Ms. Garza. What can you tell me about family, friends, acquaintances?"

Mrs. Thigpen pulled a folder from her bag and opened it across the skirt that covered her ample lap. "Umm, let's see. No family in the state. Brother, distant cousins, all in California. Some coworkers from the doughnut shop where she waitressed. None real close. Kept to herself at the apartment complex."

"She ever been married?"

"Twice. First time when she was fifteen. Divorced when she was seventeen. Second time the guy got stabbed in a gang fight, died."

"Was he Benny's father?"

"No, no, this was years ago. We haven't been able to get a line on Benny's father. The birth certificate doesn't list a name. We assume he was Hispanic, but Ms. Garza claims she doesn't know who he was. She's thirty years old, so she was twenty-one or twenty-two when she had Benjamin. She wasn't married at the time."

"So it doesn't seem likely the father will come forward and demand custody."

"Not likely."

The night air grew cooler. Daniel shivered. The sound of wedding guests murmuring in the front yard mingled with the cicadas. The band seemed to be taking a break. Daniel was thankful for that. The screen door slammed, and Marco ran down the steps. He was barefoot. Daniel wanted to yell at him to put on his shoes, but he couldn't muster the strength. "I took good care of him."

"I know that, Mr. Martinez. No one could've imagined that something like this would happen, but it did. CPS is under tremendous pressure right now with the deaths of the Torres babies. We can't afford to be lenient."

Daniel had read about that case. Twins smothered by their teenage mother and then stuffed under the foundation of the duplex where she lived. She'd had a barbecue and when guests complained of a stench, she'd blamed it on a dead dog. "I will get him back."

"Even if you do, what shape will he be in?" Her voice cracked slightly. She sniffed and dabbed at her nose with a tissue. "You and I both know some of the things children experience at the hands of adults can be far worse than a quick, merciful death."

Daniel curled his hands around the arms of the rocking chair and willed himself not to imagine all those things. Joanna Thigpen had seen them firsthand. When it came to children, she'd seen much more than he had. Things that precluded leniency or sentimentality now.

"When will you talk to Ms. Garza?" The

emotion on her face had subsided. Her professional mask was anchored in place.

"Early in the morning. If she tells us who she was doing business with, we could have Benny back by the end of the day. We might be able to find him before the deadline Monday. Even if we don't, we'll have the drugs and we'll be able to make the exchange when he does call." Or sooner.

"So much rides on Ms. Garza."

Daniel struggled to give the benefit of the doubt to Benny's mother. "If you're correct about her wanting to do the right thing for him, we've got nothing to worry about."

"Keep me posted." Mrs. Thigpen rose from the swing, the motion causing it to whip back and tap against the wall. She dropped the file in his lap. "Everything I know about Benjamin Garza is in this file. It's a copy — keep it."

Daniel put his hand on the folder to keep it from sliding off. He had to swallow twice before he could force the words to form. "Thank you."

He sat there for several minutes after Mrs. Thigpen plodded down the steps and across the yard.

God, wherever Benny is right now, please form a wall of protection around him. Soften the heart of the man who has him. Protect

Benny until we can find him. Let him feel your presence and not be afraid.

He heaved himself from the chair. Benny's return rode on his mother's shoulders now. If Mrs. Thigpen had gauged Shawna's rehabilitation correctly, they had nothing to worry about. For Benny's sake, he hoped the caseworker was right.

Even if that meant losing Benny all over again when Shawna got out of prison.

Shawna Garza swished the brush in the toilet one more time and flushed it. The smell of urine gagged her. No amount of scrubbing would get these toilets cleaned. It didn't matter how often she washed them. Everything in this place was dirty, even though it smelled like bleach.

She couldn't wait to get out, start a new life with her stash. She and the kid could go someplace far away and get a fresh start. She'd buy herself some fancy new clothes and a nice car. Yeah, a convertible. They could go to California, to Hollywood, drive around on Rodeo Drive. She'd put Benny in one of those fancy private schools so he wasn't hanging around all the time being annoying.

Grinning at the thought, she turned to grab the mop and start on the floor.

"Whatcha doin', sweet pea?" A muscular arm clamped down around her neck from behind. Hot breath touched her left ear. She recognized the voice. Gina. The inmate who had killed her husband because he cheated on her with another biker. Gina was the leader of one of the gangs in Shawna's cell block. "I've been looking for you."

"Back off." Shawna struggled to break free. She wasn't interested in being anybody's pretty girl — not unless they had something to give her in return. "Get off me!"

She had worked so hard not to be alone long enough for this woman to catch her. As a trustee, Gina could turn up anywhere on the cell block. They'd been playing cat and mouse for weeks. Shawna had let her guard down for a second. Just a second.

"Think you're too good for me, don't you, pretty girl?" The voice was low.

A shudder ran through Shawna. "I don't want no trouble."

She managed to tuck her hand in the front of her pants for a second and grab the piece of metal she had hidden there. It looked like part of a table leg. She'd found it stuck up against a bookshelf in the library one day when she was doing research on her case. Carefully, she slid the shank out, keep-

86

ing it flat behind her hand and arm. *Do it. Do it!*

She tried to raise her arm enough to strike back toward the woman's body behind her. Gina, maybe a half foot taller and thirty pounds heavier, spun her like a child. Shawna's back smacked up against the bathroom wall. Gina crowded so close Shawna could see the dark fillings in her back teeth and smell her funky breath.

The anticipation in the other woman's flat brown eyes told Shawna she had to act now. With a grunt she jerked the homemade weapon up into a defensive position. Gina's face registered surprise before she brought her thick fist down on Shawna's forearm, the blow causing the shank to clatter to the floor.

"You —" Obscenities rained down on Shawna. She tried to slide down toward the floor, toward the weapon. She had been so careful to hide it, so careful to keep it close, now it was gone.

Gina slapped her back in a bone-jarring blow that sent Shawna's head smacking against the wall. Pain ricocheted through her brain. Her sight blurry, she felt around for the weapon. Gina got there first. She grabbed the homemade knife with her other hand. "Teach you a lesson, you —"

Shawna felt the first slice, hot and bruising. *No, I'm not done yet.* The pain blossomed in her stomach. She struggled for air. Her body slid down to the floor, still sitting up.

A red convertible. Rodeo Drive. Her dreams receded until they were tiny specks on a far horizon. Then disappeared silently into black night.

CHAPTER EIGHT

Inhaling the odor of bleach, Alex stood next to Cooper, watching forensic anthropologist Jennifer McDonald carefully arrange the last of the boiled and scoured bones in anatomical order. He'd been surprised and pleased when Cooper had agreed to let him accompany him to the county morgue. Being the one — with Deborah — to find this little girl, had given him a strong, personal incentive to find out what had happened to her. Almost as strong as the desire to find Benny's kidnapper and nail him to a wall somewhere.

He glanced at his watch — at least eight hours had passed since Benny's abduction. He studied Cooper. It was the sheriff's detective's show. He needed to move faster, push harder. "Well, what do you know so far?"

Cooper's expression tightened. "What my young and impatient colleague means to say is we really appreciate you coming in on your day off." He twisted his ragged Stetson in big hands. "We don't mean to rush you, but we've got another case pending as well involving a child who's still alive."

McDonald didn't look up from her examination. She'd already explained almost two-thirds of the body's one hundred twenty-seven bones were present and accounted for. That was pretty good, she'd said. Sometimes all they brought her was a skull or a femur. "COD looks like it'll be blunt force trauma to the skull. This child received a crushing blow to the head. Massive damage to the back of the skull."

It was a beginning. A small one. They'd known from the start her death had been a violent, ugly one. Otherwise, why would someone have buried her in a secluded spot, hoping no one would find her? Resolving the more difficult issues of age, race, and identification would be necessary in order to find her killer. "So the blow caused instantaneous death?"

"There's no callus so the fracture occurred shortly before death. There are some perimortem healed fractures from much earlier." She pointed to a series of x-rays clipped to a light panel on the wall. "More than one. Here to the radius in the right arm, the ulna in the left. Two ribs broken."

"You're suggesting abuse?"

"Systematic and regular abuse."

Cooper smacked his hat against the wall. "How long has she been out there?" His voice sounded hoarse.

McDonald sighed. "That, Detective, will take some time."

Cooper responded before Alex could protest. "A timeline is critical to figuring out who did this to her. It will also allow us to eliminate certain people."

Like Ray.

"Determining how long bones have been buried or half buried is not a simple thing." McDonald's tone remained patient. It probably wasn't the first time she'd dealt with officers who wanted to try to erase the pain of seeing a child's body by bringing justice to her killer. "We'll do a chemical analysis, but it'll take time and it's not an exact science."

"Then how about her age? How old was she?" Alex turned back to the bones, trying to keep the futile anger at bay. "Can you tell?"

"We have a loss of the central incisors, but only two permanent teeth had come in. In addition, the femur bones hadn't reached full length."

"What does that mean?" Cooper sounded so much more patient that Alex felt.

"Somewhere between six and ten." McDonald touched the skull with one gloved finger. "I'd say caucasoid."

"Female, Anglo or Hispanic, six to ten. Are you going to call in Richardson?" Dan Richardson was a board-certified forensic odontologist, meaning he was one of a handful of people in the country who could identify skeletal remains using dental records. He worked in a lab two floors above the Bexar County autopsy room. "I imagine he's got some cases he can try to match to this find."

"Well, I don't know if he'll be able to help. I don't see any fillings. I'm not sure she had any dental work done."

Cooper shook his head, his face etched with exhaustion. "Well, we've got a child who isn't dead — yet — to find. You have my cell phone number. I'm sure you've both got family waiting for you at home. This will wait until Monday."

McDonald looked at the bones on the table in front of her. "She's waited a long time to be found. Long enough."

Alex followed Cooper to the parking lot. He let the cool evening breeze wash over him.

After the stale, refrigerated air of the morgue, it was a welcome relief. "We have to find Benny." He slammed his fists on the hood of the truck that separated him from Cooper. "We can't let him end up a pile of bones on a table."

"Hey, easy on the truck, partner." Cooper opened his door, but he didn't get in. "That's the plan. We also want to know who killed that little girl. If we can't show that those bones were on the property when Ray bought it, he could end up at the top of the suspect list."

"Coop." Alex adopted Ray's nickname for the detective. "No one will believe that. Ray has upheld the law for his entire career. I bet he's never even had a speeding ticket in the last twenty years. He just got married. He wants to be a minister."

"I've known Ray a few years myself." Cooper stared at a starless sky. "We've done a half dozen Habitat projects together. We fish all the time. You're not telling me anything I don't know. I'm just saying we need to find the real killer. Fast."

Alex thumped the dashboard with his hand. "Let's go, then." Something had happened at the ranch to set these two crimes — separated by time and method — in motion. The trail started at the ranch. He glanced at his watch. Almost nine o'clock and no end in sight. They still had to go over McDonald's findings with Ray and Daniel, as well as the CPS worker interview and whatever Ray had come up with on the previous owners of the property. Time to get his second wind. "I hope they have coffee made —"

His cell phone rang.

"Alex, I need a big favor." Daniel spoke softly.

"Sure, anything." Surprised, Alex waited.

"Deborah took off a couple of hours ago. She was upset, and now I can't get her on her cell or at home. Could you track her down for me?"

Alex sat up straight. A chance to connect with Deborah. Then Daniel's words sunk in. "Upset about what?"

The pause stretched. Finally, Daniel spoke again. "It was just a misunderstanding, something personal. I'm worried she might relapse."

"You're afraid she's out there drinking somewhere? That's some misunderstanding." Alex bit back the cusswords. A relapse. Only something major would cause that. And that something major involved Daniel somehow.

"Yeah. You're familiar with the bar circuit

she used to run on, so I thought maybe it wouldn't be too hard for you to figure out where she'd go."

Endless nights filled with loud music, thick smoke, and alcohol-induced rambling conversations only vaguely remembered the next day didn't interest him anymore, but Alex let the assumption ride. "I'll see what I can do. From what I've heard, Ray's brought her in a few times himself. Why don't you ask him to let me know where to start looking?"

"He and Susana are leaving in a few minutes. I don't want him worrying about Deborah — not tonight. Just try some of the usual spots."

"No problem." With everything Daniel had on his plate right now, how could he be worrying about Deborah? And how could she do this now, with Benny missing? It had to have been a major blowout of some kind. "You're sure there isn't anything else I need to know?"

Again the long pause. "Just make sure she gets home safe, all right?"

Alex disconnected. If Deborah wasn't at home, there weren't a lot of other possibilities. She tended to be a loner. He intended to change that. She couldn't keep turning him down forever.

Of course, he had to find her first.

CHAPTER NINE

Daniel listened to the phone ringing in his ear, counting. One, two, three. "Come on, Nicole, come on," he whispered. Ray shifted on the narrow couch as if he could hear the desperation in those words in his sleep. Daniel's new brother-in-law had dozed off in mid-sentence a few minutes earlier. Daniel didn't have the heart to wake him. His own eyes burned with fatigue. He should sleep, but first he wanted — needed — to tell Nicole not to give up on their marriage — to leave this other man out of it. It was after nine, but she shouldn't be in bed already. Maybe she saw his name on the Caller ID and ran the other direction.

The ringing stopped, and a rustling sound followed by clattering assailed his ears. "Sorry, I dropped the phone. I mean, hello, it's Nicole." She sounded disoriented. "Any news on Benny?"

"No. No news." Daniel beat down the

emotion that admission elicited. Just the sound of her voice sent a quiver of longing through him. He should be in his living room, on his couch, sitting next to her. They should be drawing comfort from each other. He'd destroyed that possibility with sheer neglect. Now he was in danger of losing her to someone who apparently appreciated her more. "Were you asleep?"

"No. No, I . . . I was . . . I mean . . ." She sounded nervous, maybe even guilty. About what? "I wasn't asleep."

"I wanted to talk to you. About this afternoon. I mean, you know, when we —"

"Kissed? When you kissed me?" Her tone fired up with unmistakable anger. "And then went into a bedroom and hugged another woman?"

"I told you — Deborah was trying to wake me up. There was no hug —" Daniel shut his mouth as Ray stirred on the couch and his eyes opened for a second, then he sank back, slumbering again. Daniel reeled in his emotions and schooled his voice in a whisper. "Surely you can see the irony in the accusation. Come to Pastor Wilson's counseling session. We can work this out."

Another voice — a masculine voice — spoke in the distance. Something about leaving. Daniel strained to hear. "Who is that? Is it him?"

"I have to go."

"Wait! Your new boyfriend is there? While the kids are upstairs? What do you think this is doing to them, Nicole? This isn't right —"

"I have to go."

Silence buzzed in his ear, a monotonous, irritating reminder of how far away Nicole had gone. Daniel forced himself to breath in and out for a few seconds. Then he punched a button. Christopher's cell phone number popped up and dialed. His son answered on the second ring. "Pop! Did you find Benny?"

"No, *m'ijo,* not yet."

"I want to live with you. I don't want to be here anymore."

Daniel swallowed the urgent need to probe about the man in his house. He would not use his son to spy on Nicole. "Squirt, give me time to make things right with your mom. Then we'll all live together again as a family. I promise."

A stifled sob greeted that optimistic statement. "You shouldn't make promises you can't keep. Mom has a boyfriend, and he's here. Right now. I saw them. They were . . . kissing."

Daniel let the phone sink to his lap. He

99

could hear Christopher's voice calling him, asking him if he'd heard, if he were all right. He'd heard, but he wasn't all right. Finally, he lifted the phone to his ear. He had to reassure his child. "Just give me time, Son. I'll fix this. I promise."

It took several minutes of reassurances before Daniel could hang up the phone. His exhaustion was so acute he could barely raise his hand to lay the phone on the table. The sound of the screen door slamming forced him from the vicious cycle of his thoughts. Ray's yelp of surprise reflected the fact that he'd heard it, too. He sat up straight, clutching a pillow to his chest, his curly hair sticking up all over his head. "I thought everyone headed home for the night."

Daniel stretched, trying to get the kinks out of his shoulders and neck and shake the last few minutes from his brain. "Alex said Detective Cooper is coming back to talk to you."

Ray dropped the pillow and rubbed his face with both hands. "Right. I wish I had more to tell him."

Cooper strode into the room, ragged hat in one hand. His eyes were bloodshot and his cheeks covered with white stubble, but he managed a grim smile. He sank into the rocker across from the couch. "We need to talk."

Not exactly a friendly overture, but Daniel didn't blame Cooper. It had been a long, ugly day. "Would you like some coffee?"

Cooper shook his head. He slapped his Stetson onto his lap with a half-hearted flourish. "I need to get the name of the previous owner of this property — or the family who rented it, at least. I want Alex to try to track him down first thing in the morning, while we're in Gatesville."

Ray began to massage his left leg, a look of pain on his face. "Where's Alex? I thought he was with you."

Daniel caught Cooper's curious gaze and spoke quickly. "I asked him to check on a couple of things for me and then go home. The guy was dragging."

Ray shrugged, his eyebrows lifted. "This early? He's a night owl. A couple of hours is a full night's rest for him."

Daniel glanced at Cooper, who remained silent, his gaze still on the papers strewn across the table. The guy wasn't going to give him up. Good. Ray didn't need to know about Deborah's behavior. Not tonight. "He'll be back in the morning. Let's finish this so you and Susana can check into the honeymoon suite. Detective Cooper, did you get a COD? A timeline?"

Before Cooper could answer, Susana trotted into the room, a purse in her hand. "Marco's asleep — finally. He's so distraught over Benny I'm concerned about leaving him, even if it is just for the night."

She talked fast, her cheeks pink. Daniel glanced at Ray and then averted his gaze. The pain that had been on the man's face seconds before had disappeared behind a careful mask. "We can skip the hotel and stay here, if you think it'll help."

"I'll be here. So will Piper and Samuel," Daniel broke in. This situation would not rob his sister of an occasion for which she had waited a very long time. Trying to hide his exhaustion, he picked up his coffee cup. "If he wakes up during the night, I'll sit with him. You guys go. We know where to find you if we need you."

Susana dropped onto the couch and leaned against Ray. "Sorry, I'm just so used to worrying about him —"

"Don't ever apologize for that." Ray leaned in and kissed his wife. Their embrace lasted so long it soon became apparent they'd forgotten anyone was in the room.

Cooper cleared his throat, and the two jumped apart. "Let's get this over with so you can get out of here. What'd you find?"

It wasn't much. The title transfer was from the Duane Van Pulte estate. Five years earlier, Ray had purchased the house, barn and related buildings, along with twenty acres of land and all the machinery and equipment from the Van Pulte estate. Ray had written the name Chavez and a telephone number in the margin of one of the many pieces of paper in the file.

"The guy's name is Tómas Chavez. Maddy remembers him," Ray said. "They were neighbors before I entered the picture. In fact, she's hired him to do some odd jobs since then. I only met him once — the day I walked the property with him before I decided to buy it. He received official notification by mail that he would have to vacate. He had thirty days, I believe."

This was a start. Daniel leaned forward, glad to have something to occupy his mind besides the thought of where Benny might be right now, what he might already have suffered in the hours since his kidnapping. "Did he have family? Did you meet a wife, kids?"

"I never met the rest of the family. Maddy remembers the kids, though. She says there were four of them."

Cooper snagged a small notebook from his pants pocket along with a pen and started taking notes. "On your way out, would you ask Mrs. Stover to come see me?"

Ray let go of Susana, stood, and grabbed their bags. With a wave and diffident smile, Susana followed him from the room.

Cooper seemed lost in thought for a moment. Daniel struggled against nausea. He couldn't believe stress was making him feel this bad. He worked for the U.S. Attorney's Office. He had stress for breakfast every morning.

Cooper stirred finally, his gaze sharp. "Did you find out anything from Benny's CPS caseworker?"

"Here's the file. I was just going through it." Daniel held out the papers. "Doesn't tell us much."

"Tomorrow —"

Maddy Stover sauntered into the room. "You wanted to see me, Detective?" Even without makeup or jewelry, Ray's neighbor was a nice looking woman. Daniel glanced at the detective. He seemed to think so, too. He immediately rose from his seat, his ruddy complexion deepening.

"Nash. Call me Nash, please." Cooper nodded toward the couch. "Please, have a seat."

Maddy chose a rocking chair next to the

fireplace instead. "What would you like to know?"

Cooper dropped back into his chair. "How long have you lived here?"

"At Ray's? About five months. When Ray was laid up after that car wreck, I moved in to take care of him. I had planned to sell my ranch, but I stayed when he needed me."

Daniel's mind replayed the horrible accident, the months of surgeries and rehab. Maddy had been a godsend to Ray and Susana — to the whole Martinez family — but Cooper knew that. He'd been around to take Ray fishing and watch ballgames on TV with him. "Actually, I meant how long have you had your ranch?"

"Oh, goodness, about twenty-five years, I guess."

"So you knew Tómas Chavez?"

"Yes." Her face reflected indecision, something Daniel doubted she felt very often.

"Didn't you like him?"

"He's a pleasant enough man, despite the way he looks, but he knew nothing about ranching. He bought horses he didn't take care of. He didn't feed them properly. Moldy bales of Sudan hay. Let his dogs run wild, spook our cattle. He had big parties with that accordion music — you know, *conjunto*. Always a line of cars down the road. I could never understand why he lived on a ranch. I tried to believe he was here getting a start on a new life, but that was probably wishful thinking on my part."

Daniel contemplated her description of Chavez's lifestyle. "Yet you hired him to do some work for you."

"It seemed the Christian thing to do." Maddy tucked a wisp of hair back into her braid, then folded her hands in her lap. "I ran into him in Helotes several months ago. I was coming out of the post office, and there he was. He looked a little . . . down and out, kind of grungy. He said if I ever needed a laborer, he was in need of work. With Ray laid up after the accident, I really did need someone. Tómas did everything I asked him to do without complaining. He worked. He got paid."

"Did he say anything about his kids?" Cooper asked.

"No. He didn't talk about anything. He did his work, and he went home."

"But you remember him having kids when he lived out here?"

"Yes. They were little things. All four of them. A set of twin girls and two boys, cute as all get out, but very quiet. They seemed to melt into the woodwork whenever I came round."

"Were you around when Ray bought the ranch?"

"No, as a matter of fact, my sister was quite ill when Ray moved here. I went up to Tulsa to take care of her before she died. When I came back, the Chavezes were gone, and Ray was settled in. A quiet one he was. Saw him working his rear off to get this place in shape, but he barely said a word to me the first year he was here."

Maddy had a faraway look on her face. "Of course, now I know he was grieving for his first wife. Some folks are like that, real quiet for a while."

Cooper's face had gone white. Daniel tried to remember how long it'd been since the detective's wife had died. Ray had mentioned it. She'd had a heart attack at the breakfast table a couple of years ago. Cooper finally answered. "Yes, ma'am, they are."

No one spoke for a few seconds. Cooper stood. "I should let y'all get some sleep. Thank you for your time. Daniel, I'll be here at five A.M."

Maddy started to rise. "I'll see you out."

"Thank you, ma'am, but there's no need. I know my way." Cooper slapped his hat on his head and disappeared through the door.

Quiet reigned for a few moments. Maddy

sipped her coffee. Daniel felt as if his body was floating in a sea of exhaustion.

"Do you really expect Benny's mother to cooperate?" Maddy leaned back in the chair and rocked, the squeaking sound grating on Daniel's serrated nerves. "After all, you're asking her to admit to possession of a large quantity of drugs."

"If there's an iota of motherly love left in her, she'll be willing to pay the price to get her son back." The surge of anger that flooded him felt good. It propped up his body. "If she won't do it of her own accord, we'll have to find another way, maybe offer her an incentive of some kind."

"Well, her prior behavior says she doesn't give a hoot about her son." Maddy's tone was tart. "What's plan B?"

"We'll take apart the record of her visitors. Ask the warden to put pressure on her — put her in administrative segregation. Take away all her privileges. Whatever it takes."

"Good." She tapped neatly trimmed nails on the arm of her chair. "You won't let Detective Cooper make Ray into a suspect in the little girl's death, will you?"

Daniel met her cool gaze, surprised at the change of subject. "He's a good friend of Ray's. I'm sure he's trying to do his job without bias and let the chips fall where they may. That's what I would do. Ray didn't do it, so the truth will win out."

He stood and bumped into the coffee table with his knee. Coffee slopped over the edge of his cup onto the table. He bent over to grab a napkin. Maddy beat him to it. "Go to bed, Son, you're exhausted. I'll be praying for Benny."

"Thank you." He stumbled toward the door.

"Daniel."

He glanced back, one hand on the door to steady himself.

"And for you and Nicole."

"Yes, ma'am."

For a few seconds, the darkness lifted a little and he could see a path to his room.

Deborah stumbled toward her truck. The asphalt undulated around her. Cars jammed the parking lot, forcing her to zigzag. The Saturday night crowd never let her down. She'd managed to keep up with a couple of guys she'd never seen before and would never see again. Not bad for someone who hadn't practiced drinking in a while. She leaned on the Dodge while she dug through her purse for her keys.

Stupid. How could she have been so

stupid? Her face burned with shame at the memory of Daniel's bewildered look and Nicole's frigid stare. Deborah had messed up. How could God forgive her? He'd forgiven her for so much already, and now, after she had accepted Jesus as her savior, she'd messed up all over again. It could be the straw that broke the camel's back. For her salvation. And for Daniel's marriage. That seemed even worse. She might be new at this, but she was sure it was even worse.

She had to make it up to him somehow. Find Benny. Yeah, find Benny. That was what mattered to Daniel right now. Nothing else. Tomorrow, she'd find Benny.

Her fingers curled around the pack of cigarettes she'd bought in the bar. They tasted so good, smelled so good, felt so good. Her anxiety eased a little. She'd have one more and then throw the pack away. Right now. Where was the lighter? She dug some more. Her billfold and her checkbook slid out and landed on the asphalt.

She sank to her knees, trying to ignore the slick, black Altima that glided to a halt next to her. Great. Here she was alone in a bar parking lot. She'd stashed her weapon in the glove compartment of her locked truck. The scenario had a familiar feel to it. She would have sworn it would never happen again — until the feel of Daniel's arms around her in that nightmare-induced need for assurance made her limp back to her old crutches.

"Deborah?"

She forced herself to look up. Alex Luna.

"Luna? What are you doing here?" She dragged herself to her feet and tried to shove her stuff back into her purse. Instead, her makeup bag slid out and hit the ground, spilling its contents. Groaning, she knelt again.

"The question is what are you doing here?" The sound of the door opening told her he wasn't going away. He squatted next to her. His hand came out as if to touch her. A thrill of fear ran through her. She scrambled back. No one touched her anymore. Not even a nice guy — yeah, she could admit he was nice — touched her. "What do you want?"

"Deborah, could you look at me for a second?"

Something in his voice made her heart squeeze in a painful rhythm. It sounded like disappointment. "What?"

His face, bathed in the streetlight overhead, seemed full of emotion. "You've been drinking?"

"It's a bar. Generally speaking, people

drink in bars." She worked hard to keep the words concise. She wasn't drunk. Just pleasantly tipsy.

"But not you, remember. You gave it up, along with the smoking."

"What makes you think I've been smoking?"

"The smell. At the wedding, you smelled really good. Blush, right?" Luna's tone softened. How could a guy know about women's perfume? "Now you smell like a bar."

"So. I don't care." He was a lady's man, of course. That's how he knew. "Maybe I just wanted a night off from being good. Just one night. A couple of drinks. A couple of cigarettes. I can do one night. Why are you here? Someone send you to baby sit?"

"Daniel was worried. He said you were upset when you left, and he tried to call your cell, and there was no answer. All evening."

"Daniel's foster child is missing, and he's worrying about me?" She snickered.

Luna's expression hardened. "He's got his hands full. Do you think he needs you doing this on top of it? It's pretty selfish of you, actually. I thought you were his friend. He needs you sober and working the case. Why would you do this?"

It didn't matter that Luna was only saying what she'd been telling herself for the past several hours. "Nothing's wrong with me. I'll be right there on top of the investigation all the way — just like I always am. I'll find Benny for him. I don't let drinking get in the way of my work."

"Really? I wonder if Ray would agree with that."

He posed the question without emotion, but the words crashed down on her, syllable by syllable, each one piercing her skin like a dozen sharp knives, each one a searing pain that rampaged though her. She knew the answer to that question. She'd been drunk when her partner needed her, and he'd nearly died trying to work a case alone. She could never undo that.

She staggered to her feet. "I wouldn't mind a ride home, if you're offering."

He bowed and swept his arm toward the Altima in a flourish. "Your coach awaits you, madam. Your designated driver at your service."

She weaved toward the car, trying to examine some thought, some wisp of an idea that kept escaping in the midst of the alcohol haze. "It's Saturday night. You haven't been drinking?" *Drinking* came out *shrinking*. She ducked her head, woozy.

Shame slammed over her in another huge wave.

"No, I was working." The accusation inherent in those words didn't escape Deborah. He opened the door for her. "Besides, I don't drink."

"Come on, Luna. I've seen you at parties." She sank into the smooth leather seat, relieved that the ground had stopped heaving under her. Luna's car smelled like pine trees — clean — after the smoke-filled stench of Billy Bob's. "You're at the bars more than I used to be."

"I'll let you in on a secret if you promise not to tell anyone."

She let her head loll against the seat. "Promise."

"I get lonely. Most of my real friends are married, so I hang out with guys who aren't." He leaned in to talk to her. She could see the red lines that crisscrossed the whites of his eyes. He was tired. Shame wrapped itself around her throat in a choke-hold. "And they hang out in bars."

"So you're the designated driver."

She murdered the word designated, but he didn't laugh. He leaned toward her, one hand on the roof of the car, the other on the door. "Yes. But like I said, it's our little secret."

"Nobody knows?"

"Just Joaquin and probably Lily. Joe tells his wife everything."

"Why did you stop drinking?"

"Makes me act stupid, and I don't need any help in that department."

If she weren't so tired and woozy, she'd call him on that. Had to be another reason. There always was. "I'll let you take me home, Luna, but I'm not giving you anything in return. Nothing. You got that?"

"I don't want anything from you." He paused. "I take that back, there is one thing."

She'd known it. All men wanted something.

"My name is Alex. Maybe you could see your way to call me that."

"Yeah, whatever. I have to close my eyes now." She closed her eyes. She heard the door slam. Her head swam. She opened her eyes again and grabbed the door handle. Head spins. Not good.

She'd messed up bad. If Samuel found out, she would lose her job.

Even worse, her boss would be disappointed in her. So would Daniel. She let her head drop into her hands.

She had to help him find Benny. It was the only way to make it up to him.

Alex watched Deborah's building, inhaling the smoky scent she'd left behind in the enclosed space of his car. He'd wanted to help her through the parking lot of her apartment complex and lead her up the stairs. She wouldn't want that. He thumped the wheel a few times, turned the radio, and changed stations until he found some R&B.

What was it about Deborah that drew him to her? Besides the fact that she was gorgeous. He'd never had trouble connecting with beautiful women. It was something else. Sometimes she got this crooked grin on her face, right before she let go a zinger that put some guy in his place for getting a little fresh with her. Sometimes she blew him away with her accurate assessment of a situation or a case. Times like that, he was floored by his attraction to her.

Alex shifted in his seat. What was the matter with him? This wouldn't work. He ticked off on his fingers the reasons why he shouldn't be sitting in his car thinking about Detective Deborah Smith. She didn't like him. She had a drinking problem. She didn't like him. She was a Christian. She didn't like him. She was Ray's partner, and

Ray would shoot Alex if he hurt her. Oh, and she didn't like him.

He considered banging his head on the wheel to knock some sense into himself. This was stupid. He needed to let Daniel know the mission had been accomplished and Deborah was safely home. He pulled his cell phone from his jacket pocket and punched in Daniel's cell number. No answer. When voicemail picked up, he disconnected and blew out air.

Daniel and Samuel both needed to know Deborah was all right. Telling Daniel was one thing, telling Samuel was another. He was Deborah's boss and her stumble tonight could mean her job. He wavered. She'd never forgive him. On the other hand, Samuel needed to know she was drinking again. For the safety of every officer who worked with her. He closed his eyes, opened them, and dialed Samuel's number.

"Martinez." The word was a whisper.

"Sarge, it's me. Sorry to wake you. I tried to call Daniel, but he didn't answer."

"I wasn't asleep, but Piper is. Hang on a second while I go out in the hallway."

Alex heard muffled sounds and then Samuel came back on the line. "Daniel said you were looking for Smith. Did you find her?"

"Yeah, delivered her to her apartment

about five minutes ago."

"Is she okay?"

"Well, she'll have a king-sized headache in the morning, but probably nothing she hasn't experienced before."

Samuel muttered something in Spanish Alex didn't quite catch, and then said, "I'll have to put her back on medical leave."

"I'm sure she'll be mortified in the morning, Sarge. She'll want to work Benny's case. She won't do it again."

"I can't take a chance. She's off the case."

Alex wanted to argue, but Samuel was the boss. "You gonna tell Ray and Daniel?"

"Tomorrow's soon enough for that kind of news." An odd note of hesitation lingered in Samuel's voice. "We won't be able to make our next move until Daniel talks to Shawna Garza in the morning. While he makes the trip, we're going to take an hour and go to church . . . you're welcome to join us."

Alex was glad his boss couldn't see his face. He'd gone to church as a young kid. He'd liked it okay. Pretty restful after all the arguing his parents did. He'd never been as an adult. He didn't know how to respond.

"Alex, you still there?" The hesitation in Samuel's voice was gone. "It's not a big deal. The people at Greater Good don't bite. You don't even have to get dressed up. Even Deborah goes there."

Deborah went to Sarge's church. Now there was a piece of information he hadn't had before. "She probably won't be there tomorrow."

"She'll be there. I'm calling her AA sponsor as soon as I hang up with you. So, see you there in the morning? The service starts at eight fifteen."

Ouch. So much for a leisurely pot of coffee and the Sunday funnies. "Yeah, I'll be there."

Sunday morning. Everything would be closed. Church would fill the time until they could make another move on the two investigations. And even if he didn't get anything else out of it, Deborah would be there. No one had to know his true motivation.

Well, almost no one. God would know. Alex shrugged off the thought. God might know, but did He care?

Alex put the Altima in gear and let it rip, hoping to leave that haunting question far behind in a cloud of exhaust fumes and bitter memories.

CHAPTER TEN

Benny uncurled his body and tried to stretch his arms over his head. He couldn't. They were tied in front of him. Confused for a second, he struggled to open his eyes. He looked around, trying to remember where he was. The memories pelted him. He smothered a sob. The night, full of strange sounds and ugly dreams, had finally passed. The couch in the man's house smelled like cat pee and cigarette smoke. His tongue stuck to the roof of his mouth.

He sat up. The muscles in his arms and legs screamed in pain. He took little breaths so he wouldn't cry. He was hungry. He missed Mr. Daniel and Marco and Marco's dog, Taxi. Mr. Daniel said someday, when they knew for sure where he'd be living, he could have a dog. If he ever got back to Mr. Daniel's, he was getting one. A big one that could scare away the bad guys. But first he had to get out of here. Somehow, he had to escape and get back to Mr. Daniel.

Benny peered around the room. No man. He was probably still sleeping. Benny's mom used to sleep a lot after she drank a bunch of drinks from the big bottle. Now would be a good time to get away. If the man was like Mom, he wouldn't hear nothing. He'd sleep for hours and then get up real mean.

His dad. Benny shuddered. Could that guy really be his dad? His mom had never told him anything about his dad. Sometimes Benny imagined what he was like. The dad in his head didn't look nothing like this guy. He looked more like Marco's Uncle Joaquin. Big and tough, but nice. The good guy who protected the kid from the bad guys. This man was the bad guy.

He wiggled his hands. They moved a little inside the rope. The man hadn't done a very good job of tying them. He hadn't tied Benny's feet. He said he didn't want to have to carry him. Too tired, he said. Too drunk, Benny figured. He had been laughing the whole time, his breath making Benny gag. As the memory flooded him, he struggled to his feet. He had to get away.

He took two steps forward, holding his breath. He stopped, listened. Only the tick of a clock on the wall broke the silence.

Daniel had said praying was talking to God. God could hear him, even if Benny couldn't see Him. Was God looking at him now? If He was, why didn't He help? *God, I need some help, if You have time. Okay?* There. He'd talked to God. Now he had to get out.

Slowly, he tiptoed to the front door. Just be quiet. Just be quiet. No creaking floor. No coughing. Not even breathing. He grabbed the doorknob, turned, and yanked.

Nothing.

He tried again. The door didn't budge.

Biting his lip to keep from crying, he studied the door. It had bolts on it. Deadbolts, like the one his mom used to keep the bad guys out. Only now, it kept Benny and the bad guy in. It should have a key. Where were the keys? Benny looked around. The man probably had them.

He wanted to cry so bad. Fear made his legs shake. The guy was going to wake up and see him. He would throw him back in the closet. Or maybe he'd just cut him with the knife. Or shoot him with the gun he kept in his waistband.

Back door. Yeah, there had to be a back door.

Benny crept to the kitchen. Their dirty paper plates still sat on the table and the mustard bottle lay on its side on the counter next to an overflowing ashtray. Benny tried not to inhale the gross smell. There was a little porch off to the right, where the washing machine and the dryer sat. He opened the screen door with both hands and saw the back door past the machines. Maybe the man had forgotten to lock it.

Benny rushed forward, careful not to let the screen door slam behind him. A bubble of relief wafted through him. He wanted to laugh and cry at the same time. If he could get out, he could find someone to untie his hands. He could ask directions. He'd find a taxicab, make the driver take him home. He would see Mr. Daniel again.

He pushed through the back door and felt the sun warm on his face. He'd made it.

His foot touched the last step.

Fingers squeezed his shoulder until the bone and muscle pinched in pain.

The sun had crept up by the time Daniel and Cooper arrived at the women's prison complex in Gatesville. John Katz, the narcotics detective who had originally arrested Shawna Garza, had snoozed in the backseat for most of the three-hour drive. He didn't seem too interested in the details of the case. Shawna Garza was small potatoes.

They wanted her supplier. She wouldn't give him up and had gone to prison instead.

Daniel didn't care what Katz thought. Shawna Garza was the key to getting Benny back, and he intended to rattle her cage until she gave him the information they needed.

After Cooper parked the Explorer, Daniel shoved open the door and pulled himself out. This would've been a good morning to be in church with his kids. Not standing in front of a prison. He swallowed the sour taste in the back of his throat. He had to do this for Benny. Piper and Samuel were picking the kids up and taking them to church. Next Sunday, they'd all go together, including Benny.

The sun already seemed harsh, but Daniel shivered as they started across the parking lot. The ibuprofen he had taken well before dawn was starting to wear off. Detective Cooper's cell phone rang, a strident sound in an otherwise still morning.

"Detective Cooper. Uh-huh. Uh-huh. We're standing outside your facility right at this very moment, ma'am. Maybe we best come on in and talk about what happened."

Cooper didn't look happy. A chill shook Daniel. "What is it?"

"Ms. Garza was found dead in the bathroom. Shanked. Bled out."

"She's dead?" Daniel tried to comprehend. How would they find out where the drugs were? How would they give the kidnapper what he wanted? Shawna Garza wasn't much of a mother, but she was all Benny had. How would Daniel tell him? He fought back cusswords he hadn't said in years. Instead, he tried to pray. *God, why would You let this happen?*

"Daniel?" Cooper stared at him, concern on his face. "You all right?"

"Yeah. What now?"

The detective removed his cowboy hat and ran a hand through his brilliant white hair. "It surely does present us with a problem, don't it?"

"Yes, it does. A big problem."

"Let's go talk with the staff here, see what happened."

Inside, the warden, Ellen Rockford, a woman with the complexion of someone who sat behind a desk all day, led them through a series of long hallways, locking doors, and security checks before they ended up in the infirmary. Shawna Garza's body rested on a hospital bed, covered with a white sheet. One bare foot stuck out the end.

"This is Dr. Kramer, our resident physician," Rockford said, gesturing toward a man with thick black-rimmed glasses and acne-scarred skin. "What do you have, Doctor?"

Dr. Kramer had a surprisingly firm handshake and the deep voice to go with it. "The prisoner suffered several deep wounds to the chest and stomach. One wound penetrated a lung. She drowned in her own blood. She has some defensive wounds on her hands and some bruising on her upper arms."

"Somebody grabbed her and they struggled." Daniel lifted the sheet for one brief second. Shawna Garza's slack features told him nothing. He dropped the cloth and turned back to the doctor.

"Looks that way."

"Do you have the perpetrator?"

Cooper directed the question to the warden, who shook her head. "Not yet. The prisoners in that cellblock are in lockdown. We've isolated the troublemakers. We'll let you know if we come up with anything, but chances aren't too good. The code of silence is pretty impenetrable."

"How was her record inside?"

"We hadn't had any trouble with her." Rockford pushed her glasses up on her nose and glanced at a folder in her hand. "She spent a lot of time on the computer. Spent time in the library. Did her job."

"Don't know of anyone who gave her a hard time?"

Rockford shrugged. "She was a fairly attractive woman. I would image that got the attention of the other inmates. However, she didn't complain, at least not to the staff."

"I'd like a copy of the autopsy report when it's ready."

"We'll pass that request on. Anything else?"

"Who notifies next of kin?" Daniel couldn't take his gaze from the slender bare foot sticking out from under the sheet. She'd been a sorry excuse for a mother, but still, a human being.

"The TDCJ will take care of it."

"I don't think there's any next of kin here in Texas, besides her son," Daniel admitted, glancing over at the detective. Cooper had filled the warden in on the situation.

"The records show that she has a brother and some distant family members in California," Rockford replied. "We're not even sure the addresses she gave when she came into the system are still good or were ever good. I guess her son becomes a ward of the state."

Or my child. Daniel didn't say it aloud. *God, I'd like to think prison changed Shawna. But I don't have any way of knowing. I pray that it did. Lord, it was a horrible way to die, in prison, all alone. When the time comes, help me find the words to tell Benny. Help me to give him comfort. And Lord, show Your grace and Your mercy on Shawna Garza.*

"Daniel, you ready?" Cooper's puzzled voice penetrated his reverie.

"Yeah, I just thought — a word of prayer seemed in order."

"No problem." Cooper took a step closer and inclined his head. Katz looked away, his face reddening. The doctor and the warden simply waited. "We have time if you need more."

"No. I'm done."

Not as done as Shawna Garza. She had gone into the system a drug dealer and an unfit mother. She had come out dead. They had no way to know where she'd hidden the drugs.

The one thing Daniel needed to save Benny, he didn't have.

CHAPTER ELEVEN

A pounding headache. Pounding at the door. Deborah didn't know which was worse. She opened her eyes. She lay, still fully clothed, on her couch. The pounding increased to an earth-shattering crescendo.

"What? What?" She cringed at the sound of her own voice.

"Deborah. Open up." Omar, her AA sponsor. Shame washed over her in sickening sync with her dry heaves. He would be so disappointed. She turned over and burrowed into the couch pillows.

"Deborah. Open this door. Now!"

She rolled over and sat up, then waited for the vertigo to subside. The smell of stale beer and smoke wafting from her clothes filled her nostrils. She threw a hand over her mouth as gorge rose in her throat.

"Deborah!"

"Okay! I'm coming." She shuffled to the door and jerked it open. The brilliant morning sun pierced her to the bone, forcing her to throw a hand up to shade her eyes. The pounding in her head battered her even as a powerful thirst threatened to overcome her. She ran her tongue over cracked lips, trying to bury the craving. "What are you doing here?"

The sun shone on Omar's shaved head. He looked more like an ex-con than a computer software specialist who was married to his laptop and drove a Lexus. "Chewing you out for not calling your AA sponsor last night." He had the gravelly voice of a two-pack-a-day smoker even after eight years of smokeless sobriety. "Bringing you coffee and giving you a ride to church. It's Sunday morning, in case you're too hung over to remember."

"Who called you?"

"Sergeant Martinez." He handed her a tall brown cup. "Straight up, just the way you like it."

Deborah groaned and smacked the open door with the palm of her free hand. "Wait until I see Luna. The rat. I'm gonna kick his butt."

"Yeah," Omar snorted. "Beat up the guy who saved you from drinking and driving and carted you home in the middle of the night. That's the way to treat real friends.

We'll go to church, get some breakfast, and then go to a meeting. After that I'll take you to get your truck."

Deborah's stomach lurched at the word breakfast and lurched a second time at the thought of facing her boss in the church parking lot. "I can't go to a meeting. We're trying to find a missing child." She should've been focused on Benny last night instead of puking her guts out in her bathroom. She had to make it up to Daniel, find Benny for him. "I don't have time for meetings."

"According to Sergeant Martinez, you're on medical leave."

"Medical leave?" Deborah stuttered the words. "I was drunk, not sick. And it's nobody's business." Not true. It was Daniel's business. She had probably messed up any chance he had of getting back with Nicole.

"He's worried about you, Deborah. When are you going to figure out that these people are your friends?" Omar fingered the tiny gold hoop in his earlobe as he glowered at her. She always disappointed the people around her. "Instead of grabbing a bottle when the going gets tough, grab me or one of your other friends."

She would have to convince Sarge that she was fit for duty. He had to believe her. Deborah forced herself to meet Omar's gaze. "Does Sarge — did he say anything else?"

"Your boss is a man of few words, but he sounded sick about the whole thing." Omar's tone softened a little. "You want to tell me about it?"

"No." At least it was Sunday. The liquor stores were closed, and the bars wouldn't open until after lunch.

"If you're not going to tell me, you have to go back to the shrink tomorrow. Got it?"

Deborah had been seeing the department psychiatrist for more than six months. She had told the woman everything about her childhood, the molestation by her mother's boyfriend, the alienation from her mother, everything — everything except about Daniel. "Got it."

This time she managed to sound more confident. She'd go, for all the good it would do. The psychiatrist might be able to work miracles on her head, but Deborah hadn't seen any signs that she could do anything for her heart.

"Are you going to let me in or make me stand out here while you change. You can't go to church looking like that."

The compassion in Omar's eyes belied the irritation in his voice. Deborah took a breath and pulled the door open wider.

"Come in."

"Thank you."

She still hadn't gotten used to the idea that she had friends. If they knew what she had done to Daniel yesterday, would they still be her friends? She couldn't be sure.

Daniel had sent Luna to look for her. He wasn't mad? He should be mad. His foster child was missing and instead of helping find him, she was on medical leave. She'd let him down again. Instead of pickling herself with alcohol, she should have been looking for Benny. Daniel might forgive her, but how could God? One bad thing after another. *I'm just bad, God, bad. I'll never be good enough.*

Shuddering at the thought, Deborah splashed cold water on her face in the bathroom sink. As she squirted paste on her toothbrush, she practiced taking deep breaths and trying to smile. Why was she going to church? Because Samuel would never let her back on the team if she didn't show she had the guts.

Besides, she'd rather confront Samuel at church, when his mood would be slightly mellower — if you could use that word for Samuel's clenched-jaw personality. She might have a chance — a small one — after the service.

Omar tried to make conversation on the short trip to the church, but Deborah could only focus on the impending confrontation with Samuel. At least Ray wouldn't be there. He would be so disappointed in her. The closer they got to the church, the more she wanted to jump from the moving vehicle and run as far and as fast as she could.

Instead she sat, hands fisted in her lap, while Omar pulled into a parking space and turned off the engine. He glanced at his watch. "We'll just make it in time. Let's go." He held out his hand. "Gum."

She dropped it in his palm. "I don't know, Omar, I think I need to lie down."

Omar grunted and got out of the car. When he opened her door and offered her a hand out, she couldn't raise her arm to take it.

"Deborah, get out of the car. Now. The service is starting."

"I don't feel good. I feel really bad."

"Good." His frown reminded her of the eighth grade teacher who'd caught her smoking in the bathroom. "Remember that the next time you decide to drink."

"Thanks a lot."

"You want sympathy? You're talking to the wrong guy. You think you're gonna get out of going to church because you're hung over, forget it. All the more reason to get your sorry behind in there and repent."

Omar could be a breath of fresh air. Deborah heaved herself from the seat. More like a gale-force wind. To her relief, the faith band already had the members of the congregation on their feet, singing. Her hands shook so badly she could hardly make out the words in the bulletin. Dry heaves and shakes, her old friends, had returned. She slipped into the pew where she always sat with Ray and the Martinez extended family. Except today Ray wasn't here. Or Daniel. Mercifully.

She stole a glance at Samuel. He seemed engrossed in the song even though his lips barely moved.

His gaze swung toward her. His eyes were bleak, unreadable, but he nodded. Then he lifted his gaze to the enormous stained glass window featuring the cross in front of them.

A hand slipped over hers and squeezed. Startled, she glanced up. Alex Luna stood next to her. What was he doing here? His eyes were sympathetic. She snatched her hand away and sank into the padded pew as the song ended.

After the service, she made a mad dash down the aisle, but she couldn't shake Alex. They made it almost to the doors of the sanctuary before he spoke. "Need a ride back to your truck? I mean, could I give you a ride?"

"What are you doing here?"

"Sarge invited me." His smile sagged a little. He wasn't as confident as he liked to pretend. "Need a ride?"

"No. You've done plenty." But just because he was a snitch didn't mean she had the right to be a jerk. "No, thanks," she amended. "Thanks for giving me a ride last night. Omar and I have a — have a thing we have to go to. Then he'll drop me off at my truck."

"Who's Omar?"

"My AA sponsor."

"Oh, okay. I just wondered. Hadn't seen him around."

He looked so uncomfortable she felt something almost like pity. It had been only a few months since she had been newly sober and terrified to come through those church doors. Maybe Alex was terrified, too. Daniel had helped her. Daniel. At least she hadn't had to face him yet. Not working the case would make it easy to avoid him.

And hard to make things right.

"Since we're asking questions, why are you really here today, Luna?" she asked, dragging her mind away from a dilemma that seemed to have no solution.

"Alex, remember." His gaze challenged her to say she didn't. "Like I said, Samuel invited me."

"I know, but why say yes? I didn't think church was your deal."

"Sarge said you would be here."

His gaze held hers as he said the words. It took Deborah a second to understand. "I — I" She stopped.

"See ya." Now the broad grin that transformed a plain face was back. He turned and strolled away.

She could see why some women found that smile so devastating. Not her.

She'd turned him down three times. Yet, he didn't seem to be giving up. Even after seeing her falling-down drunk. What did that say about him? Could he be trusted or did he just like a challenge?

A shudder ran through her. She couldn't help her feelings for Daniel, but he was married and she knew he'd never reciprocate. Having a relationship with someone who was available — that was another thing. Alex didn't need damaged goods in his life.

She needed to work. Clinging to the thought, she searched the crowd in the narthex. Samuel stood in front of a window that overlooked the parking lot, talking on his cell phone. The bent of his mouth said the news wasn't good. He disconnected and stuck the phone in his pocket, his shoulders slumped as he turned and stared out the window.

She approached carefully. "Samuel — Sarge." He glanced back at her, his gaze revealing nothing. She could never tell what he was thinking. The man had helped her stop drinking and keep her job, yet he'd grown increasingly distant. "Could I talk to you for a second?"

"For a second. I have *work* to do." The sarcastic emphasis on work was unmistakable.

"I know I messed up, but it won't happen again." His face remained impassive as Deborah searched for more words to convince him. "Please don't put me on leave. I want to help with the investigation into Benny's disappearance."

"Sorry, you know the deal. You drink, you're out. Zero —"

"I know, zero tolerance." Anger flared. He didn't get it. She needed to work.

"You're lucky you still have a job. Don't you get that?" She caught a flash of fury in his face, even as he kept the level of his voice to just above a whisper. "I went out on a limb for you. And you decide to go on a bender the night of your partner's wedding? The day Daniel's foster child is kidnapped? These people are your friends, and they need to be able to depend on you."

"I know. I know."

Samuel's gaze moved over her shoulder. He raised a hand and waved. Deborah glanced back. Piper was working her way toward them through the crush of people. Deborah rushed to convince him. "If you just let me work, I know I can get past it, keep it from happening again."

"I won't endanger the officers who work with you — not again." He shoved past her and took Piper's hand. "Daniel just called. Shawna Garza is dead. I need to go to the station. Can you get someone to drop you and the kids at the house?"

Piper nodded, but her gaze went to Deborah, the look on her face too knowing.

Deborah swallowed hard and tried to breathe. "You won't let me help —"

"No." Samuel turned his back to her and raised his hand again, signaling to Alex, who stood talking to Joaquin. "Guys, over here."

Deborah let the crowd surge past her as Samuel's crew converged on him for the latest word. Shawna Garza had been killed the previous evening, presumably by another inmate. Now they had to come up with another way to give the kidnapper something in return for Benny.

She took a step back, then another, until she was against the far wall. Alex glanced her way. His gaze was sympathetic, but a second later he snapped back to what Samuel was saying.

Her mood skidded past longing toward agonizing defeat. She might as well give in.

Mr. Whiskey or Omar. Omar was nice, but Mr. Whiskey danced with her and held her in a warm embrace, whispering in her ear that she was loved, that she could do no wrong, telling her she was safe.

Deborah turned her back on the knot of coworkers who had someplace important to go.

She had no idea where she was headed.

CHAPTER TWELVE

Daniel grabbed the papers on his lap to keep them from sliding into the foot well of the Explorer as Cooper accelerated through the prison parking lot. Samuel was gathering the troops at PD back in San Antonio. They'd start hunting down Shawna's visitors within the hour. With Shawna dead, the names were the only leads they had. One of those visitors knew what game she had been playing before PD busted her and sent her to prison.

Samuel had divulged his own piece of information. Deborah had relapsed. The fact that his brother hadn't shared that news with him before he left San Antonio irritated Daniel. Once again Samuel had played big brother and made a decision about Daniel's welfare.

Daniel tried to force the thought aside. Bottom line, Deborah was drinking and on medical leave. The long fingers of guilt

141

poked him in the chest. Did her relapse result from that brief embrace in Ray's guest bedroom? Daniel couldn't imagine what he'd done to make Deborah think there might be something between them. He shook his head, caught Cooper's puzzled glance, and dropped his gaze to the documents on his lap. "Shawna had quite a few visitors."

"Repeats?" Cooper whipped the vehicle onto the road that led to IH-35 and San Antonio. "We know they weren't family. Could've been business associates. Or a boyfriend?"

Daniel gripped the door handle and tried to read as his body tipped toward the window. Cooper eased up on the accelerator, a slight smile on his face. Upright again, Daniel twisted around and looked at Katz in the backseat. "Do any of these names mean anything to you? Juanita Piedras. Rachel Lowe. Miguel Suarez. Jorge Morin."

"Oh, sure. All the gangbangers register with me personally." The narcotics detective slapped a pair of reading glasses on his long nose. "Let me look through our case file — see what illustrious names I can find."

He studied the folder in front of him, silent for a moment. "Yeah, our Latin King buddies. Miguel Suarez. He's one of Eloy

Barrera's lieutenants. No wonder Shawna wouldn't talk when we arrested her. We offered her a deal, but she refused to rat anybody out. I guess she was more scared of them than she was of us."

"Anybody else on the list ring a bell?"

Katz removed the glasses and rubbed the bridge of his nose. "Now I remember — Juanita Piedras worked with Shawna at the doughnut shop. Another one who wouldn't crack. I thought sure she was in on it, but *nada.* Jorge Morin doesn't register in the memory banks, though."

"Know where we can find Barrera?"

"He's gone under. Probably at a ranch his family has north of Laredo. Suarez is running the south side for him, from what I've heard. I've got an address on the doughnut shop where Garza and Piedras worked, if you want to start there."

Daniel's empty stomach heaved at the word doughnut, but he managed to keep his voice even. "It's open on Sunday?"

"Twenty-four hours a day, seven days a week. Shawna worked the nightshift. Locked the kid in the apartment alone."

Daniel already knew the details of Benny's life with his mother, but he let Katz drone on, thinking of Benny's scared, bruised face the day Daniel had picked him

143

up from the group home. He'd squeezed into the corner of the backseat in Daniel's car, his emaciated arms crossed tight against his undersized body, a defiant look on his face as he stared out the window.

It had taken weeks to get him to trust Daniel enough to touch him. A quick pat on the back first, then a small hug at bedtime, until finally, Benny had thrown himself into Daniel's arms for a full-fledged hug over an infield single.

The ring of his phone broke the reverie, forcing Daniel to abandon the memory of Benny's grinning face.

"Daniel, it's Samuel. I'm on the road to the station. Find anything?"

Daniel reeled off names. "Ask Joaquin about Suarez. Maybe he can track him down through his gang unit contacts."

"Right." Samuel paused. Daniel heard a horn blare and tires screech. "So we don't have Shawna and we don't have the drugs. We need to come up with a strategy to keep this guy from going ape on us." His brother's inflection hadn't changed.

"Agreed." Daniel flexed his free hand in a fist, hoping his brother had some ideas. "I'm thinking we offer to pay him the value of the drugs in cash."

"Who comes up with the cash?"

"Katz is talking to his guys, see if they might want a stake in it. The DEA might be interested if they think they might get Barrera out of it." They would get access to key information that might break Barrera's operation, and Daniel would get Benny back alive. Everyone benefited.

"*Está bien.* What's your ETA?"

"We're going to stop for doughnuts before we meet you guys."

"Doughnuts? I guess you're feeling better."

Daniel wished that were true. Nausea and a pounding headache were his constant sidekicks. "Shawna Garza's last legitimate place of employment was a doughnut shop. We're hoping to get a lead on her stash. Maybe somebody else was in the game with her."

"Be safe."

Benny wasn't safe. Until he was, Daniel didn't care about being safe. "You, too."

Light traffic and Cooper's lead foot put them in San Antonio a mere two hours later. Daniel's fingers slid down the greasy handle of the doughnut shop door. A wave of warm air hit him in the face, bringing with it the smell of fried dough. Doughnuts. Old grease. Coffee. He tried to keep his breathing shallow, not sure how his stomach would react to the aroma of food. He couldn't remember the last time he'd eaten.

Cooper slid onto a stool at the counter, Katz next to him. Daniel paused for a moment, eyeing the area behind the counter. Two waitresses pulled *pan dulce* from long trays and stowed them on shelves in a huge display case. The one with the long platinum blond hair glanced his way and returned to her task.

The one with the red hair that screamed bad dye job stared at him a second, looked away, and then at the two men at the counter. She leaned in and whispered to her coworker as she wiped her hands on a semi-white apron. She trotted the length of the counter to where Katz and Cooper sat. "Coffee, gentlemen?"

"Sure," Katz spoke first. "Coffee and a side order of information."

"Coffee's a buck, free refills. Information will cost you more."

"How've you been, Juanita?"

Juanita Piedras's bloodshot gaze sharpened. Her lined face, cankered lips, and stained teeth revealed hard living despite her youth. She had the skinny frame of a habitual user. "Fine, until now. You narcs?"

"Some of us. Don't you remember me?" Katz smiled.

Her face darkened. "You arrested Shawna. What do you want?"

Daniel picked up a menu. They served breakfast as well as doughnuts. The words swam in front of him. He dropped the menu and gripped the counter. "We want to talk about Shawna."

Juanita slapped her order pad on the counter. "Her again. You put her away. What more do you want? Let the poor woman do her time in peace."

"We would. Except we think she arranged to have her son kidnapped."

"Benny?" The woman's thin lips pulled down in a deep frown. "Don't sound like something Shawna would do. She ain't crazy about being a mother, but she wouldn't put him in danger."

Just sell drugs out of her apartment, invite strange men to spend the night, and send her son out to deliver crack on his bike. Anger surged through Daniel. He tried to breathe through it, but the smell of grease made him want to gag. "You've been visiting her on a regular basis."

"So? Visiting a friend in prison a crime?"

"Not yet. What did the two of you talk about?"

"None of your business."

"She's dead." Detective Cooper spoke for

147

the first time. He placed his hat on the counter in front of him and ran his hand over the top as if to remove any dust particles.

The coffee cup Juanita set on the counter in front of Katz clanged against the saucer, sloshing liquid over the side. "You're lying. I just saw her last week. She was fine. She was putting together an appeal. She was gonna get out and get her kid back."

"Not anymore." Katz smirked and dumped sugar in his coffee. "Guess that leaves you with the stash."

"What stash?" Juanita picked up a washcloth from the sink. She began wiping around the large coffeemakers that lined the back wall.

"Barrera's product."

"I don't know nobody named Barrera. I ain't got nobody's product." She twisted the washcloth between bony fingers. "I told you guys when you arrested Shawna, I didn't have nothing to do with her side business."

"I didn't believe you then, and I don't believe you now." Katz took a sip of his coffee and grimaced. "You make this last week?"

"Fresh every morning, just like the sign says."

Daniel didn't have the patience for this small talk approach. "I believe that as much as I believe you don't know what Shawna was up to. Who else knows where the stuff is?"

"I have no idea."

Katz chuckled. "Juanita, I bet if I get a warrant to search your apartment, I'm gonna find your own little stash. I bet you've got some in your purse. I bet I'd find a dime rock in your pocket right now. Detective Cooper, what do you want to bet?"

"Well, I'm not a betting man. However, I'm fairly certain you're right, Detective Katz," Cooper said. "I think you should get yourself that warrant. Maybe we'll find what we've been looking for."

"I ain't got it." Juanita's face puckered. "I ain't."

"Something happens to Benny, you'll be responsible." Daniel let the heat of his anger fuel the words. "You said Shawna wouldn't endanger a child. What about you? Do you want to be responsible for the death of a child? Can you live with that? What kind of monster are you?"

The woman rubbed red-rimmed eyes. "All right. All right! I bought from Shawna. But I never sold. I wasn't involved in her business. I told her she was making a pact with the devil when she got involved with Barrera, but she wouldn't listen. She wanted out of this hole so bad, she would've made a deal with anybody."

"What was she planning before she was arrested?"

"I don't know exactly, but it was big. She was excited. She said she had her ticket out of this joint, and as soon as she had her score, she'd be gone. Her and the kid. She was going to California. She was going to get a job on Rodeo Drive. She talked big. It was just garbage."

"She have a partner? Somebody she was working with?"

"I don't know."

"Juanita, you might want to think a little harder." Katz pulled a pair of handcuffs from the back of his belt and laid them on the counter. The woman's gaze fastened on the shoulder holster visible under the detective's jacket when he moved. "I can charge you with being an accessory to kidnapping. Mighty hard to get your fix in jail."

"No, you couldn't. You got no evidence. I ain't done nothing." Her gaze darted from left to right as if searching for an escape route.

Katz stood, shook out the handcuffs, and took a deliberate step toward the end of the counter. "Watch me."

"Okay!" Juanita began to back up. "There was a guy. A skinny Mexican. He came in here a lot toward the end. Always sat in the back, in the corner. Shawna never charged him. He always ate half a dozen doughnuts all by himself, one right after the other. It was kind of sickening to watch."

"Name, Juanita, name!" Katz eased around the corner of the counter, ignoring the glare from her coworker, who stood watching the exchange with obvious interest.

"She called him Jugo. That's all I know." Her hands fluttered to her face and dropped to her apron. "I'm telling you, that's all I know."

"Jugo as in Juice? Describe him."

"I told you — tall, skinny Mexican."

"Mexican national or Latino?"

"I didn't ask him for no papers." Her gaze swung over Daniel's shoulder, toward the front door, her watery eyes squinting as if the guy might walk in any second. "He talked like he was from around here. All Tex-Mex. Tall, real brown, light blue eyes, made him look weird. A gold tooth that showed when he smiled. He was always smiling at Shawna. I thought he had a thing for her. But Shawna said that was in the

151

past. I guess she'd known him for a while."

Katz pulled his cell phone from his pocket. "Get me an address for a Juanita Piedras. Yeah. Home address. Yeah, then see what you can do about getting me search warrants for the All Night Donut Shop and for that home address. See if we can get a sketch artist. Yep. That's right."

"You said if I told you —" Her face white, Juanita's mouth worked and her voice rose to a high-pitched scream that grated on Daniel's decimated nerves. "You're a liar!"

Daniel leaned over the counter and grabbed her arm so he could pull her face close to his. "Shut up and listen. You were the last one to visit Shawna. You saw her at least once a week. That's no casual friendship. It's a long drive to the prison. If you had something going with her, I'll find out what it was. If you had something to do with this little boy's disappearance, you're doing time. Until we find Mr. Weird Eyes, you're a prime suspect. Get used to it."

Juanita jerked from Daniel's hold and tried to lunge past Katz. Coffee cups flew. Liquid splattered. A pot slid from the counter and crashed at their feet in dozens of pieces on the cracked, greasy linoleum.

"Juanita Piedras, you're under arrest for assault on a public servant." A lazy grin on

152

his face, Katz grabbed both her arms and pulled them behind the struggling woman. The handcuffs made a satisfying clink when they snapped around her wrists.

Holding her with one hand, Katz grabbed a coffeepot with the other. "Care for some more coffee, gentlemen?"

Shaking his head, Daniel slid from his seat. He shoved through the front door of the doughnut shop and stood on the sidewalk. The afternoon sun warmed his face, but he was still freezing. Cooper pushed through the door behind him.

"She doesn't know anything."

Cooper chewed a toothpick, one hand shielding his eyes from the sun. "You don't know that."

"She wasn't in on it."

"No, but she may know who was."

"She didn't give us much to go on."

"We got this guy Juice."

"He could be one of the names on the visitors' list," Daniel conceded.

"Katz will have his guys run the names through the database and start pulling up pictures. Give her a couple of hours without her rocks and she'll cooperate. If that doesn't work, we'll get a sketch artist. One way or the other, we'll get an ID."

Daniel started toward the Explorer. They

didn't have Shawna Garza; they didn't have the drugs. All they had was a name. Jugo. Juice.

It would have to be enough.

CHAPTER THIRTEEN

Alex slapped another folder on the stack of paperwork he was digging his way through. Tómas Chavez had a record a mile long. Most of it preceding his short stint as the lease holder on Ray's ranch. Alex's gut said there had to be a connection to the little girl. Finding it was the problem.

He shifted in the hard chair the sheriff's deputy on duty had allowed him to use. They weren't too thrilled at having a PD homicide detective in their workspace on a Sunday afternoon, but Coop had paved the way like a bulldozer. Who cared about jurisdiction when the minutes were ticking — for Benny? Even with the clock banging in his head, Alex had to squeeze in time for a little girl who had been killed and dumped into an unmarked grave like unwanted trash. On the flip side of the coin, working a kidnapping and a murder case simultaneously had the dubious benefit of making it possible for Alex to forget Deborah's brush-off at the church. Almost.

The things a guy did for a woman. Like spending an hour in church fighting off memories that refused to remain at bay. His sister in a white confirmation dress. Sitting between his parents who refused to look at each other throughout the entire service. Mouthing songs that had no meaning as he dreaded the silent ride home and the explosion of argument that started when they pulled into the driveway and rocked the house for hours afterward. No place to hide. All he could do was run. Neither of them ever noticed he was gone.

Alex's stomach growled. He ignored it and began combing through the files. The former tenant at Ray's ranch had done various stretches in the Bexar County jail on misdemeanor drug possession charges. Chavez's pen pack at the jail showed he'd admitted to an affiliation with the Latin Kings, a local gang with an increasingly violent hold over a good chunk of the south side's drug trade.

The next time he'd been busted, Chavez had graduated to the Texas Department of Criminal Justice for possession with intent to distribute. The stay must have done him good or made him smarter. He hadn't been in the system in almost five years until a recent arrest for drunk and disorderly and assault after a bar fight.

Alex slapped the folder shut and reached for the next one. It was more interesting. Deputies had been out to Spanish Oaks Ranch half a dozen times on domestic dispute calls over a two-year period that ended five years ago. They'd made Chavez leave the property twice. No charges had been filed.

Sheriff's deputies had escorted CPS workers to the ranch on one occasion. A young child had been removed. A little girl named Nina Chavez.

Sick excitement rolled through Alex. His hand hovered over the phone. One more folder, thicker than the others. He opened it. Tómas Chavez had filed a missing person report about six months after the CPS visit. Missing persons, actually. His wife and five children.

He claimed to have left the ranch to run some errands and came home to find them gone, along with their clothes, suitcases, and the family minivan. The deputies had done a detailed investigation. They'd concluded that Clarisse Chavez had probably fled and was in hiding from an abusive husband. The family was never found, and the case was still open but not under active investigation.

Chavez called periodically to harass them about finding his family, and the calls were duly noted in the file. Alex now had the man's home address in Helotes.

He rose and scooped up the folders. Sarge wouldn't be happy, but Alex had to make a detour before going to the station. "Thanks," he called to the deputy as he loped toward the door.

"Hey, you can't take those folders —" The deputy stood. He seemed to think twice of the effort and sat down.

Alex took the steps two at a time. It wasn't just one little girl, it was five kids. If the little girl had met this end, what had happened to the other four? Were there more graves somewhere, graves they hadn't found yet?

All those little graves. The image drove Alex to keep the accelerator to the floor on Highway 16 all the way to Chavez's address on the outskirts of Helotes. The man lived in a trailer set back from a dirt road. A patch of tall grass and weeds almost obscured the set of steps leading to the door. What looked like a garage and a falling-down shack were half hidden behind the trailer. An enormous Dodge Ram sat in the dirt driveway. Nice ride for a handyman. When Alex identified himself as a police officer, Chavez didn't flinch.

"Come in. *Mí casa es su casa.*" He held the door for Alex, his arm extended in welcome, despite the sardonic tone. Alex guessed his age as close to fifty if the wrinkles around his eyes and the thinning hair shot through with gray were any indication. "Beer? *Está fría.*"

"*Gracias, señor,* but no."

"Some water then?" Without waiting for an answer, he shuffled to the kitchen on bare feet. The trailer was so small from where Alex stood, he could see Chavez pull the glass from the cupboard. "You here about my kids? After all these years, did you find Clarisse?"

Alex hesitated. The remains hadn't been definitively identified. "Sir, you haven't had any communications from your wife in the last five years?"

Chavez handed him a huge plastic tumbler of ice water. "Not a word. Hard to believe six people could disappear from the face of the earth like that." A spurt of anger flickered in his face and then disappeared. "The police are real good at their jobs around here."

Alex ignored the dig. "Did you try looking for them on your own?"

Chavez's expression remained serene, but something about his eyes struck Alex as hard. "I spent some serious moola on a private investigator after the police sat on their hands and did nothing. He came up with squat, took a trip on my dime, and then bailed. His partner gave me my money back. What's this all about?"

No choice but to go out on a limb. "You leased Spanish Oak Ranch for about a year, didn't you?"

The man's sudden stillness reminded Alex of a cornered animal trying to camouflage itself in the landscape. "Yeah, I did. How'd you know that?"

"A friend of mine bought the ranch five years ago."

"And what does that have to do with me?" The question came a little too quickly. He was quiet a minute, and Alex let it ride, waiting. "Hey, I read about this in the paper this morning. About the kid who disappeared at the ranch. It caught my eye since I lived there. Brought back some memories." He shook his head as if reviewing those memories again. "Shouldn't you be out there looking for him instead of chasing ghosts from five years ago?"

Ghosts. Interesting choice of words. "Well, there's more to it than you read in the paper." Alex held off giving him the details. "You actually have been back to the ranch since you left it five years ago, haven't you?"

Chavez scratched his neck over the collar of a ragged T-shirt. "Yeah, a few months ago. I did some work for the lady who has the place next door, *Señora* Stover. Mostly I worked at her ranch. She had some heavy stuff she needed moved. Once or twice I went to the Spanish Oak, but I never see the new guy who owns it. He was in a wreck or something. He never come out of the house. He couldn't walk good, she said."

"But you spent time on his property."

"A few hours, here or there. Is that against the law? I worked. I got paid. Ask *Señora* Stover."

"When we were searching for Benny Garza, we found someone else." Alex quickly laid it out, omitting the details.

The man went still again. Alex waited, studying his face. Not a muscle moved. After several seconds, Chavez's hands went to his face. "Mr. Chavez, should I get you some water?"

The hands dropped. Chavez's eyes were dry. "No." He stared at Alex. "Are you saying one of my kids has been buried out there on the ranch for the last five years?"

"Maybe you should tell me." Alex said the

words gently, never taking his gaze from Chavez's face. Not a single crack in the façade.

"Detective, my wife packed up my kids and left me five years ago. I came home one day, and she was gone. As far as I know all five of them went with her. If you're accusing me of something, why don't you just come on out with it?" He spoke as if he were offering Alex another beer. "Are you doing some kind of tests on the remains to see who it is?"

"A forensic anthropologist is doing the work, but we know she was a little girl, no more than five or six."

Chavez rose from his chair and went to the window, his back to Alex. "Nina. It had to be Nina."

"She was your youngest?"

"Yes. Five years old the last time I saw her." Chavez turned and faced Alex, his lips tight across teeth that protruded slightly, giving him a wolfish look. "Maybe that explains why Clarisse left. She was always whacking the kids — no patience at all. She popped out those puppies too close together, and then she couldn't handle it. She kills Nina and blows out of town . . ."

"That's interesting speculation." Alex tried to keep his disdain for the man out of his voice. "But like I said, we don't even know for sure the identity of the victim. Did Nina ever have dental work done?"

"Of course, we were good parents. Good parents." A flash of anger.

"You just said your wife was always whacking the kids — which is it?"

"So she was short on patience. You got kids?"

Not yet. At the rate he was going, maybe not ever. "You have an extensive criminal record, Mr. Chavez." Alex opened the folder in his hand, even though the contents were firmly established in his head. "A couple counts of domestic battery, DUI, public intoxication, possession, possession with intent to distribute, carrying a firearm without a permit, assault. Very colorful."

"I had a drug problem."

"Trying to forget something?" *Like killing his daughter?*

"Life in general. It's under control now."

Tires screeched, and a car door slammed. Chavez moved toward the door. He glanced through the octagon-shaped window and then back at Alex. "I don't remember the dentist's name, it's been so long, but I'll get it for you. Could I call you later?"

"Certainly, Mr. Chavez, and thank you." Alex stood and handed Chavez his card.

"My cell phone number is on there. Call me anytime."

"Will you let me know as soon as you know if it's my kid?" The pounding on the door didn't faze him. Alex could see a man's face in the window. "When can I bury her?"

"We'll need her dental records. The sooner you give us the information we need, the better. This is a murder investigation. That little girl died from blunt force trauma to the head. Someone hit her hard enough to kill her."

Chavez nodded, but the frown on his face deepened. "Someone like me? Listen, *ese*, I told you, Clarisse had a bad temper, and she had five kids too many."

"We don't know who did it, but we'll find out." That was a promise. The pounding got louder. "Do you want to get that?"

"He'll wait." Chavez's gaze didn't waver. "You think I killed my little girl — arrest me. Or is it just a feeling? Maybe you don't like the way I dress. Or my tatts, eh, *hermano.* But you can't arrest me because you ain't got no proof. So maybe you should come back when you do."

"That's the plan, Mr. Chavez." Alex stopped at the door and looked back. "By the way, are you working now? That's a very nice truck you got out there."

"I like to play the slots in Vegas. The truck's paid for." Chavez towered over Alex. His eyes were like bullets. "But I also work regular now. At Chuy's Auto Repair Shop. I'm good with my hands." This time his mouth formed a tight grin. "If you need help looking for that missing kid, let me know."

Right. "By the way, what was the name of the PI you hired? Do you remember that?"

"The guy was a deadbeat — I won't forget his name ever — Simon . . . yeah, Simon Phillips."

"Fine. We'll be in touch. That's a promise, Mr. Chavez."

"*Bueno.*" Chavez shrugged and finally opened the door.

The man who had been pounding gave them a surly look. "You deaf or what, *vato?* I was knocking." His gaze flickered to Alex. "Who are you?"

Alex introduced himself and waited. The newcomer didn't offer an introduction and neither did Chavez. "Well, I was just heading out. Give me a call if you think of anything that might help us identify this little girl."

"Little girl —" the man sputtered. Chavez gave him a look. He shut up.

Once he was on the road, Alex dug out

his cell phone and called Cooper. He told him about Chavez's history of domestic disputes and the disappearance of the wife and children. "We could be looking at more graves. We gotta get an evidence crew out to Ray's." A cold chill rippled through Alex. "Maybe he killed them all."

"Whoa. We haven't even established the identity of the first body." Coop's voice sounded muffled like he had the phone in the crook of his neck. "Let's not go off half-cocked. Did he seem nervous or upset?"

"He jumped to the conclusion that the remains belong to his youngest daughter, but he controls his emotions extremely well. Until this other guy showed up. Then he got a little nervous."

"I'll call out the canine unit and have them cover every inch of Ray's place to make sure there aren't any more graves out there. I —"

"And Coop . . ." Alex broke in. "That lets Ray off the hook, right? I mean, we're sure it's gotta be related to Chavez somehow."

"If the body belongs to Chavez's daughter, Ray's off the list."

"Good." Ray had never really been a suspect in anybody's book, but Alex wanted the record very clear with Cooper. Not that Ray and Susana would leave on their honeymoon anytime soon. Not until Benny returned home safely.

At least they had a plan of action. Alex eased onto the highway and shifted the phone from one ear to the other. "In the meantime, we should also follow up with the PI he hired. Either the rest of those kids are dead and buried or his wife made a run for it and hid them to keep him from killing them, too. We have to find them, one way or another, to make a case against him."

The line was quiet except for a faint buzz. "Or maybe the wife did it and then ran."

"Either way, we have to find them."

"If I had my druthers, it'd be alive and hiding." Cooper sounded tired.

"Me, too, Coop."

"The next step is the canine unit and then the PI."

"Right. See you at PD when you get back to town."

Alex disconnected. Benny missing. The four Chavez children missing. He hoped more of them were alive than dead, but the weight of his experience bore down on him.

So did the image of little bones arranged on a slab at the morgue.

CHAPTER FOURTEEN

Alex pulled the cell phone from his ear. He steadied the wheel with his other hand. He'd barely ended his conversation with Coop when the phone had vibrated on the dashboard. Joaquin's loud voice held irritation. "Samuel wants you and me to check out a guy. You're holding me up, man."

"Sorry, I'm working the Jane Doe case, too. I —"

"Sarge says let Cooper handle the Jane Doe for a couple of hours."

"Right." Alex hadn't had a chance to brief the boss on the latest developments, but now wasn't the time to argue — not with Benny's life on the line. Coop would keep him posted on the canine search at the ranch. "I'm five minutes from the station. I'll slow down to fifty and pick you up."

Joaquin laughed. "Where we're going, you ain't gonna want to take that fancy car of yours."

"Bad roads?"

Joaquin chuckled again. "I was thinking more along the lines of bullet holes."

Ten minutes later they were headed out of downtown in Joaquin's ancient Blazer.

"So, where're we going?"

"I've got a couple of uniforms meeting us at Miguel Suarez's last known address." Joaquin swerved to avoid a massive pothole, swore, and grinned. "Sorry. We're gonna do a knock-and-talk. If the guy's around."

"So, who is he?"

"Suarez is Barrera's muscle. Middle management. He dabbles in firearms, prostitution, a little extortion, a little gun for hire. Full-service bad guy."

Alex touched his holster, glad he'd spent some time at the firing range the previous week. "Great."

"Yeah, Eloy sends old Miguel out when he's upset with you — when he needs to set something straight. He spanks you, you know you've been spanked. We're thinking the drugs the kidnapper is after actually belong to Barrera and he sent Suarez to try to shake their location out of Benny's mother."

"I guess we should be happy we've found some connection." Alex leaned back in the seat and tried to relax. "But I hate to think whoever has Benny is connected to Barrera. They'll have no scruples about killing a kid."

Joaquin's face hardened. "They hurt a hair on that kid's head, there won't be any place they can hide."

It was a good thing Joaquin had chosen the right side of the law — he'd be one scary bad guy. He drove through two green lights before he spoke again. "So what's up with you and Deborah Smith?"

Alex tensed. "What?"

"I saw the look you gave her at church. So did Lily. What's going on with you two?"

"Nothing as far as I can tell."

Joaquin snorted. "Oh, man, you *like* Deborah Smith."

Something in Joaquin's tone stung and made Alex want to defend Deborah. "You have a problem with that?"

"No. But you will."

"What do you mean?"

"The woman's trouble."

His desire to find out what Joaquin knew about Deborah overcame Alex's natural reticence about his personal life. "What do you know about Deborah's problems?"

"I have ears and eyes. She has a reputation for getting around. That seems to have died down a little since she supposedly quit drinking, but when she drank —"

"She doesn't drink anymore."

Joaquin snorted. "Except last night."

"I thought she was your friend."

"She's Ray's partner, and she's a police officer. I don't dislike her, but I know what it's like when someone's got a drinking problem. She'll drag you down, dude."

The stony look on Joaquin's face said this wasn't the time to probe his experience with people who drank too much. Alex squirmed in his seat. "She's trying."

"Sure she is, and she has my wife's family and Ray to help her. That makes a big difference."

"And she goes to church."

"Yeah, don't make her an angel." Another stony look.

"What's up with you, Joaquin?"

"Nothing."

"You seem a little uptight about the church thing."

"No."

Joaquin fiddled with the knob on the radio. A voice droned on about the importance of recycling. Alex turned the volume down, ignoring Joaquin's dark look. "You sure?"

"I'm just saying be careful. You get involved with an alcoholic, it'll come back to bite you in the butt."

"I'll keep that in mind. But you don't specifically know anything about Deborah?"

"She's an alcoholic. That's all I have to know. Just leave it at that. Can we talk about something else?"

"Sure." Alex didn't bother to point out that his friend had brought the subject up. No need to get the guy more riled up.

It took them almost twenty minutes to get to Miguel Suarez's neighborhood. They pulled onto a street pitted with potholes and littered with trash, one junk pile of a car parked in the middle of the block. A stray dog, so skinny every rib showed, shot across the street, forcing Joaquin to brake hard. Alex's chest slammed against his tightened seat belt. "Easy, dude."

A marked SAPD unit idled at the corner half a block from the residence. "There's our backup." Joaquin pulled alongside the Crown Victoria and put the Blazer in park.

Alex rolled his window down. He'd met the driver a few times before. "Hey, Diego. Anybody home?"

The officer shrugged. "We did a roll-by. No vehicle in the driveway. Nobody outside. You gonna knock and talk?"

"Yeah, let's hit it."

Alex scanned the street and walked along the sidewalk toward Suarez's front yard.

Very quiet for a Sunday afternoon. The sun was already making its way down in the distance. It should have been time to fire up the mesquite wood in the barbecue pit. Turn up the *corridas* on the radio. Nobody sat on the porch reading the paper. No kids playing hopscotch on the sidewalk.

Tires screeched in the distance. Someone screamed, "Shut your mouth, *idiota.*" Now that was more like it.

Joaquin shoved open a rusted metal gate, swinging it back until it stood open on its own, a squeaky hinge protesting the entire way. He rapped on the door. Diego and his partner, a black guy Alex didn't recognize, stood back on the porch steps.

No answer. Alex eased his head down to peek in one of the front windows. Dirty glass revealed little. Joaquin pounded on the door. "SAPD, open up."

Glass and flying debris exploded through the window. He dove to the porch floor, Joaquin next to him. Diego and his partner bolted down the steps and slammed to the ground next to the foundation of the house.

"Jerk," Joaquin muttered.

Alex didn't feel much happier. Getting shot at in broad daylight on a Sunday afternoon didn't suit him at all. Joaquin crawled toward the end of the porch. "He's gonna try to get out the back. You watch. We'll have to chase the guy."

"Call for additional backup," Alex yelled at Diego. "Then secure the house from the front. We'll take the back."

He loped after Joaquin, trying to stay low and still move.

The back door stood wide open. A flash of color — a red T-shirt — caught Alex's gaze. A man hurled himself over the slatted wooden fence that marked the boundary between the yard and the alley.

"There!" He pointed. "He's going over the fence."

"That's Suarez. Stop, police, stop now!" Joaquin shot across the yard and hurdled the fence pole vault style. "Stop!"

Since Joaquin ran several miles a day and Alex only thought about doing it, he found himself lagging a few yards behind. He managed to take the fence without impaling himself and churned down the alley, trying not to stumble over tree limbs, trash, and tires. He couldn't suck in enough air to fill his lungs. The muscles in his thighs and calves burned.

Suarez took a hard right at the end of the alley, Joaquin only a few strides behind him. For a long second, Alex lost sight of both men. He picked up his pace, ignoring the

pain in his side and the excruciating in-
ability to breathe.

He hit the corner full-tilt.

Gunfire erupted.

CHAPTER FIFTEEN

Alex dropped to the pavement, his tortured breathing loud in his ears. He sucked in air and flung himself behind a Tahoe parked on the street. His stomach clenched. He hated getting shot at. And where was Joaquin?

Another quick one-two punctuated the still air. Then two more shots farther apart. "Joaquin! Talk to me."

Nothing. The seconds ticked away in Alex's ears. One-thousand-one. One-thousand-two. "Joaquin?"

"He's gone! He got away from me." Joaquin sounded like a kid who'd been denied a trip to the zoo. "Man, I thought I had him."

Alex poked his head around the bumper, then stood. Joaquin trotted down the sidewalk, his weapon hanging from one hand. He wasn't even breathing hard. "That sucker's fast. He took a couple of shots at me and when I returned fire, he ducked behind a car. I don't know if he went left or right. Call Diego and make sure they have the house secure, will you?"

"You all right?"

"No. The dude got away, man. That irritates me big time. Now I'll have to deal with the shooting team and I didn't even hit the guy."

Alex studied Joaquin as he listened to Diego confirm that everything at the house was under control. Something wasn't quite right. Joaquin's lips were pursed in a tense, thin line. Discharging his weapon meant an investigation by the shooting team, but that wasn't the problem. His breathing was shallow. He winced. His free hand went to his forearm in a tight grip. Alex took a closer look. Blood ran down his colleague's middle finger and dripped on the sidewalk. "You're bleeding."

"And you're very observant." Joaquin's laugh trailed off. "The bozo winged me — just grazed my arm. I really hate getting shot. It upsets Lily."

"I'm calling nine-one-one."

"I don't need no stinkin' ambulance." The bravado didn't keep Alex from noticing the gray tinge to Joaquin's skin. "I just need a bandage."

After completing the call, Alex grabbed

Joaquin's good arm and steered him back down the alley. "You're dripping all over the sidewalk."

"You like to exaggerate, don't you?" Joaquin stumbled.

Alex tightened his grip, silently berating himself for letting the chase get away from him.

"Let it go, Alex. Stuff happens."

Now the guy read minds. "I should've stayed closer."

"Hey, you could work out everyday and still never be able to keep up with me." Joaquin's laugh ended in a sound that might have been a groan. Alex walked faster.

The house smelled faintly of chicharron and corn tortillas. A baggie of pot lay on the kitchen table next to a pipe, matches, and a bottle of Corona. "Poor guy, we caught him in the middle of relaxing." Joaquin gritted his teeth, pain etched around his lips and eyes.

"Go outside. Find a place to sit down where you don't drip on evidence."

Joaquin backed away to the kitchen counter where he picked up a dish towel and wrapped it around his arm. "I'll stay back. I want to see the weapons."

He staggered ahead of Alex into the living room. Diego and his partner examined a cache of weapons laid out in rows on the floor. Three AK-47s, two 9mm handguns, a couple of MAC-10s, and a silencer. Variety is the spice of life. "You didn't touch anything, did you?"

Diego growled. "We'll secure the perimeter and wait for the evidence unit outside."

The smack of the screen door let Alex know what the officer thought of his question. The room was quiet except for Joaquin's labored breathing. And something else.

A tiny, muffled sob.

Alex's hand went to his gun. The uniforms had been so interested in the weapons they'd apparently missed another important aspect of the scene. He let his gaze sweep Suarez's living room. Aside from a slick, leather sectional and big screen TV, the room was empty. He strained to hear movement. Joaquin pointed his weapon at the drapes behind the couch and jerked his head. Alex nodded.

The sob came from behind the curtain that covered the largest of the three front windows. Alex eased forward, his weapon ready. Joaquin took the other side.

Alex whipped the curtains open.

"*Por favor. Señor.* I didn't do anything." A girl crouched under the broken window. She spoke in Spanish. *"No hice nada.* Don't kill me, please!"

"Soy policía. I won't kill you, I promise." Alex moved around the sofa, gun pointed at her. "Do you speak English? Get up, please. *Pare, por favor."*

The girl did as he commanded and stood, her trembling hands raised over her head. *"Me llamo Marta. Soy de Nuevo Laredo."*

"Habla inglés?"

"Sí. I speak little. I am Marta."

"I got that. From Nuevo Laredo. Why are you in Miguel Suarez's home?"

"The men with the machine guns took over the coyote's route. They killed him, and they said everyone had to pay again. I didn't have any more money so they sold me to *Señor* Suarez."

As Homeland Security had tightened up the border, the drug cartels had begun taking over the illegal alien smuggling routes, trying to control all illegal entry into the country for their own purposes. Marta's dilemma was a reflection of a post nine-eleven border reality. "How old are you?"

Two tears trickled down the girl's face, one on each bruised cheek. The bruises deepened from yellow to purple and green. "Fourteen *años."*

"Sit down, please."

She dropped to the floor on her hands and knees.

"On the sofa, Marta, *aquí*." Alex helped her up and led her to the sofa. Joaquin eased in next to him. "Sit here a minute while I get some help."

He needed a lot of help. His best friend was trying not to bleed on the furniture and a traumatized girl who'd left home searching for the American dream looked like someone had used her as his personal punching bag.

The EMS unit arrived moments later, sirens and lights blazing. The paramedic insisted Joaquin needed to be transported to the hospital. "It's more than a graze — it's a through and through."

"The bullet barely nicked my arm," Joaquin insisted through clenched teeth. "I'm not getting in that ambulance. I'll see my doctor for the antibiotics. I'm not gonna freak Lily out by making her come to the ER."

Alex shared an exasperated look with the paramedic. "Like she won't freak when she sees that bandage?"

"I'll wear long sleeves."

"To bed?"

Joaquin grinned. "None of your business. And shut up."

"You don't go in the ambulance, you gotta sign some paperwork for me." The paramedic stalked away.

"Hey, I promise not to sue you if my arm falls off." Joaquin called after him. His laugh faded into a grimace.

Alex followed his line of sight. Samuel and Ray approached. It was hard to tell whose face was surlier. Alex had given Ray the bare minimum over the phone. He'd rather Ray tell Sarge these things. Samuel Martinez was a fair man, but when it came to family, he was worse than a cornered rattlesnake.

Joaquin threw up a hand. "Don't worry, *cuñado.* It's already taken care of." A look passed between Samuel and his brother-in-law and the emotion on Samuel's face eased.

"Suarez?"

"They're still searching the neighborhood. I suspect he's long gone."

"Left a nice stash, though," Alex chimed in. He nodded toward the couch. "And a girl."

After making contact with the sergeant in charge of the shooting team, Ray took Joaquin to his doctor, leaving Alex with the Blazer. Alex was glad he wouldn't be at the Santos house when Lily discovered why Joaquin had come home early.

In the time it took a uniformed officer to find a soda and *tacos de picadillo* for the girl, Marta didn't say one word. She sat at the table, silent, her eyes red, her expression flat. Alex set the food in front of her. She grabbed a taco and wolfed it down. She kept looking at him as if she were afraid he'd steal her food. The paramedics said she was dehydrated, malnourished, and had bruises in a number of places aside from her face.

Sarge sat across from the girl, his hands clasped in front of him on the table.

His face exuded patience, but Alex knew better. They needed answers and quickly. Benny's kidnapper would be calling later in the day, and they still didn't have a solid lead on him.

"Marta, how long have you been in *Señor* Suarez's house?" Sarge's Spanish sounded like pure Mexico, unlike Alex's broken Tex-Mex.

The girl swallowed the bite of taco and took a sip of her soda. "Three day, I think. *No sé.*"

"Did Suarez have any visitors during that time?"

She nodded before taking another bite and chewing. She swallowed hard. "Did you call *La Migra?* I go back to *Mejico,* now? *¿Sí?* I want my *mama y papa.*"

183

"After the doctors take a look at you at the hospital."

Alex pulled up a chair and sat down, close to the girl. He took a shot at it. "Was it a man? Did you hear what they talked about?'

Marta rolled the second taco up in the foil, the look of fear on her face deepening. She said the two men talked loudly, arguing sometimes. "The man said he would get the drugs back if he had to kill a man named Juice." She frowned as if trying to figure out why a man would be called Jugo. "He said the man had called him. Said he was working on getting the drugs from a woman. He said he knew where to find a man named Juice. Then he left. He didn't come back."

Alex and Samuel exchanged glances again. Juanita Piedras had said a man named Jugo had visited Shawna at the doughnut shop.

"Marta, did you hear *Señor* Suarez say the man's last name?"

Marta studied the taco in front of her for a few seconds. "I think he say Morin. Yes, Morin."

Juice Morin. A Jorge Morin had visited Shawna Garza in jail. Jorge and Juice were one and the same man, and he was a suspect in Benny's kidnapping. Connected to a vicious drug dealer. Alex didn't know whether to be happy they had a name or scared sick

184

for Benny.

"What happened after the man left?"

"*Señor* Suarez paid attention to me. He said he liked me. A lot. I told him I wanted to get a job and send money home to my parents. He laughed. He said I had a job. My job was to make him happy."

Marta started to cry. She shoved the remaining taco across the table toward Alex. *"Ya no tengo hambre."*

Alex tossed the taco in the wastebasket. He'd lost his appetite, too. They had a name. Jorge "Juice" Morin.

If Morin couldn't come up with Barrera's product, Benny's fate could be in the hands of the most hardcore drug dealer in South Texas.

CHAPTER SIXTEEN

Daniel paced, his steps a monotonous thud on the thick, brown carpet in his apartment. The kidnapper was supposed to call with the time and place of the meeting. Three o'clock and still nothing. After the long round trip to Gatesville, his legs and back ached so he could barely stand, but he couldn't sit still. How long would he have to wait to tell this man that Shawna Garza was dead? That they never had a chance to ask her where the drugs were.

"Daniel, do me a favor." Samuel's voice held irritation mixed with a gruff affection.

Daniel glanced up. "What?" Ray and the DEA guys all seemed to be studying the floor.

"Sit."

Daniel sank into a nearby black, leather recliner, trying not to think about how Benny loved to sit in the big chair, crank the lever, and snap it back for a little nap.

Samuel consulted his notebook. "Jorge Morin is Jugo. He's done time for possession, intent to distribute, DUI, assault, burglary, theft. Lots of little junk. Nothing big — until now."

Daniel tried to stave off impatience brought on by stress combined with a lack of sleep and food. "He's connected to Barrera through the Latin Kings. He visited Shawna at the doughnut shop and in prison. It's him. We need to find him."

"His last known address was a bust." Samuel's tone stopped short of a patronizing big brother. "We're working on tracking him down, but right now we need to discuss what you'll say to him when he calls."

"I'll tell him to return Benny to us, or I'm going to find him and turn him into ground sausage." Daniel jerked up from the recliner and stomped from the room. He needed air, or coffee, or something.

At least the kitchen was quiet — and not so crowded.

He pulled a glass from the cabinet and filled it with water. A bottle of syrup on the tiled counter caught his gaze, reminding him of a recent Sunday morning when he'd fixed pancakes for Benny, Christopher, and Phoebe before church. Benny had begged to pour the batter in the big, electric skillet, marveling at how it turned into a solid. He thought all pancakes came from toasters. Christopher and Phoebe egged him on. Batter ended up splattered all over the stove, countertops, and all three kids' grinning faces.

Daniel grabbed the nearly empty coffee pot, the smell of the cold liquid turning his stomach. Might as well make himself useful. The kitchen extension phone rang as he turned on the water faucet. He set the pot in the sink and left the water running.

"If you hurt him —" Daniel said into the receiver as Samuel barreled into the kitchen.

"Is it him?" Samuel mouthed.

"Hurt who? Martinez? This is Bergstrom." Daniel gritted his teeth until his jaw hurt and shook his head at Samuel.

Bergstrom. Work. He hadn't called to tell them about the situation. He'd totally forgotten. He turned off the water. "I planned to call you. I won't be in tomorrow."

"Reiger wants us to leave for Laredo at five A.M. tomorrow. I'll pick you up. The Ruiz case."

"I can't. My foster child was kidnapped yesterday. Plus I have an appointment with my wife." An appointment that Nicole might or might not keep. Still, Daniel had to be there in case she did. "I'm taking a day off."

"Reiger will go ballistic."

Bergstrom knew his boss well. It didn't matter. "He'll just have to get over it."

"Reiger?"

Bergstrom was right. Their boss had a one-track mind. Daniel had learned it from him. That thought hit Daniel squarely between the eyes. Everything . . . everything that had been happening in his life had led to this very point. His skewed priorities. Daniel sucked in air and lowered his head. "Tell Reiger I'll email him my letter of resignation."

"Whoa, whoa, that's not necessary." Bergstrom sounded as if he were picturing the conniption fit the boss would throw at being a man down. "I didn't mean — I mean, I'm sure we can get another investigator to fill in."

"No, thanks. I've got to think about my wife and kids from now on." It might be too little too late, but Daniel had to try. "I need to keep this line open. The kidnapper is supposed to call."

"But Dan —"

Daniel laid the receiver in its cradle and looked up at Samuel. His brother's expression was quizzical. "You're giving up the job?"

"Yeah."

Samuel's eyebrows shot up and down. His rueful half-smile made him look almost envious. "Good for you. Come on, let's get ready."

A few minutes later, the phone rang, the shrill notes sending Daniel's heart into triple time.

"Go ahead." Samuel sat on a folding chair across from Daniel, a card table they'd set up in the living room, between them. His brother's voice was calm, his expression full of encouragement. Ray leaned against the wall, his head down. Praying. DEA guys and their equipment filled the room until it might explode with the contained energy. Daniel closed his eyes for a second and tried to shut them out. He had to narrow his focus to his goal. Benny.

He ran through the strategy again. Without the drugs, Plan A was to try to bluff Morin into bringing Benny to a meeting place for an exchange. Plan B would be to offer money so Morin could pay off Barrera. Where that money would come from was still open to discussion. Both options included confronting Morin about his identity. It didn't matter if he bolted from his current location since they had no idea where he was. If they could confirm his identity, they could more quickly narrow down the possible locations to which he might run.

"That you, Martinez?"

The guy sounded like he was talking to an old friend. Daniel wanted to reach through the phone line and rip his head off. "I want to talk to Benny."

"Now, now, let's not get ahead of ourselves, *ese*. Did you get the product?"

Daniel choked back frustration. "We have information on the product. We want an immediate exchange. You pick the location. Give us the boy. You get the information. Face to face."

"I don't want no information. I want the product."

"We tell you where it is. You pick it up."

"That's not the deal. I thought you wanted the kid back."

"I do. Let's meet and we'll talk."

"I want you to listen to something." The kidnapper's voice took on a gleeful quality that made Daniel's skin crawl. The line crackled with movement. Something banged. Then another sound floated over the line. A soft groan.

"No, no." Benny's voice, high and filled

191

with fear. "No more. I promise I won't try to get away again." A sob. Another.

Anger swallowed Daniel's vision in a red wave.

"Benny, it's me, Daniel," he shouted into the phone. "We're coming for you! We're coming for you!"

The line went dead. "No. Don't hang up! Don't you hang up!" Daniel shot to his feet, shouting into the receiver. He smashed it against the table once and then hurled it against the wall.

"Daniel! Danny!" Samuel grabbed him by the shoulders and forced him back into the chair. Ray pushed away from the wall and slid in next to Samuel. They were twin giants towering over him. The other men receded into the background. "Easy, *hermano,* easy." Samuel kept a tight grip on Daniel's arm. "He'll call back."

"He's hurting him, Samuel. He's hurting him," Daniel shrugged away from his brother. Samuel was bigger, but Daniel had fury and frustration on his side. He shoved him away and paced around the room, his back to all of them.

Samuel muttered something. The room began to clear. Feet tromping. The door clicked shut. Quiet.

Daniel wanted to smash a fist into a wall.

192

He came to a stop in front of the window. The sun hurt his eyes. He looked back at his brother. "Right now, while we're standing here talking, he's hurting Benny."

Ray picked up the phone and set it back on the table. Samuel stood in the middle of the room, his hands limp at his side, his face blank. Finally, Daniel dropped onto the sofa and put his head in his hands.

After a few seconds, Daniel heard his brother move and ease onto the couch. A hand touched his shoulder for a brief second. "He'll call back."

Another hour passed before the phone rang again. Daniel spent it in his bedroom, on his knees.

"Martinez." He kept his gaze fixed on Samuel's face. They would get this guy and when they did, he'd never hurt anyone again.

"You in the mood to talk?"

The kidnapper's voice wasn't so gleeful now. Daniel shifted his focus. The guy knew. "Yes."

"You ain't got no information. You don't know where my product is."

"What makes you say that?"

"A little birdie told me Shawna baby's dead."

"Yes. She's dead. But that doesn't mean

we can't still deal."

"She tell you where my product is?"

"No, but —"

"How you gonna help me if you don't know where my product is?"

The man's voice had a whiny quality that rubbed Daniel's nerves raw. He counted to three, studied the floor, then answered. "We can pay you the value of your product. You can pay your debt."

Silence bounced across the line. The clock on the living room wall ticked. Morin cleared his throat, a dry grating sound. "I'll have to think about that. Make some calls. Deliberate."

The man drew out the syllables of the last word like he was rolling them around on his tongue, trying them out for size.

"What's to deliberate?" Daniel felt panic starting to swell in his gut. He wanted a definite plan, a definite time for getting Benny back. No more waiting. "We'll get you the money."

"My price."

Anger clawed at Daniel's insides, trying to get out. "What's a little boy's life worth to you, Juice?"

The sound of the line disconnecting was pronounced in his ear. "Son of —"

"Easy, easy." Samuel took the phone out

of his hand and laid it on the table. "You did fine."

"It was a mistake. What if he skips town and takes Benny with him. Or kill — we may never find him."

"He's too greedy for that, Danny. Think. He's desperate. He's got to pay up. He needs us. We'll check out his family and his known hang-outs. Check out his friends. We can definitely narrow our search down to Jorge Morin. This helps a lot. We can figure out where to look for him — his family, known associates, previous addresses. We're good."

Daniel wiped his face with the back of his sleeve. The room seemed to get steadily colder. A chill invaded his body so intense that he wanted to pull blankets from the linen closet. "It depends."

"On what?"

"Whether fear or greed is bigger with this guy. We know he's a coward. Will he cut and run? He knows Barrera will come after him." Second-guessing fueled his doubts. The plan had big holes in it. "He won't take a kid with him if he runs. He could be killing Benny right now."

"No." Ray spoke up.

"How do you know?"

"Greed will win. He'll want the money

before he skips town. With a guy like this, greed will force him right into our hands. Benny is his golden goose. He'll hang onto him until he gets what he wants."

"Look, you need to get out of here." Samuel moved toward the door. "Let's go to the station, do some research. You'll feel better if you keep moving."

Twenty minutes later, Daniel sat at Samuel's desk and peered at his brother's computer screen, tempted to ask for his reading glasses. "So Juice Morin was in the county jail for nearly six months on the DUI and possession charges."

Samuel sipped on his third or fourth cup of coffee before he answered. "He ended up with a plea bargain, probation, and time served. That must have been what he was talking about when he said he had a little problem and was away."

"Yeah." Ray swallowed coffee and grimaced as he perused the folder in his hand. "The address he listed is fictitious — no such street. It says here he's got a brother in Huntsville and a sister who works Broadway, gets busted regularly for soliciting. Wait a minute!"

Samuel's coffee sloshed on his hand. "What?"

"I don't believe it. There was a disturbance

on the pod where Juice Morin was incarcerated. Several inmates got into it in the common area. Guess who one of the other guys was?"

"I give." Daniel didn't have the patience left to play a guessing game. "Who?"

"None other than Tómas Chavez."

Daniel stood. The muscles in his legs cramped. He sank back into the chair. "Your predecessor at the ranch? Tómas Chavez and Juice Morin were in the Bexar County jail at the same time?"

"Same pod. Their paths definitely crossed. And they're affiliated with the same gang. Latin Kings."

Daniel grabbed a folder and leafed through its contents. "The last time Chavez was in was for drunk and disorderly, aggravated assault — bar fight. He couldn't make bail so he was in about six weeks before he finally took a plea. Probation, community service, fine, and time served. Slap on the hands."

Daniel's gaze connected with Samuel. "So what do you suppose they talked about?"

"I'll call Alex. He's out at the ranch with Cooper and the canine unit. He's already had contact with Chavez. He can go back and interview him again."

Ray tossed the folder on the desk. "What

about the sister — Rita Morin?"

"We'll see if we can get an address on her. Maybe Morin's holed up with her." Samuel got to his feet as well. "We'll work that end. You coming, Daniel?"

Daniel's cell phone rang before he could answer. He glanced at the Caller ID. His name came up. Ironically, it was still on all the accounts at the house. He worked his way between the desks, girding himself for the conversation. "Nicole, what's up?"

"Pop."

His son's voice was small. He sounded even more tense than he had the night before. "Squirt, what's the matter?"

"I can't stay here anymore. I . . . I miss you, Pop."

Daniel's throat closed. "I miss you too, *hijo.* I'm doing the best I can to work this out." Christopher sounded way too old for twelve. And so despondent. Daniel never imagined he'd do this to his own children. Divorce. The children paid . . . and paid. The pause stretched. "*Hijo,* are you still there? Did something else happen?"

"Me and Benny could share a room. I'd help keep it clean and everything."

Daniel saw Samuel and Ray exchange concerned glances. He moved into the break room. "Look, kiddo, it's not about the room, it's not about the cleaning."

"Benny lives with you. Why can't I?" Anger mixed with hurt bled through the telephone line.

Daniel made a fist and pounded lightly on a countertop. His hand hurt with the effort not to smash something. "You know I love you, and I want you to be with me. I'm just afraid your mother —"

"She won't care. She doesn't care."

Sniffling sounds filled the line. At twelve, Christopher never cried in front of him anymore. A well-adjusted macho Latino kid. "Did you try to talk to your mom about her . . . about the . . . about her friend?"

Silence. Prolonged silence punctuated by small sniffs. "She says he's just a friend. She says not to worry." His voice cracked. "She's just like you. She says don't worry like I'm some dumb kid who can't figure things out."

"You're not dumb. You're smart. Your mom knows that and I know that. I would love to have you live with me. But if I fight your mom on this, we might never get back together. Don't you want us all to live together again?"

"Yeah, but I don't think Mom does."

"She does. She just doesn't know it."

"He came and picked her up for lunch. They still haven't come back."

Daniel swallowed words he hadn't used in a long time. Reconciliation seemed farther away than ever. "They work together. Maybe they're reviewing a case that they have a court setting for tomorrow."

"Maybe."

He wasn't convinced and neither was Daniel. "I'll talk to your mom. But you have to sit tight, let me do it. And try not to worry, okay? I love you, Squirt."

"Stop calling me that."

"I always call you that." Christopher had been a preemie, born almost two months early. A tiny wizened monkey, who'd suddenly taken off and grown like crazy with the help of his mother's milk. Daniel had called him Squirt from day one.

"I'm not little anymore." Stubborn determination in his voice told Daniel his son had been wanting to get this off his chest for a while.

"Got it. I love you, Christopher, or would you prefer Chris?"

"Chris is fine. Love you, too, Pop. You're gonna talk to Mom soon — right away — today, right?"

"Tomorrow. Tomorrow, at the counseling session. I promise."

Daniel disconnected and leaned his forehead against the wood of the cabinet, willing the room to stop spinning. He hadn't been able to swallow the croissant sandwiches Piper had brought over for dinner. His stomach roiled at the thought.

He shivered, turned the faucet, and splashed water on his face. Then he let water pour into a glass, took a drink, and immediately heaved into the sink.

"Are you all right?"

He grabbed a paper towel and wiped his face before he turned to face Samuel. "I'm fine. Just washing my face."

His brother studied him, disbelief written across his face. "Ray will monitor the phones. He's in contact with Alex about Chavez. Juice Morin's sister works a corner on Broadway. Let's see if she knows where her brother is staying."

Alex pulled on to the dirt road that led from Ray's ranch to the highway. After the scene at Suarez's place and a couple hours of watching dogs sniff at nothing on a property that covered fifty acres, he was hot, sweaty, and hungry. Oh, and tired, and unsure whether he should be elated or disappointed that the search had turned up no clue as to what had happened to the Chavez family — so far. "You know what's weird?"

Cooper snorted. "Besides the disappearance of a woman and five children five years ago and we can't find a single piece of information that tells us what happened to them or where they went?"

Alex swerved to avoid a possum crossing the road. "It's weird that I can't find any information on the private investigator Chavez hired. I had a coworker run a background on him. The address is still good for his office, but she checked out the home address and he hasn't lived there for four years. The apartment manager is new — says he never heard of the guy. Claims the rental records were destroyed when a pipe broke in their storage facility. Phillips hasn't renewed his driver's license or private investigator's license in the last four years. He's divorced, no family, doesn't own any property. He slid off the radar."

Cooper adjusted his seat belt and leaned back against the headrest like he might take a nap. "One thing at a time, Alex. We'll track him down. His shop is still there. It's on the to-do list for tomorrow."

Right. Alex wanted to move faster. He really wanted to be in two places at once. Too bad Deborah messed up. They could use her help. He'd tell her that — next time he saw her. Which, with these two cases now apparently intertwined, might be a while.

He forced himself to focus on the road. And the case. Both cases.

A few minutes later, he slowed on the rutted road that led to Chavez's trailer. A dozen trucks and cars dotted the driveway. Alex eased his car in behind the last one. He jabbed the button to roll down the window. The sound of accordion-driven *conjunto* music blared from the trailer's open windows, accompanied by the smoky odor of sausage and chicken being grilled somewhere behind the structure. "A lot of company for a Sunday night."

Cooper nodded. "I imagine they've had a few. Do you think we need backup on this?"

"We just want to talk." Alex shoved his door open. "We're not accusing anyone of anything — yet."

Cooper shrugged and got out. They didn't quite make it to the trailer door. A skinny Latino man jerked it open and tumbled out. "Who are you?" The slur was thick.

Alex waved his badge under the guy's nose. "We're looking for Tómas Chavez."

"Right here, *vatos*." Chavez stood in the doorway, one hand wrapped around a longneck Corona, the other around the waist of a pretty, young girl wearing too much makeup and not enough clothes. "Come on in, have a beer."

Chavez sounded as if he'd had enough for all three of them.

"No, thanks. Why don't you come on out? We need to talk."

"What? You get a positive ID on my little girl?" Chavez gave the girl a slight shove, and she disappeared into the trailer. "We're having a little wake for her this evening."

"We're still working on it." Alex introduced Cooper as the lead investigator on the two cases.

Chavez stomped down the stairs, the bottle dangling from two fingers. "Must be a big man, head honcho over two investigations at once."

Alex ignored the challenge in the man's voice. "So how well did you get to know Jorge Morin when you were in jail?"

Chavez halted. "Jorge? I know lotta guys named Jorge."

"Maybe you knew him by the name of Juice or Jugo."

"Nope. *Nada.*" Chavez took a long swallow from the bottle. "Why don't you *señores* pull up a couple of chairs. We got sausage, we got chicken, *arroz con frijoles borrachos.* We feed you good."

"Thanks, but we're working." Alex held out a mug shot of Juice Morin. "You were in at the same time as Morin. You were involved in an altercation in the jail. Both your names are in the report. Your paths crossed. So why not come clean and tell us about it?"

Chavez sat down on the step and pulled a cigarette from his pocket. "So what? I got nothing to say about Jugo."

A huge guy with a bandana wrapped around his head appeared in the doorway. "You need some help, *ese?*"

"Tranquilo." Chavez jerked his head. The man disappeared.

"What was the fight about?" Alex took his hand from the butt of his weapon.

"Somebody got in somebody's face. I don't remember, man. It was no big deal."

"You and Morin know each other before you got arrested?"

"Seen him around."

"You're both Latin Kings. You're in business together."

"I got no gang business. I stopped that stuff. I got a legit job, *ese.*" Chavez's eyes were so dilated you couldn't see his irises anymore. "All I did was give the dude some advice. He got ripped off by his old lady. He was having some problems with . . . with his boss . . . needed to take care of a situation. I gave him some suggestions. That's all."

Alex rocked on his heels. He wanted to wrap his hands around the guy's neck and squeeze. The guy with the bandana was back in the doorway. This time he leaned against the frame, his biceps bulging from the cut-off sleeves of his faded shirt. Alex forced his gaze back to Chavez. "You said you did some work for Mrs. Stover a few months ago, before you were in jail. You probably heard her talking about the wedding coming up. Maybe you picked up some information that you passed onto Juice. Maybe those suggestions involved kidnapping a kid?"

"*N'ombre,* I don't know nothing about no kidnapping, and I don't know nothing about what Morin's been doin'. I only talked to him a couple of times. Never saw him again."

"That's a nice truck you have. A little high end for a handyman. Maybe you both work for Enrique Barrera. That's why Morin came to you for advice. How to handle Barrera while he tried to get the product back."

"I don't do no drug business. I told you, I hire out as a handyman for people like *Señora* Stover. I won some money in Vegas the last time I was up there. I used it to pay for the truck."

"I find out you're lying to us, I'll be back."

206

Alex walked away before he did something they'd all regret.

Back in the Altima, the silence lingered until they made it back to the main road. "Any chance we have enough to get a search warrant?" Cooper spoke first.

"For what?"

"I smelled more than sausage and chicken cooking out there."

Alex swung his gaze toward the older man. "The guy's not making payments on that truck with what he makes changing oil and tightening belts, and he probably hasn't been to Vegas in a long time."

"Let's see if we can get a warrant."

CHAPTER SEVENTEEN

"That's her." Daniel studied a mug shot of Juice Morin's sister, Rita Morin, stapled to the file Samuel had propped against the wheel of his pickup truck. He looked back at the woman standing on the curb at the bus stop. Rita, who used the name Roxanne Diablo on the street, was working it on the corner of Broadway and Travis. She'd seen them pull up in Samuel's truck. Now she was prancing up and down in four-inch stiletto heels, letting them see the merchandise.

At a distance, she could've been a model, with her long, lean legs, slim hips, and curves, but when she sashayed up to the passenger side of Samuel's pickup, Daniel got a good look at her face. He could see no similarity to the photo he'd seen of Juice, though the file said they were only a year apart in age and had grown up together on San Antonio's south side, the children of a waitress and a missing-in-action, unnamed father.

Thick makeup and a slash of red lipstick couldn't hide the ravages of age and hard living. Rita wore a long red wig that sent curls cascading down her back. Her pupils were dilated when she shoved her face through the window. Apparently she shared her brother's taste for illegal substances. "Hi, sweet pea. Looking for a date?"

He could smell rum on her breath and cheap perfume permeated the air, making him want to sneeze. "Are you Rita?"

"Who wants to know?" The inviting smile slipped a little.

She started to back off. Daniel grabbed her wrist. "A friend of Juice's. He recommended you."

She stopped struggling, her expression guarded. "I ain't talked to Juice since he went to jail."

"He's out."

"Really. Good for him. I'll have to give him a call. Buy him a steak." She leaned in again, her breath warm on his face. Her gaze skittered to Samuel and back. "He was always good for a referral. You looking for a twosome? You want me to call one of my girlfriends over?"

"We just want you." Daniel was careful to

keep his disgust from his face. Samuel hadn't moved or spoken.

"Well, that'll cost you extra. Get out. I'll sit in the middle. Where you wanna go, sweet pea? I've got a room, but it ain't nothing special. You two look like you might want something special. Your buddy there is a mighty fine looking specimen. I bet he'll want something extra."

Daniel got out and let her slide in. He pulled his billfold from his pocket before he got back in the truck. "So how much you charge?"

"For something like this?" She bit her lip, contemplating. "Cost you at least a couple of hundred bucks."

Daniel handed her three twenties. "A down payment."

She took them. "Wow, don't get many johns who offer to pay before we get to the room." Daniel watched as comprehension slid over her face. "Ah, man, you're cops. I shoulda known. Ah, you gonna bust me, aren't you? I knew it was too good to be true. You're clean, you smell good, and you got nice fingernails. You probably carrying your own protection."

She shook her head, looking amazingly disappointed.

Daniel almost felt sorry for her — almost.

"We're not looking to bust you. We just want some information."

"Of course, if you don't feel like cooperating, we can take you in." Samuel flipped out his badge for her to see.

"SAPD. I should have smelled it on you." She sounded bitter now, but she relaxed on the seat. "So what do you want? A freebie? I'm not giving you the sixty bucks back."

"I'll write it off." Daniel twisted in the seat so he could read her face. "We're looking for your brother. His last known address is a motel on Zarzamora Street. He hasn't lived there since before he went to jail."

"Man, I didn't even know he was out."

"I don't believe that." Samuel's voice was hard. "You visited your brother at the jail a number of times. You hired his lawyer, didn't you?"

"He ain't much, but he's blood." Rita pulled a cigarette from a crevice Daniel had avoided looking at throughout the conversation. "He'd do the same for me — maybe."

"So, you have talked to him."

She shrugged and lit the cigarette, taking a long drag. The plumes of smoke turned the inside of the truck into a hazy space worse than a nightclub. Samuel plucked the cigarette from her fingers and tossed it out the window. "Sorry, this is a no smoking establishment."

"So you're playing the bad cop." She gave him a slow grin. Daniel wanted to laugh, but he was afraid he would vomit. The stench of cigarette smoke sent his nausea off the charts.

"Yeah, so either you talk or I arrest you. That pretty much covers it."

"He used to dig a chick who lived over off Martin Street. West side. I think they worked together. Her and her brother and Juice."

"Worked together?"

"Yeah, worked together. Had a little business going. Entrepreneurs."

"Name. Address."

"Hmmm." Rita pursued her lips. "Let me think. You ain't gonna arrest me, right?"

"You have my word."

"Okay. Her name was Mica. Mica Jordan. He was, let me see, let me see, umm, Seth. That was it. Seth Jordan. The address. I don't know. Off of Martin and Thirty-Sixth Street. Up in that area. Okay. Becker. That's it Becker. 1012. 1011. 1112. Something like that. The ten-hundred block. Like that."

"Thank you."

Daniel shoved the door open, relieved to get her out of the truck. Relieved to have something to go on. Anything. She leaned into him and sniffed. "You smell really good, officer."

"I'm not an officer." Technically.

Her hand drifted up, touched his chest. "Then you smell even better. Sure you don't want a taste of me?"

"I can still arrest you."

"Oh, well. Your loss." She smiled, swiveled, and sashayed across the street, tossing glances his way every few steps. Daniel stood there, frozen, thinking about losses, not seeing her anymore.

"Daniel, get in." Samuel's voice penetrated the gloomy reverie. "I called dispatch. They're looking up that address for us. Let's go."

"Yeah." Yeah. Benny. They were getting closer.

No outside lights illuminated the house at 1011 Becker. Samuel called for backup. The wooden porch creaked under their weight. Daniel stood for a second, listening. A dog barked continuously in the backyard of the house next door. "Nobody home?"

Samuel jerked his head toward the driveway. Somebody had parked a VW bus with gray primer on the door across the sidewalk. "Wait or go?"

"Go."

Samuel pounded on the door. No answer. No movement. "Let's try around back."

In the backyard, a naked bulb over a slab of concrete illuminated a landmine of tools strewn on the ground, an abandoned mower, and an assortment of straggly lawn chairs. Another light peeked through open curtains to the kitchen. Daniel peered in, then ducked down. A man sat at a table that held a scale, a couple of boxes of baggies, and other paraphernalia. He had his head back like he'd nodded off.

"He's dead." Samuel jerked his Glock from his holster and grabbed the doorknob. He smashed his shoulder into the wood. The door gave with a groan.

Daniel followed him in and crossed the kitchen in two strides. He put two fingers on the man's neck. The guy had a large hole in the center of his forehead. Blood and brain tissue had seeped down his back onto the chair and pooled on the floor below him. "Where's that backup?" Sirens roared in the distance as if in answer to the question. Daniel eased toward the kitchen door, trying not to inhale the odor of gunpowder, urine, and dirty dishes. "I suppose that's Seth Jordan?"

"So where's Mica?" Samuel strode from the kitchen, Daniel right behind him as they swept the hallway, dining room and then hit the living room. The place had been trashed.

Overturned chairs, lamps, broken glass, littered the floor.

"Overkill?" Daniel pointed at the spray of bullet holes that decorated the walls of the living room. Posters of The Doors and Jimmy Hendrix had been ripped to shreds by repeated blasts. "Somebody was having a good time."

"Yeah —" A moan fractured Samuel's response.

A woman lay facedown at the foot of the stairs. Daniel got to her first.

"I'll clear upstairs." Samuel took the stairs two at a time, his gun trained ahead of him.

Daniel touched the woman's neck. The pulse was thready and fading. "Mica? Mica Jordan?"

She gasped. A tiny bubble of red saliva burst on her lips. "Help me, please, please help me."

"Hang on. An ambulance is on its way." Blood soaked her shirt and pooled under her. She would bleed out before help arrived. Daniel darted into the kitchen, grabbed dish towels from the counter, and raced back into the hallway. He dropped to his knees and applied pressure. "Hold on, Mica, just hold on. Can you tell me who did this to you?"

Her eyes were closed, but she mumbled a

response. He leaned in, trying to hear. Blood soaked the towel at an alarming rate. "Mica, stay with me. Who did this?"

"He wanted the stuff." Her blood-covered fingers sought his and contracted in a tight, painful squeeze. "We didn't have it. Juice . . ."

"Juice Morin shot you?"

"No. No, his stuff . . . not here. They wanted . . . the stuff."

"Who, Mica, who?"

She sighed and stopped talking.

CHAPTER EIGHTEEN

Alex tugged his ringing cell phone from his pocket and stopped in front of the building that housed the Department of Family and Protective Services. A slight chill hung in the morning air despite the sun's peeking through drifting clouds. Monday morning rush-hour traffic had delayed him longer than he'd hoped. Sarge's name popped up on the Caller ID.

As usual Samuel eliminated the preliminaries. "You're gonna have to work fast. Macon is on my back about the three cases you haven't closed. And we picked up two more last night with Seth and Mica Jordan."

"Did you tell him the Jane Doe death ties into a kidnapping and a drug ring and that could even include the bodies last night?" Alex couldn't contain his irritation. Of course Samuel had told him. Lieutenant Macon was under pressure from the higher-ups over a steadily declining closure rate on homicide cases. Instead of recognizing the result of too few detectives, a growing population, and a steady increase in violent crime, the brass wanted the eleven homicide detectives on staff to work miracles.

"I'm down staff with Deborah and Ray both out." Sarge's tone was stiff. "At least, since Ray is still in town, he can help unofficially with Benny's kidnapping and that frees me up to work here, but we can't let the backlog grow."

"I'll be back as soon as I can, boss." Alex grabbed the door and jerked it open. "Coop says the judge won't give us a search warrant on Chavez's property. He wasn't impressed with the Sunday night barbecue scenario. We've got to keep working this or Chavez will get away with murder. And he's connected to Benny's kidnapping. We still need to run down the lead on the PI who worked the missing persons' case for him."

"Just — wait a sec —" Samuel's voice became muffled. A second later he was back. "Gotta go. Macon wants me in his office. Keep me posted at all times. And get back here as soon as you can."

Dead air hissed in Alex's ear. Fine. He focused on his mission.

They needed more evidence to nail Chavez — something to connect him to

Juice Morin after they both were released from jail. If they had something to hold over his head, they might be able to get him to talk about Morin. And it would give them time to prove the skeletal remains belonged to Nina Chavez.

Alex freewheeled past the image of the other four Chavez children. The file said two girls, twins, who'd been nine when they went missing. If they were alive, they'd be fourteen now. And the two boys, twelve and ten.

If they were alive.

He tried to latch onto a more positive train of thought. Deborah. Nope. That wasn't it. He'd called her apartment before he hit the sack the previous evening. She hadn't answered. Caller ID. She didn't want to talk to the rat-snitch. Or maybe she was with Omar. Or at a bar.

Think positive. Think about the case. Cooper was back out at the ranch where the canine unit had resumed its search of the property. In the meantime, Alex had the CPS angle.

No pressure.

Joanna Thigpen didn't look happy to see him. In fact, the caseworker looked exhausted, despite the fact that it was only Monday morning. The stacks of files on her desk might have something to do with that. The woman was clearly overworked, as were all the caseworkers employed by CPS in the state of Texas. "I really don't have a lot of time for this, Detective. I have actual current cases that need my attention."

Alex eased into the chair across from her desk even though she hadn't invited him to sit. "I promise to make it quick. Sheriff's records show officers escorted a CPS worker to Tómas Chavez's home a couple of times. At least one child was removed and then returned after CPS did an evaluation."

Thigpen moved a folder from one stack to another. "And you want me to find out what was in that evaluation."

"Mrs. Thigpen, there's a little girl's skeletal remains lying on a table in the morgue right now. Someone got away with murder five years ago — that's how long Ray Johnson has owned the property. Tómas Chavez leased the property before Ray bought it. I just want to find out what kind of parent he was and what kind of problems brought your department into the mix. I've spoken with the man, and he claims to have been a model parent. He claims to not know anything about his youngest daughter Nina being the victim of a brutal murder. I want to find out if he's a liar."

Thigpen stared at him, her pudgy face morose. "Detective, do me a favor. Go to Starbucks, get a café latte — you know what, make it a double."

Fatigue, frustration, and a certain degree of sadness mingled in the woman's face. Thigpen teetered on that thin line between dedication and burnout.

"Would you like a chocolate chip cookie with that?"

"That would be lovely." Her voice wobbled. "Give me about thirty minutes."

Twenty minutes later Alex set the coffee and the cookie in front of Thigpen.

Thigpen took a ginger sip of the steaming coffee and closed her eyes, an ecstatic look on her face. "Tómas and Clarisse Chavez ended up on our radar after the schools reported chronic absenteeism, a lack of immunizations, and neglect of at least one of the children."

"Just one child showed neglect?" Alex frowned. "Ray said there were three or four running around."

"The Chavezes had five children. Three girls and two boys. They all missed school and they all needed immunizations, but only one — the youngest one — presented a potential abuse scenario. A teacher reported that she came to school with fingerprint-shaped bruises on her arm. When she tried to talk to her about it, the little girl freaked. Nina was five at the time."

She broke the mammoth cookie in half and offered the larger piece to Alex. He took it. "What else?"

"She was underweight, apparently undernourished. Suffered from anemia." Thigpen flipped through the pages of the file in front of her. "The foster parents reported that she refused to sleep on a bed, kept sliding down on the floor after they left the room. They'd return and put her in the bed. She cowered every time they came in, but got back on the floor after they left."

"Bizarre."

"It's the kind of thing we see." Thigpen dropped her reading glasses on the desk. "A child who's been abused will continue behavior conditioned through punishment. She undoubtedly had been taught that she was not allowed to sleep on a bed and would be punished if she did."

"Maybe they didn't have enough beds."

"Her speech was delayed. She hadn't developed the basic skills needed to learn to read. Her social skills were poor."

"And y'all sent her back."

Frowning, Thigpen leaned back and steepled her chubby fingers. "Let me tell you something. In the last fiscal year, there were 3,249 cases of confirmed child abuse in the state of Texas. Those are just the confirmed ones, not the thousands that have to be investigated. Of those, nearly nine hundred children were removed from their homes.

"In Bexar County, the number of children abused was four percent higher than in the rest of the state. That means something like thirteen of every thousand kids in this county were abused or neglected last year. Should we remove all of them? And what would you have us do with them? Do you understand the state of our emergency shelters and our foster care system?"

She stopped and took a long breath, bright red spots glowing on both cheeks. Neither of them spoke for several seconds. She sniffed. "The answer to your question is we can't remove children unless they are in imminent danger. Because of the bruising and the fact that Mr. Chavez became belligerent when the workers approached him, Nina was removed. He committed to attending an anger management course and making sure Nina was in school each day. The children received their immunizations. Nina was returned. That's the way the system works."

She snatched a tissue from her desk. Instead of using it, she began shredding it. "This wasn't my case, Detective. I'm just telling you what's in the file." She went back to the paperwork in front of her. "Chavez completed the class. The other children all seemed fine. I guess the caseworker figured four out of five wasn't bad. Sometimes one child is just smaller and slower than the others. It could go either way. As for attendance at school — we didn't receive any more complaints from the school."

"Mrs. Thigpen." Alex stopped to rub his eyes for a second, trying to remember the exact conversation. "The neighbor, Maddy Stover, lived next to this family for about a year. She told us they only had four children. She only saw two girls and two boys when she dropped by the ranch."

Thigpen pursued her lips, staring at the report. "She was mistaken. It's right here in black and white. Twin girls, age nine, Esperanza and Estrella. Domingo, age seven, Francisco, age six, and Nina, age five. And it's also in color. Here's the photo."

Alex took the photograph. An ugly, cold chill wrapped itself around his neck. The face of a dark-haired little girl stared up at him. Nina Chavez looked like an elf. She had wispy black hair that fell to her shoulders, one plastic barrette on each side. Uneven bangs spoke of a home haircut. Her skin was olive and her eyes green. This could be the face that belonged to the bones. Nina Chavez had been a cute kid.

"Poor Mrs. Chavez." He dropped the photo on his desk, hoping she hadn't noticed the sudden shaking of his fingers. "She had her hands full."

"You've got that right. According to this, Mr. Chavez didn't see any need to assist her in caring for the children."

Chavez's cold stare lingered in Alex's mind. "Or maybe he found another way to help her out."

Daniel clasped his hands in his lap, his fingers clenched so hard they hurt. Nicole sank onto the couch next to him in the pastor's miniscule office. He'd almost given up. She was fifteen minutes late. Now she sat so close he could smell her fragrance, sweet jasmine. His legs felt shaky, and his head was swimming. It had to be nerves. Or the billowing anger he felt every time he imagined her kissing another man. Especially in their home . . . in front of their children.

Or maybe it was the stress of knowing Sunday had turned into Monday and still no follow-up call from Juice Morin. The kidnapper had either killed Benny and run, or he was still "deliberating." Daniel tried not to think about which it was.

Ray was monitoring the phone, and they would put the call through to Daniel if it came while he was at the counseling session. He had debated coming at all, but he couldn't take the chance that Nicole would show up and find him absent. Not when this new man threatened to take his place in their home and at his wife's side.

Too much was riding on this — his marriage, his family, his life.

Nicole leaned toward him slightly, her face anxious. "No word on Benny?"

He shook his head, afraid to trust his voice.

"I'm sorry." Her hand touched his for a second. Then she withdrew before he could react.

"Are we ready?" Pastor Wilson smiled the same gentle smile he displayed at the beginning of each session. The accusations, the shouting, the bitter recriminations, none of it seemed to faze him. He just kept smiling and nodding. Sometimes Daniel wanted to punch him to see if he would react. "Daniel, let's start with you. Did you give some thought to how you would approach your marriage differently if you and Nicole were to reconcile?"

Daniel sucked in air, willing the anger to subside. It grew instead. "I don't think reconciliation is what Nicole has in mind. I think she's already moved on. I think this whole counseling thing is a bust. She's just doing it to make her boyfriend happy."

Pastor Wilson slipped his silver-rimmed glasses from his face with maddening calm. He snagged a tissue from a box on the corner of a cluttered oak desk and wiped his lenses. "Nicole, is there some new development in your life that impacts the conversations we're having here?"

Nicole's face reddened. She glared at Daniel. "It's not like it sounds —"

"Yes, it is. It's exactly like it sounds," Daniel broke in. "The man was in my house. Kissing my wife."

"Have you been spying on me?"

The outrage in her voice fueled Daniel's own fury. "No. I didn't have to. You couldn't be bothered to conceal your affair. You made out with your boyfriend in front of my son. My twelve-year-old son. He wants to come live with me now. I think he should . . . I think —"

"No! Stop!" Nicole's face crumpled. She burst into tears. Her sobs cascaded around him. She jumped to her feet and faced a wall of books, her back to both of them. After a second, she whirled around. "I didn't know Christopher was in the room. You have to believe me. I would never do that to him. I didn't kiss Joshua. He kissed me! There is no affair."

Daniel stared up at her, his heart racing. At moments like this, her effect on him only multiplied. "He kissed you. You kissed him. There's no difference, and that is an affair in my book — in God's book."

Daniel tore his gaze from Nicole and looked at Pastor Wilson for confirmation. The pastor's compassionate gaze was on Nicole, not him. "Isn't that right, Pastor Wilson?"

The pastor tapped his pen on the desk in a slow, deliberate stroke. "Why do you think Nicole sought the company of another man, Daniel?"

No way. "So this is my fault?"

"No fault is being laid. No blame assigned. I'm asking you to examine the cause behind the effect. The relationship between a husband and wife is a complicated dance. Sometimes we forget the steps. Or we decide to sit it out without realizing it. Doing nothing has consequences."

"So you're saying it's okay for her to cheat

— because I checked out for too long."

"No, I'm not saying it's all right to cheat. I'm saying let's understand your wife's need for attention and affection — something she says she wasn't getting from you. Let's see how we can repair the damage."

Daniel stood. Pastor Wilson wasn't helping. He was giving Nicole the ammunition she needed to make this split permanent. She already had a replacement lined up. "Fine —"

"Sit down, Daniel." Daniel had heard Pastor Wilson preach a few times. He could command. Daniel sat.

"Nicole, you came here today. That tells me you're still trying. You haven't made up your mind. That's good. Have you been talking to God about this new development?"

Daniel glanced sideways. Enough to see her face. It was soaked with tears. Her chin shook with the effort to control her sobs. A bizarre desire to comfort her blossomed inside him. No matter what she did, he couldn't stop loving her. She raised her head and spoke directly to the pastor. "I don't think He's talking to me anymore."

Pastor Wilson chuckled, a dissonant sound in the midst of so much tension. "Oh, He's talking. Are you listening?"

"What do you think He's saying?" Nicole's voice quivered with emotion. "Whatever it is, I can't hear it."

"Start with Ephesians 5:22."

Daniel wanted to throw up his hands and surrender. Surely Pastor Wilson knew Nicole well enough to realize this strategy wouldn't work. She was too independent to be the submitting type.

"Wives, submit to your husbands?" The disdain in her voice told Daniel he was right on the mark. "So you think God intends for me to be miserable the rest of my life because my husband is married to his job? Tell me He isn't that cruel."

His job would no longer be a problem. Now was the time to tell her. "I gave no—"

"Wait, Daniel, let me finish, and then you'll get a turn," Pastor Wilson interrupted. "That's not the whole passage, and I suspect you know it. Both of you." He picked up the open leather-bound Bible on his desk, adjusted his glasses, and read, " 'Husbands love your wives, just as Christ loved the church and gave Himself up for her.' It's a two-way street. Relationships take work and sacrifice. When you start thinking of what your spouse wants and needs first, you'll find the love you once felt for each other."

Which was exactly what Daniel had done — a little late, but better than never. He opened his mouth to tell them. A sneeze shook him, and then another. "Excuse me, I'm so sorry." Dizzy, he reached for a tissue box. The room rocked. His body swayed. Swallowing against swelling nausea, he stood. He needed to get to a bathroom.

"Daniel, are you okay?" Nicole's voice sounded distant and oddly distorted.

He couldn't answer. If he opened his mouth, he would vomit. He took one step, teetered. The rattling of his bones and the crack of his head against the wooden floor told him he hadn't made it to the door.

"Daniel! Daniel?" Nicole crouched next to him, her cool hand on his face. He wanted to grab it and hang on, but his limbs were too heavy to lift. Nicole's face wavered over him. "You're burning up."

Darkness seeped in around her face. Daniel fought to keep from losing consciousness.

"I quit my —" the rest of the words sounded garbled to his own ears.

He couldn't remember what he was saying. Then he couldn't say anything at all.

Pain.

Benny's neck hurt where the hands had

tightened. He tried to take a deep breath, but his nose was swollen, making it hard to get any air. His lip was bleeding. He could taste the blood in his mouth. He had cried until no tears were left. He couldn't help it. He wasn't a crybaby, but it hurt. It hurt so much he was still rolled up in a ball in the dark, little hurt sounds coming out of his mouth. He tried to stop, but he couldn't.

Mr. Daniel would come get him. Soon. Benny was sure of it. The man had brought the phone in, and Mr. Daniel had heard him. He would know, and he would come soon.

The man sounded very mad. He threw things around, yelled, slammed doors. Benny tried to move. He needed to go to the bathroom, and his stomach growled. He hadn't eaten anything since the hot dog.

A banging sound. He wanted to cry again. No more crying. The door swung open. A bright light blinded him.

"Get up, boy. Get up now. We gotta go."

The man grabbed him by one arm and dragged him to his feet. Pain shot through his arm and shoulder. "Mister, please, please, don't hurt me anymore."

"I ain't gonna hurt you, boy. Leastwise, not if you do what you're told. Don't try nothing stupid again." The man lifted Benny up and threw him over his shoulders so his head dangled. Benny squirmed and tried to look around. The guy had messed up the place even more. A lamp lay on its side. Things were broken like the man had smashed them.

A crashing sound rang through the living room, banging, the sound of wood ripping. The man grabbed the gun from the waistband of his jeans.

Benny sailed through the air. His skull cracked against the wall with a popping sound. The scream that hurt his ears came from his own mouth.

He struggled to sit up. His hands were tied, and he couldn't get his balance. He teetered for a second and then smashed to one side. Tears filled his eyes. Pain pounded through his ear and up the side of his face, filling his eye sockets.

A huge man dressed in army pants and a green shirt with no sleeves filled the space in the living room. A big gun with a long barrel hung from one hand. Benny froze. He wanted to crawl away and hide, but his legs wouldn't move. His heart banged inside him, the sound loud in his ears.

The guy who said he was Benny's dad dove behind the wall that separated the kitchen from the living room.

The big brown man swerved from side to side, training the gun in one direction and then the other, like he was hunting an animal. "Morin! Get your butt out here." The man sounded like he was trying not to be mad. But Benny was sure he was mad. Very mad. "We gotta talk, *ese*. Time to pay up. I ain't gonna hurt you, Juice. We just gonna do business."

His kidnapper had a name. Juice Morin. Benny didn't have too much time to think about how weird the name was. The man had his finger on the trigger. His black eyes glowed. He smiled a little smile under his bushy mustache.

He clomped forward three steps. He was even with Benny now, but he didn't look down. Benny stared at the black, shiny combat boots. *Please don't look down. Please don't look down.* "Get out here, Morin. Don't make me get mad. Cops came to my house. I think you got something to do with that, *ese*. We need to talk about it. Barrera is tired of waiting. He wants his product. Or his money. You got to pay. Time is up. Give me his stuff or give me the money. Your choice."

No answer. Benny thought for a minute maybe Juice had ducked out the back door and escaped. He tried not to think about what that would mean. Him alone here with the big, brown man.

He didn't move. He didn't want the man to see him. To hear him breathe even. He gritted his teeth to keep from crying. *I want Mr. Daniel. Please. Mr. Daniel.*

Juice rolled across the floor into the doorway, sprang to his feet, and opened fire. An explosion of gunfire burst all around Benny. He collapsed into a ball. He tried to make himself small. He wanted to disappear up against the woodwork of the wall. The smell of smoke and guns filled the air. The spatter of bullets pinged against walls.

The big, brown man screamed cuss words. His mouth flew open wide in surprise. Red splotches grew on the front of his T-shirt.

Benny wanted to squeeze his eyes shut, but they seemed frozen wide open, staring at the red color ballooning over the front of the shirt.

The big, brown man teetered, then stumbled forward in his black combat boots. Benny stared at the boots. They were untied. *He's gonna fall.* Then the big brown man did it — he fell. Right next to Benny. Screams tore from his throat. He bucked, trying to get away.

Loud sobs punctuated with hiccups filled the sudden silence. Benny tried to stop, but he couldn't. He wanted to run, but he couldn't move.

A hand grabbed the back of his shirt and pulled. He rolled over onto his stomach, knees pulled up under him, not wanting to get up. Not ever.

A slap connected with the back of his head. "Get up, boy. We gotta go." Juice's voice, high and breathless, shook. "Now, *chiquito,* I ain't got time to mess with you. Get up."

Benny let the hand pull him up. He didn't want to stay on the floor with the big, brown man staring at him with eyes that didn't close.

Better to go with Juice.

Juice dragged him to the back of the car. The trunk again. "No, please. Please don't put me in there." His lips were swollen thick, making his words sound muffled.

"Ain't got no choice, *chiquito.* You be safe in there."

Bags of clothes and groceries crowded the backseat of the car. The clothes were stuffed into paper bags like someone was in a hurry. No room for him. "I promise to be good. Please let me sit up front with you."

Juice's face twisted in a snarl. "Shut up and get in, *m'ijo.* You ain't getting the chance to do something stupid. No sir. Get in. I

236

ain't got time to mess around. *Vámanos!*"

Juice grabbed Benny by the seat of his pants and hoisted him into the trunk. His nose hit the bottom. Blood spurted out. A second later, he tasted it. The trunk banged shut. Darkness again. Benny almost liked it now. The dark seemed safe.

Safer than out there.

CHAPTER NINETEEN

Abilene, Kansas

Esperanza Chavez dropped to her knees on the sidewalk in front of the grocery store and tried to grab the cans of beans rolling toward the street. No matter how much Momma insisted they call themselves Dodge, Esperanza clung to her old name. Momma couldn't get in her head and take that away from her. The sack had been too heavy for her, and then the brown paper had given way at the bottom, sending cans hurtling in all directions. Momma would kill her. Esperanza would die right here in front of the Abilene IGA, across from the public library. The bottle of pickles had broken, filling the humid morning air with the smell of dill and vinegar. The juice soaked into the hem of her jeans, making an ugly wet patch.

"You clumsy cow." Momma's sharp whisper sent fear scurrying through Esperanza.

Her long shadow blotted out the sun, making the fall morning go dark around Esperanza.

Estrella, her twin, stood frozen next to Momma, that funny look on her face that she always got when she was trying not to cry. Dom set his bag on the ground. Momma's fingers wrapped around his skinny arm. "No. She made the mess, she cleans it up. No child of mine could be that clumsy. Get that stuff picked up. Now."

"Good morning, Ms. Dodge." Another long shadow met, mingled with Momma's. The man towered over them, his belly hanging over a belt that had a gun holster on it. His hand rested on the gun. Esperanza risked a look at his face. He wasn't smiling. She scurried after a can of peaches that had rolled all the way to the curb. The man chewed on a toothpick, a strange fierce look on his face as he stared at her momma.

He had on a uniform and the patch on his pocket said Sheriff's Office. He reached for a can. "Let me help you with that, sweetheart. Look's like you're gonna need another sack. This one's got a big old hole in it. Those pickles smell mighty good, don't they? Shame they ended up on the ground."

"Frankie, back up, before you step in it. Dom, run in and get another bag. Now. And come right back, you hear me." Momma's voice had that dangerous note in it. She didn't like for anyone to pay attention to them. She was so afraid. Afraid *Papi* might find them. "Thank you, Deputy Baker, but there is no reason to trouble yourself helping this girl. She's a clumsy one, but she'll get it picked up."

"It's no bother. It's just the gentlemanly thing to do, helping out a young lady in distress." He rose, took Esperanza's arm, and helped her to her feet. "You ain't had no more trouble with the law, have you, Ms. Dodge?"

He had a twang like people from the south. Esperanza liked that sound. It reminded her of San Antonio. San Antonio was a distant memory. She wasn't sure how much she remembered and how much she'd made up to block out the miserable present. They'd moved to the farm outside Abilene right after she turned nine. She and Estrella turned fourteen in February, but they hadn't celebrated because Momma said they were too old for that silly stuff. Not like when *Papi* would stick a piñata on the tree and let them whack at it while *conjunto* music played and his friends drank beer in the front yard. They didn't have anyone to invite to a party, anyway. None of them —

not she nor Estrella nor Dom nor Frankie — was allowed to have friends. Momma said it had to be that way, for their safety. *Papi* might find them.

"No, sir. I told you that whole business with the overdraft was a simple bookkeeping error. I had no intention of writing a hot check." Momma didn't look happy. The man had made her mad. Things would be that much worse when they went home.

"Mr. Carpenter is gonna come out and pick up the glass and hose down the sidewalk." Dom rushed between Momma and the sheriff's deputy. He handed Esperanza the paper bag. Their gazes connected. His eyes said he wanted to help her. Esperanza shook her head at him. She didn't want him getting a whupping, too.

She began shoving the food into the bag. In her hurry, she rammed her hand into the broken pickle jar. "Oh-oh-oh." She slapped her hand against her chest in a sudden agony of pain. Blood gushed from the cut and soaked into the T-shirt. "Ouch."

"Now look what you've done, you idiot." Momma yanked her to her feet in a bone-jarring motion. "You got blood on your shirt. That won't come out."

Esperanza swallowed a sob. Her gaze caught the sheriff's deputy's. He took a step toward Momma. Stopped. Momma dropped her hand. The deputy turned to Esperanza. "You've cut yourself, little girl. Maybe I should take you over to the station and patch you up. It's just right across the street."

His face was so kind. Esperanza wanted to put her hand in his and let him lead the way. If she could just get to the station, maybe she could tell him about the things that went on in her house. He looked like the kind of person who would listen and who would do something about it.

"Not necessary. We'll get her home. We've got a first aid kit at the house. She'll be fine." Momma thrust a wad of tissues at her. "Put pressure on it. Dom, get your bag. I'll carry Esperanza's. Y'all get in the car. Now!"

Without risking another look at the deputy, Esperanza rushed with the others to the car. The girls squeezed into the front seat while Dom and Frankie climbed into the back. Esperanza dared to peek out the window. The officer stood on the sidewalk, not moving, staring after them. She could almost imagine from the look on his face that he knew . . .

. . . knew that whatever Esperanza would be when she got back to the farm, it wouldn't be just fine. In fact, she would never be just fine. She tried to send the deputy a message with her mind. Like the prayers she said every night before she went to bed.

Help us, please. Help us.

CHAPTER TWENTY

Inhaling the smell of fresh dirt and grass, Alex touched the dry, disturbed earth near the patch where little Jane Doe had been found. After dropping Samuel off at the hospital, he'd returned to Ray's ranch to check on the canine search. It was winding down. Still nothing of note. The doctors weren't saying much about Daniel's condition, other than he should've sought medical treatment much sooner. Duh. At least Alex could help relieve Samuel's stress by staying on top of the Jane Doe case so Samuel could focus on his brother and family issues.

Not that the search had been fruitful. Officers from SAPD and Bexar County hadn't turned up any more unmarked graves. Alex scooped a few clods in his hands, squeezed, and let dirt seep between his fingers. Cooper walked the fence line in the distance with two deputies, a frustrated look on his face.

The same frustration ballooned in Alex. The teams continued to comb the area, but with no results.

Alex stood and stomped his feet. Physical action might disperse the melancholy that weighed heavily on his shoulders. His stomach growled, reminding him he hadn't eaten all day. Between hunger and exhaustion from a very long night, his body kept trying to crash despite his best efforts to stay alert.

"Detective Luna!" Maddy Stover strode across the field, looking like a farm wife from a John Wayne western. "Find anything new?"

Alex looked over her shoulder at the open field where Ray's horses trotted along the fence, staring their direction, maybe hoping for an apple or a carrot. "Nope. *Nada.*" He smacked his dusty hands on his slacks. "Not a thing."

"I thought y'all might want to come up to the house for some coffee, but I guess you're still busy."

"I'm dying for some coffee." Alex fell in step next to her. "Coop will come up when he's done, don't worry. I think he can smell caffeine a mile away."

She smiled and picked up her pace. "What I don't understand about our little Jane Doe is how the schools and CPS could not notice when a child disappears."

"The children sometimes have health or emotional problems," Alex said. "They're absent from school a lot anyway, so the district loses track of them. They may figure they're back in foster care in another school district. They simply slip through the cracks."

"Yep. I guess it could happen more than most of us would like to admit." Her pace increased, apparently in keeping with her agitation. "It's a sad world. I'm thinking about selling the ranch. Ray doesn't need me around anymore. I might go up and live with my son in Dallas, spend time with my grandchildren."

Alex pictured the look on Coop's face whenever he got within a few yards of Maddy. "Ray might be married, but he'd still miss you. I imagine a lot of people would. From what I've seen, you're an honorary member of the Martinez-Johnson family."

"That's sweet of you, Alex." Her smile didn't make her look any happier. "Have a seat on the porch swing. I'll bring out the coffee."

He gave the swing a push with his foot and stared at the horizon, wondering what it would be like to have a child to rock to sleep at naptime. Deborah's face floated in front of his. He wanted a woman he could put his arm around at night and drift off to sleep. A woman he could count on. Deborah had an alcohol problem. She could kick it. He could help. Or was that more pie in the sky?

Maddy pushed through the screen door, forcing him to abandon that dangerous line of thought. She handed him a huge mug of coffee. "Tómas Chavez was an odd character, all right." She picked up the conversation as if there'd been no pause. "I was thinking about it last night as I was washing dishes. Thinking about things I haven't thought about in years. Things I really didn't want to remember."

Alex swung some more. "Like what?"

"Like the shed out there. The bigger one behind the barn." Maddy stood and walked to the split-log porch railing, her back to Alex. "I came up here one evening to return Mr. Chavez's dog. For some reason, the poor old thing — it was a mutt really — had attached itself to my place. I kept having to bring him back over here. Chavez had a bunch of friends out in the yard. They were sitting around in lawn chairs, drinking beer, music blaring."

247

"Were the kids around?"

"They were sitting on the porch when I drove up, but they disappeared in the house right away when I got out. Two girls, two boys. All of them dirty, barefooted, needed haircuts."

Alex kept quiet, thinking of that fifth child. Maddy turned and leaned against the railing, the cup of coffee half raised. "The dog ran off, but I went out to the shed to tell Chavez I'd returned his dog." She stopped, her mouth closed tight for a second. "Chavez pulled a thirty-six Smith & Wesson from his jean jacket and aimed it at me. 'Course I immediately called out, 'Hey, it's me, your neighbor.' He got this funny look on his face, real foolish-like, and stuck the gun back in his pocket."

Alex joined her at the railing. "Strange reaction to seeing a neighbor."

"He was higher than a kite. His friends laughed like it was the funniest thing they'd ever seen. He offered me a drink. Of course, I turned him down and got out of there. I could hear them cackling all the way back to my truck."

"Scary."

Maddy nodded. "And you have to ask yourself why a law-abiding citizen with four kids would feel the need to carry an S&W

in his coat pocket."

That was a fair question. But how did it tie back to their Jane Doe? "We don't even know for sure this little girl is Nina Chavez."

Maddy cocked her head to one side, her lips pursed. "Well, CPS did come out here."

"True and we've already been over how the system works." Alex set the coffee mug on the table next to the swing. "We think we may have a lead on where Chavez's wife and kids are. I'm headed out to talk to someone who might know. I hope we're on the right track."

"Have faith."

He stomped down the steps. It seemed that everyone had decided to push the faith issue with him. "Faith isn't something I know much about. Good police work will solve this case."

Maddy fixed him with a fierce look. "You can't do it on your own, not even with the help of good men like Cooper, Ray, and the others. You need more. You need faith."

"Yes, ma'am." He didn't want to argue with a woman old enough to be his grandmother. She had no way of knowing faith had stopped entering the equation long ago. "I'm sure Cooper will be up for coffee soon. Do me a favor, please, and tell him I went to run down the PI lead. He'll know what

I'm talking about."

Maddy nodded, but he had a feeling her sharp gaze missed nothing.

Anger shot through him, more effective than the caffeine. Only he wasn't sure why he was angry. Something. About everything. "I'll figure it out," he said aloud as he jammed the key in the ignition. He just wasn't sure what it was he was trying to figure out. He backed out and let the Altima rip.

The address for Simon Phillips's office led Alex to a storefront door in a strip shopping center between a hair salon and a Java Shack. The sign painted on the window read PHILLIPS & HAMILTON PRIVATE INVESTIGATIONS. Inside, a window unit air conditioner rattled, but the air was lukewarm and damp. A platinum-blond woman wearing pink lipstick sat at the desk, sipping coffee and playing solitaire on the computer.

"I'm looking for Simon Phillips."

She chuckled and took her hand from the mouse. "You and every other customer he ever stiffed."

He held his badge out. "I might have more cause."

She eyed it. "I'm his former partner. BeBe Hamilton."

"So would that be a lot of customers?"

She waved a hand toward a straight back chair on the other side of the desk. "No, just the ones he was working when he decided to up and retire on a moment's notice."

"When did that happen?"

"About four years ago. He was all hot on a missing persons' case, went up to Kansas to check out a lead. Next thing I know, I get a letter from him saying he's decided to retire and he isn't coming back. Asked me to clear out his apartment and take everything to the Goodwill. He was cutting all ties, according to the letter. Apparently they got some sweet deer hunting up there and land prices are cheaper."

"The missing persons' case — was the client a man named Tómas Chavez?"

Hamilton's mouth dropped open. "What are you — some kind of psychic? How'd you know?"

"I'm looking into the same case."

"Huh, after all these years?"

"Didn't you think it was sort of strange, Mr. Phillips deciding to retire like that?"

"Naw, not at all. He was a bitter, old man, and he was tired. His wife took him to the cleaners in the divorce. He had no kids, no family to speak of. He could retire if he wanted to."

"What about the money Chavez paid him?"

"I told Chavez that Simon had exhausted all leads and gave him the retainer back. I didn't give him any details. The guy was a scary dude. I would never have taken the case, if it'd been up to me. I didn't want him to go looking for Simon or following me home one night after work."

"You never tried to get in touch with Mr. Phillips again?"

She picked up her fingernail file and went to work on her thumbnail. "Actually, I did, but they said he'd already checked out of the hotel. I didn't have an address or a telephone number. I figured he'd cut the ties."

"And you got the business?"

"Such as it is." She waved the nail file around. "It ain't much, but it's home."

"You wouldn't happen to have a file on the Chavez case, by any chance."

She made a *help-yourself* gesture. "I imagine it's in one of the boxes in the back room there. Simon would've taken copies, left the originals. He was real careful about stuff like that."

After an hour of pawing through boxes haphazardly stacked around a desk that still had Simon Phillips's nameplate on it, Alex came up with the file. He sneezed twice and wiped the dust from his face with the back of his hand before he sat down in the only chair in the room.

Bingo. He had to read the certificate and Phillips's notes twice before it sank in. A marriage certificate issued in Dickinson County, Kansas, to Clarisse Berger and Ezra Dodge four years before she married Chavez. Phillips had been unable to find any record of a divorce or of Dodge's death.

Clarisse Dodge slash Chavez was a bigamist.

Phillips further theorized that when she disappeared, it was to go back to her first husband.

In Abilene, Kansas.

CHAPTER TWENTY-ONE

Deborah slammed the cookie tray on the kitchen counter and jerked off the oven mitt. She'd burned another batch, filling her apartment with the acrid smell of burnt peanuts. She should've gone to the movies instead of pretending to be Betty Crocker. An hour of AA at the crack of dawn followed by another hour in her therapist's office, and two hours at the gym, and then another hour of AA — that left an endless nineteen hours of every day to fill.

A rap on the door sent the thought careening away. Someone — she didn't care who it was at this point — to interrupt the dreadful, lazy tick tock of the clock. Deborah sped to the door and flung it open. "Oh. It's you."

Alex shifted from one foot to the other. "Nice to see you again, too."

"Why — never mind. Come in. Please." She whipped the door wide, glad to have something besides her own insidious thoughts to entertain her.

"Here." He thrust a brown paper bag at her as he slipped through, within inches of touching her even though the doorway was plenty wide for both of them.

She took the bag and backed away from him. "What's this?"

"Candy."

"Thanks. Did it occur to you that you might want to call before coming over?"

"I did. There was no answer. The candy is supposed to help you quit smoking."

Belatedly, Deborah remembered she'd unplugged the phone after the third "just wondering how you're doing call" from Teresa and Omar and Ray — everyone but Daniel.

"Candy's bad for my teeth. I chew sugarless gum." She peered inside the bag. Peppermints, lemon drops, root beer balls, an assortment of Brach hard candies. Not bad.

"All that chomping is so attractive." He plopped down in the only decent chair in her living room before she could offer him a seat. He looked good. Dark blue shirt. Gray dress slacks, nice silk tie. "What smells? Like something burned?"

She popped a peppermint in her mouth and headed for the mini-kitchen without answering. Normally she liked the tight efficiency of her tiny apartment. Now it seemed way too small for her — and him. He filled up the space with a coiled energy that radiated masculinity. She peeked at him over the counter as she swept the burnt cookies into a wastebasket and stuck it under the sink. "Aren't you working?"

"I've been running all over the place, and I realized I forgot to eat. So I thought . . . well . . ." He ducked his head and looked at his shoes.

Deborah took the opportunity to study his face. He looked exhausted. Dark circles around big dark eyes in a face that didn't seem as plain to her as it had before. "So what are you doing here?"

"Inviting myself to have a late lunch with you. Or an early dinner." His tone sounded more resolute. He stood and followed her into the kitchen. The passage between the counter and the sink shrank. "You have the makings for sandwiches by any chance? I'll make one for you, too. Or we could go to the deli, if you'd rather. I'll buy."

"Why me?" The question was out before she could reel it in. Nice. Couldn't she be nice just once?

He didn't seem deterred. "I —"

"I don't care why," she interrupted him. She knew why. Sarge sent him to make sure she wasn't backsliding with a bottle. To babysit her. "You promise to tell me what's going on with the investigation, and I'll feed you. You can even have a homemade cookie."

"You made cookies?" He laughed. "Hence the burnt smell."

"Why are you laughing? Some of them turned out okay."

He threw a hand over his mouth, obviously trying to hold back the guffaws.

"What's so funny? This was your idea. If you don't want to eat with me, fine. Leave."

"No, no. I'm sorry, Deborah. I'm not laughing at you. I'm just tired."

"Sure you are. So where are they on finding Benny? And have they ID'd that other child's remains?" She eased past him and inched her way to the other side of the counter. Alex's gaze took in her gym shorts and tank top, then slid away. "What are you looking at? It was hot in here with the oven on."

"I'm not — nothing, I'm not looking at anything." He stuck his hands in his pockets and hunched his shoulders. "Feed me and then you can pump me for information."

"There's ham and turkey. I'll be right back." She started toward the bedroom. "Start the sandwiches. I want to know everything."

"I think I better have turkey. It would be appropriate." His wry tone wafted after her.

Deborah contemplated his presence as she changed into jeans and an oversized T-shirt. No way he'd shown up at her door for a sandwich. Something was up. Was Benny dead and he hadn't found a way to tell her yet? He better not be holding out on her.

If something had happened to Benny, Daniel would be devastated. She would go after anyone who hurt him. Her chest tightened at the thought. Only she couldn't because she'd messed up and gotten tossed from the case.

She'd let her friends down. Again.

Trying to shake the thought, she hurried back to the kitchen. Alex was rummaging through the cabinets. "Where's the —"

"No, not that one!"

It was too late.

His hand froze on the door handle. His other hand came up and grasped the bottle of whiskey and pulled it from the top shelf. He turned slowly, his gaze hard. "So, what's this doing here?"

"You don't understand —"

"You don't get it, do you?"

He pushed past her, taking the bottle with him.

"Wait. Alex, please, wait." She put her hand out to stop him, but even in that desperate moment, she couldn't bring herself to touch him. "I didn't open it."

"So why'd you buy it?" He whirled and slammed the palm of his hand against her door. There was more than anger in his face. She couldn't define it. Pity? Fear? Why did he care so much? "Why have it in the apartment?"

"It's . . . it's like a security blanket." The words tumbled out in a rush. "Didn't you do that when you quit smoking . . . keep two or three cigarettes in a drawer just so you knew they were there and you didn't feel so panicked? Like you didn't have to run out and buy some when you couldn't stand it anymore. They'd be there, if you needed them. Just knowing that, kept you from doing it, right?"

Alex had one foot out the door. His fingers gripped the knob. "It sounds dangerous to me."

"It is."

The silence stretched for several long seconds. If he left, they were done as friends — or anything else. Still, she refused to beg.

He stepped back into the room. "It's going with me when I leave."

She tried for a smirk. "No biggie. It's all

259

yours. Share it with your buddies . . . or your girlfriend, whatever."

"I told you. I don't drink. And I'm between girlfriends at the moment."

The sudden lightness of his tone belied the bleak look on his face. He set the bottle on the end table next to the couch. She allowed herself one longing glance at it. Maybe he'd forget to take it with him.

The set of his jaw told her it was unlikely. Another trip to the liquor store loomed in her future.

"I'd like mayo and mustard on the sandwich." Alex waited until Deborah turned to pull something from the refrigerator to wipe the sweat from his forehead on his sleeve. He struggled to get his bearings. Her tiny apartment didn't give a person much room to navigate.

"So tell me, what's the news on both cases?" Deborah pushed her long, blond hair back behind her ear with one hand. She had thin, tapered fingers that ended in nails painted a pale pink. No rings. Beautiful hands. They were shaking.

Alex tore his gaze from them and studied the countertop. He'd always had profound respect for Omar and his AA counterparts — now even more so. He ran through the facts on the Jane Doe he had come to believe was Nina Chavez, including his find at the PI's office. Deborah's hands stopped moving. She laid down the knife and gripped the edge of the counter. "So, Phillips went to Kansas to find Clarise Chavez and then suddenly decides to retire and never come back. Doesn't tell Chavez what he found out. Doesn't tell his partner. That's just bizarre."

"I know. The trail is plenty cold, but it's still there. Follow it to the end, and I think we'll find Clarisse and those kids."

"Yeah, but Benny is in imminent danger. We — you have to find him first."

On that, they agreed. Alex ran through the Barrera-Morin-Chavez connection.

Deborah resumed making the sandwiches. "Daniel must be all over this guy, then."

"He will be, as soon as he gets out of the hospital. We're hoping —"

The jar of mayonnaise hit the floor and shattered. The knife clattered on the vinyl next to it. "What did you say?"

Her face was white. Alex froze. First, Daniel had been all out of whack because he couldn't find her, and now she was freaking because Daniel was sick. That was more than friendship. "I thought Ray told you. He's got some kind of flu or something."

Alex had the urge to practice his gobble. "He passed out at the counseling session. They took him to the hospital by ambulance."

"Is he all right? What did the doctors say?"

"He has some vicious strain of the flu. He didn't take care of himself. They're having trouble getting his fever down, but he'll live. Nicole's with him and Susana and the whole clan."

Alex began picking up the glass, not wanting to watch the emotions dance across Deborah's face. Fear and relief coupled with guilt and remorse.

"Leave it. I can clean it up. I don't need your help." She reached for a piece of glass. The color had returned to her face, but she didn't make eye contact.

"Fine. Look, maybe I should just go."

"Yeah. Maybe you should just go. I don't know what you're doing here anyway."

She stood at the same time he did. She seemed angry. Why should she be angry with him? He hadn't done anything. He wasn't married to someone else.

"I don't know either." He strode to the door and reached for the knob. "I know the way out."

"Don't go." Her voice had the slightest quiver in it.

"Why?"

"You haven't had your sandwich."

"I lost my appetite."

"Don't be stupid, Alex. You came here for a sandwich, and you're not leaving until you have a sandwich."

Alex glared at her. She glared back. "Fine, but no more talk about the investigation."

Did he see a tiny hesitation? Maybe. "Fine."

"Let's start over — one more time. Why don't I make the sandwiches and you tell me what you've been doing?" Alex wiped up the mayonnaise with a wad of paper towels.

A morose look on her face, she plopped down on the barstool at the counter that separated the kitchen from the living room. "Burning cookies."

He dumped the dirty paper towels in a wastebasket that reeked of burnt cookies. "They say practice makes perfect."

"Did Sarge send you to check up on me?"

"No, Sarge did not send me." Alex added slices of cheese to the turkey he'd slapped on two pieces of wheat bread. He forced himself to look at her. "He doesn't know I'm here."

She dusted crumbs from the countertop. "Any chance you'd go to bat for me? You know, ask him to let me come back."

Alex bit his lip, trying to think. Was she ready? She had a bottle of booze hidden in her apartment. His desire to get close to her could not cloud his professional judgment. On the other hand, working might be the one thing that allowed her to stay sober. On the other hand, she needed time to work out her issues. He was no expert. "Deborah, I —"

"Forget it. Obviously you don't get it."

"No, because you won't tell me what's really wrong."

"Nothing's wrong, I just need to work. I need to be useful. I can resolve my issues and work at the same time." She slapped both hands on the counter. "If you can't understand that and try to be supportive of a fellow officer, I don't know why you're even here."

"I'm trying to be your friend." Or something like that.

Her forehead wrinkled over blue eyes that looked puzzled. "Why?"

He added lettuce to the sandwiches so he wouldn't have to keep looking at her. "Because I like you."

She snorted. "Why?"

"It's beyond me."

"Nice."

"Nicer than you are to me."

"You sound like you're six."

He smiled in spite of himself. She was right.

She tossed her hair over her shoulder, her gaze defiant. "Let's get something straight."

He sliced a tomato, narrowly missing his thumb. "What's that?"

"I'm a Christian now. I know it doesn't look like it. But I'm trying. I need to be around other Christians. And I'm not doing the stuff I did before. Saturday night, I fell down, but I'm picking myself up. You may have heard stuff about me and men, but that's all in the past. In case, you have some ulterior motives or plans —"

Anger dovetailed into a crazy, hurt feeling. He dropped the knife on the cutting board. "I really should go. This was a mistake." He headed for the door again. Stupid. He was too stupid to understand women. Especially this one.

"Alex. I'm sorry. I didn't mean that the way it sounded."

He didn't answer. He reached for the doorknob. The palm of her hand slapped against the door, keeping him from opening it. "Don't go."

He whirled and grabbed her shoulders, looking into her startled blue eyes. "Who told you I was the bad guy?"

Her face blanched white. She struggled from his grip. "Get your hands off me." Her voice quivered with fear.

Alex dropped his hands and backed away. "I'm sorry. I'm sorry, Deborah."

She stumbled back, her hands rubbing her shoulders. "I don't like to be touched. You know that."

He held up both hands. "I would never hurt you. I promise. Never. You know that."

She kept backing away until she was up against the far living room wall. She slid down on her haunches and put her hands over her face.

"Deborah?" Confused, Alex crept closer and knelt. "I'm so sorry. I didn't mean to scare you. You make me nuts because I — I guess I have a crush on you."

A hysterical sounding giggle escaped from behind the hands covering her face, but she still didn't speak.

"You think that's funny?" He peeled a hand from her face. She flinched.

"Deborah, who hurt you?"

Her gaze didn't connect with his. "It was a long time ago. It doesn't matter anymore."

"Obviously, it does."

"Only if we were . . . if we were dating or something like that."

He swiveled around on his heels and leaned against the wall, careful not to touch her. "Even if we just become friends, it'd be important to know."

"We can be friends."

"Yeah? As long as I don't touch you?"

"Yes."

"Sometimes friends hug. Sometimes they pat each other on the back. They might even hold hands."

"Not me."

"You need physical affection as much as the next person."

"Not really."

"What if you had a boyfriend? You've had boyfriends." The memory of her, a drink in one hand, a cigarette in the other, leaning into the space of some tall, blond guy at the Cadillac Bar surfaced. Her smile had never wavered.

"When I was drinking."

"Ah. But not sober."

"No. Not sober."

He hadn't seen her with anyone in recent months, but then their paths rarely crossed in social situations now that neither frequented bars. "Have you given it a chance?"

"The opportunity hasn't come up."

"And then when it did, I was angry, and I scared you."

"I'm not scared of you."

She sounded more like herself. Alex stuck his legs out and relaxed against the wall. "Right."

"Could you please leave me alone?"

Now she sounded tired and sad. This wasn't at all what he had planned. Food and some light conversation. The getting-to-know-you phase. "I don't want you to be alone."

"Please. Some other time."

"You promise?"

This time she looked at him. "You want there to be another time?"

"Yes, I do."

"Even though I'm like this."

"Human?"

"Stone cold frigid."

Cold didn't enter into the equation when he thought about Deborah. Only heat. "You may be a lot of things, but that's not one of them." This might be his only chance to convince her he was serious. He forced himself to verbalize something even he didn't understand. "I think of you as lightning on a dark night. You walk into the room and no matter how dark it is, you light up the place."

Her cheeks darkened to the color of a dusty pink rose. "Maybe we could —"

The shrill ring of Alex's cell phone shattered the air. They both jumped. Alex ripped his gaze away from hers and tugged the phone from his pocket. "Yeah."

Cooper's voice filled his ear, telling him they'd made contact with the foster parents who had taken Nina Chavez into their home for a few short months prior to the disappearance of Clarisse Chavez and her children. "You want in on the interview?"

"Absolutely." Alex glanced at Deborah. She had her forehead resting on arms crossed over her knees, her long hair cloaking her face. This conversation would have to wait for another time — but soon. "Give me the address. I'll meet you there."

He pulled himself up from the floor, again careful not to touch her. At his movement, she shifted. "News on Benny?"

"No. Jane Doe. I have to go. Deborah, we need you on both these investigations. If I have the chance, I'll tell Sarge that. He's really shorthanded, and Macon's on his back." Shorthanded because Deborah had chosen to drink. Sarge was unlikely to forget that. "Don't mess up again. If you need somebody to talk to, call me, night or day."

She didn't answer. He picked up the whiskey and opened the door.

"Alex?"

"Yeah?" He looked back. She still sat hunched against the wall, her knees in her face.

"Now let me give you some advice. Go back to church — and not because you think I'll be there."

"Hey, I thought it was a pretty good reason." Church belonged to that distant part of his life that had involved two parents and two children attending as a family.

"I mean it."

"I know you do. I'll think about it."

"Good-bye."

"Not good-bye. *Hasta luego.*"

"Until later?"

"Yeah." He closed the door, then closed his eyes for a second. No sounds from the other side of the door. He'd almost gotten away with the feeling that they had cleared a hurdle. Then she had to go and mention church.

CHAPTER TWENTY-TWO

Daniel struggled to open his eyes. They were glued shut. His cracked lips burned. His tongue stuck to the roof of his mouth. The familiar smells of coffee and doughnuts that usually filled Pastor Wilson's office were gone, replaced with antiseptic odors. He tried to remember what had happened. He'd been in the office and then . . . something . . . with Nicole. "Water. Please, somebody, I need water."

A cool hand brushed against his cheek. "I'm right here, *mi amor.* Can you open your eyes?"

Mi amor. He hadn't heard those words directed at him in a long time. Nicole's voice had a gentle quality that took him back to the days when she'd sat in the rocking chair with Phoebe in her arms, cooing little sweet nothings to her newborn baby.

Tears formed and seeped from the corner of his eyes. They slipped into his hair. He forced his eyes open. Her face filled his vision. Tousled hair and smudged makeup did nothing to detract from her classic beauty. He closed his eyes and opened them again to make sure it wasn't a hallucination brought on by fever. She was still there. Why? If she was leaving him for another man, why was she still here?

He opened his mouth to ask, but the worried faces of Samuel and Susana, side by side at the foot of the bed, made him stop. "Am I in the hospital? You didn't let them admit me, did you? What about Benny? I have to find Benny."

"Yes, you're in the hospital, Danny. Alex and Joaquin and the rest are working the case. You're sick. You passed out. You have a temperature of one-oh-three. You scared me to death." Nicole dropped her hand. "Do you feel any better?"

"Why are you here?" He couldn't keep the sarcasm out of his voice. "Still."

"To make sure you're all right."

"I didn't know you cared." He tried to sit up. "I want out of here. Now."

Samuel moved around so he was closer. "The doctor says you're dehydrated, and the fever is out of control. You're to stay in bed until they can get it down. Let us worry about Benny."

"Ray and the rest of the gang will find him," Susana chimed in. She crowded Nicole, without looking at the other woman.

Nicole held her ground. "What can I do for you?"

Besides let him come home? "I need a drink of water."

Nicole beat Susana to the pitcher on the stand by the bed. A few seconds later she handed him a glass with a straw in it. He sipped greedily, making slurping sounds. His hand shook and water spilled on his gown. Her hand covered his, steadying the glass. "Is that better?"

"Yeah." He looked at the ceiling, breathing for a few seconds. Anger and fear fueled the nausea. "Samuel, Susana, could I have a few minutes alone with my wife?"

Susana's mouth came open, but Samuel grabbed her arm and hustled her toward the door. "We'll be right outside if you need us," she called back before the door closed behind them.

Daniel laid his head back, coughed, sat back up, coughing so hard, he was afraid he'd vomit. Nicole patted his shoulder. "Should I get the nurse?"

"No. No." He lay back again, gasping for air. "What's wrong with me?"

"Severe case of a nasty strain of the flu."

She smoothed his sheets and fluffed his pillow. "I'm surprised. You always get your flu shot — you hate missing work."

"You make that sound like a character defect." Another wave of anger added to his lightheadedness. "Some people think being a hard worker is a good thing."

"It is. It's one of the things we have in common." She plucked at the sheet again. "Look, Daniel, I don't want to argue, I just want you to get better."

"How are the kids?"

"Worried about you."

"Chris wants to come live with me."

"Daniel —"

"I know. It's impossible. As it is, Benny spends most of his time at Lily's or with Marco. I'm not there enough for him. But Chris was so upset with you." Daniel stopped, each breath causing his chest to hurt. "I'll do whatever is necessary to make it happen if you plan to continue to see that man."

"It's not like you make it sound. Joshua just stopped by to make sure I was all right after the wedding."

Daniel coughed. "Another man in my house, checking on my wife. Did you tell him I abuse you or something?"

"Of course not. And it's my house. We just talked."

"You kissed him, Nicole. Coworkers don't kiss. Did he spend the night?"

She gasped. "You're intentionally trying to hurt me now because I hurt you." Nicole backed away from the bed, her face set in angry lines. "Not that it's any of your business, but we haven't even had a date yet."

"It is my business. You're still married to me. Chris should live with me." Daniel's anger raged as hot as his fever. "I could get a housekeeper. Get a bigger apartment. For when we get Benny home. We'll bring him home, and they'll be real brothers."

He began coughing again. "I'm going to be sick."

Nicole grabbed a disposable container from the bed stand and thrust it at him.

"Get away from me." He desperately wanted her to stay, but that would only make it hurt more in the long run, when she left him for good. "Just get out! Get out!"

"Daniel, stop. You're making it worse." She pushed him back against the pillows. "You shouldn't get excited. You need to rest. We can talk about this later."

"I don't need you here. I have family here."

She turned and rushed to the door. He vomited into the tray. "By the way." His voice sounded harsh and raspy in his ears. "By the way, I quit my job. I meant to tell you at the counseling session. I quit my job."

She stopped, her hand on the door, but she didn't turn around. A second later, she disappeared through the door. It swung shut behind her.

Daniel sat up and threw off the covers. The flu. It wasn't like he was dying. He had to get back in the field. Benny needed him. He tottered to his feet. And crumpled to the floor.

CHAPTER TWENTY-THREE

Kim Glover handed a tall tumbler of lemon-
ade to Cooper and then turned to Alex with
a second glass. He sipped and let the cold
liquid slide down his parched throat. He
could barely hear the foster mother's offer
of brownies over the noise emanating from
the hallway of a house that looked as
rumpled as its owner. It sounded like several
children were playing a rousing game of
Hokey Pokey. How had Nina Chavez fit into
this noisy, homey environment, apparently
very different from the one she'd been born
into?

He set the glass on the corner of a coffee
table covered by half-folded laundry and
got down to business. "What can you tell us
about Nina Chavez?"

"Nina was one of our easy-to-handle
foster children, but she wasn't here long
enough for me to establish a real bond. Only
about a month, I think. Sweet little thing,

afraid of her own shadow." Sadness blurred Mrs. Glover's chubby features. "I always wondered what became of her. Did something happen to her?"

It would be nice to avoid answering that question. Alex glanced at Cooper, whose lifted eyebrows said *be my guest.* "Were you afraid something would happen if she went back home?" He was ninety-nine percent sure the little girl in the grave was Nina Chavez. Sweet little thing, afraid of her own shadow, and dead. "Did you see signs of physical abuse?"

Mrs. Glover shoved aside a doll and a stuffed rabbit and sat down on the love seat across from them. She had a smudge of flour on her cheek. The house smelled like cinnamon rolls baking. "You always wonder, Detective. These children are in the system for a reason. CPS doesn't take kids out of the home on a whim."

"You have a lot of experience with CPS and foster children?"

"My husband Fred and I have been foster parents for almost twenty years," she said with an expressive shrug. "We know all the games biological parents play. We know the whole gamut of ways they inflict pain — physical and emotional — on kids."

"What specifically —"

Before Alex could finish the question, a small girl burst into the room. "Mrs. G, can we have cinnamon rolls now? We're starving. We want milk with them. Can we have milk, too?"

Two boys peeked through the door, their faces eager, but they didn't enter the room. Alex waved as Mrs. Glover answered the girl. "Belle, I told you I would call you when they're ready. Did you hear the oven bell ding? No? That's because they're still baking. You have to be patient. Now go. I'm in the middle of talking to these gentlemen. You shouldn't interrupt."

"But I'm so hungry."

"Belle, did you or did you not have two PB and J sandwiches, a banana, and a glass of milk for lunch?"

"I did, but —"

"Go." Mrs. Glover enveloped the pigtailed little girl in a hug, spun her so she faced the door, and gave her a gentle nudge forward.

Alex exchanged an amused glance with Cooper. Little kids were cute. He'd never spent much time around kids, but he wouldn't mind giving it a try. Someday.

Mrs. Glover chuckled. "Sorry about that."

"Your kids?"

"Belle's mother chained her to a bed every

279

night while she went to work as a stripper. Said she didn't want her running off while she was gone." Mrs. Glover's voice quivered with indignation. "Neighbors heard her crying one night and broke into the apartment. She had a fever of a hundred and two and she'd soiled her bed. Had diarrhea. She had sores on her ankles and wrists from the handcuffs. Her mother's in jail now on drug charges as well as child neglect and endangerment."

Alex had heard these stories many times before — except his involvement usually meant the child was dead. Thank God for people like the Glovers. "How many kids are you caring for right now?"

"Three foster. And then the four we've adopted over the years. The oldest one is a senior in high school now."

It was a shame Nina Chavez hadn't had the good luck to remain in the Glover home. "So what brought Nina Chavez to you — and why did she get sent back home?"

"Whatever was happening with Nina apparently wasn't so overt. At least, CPS couldn't make a determination that she was being abused." Mrs. Glover's gusty sigh made her double chin sway. "But something was going on. She cowered if I got too close to her. She refused to talk. When I put food

280

on the table, she ate so fast, she choked and she kept looking at me like she was sure I would take it back before she could get enough to eat. She gained three pounds in the month she was here."

Alex flipped through the pages of his notebook — an excuse to keep his gaze lowered until the sudden emotion that flowed over him subsided. "The report I saw said she refused to sleep in a bed."

"Yes. And she always waited for permission to come out of her room, to start eating, to leave the table, everything. She did nothing without permission."

He didn't have a whole lot of experience with children, but he had some. "Not like most five-year-olds, I guess."

"No, it's not." Mrs. Glover plucked at her denim dress. "What happened to her?"

"We don't know anything happened to Nina. We're just following up on a lead."

"You're homicide detectives."

"Yes, ma'am."

Mrs. Glover's face crumpled. "Poor Nina."

Cooper didn't have much to say on the ride back to the sheriff's office. Alex let the silence build. They both needed time to contemplate their next move. In Cooper's office, Alex borrowed his computer and did some research while Cooper pushed paper. After about fifteen minutes, Alex stood and stretched his arms over his head before cranking it from side to side. "On the Attorney General's Web site, it says some of the experts call it 'Vulnerable Child Syndrome.' Others call it 'Targeted Child.' "

"It has a name?" Cooper sounded tired.

"Yeah. Targeted Child is when a parent sees something in a child that he sees in himself and doesn't like."

"We're just speculating at this point." Cooper stuck some papers in a folder and shut it.

"But it does happen, is what I'm saying. With Vulnerable Child Syndrome, parents pick out one child who is mentally slower or physically handicapped in some way or just has a personality that the parent doesn't like, and they abuse that child. The other siblings are treated fine. It's fairly common."

"I can't understand that." Anger flashed across Cooper's face. Alex imagined the guy was a good dad. The kind of dad every kid would love to have. His own dad was as distant as his memory. "How could a parent pick on one child — or any child? I just don't understand it."

"Nobody in his right mind can understand it." Alex stood. "Look, I've got an errand to run. I'll be back here in time for the evening round-up. Call me if you get that report back from the ME."

Nobody in his right mind. Like a meth-producing gangbanger? Alex wanted a definitive ID. Then he'd pay another visit to Tómas Chavez.

CHAPTER TWENTY-FOUR

Alex wandered through the house looking for Ray. According to Maddy, who had been sitting on the front porch reading a book when he had trotted up the front walk, Ray and Susana were in the study. He tapped on the door. No answer. The newlyweds were hiding out. He couldn't blame them. Between Benny's kidnapping and little Jane Doe, their memories of the early days of their marriage would be very interesting. He had to ask Ray two questions, and then he'd leave them alone. One dealt with the case, but the other question had been eating at him since he'd left Deborah's apartment and dogged him as he'd done the Glover interview.

Late afternoon sun shone in his eyes as he opened the screen door off the kitchen and stepped onto the side porch. Giggles floated through the air. The couple shared a lawn chair. Ray had both arms around Susana, who sat on his lap. They were kissing. Rocky rested at their feet. The dog raised his head and growled.

Alex dropped his gaze, trying to identify the emotion that ran through him. It felt like envy. He started to retreat through the screen door.

"Hey, Alex! Where are you going?" Ray waved a big hand. "Did you need something?"

"It's all right. I'll come back later."

Susana planted another kiss on her husband's lips and jumped up. "No, we were just taking a little break. Time to get back to work."

"I could see that." Heat burned Alex's face. "I'm sorry. I didn't mean to interrupt. I know you guys aren't getting a lot of privacy these days."

"Don't apologize, Alex. We have the rest of our lives for privacy." Susana sounded so much like Samuel that Alex had to smile. She pushed past him and then called back, "I'll bring you guys some sodas. Dr Pepper or root beer?"

Alex needed caffeine. "Dr Pepper."

Susana laughed. "Two caffeine boosters coming up."

Rocky at her heels, she disappeared into the house. Alex stayed in the doorway.

"You coming out, bro?" Ray stretched back in the patio chair, his hands behind his head. "Or do I need to come in?"

"I'm coming out." He went as far as a second lawn chair and plopped down in it. The breeze had a cool chill to it. Fall had finally arrived in South Texas. He closed his eyes for a second and let it blow over him.

"What's up?" Ray cranked his head from side to side and rolled his shoulders. "You look . . . stressed."

"Where's Marco?" Alex stalled.

"Spending the night with his cousins. Susana thought it would help take his mind off Benny."

"What about Daniel?" He stalled some more.

"Not great. He tried to get out of bed and passed out again. Lily thought Nicole had done something to upset him, but that's probably just the protective sister talking."

Time to get down to business. Even if it led places Alex didn't want to go. Places Ray probably had worked hard to forget. "Has Morin called?"

"No. Not since he found out we know who he is."

Alex shook his head. "That's not a good sign."

"No. We were hoping he'd go for the

money."

"Maybe he still will."

"Maybe." Ray didn't sound optimistic. "In the meantime, we're trying to figure out some places he might go. The Evidence Unit matched a fingerprint at the Jordan house to Miguel Suarez, which tells us there's definitely a connection between Barrera and Morin. But with the Jordans dead, we got no new leads on Morin's whereabouts. What about the connection to Tómas Chavez?"

"Chavez knows more than he's saying." Alex leaned forwarded and propped his elbows on his knees. "Morin confided in him in jail. We tried to get a search warrant, but the judge didn't think we had enough probable cause. If we nailed him for cooking meth and selling it, he might be willing to deal Morin to reduce the charge. I wish we'd get the ID back on the little girl's body. It'd help to know for sure she's Chavez's daughter."

Alex took a breath. Ray would probably recognize his rambling for what it was. Nerves. He didn't like delving into Ray's painful personal history. "Nobody remembers seeing Nina Chavez after she was returned to the ranch by CPS. Then the whole bunch disappears. Chavez hired a private investigator who went looking for them in Kansas and never came back. Right around the time you bought the property."

Ray was quiet for several seconds. "So they disappeared around the time I bought the property, and you're wondering how I couldn't have known that and why I didn't bring it up."

Alex shifted on the lawn chair. "A little. I mean, it would have been investigated by the sheriff's office, not PD, but even if it didn't make a big media splash, it was property you were buying."

Ray's hands slapped the metal arms of the lawn chair, making a hard, angry sound. "Five years ago, I was still in patrol on the south side. I was burying myself in work — among other things — trying to get past my first wife's death."

He stopped. Alex waited, letting Ray wrestle with emotion. "I drove myself into the ground working during the day and buried myself in bars and bottles at night. Some mornings I woke up in strange places and didn't know how I'd gotten there — and with women whose names I didn't know." His voice dropped to a hoarse whisper. "By the time I took possession of the ranch, Chavez was gone and I didn't give him a second thought. I started fixing the place up and getting myself straight instead of drowning in a bottle of bourbon every night."

A few oblique references in the past had made Alex aware that Ray's first wife had died. This was the most his friend had ever told him about that era in his life. "Sorry. I didn't mean to pry."

Ray's smile was wry. "The point is there could have been a massacre, and I would've been too blitzed to have known about it."

They were quiet a minute. Ray seemed to be contemplating his hands on the lawn chair. "Was there something else you wanted to talk about?"

He seemed to have a homing device when it came to stuff like this. "I wanted to ask you a question." Alex's nerves revved some more. Ray was Deborah's partner. He was also her chief defender, despite having suffered through her worst alcoholic episodes. He had nearly died in a car accident, chasing a murderer, before she had checked herself into rehab.

"Ask away."

"Deborah."

"What about Deborah?" Ray leaned back so his face was in a shadow, but his tone conveyed steel.

"Well, I wanted — I tried — I mean — I went over —"

"Did you do or say something to her?" Ray's tone had turned downright unfriendly. "She's a lot more fragile than she looks."

"Whoa!" Alex threw up both hands. "Why does everyone assume I'm some kind of lady killer?"

"Sorry." Ray's tone tapped down a notch. "I didn't mean to jump to conclusions. I know a little bit about reputations. In your case, the rumors fly."

"Why?"

"I don't know, but every time your name comes up it's in connection with a jilted woman."

"Don't believe everything you hear."

"I don't. I just wonder if maybe you have some commitment problems."

Alex snorted. "I don't think so. I'm ready to have myself committed over Deborah."

Ray laughed, a deep full-blown chuckle. "Kind of grows on you, doesn't she?"

"Like a rattlesnake."

"So what happened? Did she give you the tough girl routine?"

"She freaked out on me a little. I touched —"

"Did you hit on her?" Ray sat forward in the chair, as if poised to stand.

"Let me finish, will you?" Alex rushed on. "We were arguing about why I showed up there, and I put my hands on her shoulders to make my point. She freaked."

Ray didn't say anything. He leaned back again, fingers tight around the metal arms of the chair.

"What happened to her?" Alex couldn't read Ray's expression. "She wouldn't tell me. I need to know."

"Why?"

"What do you mean why?"

"Why do you need to know? Is the physical thing what you're looking for?"

"No, man. What kind of person do you think I am?" Alex tried to put the hurt feelings aside. Somehow he had to overcome this perception. "I'm trying to get to know her."

"Good luck with that. If you want to know what her deal is, you'll have to ask her."

"I did. She said it didn't matter."

"It does matter."

"Yeah, I can tell."

"The man who takes Deborah on will have to give her a lot of room and take things very slowly."

Ray wasn't giving him any information, but the advice was good. "Sounds like you've given this a lot of thought."

Ray's laugh was gruff this time, embarrassed. "People talked about us, but we were never more than partners. Susana is it for me."

"You're a lucky man."

"I got a second chance. I'm thankful for that every minute of every day."

Alex rose and turned to go, but Ray's voice stopped him. "Deborah needs a man of God."

Alex turned back to face his buddy. "I believe in God."

"A lot of people who believe in God aren't men of God."

Maddy, Deborah, now Ray. Was it gang-up-on-Alex day? "Look, I went to church as a kid. I know all the stories. But that's all they are to me — stories."

He realized his hands were clenched in fists and tried to release them. He hadn't wanted to stir all this stuff up. He'd avoided it for years. Here it was slapping him in the face again. Because of a difficult woman. Now Ray would give him the big speech, and he'd have to stand there and listen.

The silence stretched. When Ray finally spoke, he sounded surprised and delighted. And totally nuts. "You and Deborah are perfect for each other."

"What?"

"She's like the woman at the well. Jesus spoke to her and she said she would go tell the others. She's gonna tell you. God's using her. I never cease to be amazed with how big His plan is."

"His plan?"

"A recovering alcoholic will bring one of God's lost sheep home, buddy. Tag, you're it."

"I have to go back to work."

"Alex, one other thing." Ray rose and stretched to his full six-foot-four-inch height. "Hurt her, and you'll answer to me."

"I had that part figured out." Alex headed to the door.

Susana opened it before he could. Instead of sodas, she had a cell phone in her hand. "It's Samuel. They've got a lead on Jorge Morin. He wants you and Alex in on it."

Ray grabbed the phone and started talking.

"When you're done, don't hang up. Let me ask him something," Alex said, waving his hand to get Ray's attention, the words out before he could think about it. Samuel was the boss, but he was fair. He'd listen. After a minute, Ray handed the phone over, his eyebrows raised.

"What?" Samuel sounded about as friendly as a feral hog.

"Maybe you could let Detective Smith back on. She's doing AA twice a day and seeing her therapist. Working would make her feel useful. And we could use her. We have two related cases going, and we need all hands on deck." Alex talked fast, hoping he wasn't so far out on a limb it would break under his weight. "She's going crazy, sitting around doing nothing. And you need another body."

Silence greeted the suggestion. The seconds ticked by. Alex debated expanding on his plea. He decided against it. With Samuel, fewer words were best.

"Put Ray back on the phone."

Was that a yes or a no? "Yes, sir."

Alex watched as Ray walked around the backyard, his limp only slightly noticeable. He made a circle as he passed trees and bushes, talking rapidly, his words dissipating in the distance.

When he disconnected, he smiled. "Let's go."

"What'd he say?"

Ray increased his speed, his bad leg making his gait uneven. Alex broke into a trot. "He told me to call Deborah and get her over there. He wanted to know why you spoke up for her."

"What'd you tell him?"

Ray grabbed a baseball cap from the table in the foyer and slapped it on his head. "You were looking out for a friend."

"Thanks."

"Didn't do it for you. Did it for her. She needs people to have faith in her. I'll call her on my way."

Whatever the reason, Alex was glad. He headed through the front door, Ray at his heels as they raced toward their vehicles. Alex tried to focus on the task at hand, but his mind was still on what Ray had said. And not said. He still didn't know what had happened to Deborah, but whatever it was, it had been bad. Bad enough to send her back to the booze over and over again. Bad enough that she couldn't bear to be touched — not even by someone who cared about her. *God, help her. Help me help her.*

Alex stopped in his tracks, keys in his hand, frozen. Ray plowed into him.

"Hey, man, what are you doing?"

"Nothing. Sorry. I just — nothing."

How could he tell Ray he had prayed? A puny little prayer, but still. After more than fifteen years of silence.

So he had prayed. He was sticking his neck out. He expected an answer.

The right answer.

CHAPTER TWENTY-FIVE

Alex skidded the Altima to a stop just short of the curb. Two marked PD units, a DEA unit, and Detective Cooper's vehicle all rolled in at the same time. Alex slammed from the car and raced toward the house. Samuel and Ray beat him by a few steps. Joaquin brought up the rear. Deborah slid from her truck and joined them. Her glance never came his way.

Mica Jordan's sister said Jorge Morin had fought with Mica's husband after making a pass at Mica. He'd moved out of the house about three months before going to jail on the drug possession charge. According to the sister, he'd moved in with a cousin who lived at this address.

"SAPD. Anybody home?" Samuel nodded toward the front door. It stood battered and bruised, half off its hinges. No need to break it down. Somebody already had. No one answered Samuel's question.

A dog's bark punctuated the silence. Alex watched Samuel's face. His boss's eyes were black with fierce concentration. All emotion had fled. Knowing what they might find on the other side of the door, Alex anchored his own face. Samuel nodded. They moved.

The smell of stale beer, cigarette smoke, and rotting food permeated the air inside. Along with a few other equally unpleasant things. Blood and urine. The body of a large, Latino man sprawled across the living room floor, his face frozen in perpetual surprise. A Norinco assault rifle laid across his blood spattered T-shirt.

"Not Morin." Ray snagged the weapon. Dead or not, the bad guys didn't get to keep their guns. Agents darted into the kitchen and down hallways, yelling "clear" as they moved from room to room.

"Nope." Samuel smacked the palm of his hand against the wall. Disappointment flickered across his features before he shuttered it again. Alex knew how he felt. They all wanted to walk away with Benny safe and alive.

Ray slid his weapon into his holster. "Anybody recognize him?"

"Yep." Joaquin spoke first. He had been the last in, Deborah at his side. Alex's glance collided with hers, finally. She looked away, her face unreadable. "That's Miguel Suarez, the guy who shot me."

"Now he knows how it feels." Samuel sounded satisfied at the thought. "So he killed Seth Jordan to get Mica to tell him where she thought Morin might be hiding. Then he killed Mica. Now he's dead. Morin must've gotten lucky to take him out."

Alex shrugged off the icy feeling he'd gotten from Deborah's blank stare. He let his gaze roam. Had Benny been in the room? How had he felt, watching a gunfight go down? Had he survived? Had he been hit in the crossfire? If he had, wouldn't his body be here, next to Suarez's? The thought was cold comfort. The trauma alone meant the kid might never be the same — even if he did survive.

Ray moved toward the hallway. "Morin is one desperate dude. He knows Barrera is gaining on him. If Suarez got this close, the others can't be far behind. Once Barrera finds out Suarez is dead, Morin's life isn't worth two corn tortillas. I'll take the back. The Evidence Unit and the ME are on the way."

"I'll take the bedrooms." Deborah started in the opposite direction. Alex glanced at Samuel. The boss stared back. He didn't look happy. He probably figured his detectives should keep it professional. Too late for that. For Alex, anyway. He headed down the hallway after her, finally understanding the phrase *glutton for punishment.*

"So Ray says you put in a good word for me." She surveyed a bedroom that stank of musky bedding and wet cigarette butts. "With Sarge, I mean."

The chip-on-the-shoulder routine irritated him. He stuck his head in the bathroom and found nothing but a ring around the tub and an empty tube of toothpaste on the sink. "You have a problem with that?"

"No. Thanks." Her tone had softened. She meant it. "I really needed this."

He counted to ten, twice, angry with himself. "Over here." He squatted and shone a flashlight into the closet.

"What is it?"

"Looks like blood on the carpet." He fought to keep his face neutral. Deborah squeezed in next to him. Color seeped from her face. The skin tightened around her eyes. Alex had never worked a case before where he knew the victim. Especially a little kid. Alex liked little kids in general, but Benny in particular.

"Benny's blood?" Deborah's voice cracked a little on the boy's name. "Get the evidence tech over here."

Alex stood, wanting to get away from those stains. He'd examined hundreds of crime scenes. This one was different. Maybe it shouldn't be, but it was.

"And what about this?" Deborah looked up at him, her gaze quizzical. She used the end of her pen to point at three blue-green marbles lined up against the back wall of the closet.

"Benny." Alex let his breath out. He'd almost hoped Benny hadn't been here, but the marbles, like the ones left on the road to Ray's ranch, told another story. "Daniel bought him marbles last week. He left some at the other scene."

"Kid's leaving us bread crumbs — so to speak."

"He's smart." Alex said it to himself as much as to Deborah.

"He's a survivor."

"Let's hope so." Deborah had closed her eyes. She looked as if she were praying. He hadn't even thought of it. "Given his background, I think we have to assume he's figuring out how to deal with it."

"These are seriously warped men who are after Jorge Morin." Deborah whispered something he couldn't quite hear and straightened up. "They won't think twice about killing a kid."

"So we not only have to worry about Jorge Morin hurting Benny, but we have to worry about drug thugs." He had to understand the dynamics of a situation whether he liked them or not. "I'll get the EU guys in here."

He left her in the closet. He glanced back. Her eyes were closed again.

He trotted into the living room. Samuel was on the phone.

"He's got Morin on the line." Ray spoke softly. "The agent who took the call told Morin Daniel was in the hospital, temporarily out of the picture. He agreed to talk to Samuel."

Samuel stood very still, one hand arrested in mid air as if he couldn't remember what he planned to do with it — scratch his forehead or rub his aching head?

"I'm Daniel's brother. Samuel Martinez, SAPD Homicide. I'm standing in for him." Samuel's voice was cool. "He's sick, hospitalized. He asked me to negotiate with you."

A pause.

"We're willing to deal. We can pay you the value of the product Shawna Garza took from you. Just tell us how much, when, and where. We'll get it to you. In exchange for Benny Garza, unharmed."

Samuel was quiet then for several beats. The furrow on his forehead deepened. His jaw jutted. Ray shifted next to Alex, his hand on the butt of his gun. Deborah trotted into the room, looked from Alex to Ray to Samuel and stopped. She didn't speak.

Samuel's next words were simple. "Name your price." Followed by "When and where?" A few seconds later he disconnected and bent over, both hands on his knees, his head down.

Ray put one hand out as if to touch Samuel's back, then let it drop. "What'd he say?"

Samuel straightened, his expression blank. "He says he has to be compensated for his time and his aggravation. Shawna Garza aggravated him. Daniel aggravated him. And he says Benny is his son, and he should be compensated for giving him to Daniel."

No one spoke for a long moment. Ray shook his head, disbelief on his face. His knuckles were white where his fingers gripped the weapon at his side. "No way. In the first place, no way Benny's his son. And, if he is, basically he's asking Daniel to buy his kid."

"That's beside the point right now. We're not in any position to turn our noses up at his offer." Samuel smacked his fist against a wall. "He claims he and Shawna had a fling several years ago and if Daniel thinks Benny's better off with him, Morin wants to be compensated for all his trouble and for the product he no longer has access to."

Fury rolled through Alex. "His trouble. My guess is he's probably never seen the kid before in his life. He just abandoned him, and then he comes back and kidnaps him, scares him to death, hurts him, and thinks he should be compensated? I'll be glad to compensate him. Give me five minutes with him alone."

He stopped. Everyone was staring at him, varying degrees of surprise on their faces. Even Deborah. The only one who didn't look surprised was Joaquin. His friend laid a hand on his shoulder for a second. "Easy, dude. We'll take him out together."

"Yeah." Alex wiped sweat from his face with the back of his shirtsleeve. "Sorry."

"Don't be." Ray grinned at him. "Good to see you're passionate about something besides cars and women."

Alex tried to relax. "How much does he want? When and where?"

"Midnight, tonight." Samuel glanced at the DEA agent standing next to him. "The entrance to Mission County Park. He wants a million dollars."

The chorus of agitated words didn't seem to faze Samuel. He held up a hand. "Let's focus, people. We've got six hours to put together a million dollars and figure out our strategy for the drop."

Alex let his hand rest on his holster. Six hours until they had the man who kidnapped Benny in their crosshairs. He would be first in line to take the guy out — only if necessary, of course. His hand tightened involuntarily on the butt of the gun as his gaze met Ray's. The look in his friend's eyes told him they were thinking the same thing.

Jorge Morin better be ready for them.

Chapter Twenty-Six

Alex stopped, his turkey sandwich halfway to his mouth. He hadn't even taken the first bite. He was finally getting the sandwich. With Deborah. True, they were sitting in his car outside a sub shop a few blocks from the station, where they had to report in ten minutes for a strategy session on Benny's case. But technically, they were alone. And now that they were about to eat, his phone was ringing.

"Go on, answer it." She bit into her Italian sub, her gaze returning to the window. "Maybe they've got news about Daniel or Benny."

"Alex, it's Cooper." The detective's voice lacked its usual verve. "We got the ID."

Alex dropped the sandwich on the napkin in front of him, his appetite gone. "The dental records matched. It's Nina Chavez."

"Yep."

Alex sucked on his iced tea to dissolve the

hard knot in his throat. "We have to locate Clarisse Chavez and the rest of the kids. It's the only way to find out what happened at Ray's ranch."

"My buddy in Kansas is checking out Clarisse's first husband, Ezra Dodge, for me. He lives on a farm outside Abilene with his sister and her four kids."

"Sister. Yeah, right." Alex tried to keep his tone dispassionate. Professional. "Ex-wife Clarisse. And her four children, not five, but four."

"Detective Baker will pay him a visit, get the lay of the land. He says there's nobody by the name of Simon Phillips in his town. In fact, he doesn't remember a PI paying him a visit. He's checking into that as well." Static broke up some of Cooper's words but Alex got the gist of it. "My boss wants me back at the sheriff's office on another case — one where the victim hasn't been dead five years. Can you take a shot at Chavez with the notification?"

Alex would like to take a shot at Chavez. "Sure. I want to see how he reacts."

"I would, too. Keep me posted."

Alex stuck the phone in his jacket pocket. His hands shook. The image of a dark-haired, elfin girl with a bad haircut and green eyes floated in front of him. He glanced at Deborah. She met his gaze, the expression in her eyes unreadable. "It's her?"

"Yeah. It's her. Five-year-old Nina Chavez has been buried on Ray's property for at least the last five years."

"Poor Ray."

"Yeah, I'm sure he feels plenty guilty. I know I would." Alex rewrapped the sandwich, pain shooting through his temples as he gritted his teeth. "I've seen a lot of things in my life, but this really sucks."

"I keep thinking of those other kids." Deborah's voice hardened. "Nina may have gotten off easy. For the last five years, it's possible the rest of them have been living with the parent who murdered their sister. It doesn't have to be Tómas Chavez. It just as easily could've been Clarisse. She killed Nina, and she took off. The rest of those kids could still be suffering."

Alex struggled to connect the dots. "That sounds like the voice of experience."

Her head turned so her long hair blocked his view of her face. "I'm a police officer. Of course I have experience."

"You know what I mean, Deborah. What happened to you? Did someone abuse you when you were a child?"

The silence went on and on. Finally, she

cleared her throat and sniffed. "Do you like kids?"

She didn't trust him. Not yet. Maybe never. The question still deserved an answer. "Yeah, I like kids. If I thought I wouldn't mess them up, I might even want some of my own."

She tossed her hair back and their gazes met. "Alex —"

"You asked."

"But —"

"We gotta get back." Alex shoved the key in the ignition and turned it.

"What are you so cranky about?" She took another bite of her sandwich and chewed slowly, as if the conversation had never occurred.

"Dead and missing children."

Her blue eyes bore into his. "It's not personal, Alex."

"It is to me."

"Come on, kid, out."

His eyes too swollen to open, Benny didn't fight the hands that slid under his arms from behind and pulled him from the trunk of the car. The car ride had been too short. He'd felt safe in the trunk. No shooting. No dead men. Nothing in the dark. The back of his legs hit the edge of the trunk. Pain tore through his calves.

"Mama. Mama!" Juice called as he slung Benny over his shoulders like a big sack of dried pinto beans. "Mama?"

Benny forced his eyes open. Did Juice have a mom, still? Would she like it that her son had a gun? What would she think about her son kidnapping a kid and beating him up? Juice leaned forward. Benny tensed. Juice dropped him to the ground on his back. He gazed up at blue sky behind Juice's face. There were trees, and the air smelled clean, like Mr. Ray's ranch.

"Get up, kid. We're here."

"Jorge Manuel Morin, what you doing here, *m'ijo?* I told you not to be coming round, bringing me your trouble." A skinny lady who reminded Benny of the *señoras* who sold used clothes at the flea market, threw open the screen door. It smacked Benny hard in the side. "Who's this? You didn't bring me another of your boys, did you, Jorge? I told you, no way I could feed another mouth with my social security check."

"No, I didn't, Mama, I —" The lady smacked Juice in the face. The sound of skin hitting skin made Benny flinch.

"Mama," Juice screeched. "What'd you do that for? Just let me tell you what —"

"You ain't telling me no more stories. Last time I listened to your stories, I ended up with the *policía* at my door." The lady threw in some Spanish words Benny didn't understand, then went back to English. "Get this dirty *chiquito* off the ground and into the house before somebody sees him and decides to ask questions. And get that rope off him. You crazy, tying up a child like that. Somebody gonna turn you into CPS."

Juice once again heaved Benny to his feet, but his legs didn't want to hold him.

"*Pobrecito,* what's he gone and done to you?" The lady steadied Benny with one claw-like hand as she opened the screen door and shoved him inside.

The house, dark after the bright sun outside, smelled like burnt rice and something else Benny had smelled sometimes when his mom had friends over. A sweet, thick odor that made his stomach feel sick. He stumbled and took a step, slid, and fell to his knees. A film of grease covered the faded kitchen floor. A yellow cat mewed in the corner where it hunched over a dirty, empty dish. Juice disappeared into the other room without looking back.

"You hungry, boy? You can call me Mari. Everybody does. Real name's Maricela. Sit down right there." Mari grabbed a butcher knife from the kitchen table and lifted it over Benny's head. Benny cringed and shrank against the chair, no place to go, no place to hide.

"Ain't gonna hurt you, *m'ijo*." She sliced the rope around his hands with one clean sweep.

"You gotta name, *m'ijo*?" She shuffled in green Kermit the Frog slippers to the sink, filled a smudged glass with water from the faucet, and shuffled back. "Ain't got much to eat in here. Might be some *pollo asado* from last night. Mebbe that was the night before, can't really remember for sure."

"Name's Benny." His voice had a funny croaky sound to it. Like it belonged to someone else.

"Benny? Had a son named Benny. He died in prison. Which is where you'll end up, you keep hanging around with the likes of Jorge. He's my son, but he ain't got no common sense."

"I ain't —"

"Don't say ain't. It ain't a word." The woman snickered.

"Where's your stash?" Juice stood in the doorway, a bottle in one hand and a gun in the other.

"Don't be carrying that gun around in the house. You'll shoot your foot off."

"Mama, I need a fix bad. I done killed one of Barrera's dudes. He's gonna send somebody else after me. I gotta get my money and get out of here."

"You killed a guy over drugs, and then you come to my house?" The woman looked like she would fall over, her eyes and mouth got so big. She looked like a fish, all puffy eyed, mouth working in and out to breathe.

"I had no place to go. I just need a little time. Just enough time to get what's mine. I've got it all set up. I've got a meeting tonight. But first I need a hit, just a little, Mama."

Maricela slapped some barbecued chicken on a plate and slammed it down in front of Benny. She stuck both hands on her hips and gave him a hard stare. "Eat."

The gray, greasy-looking chicken had fat, white and thick, around the edges. Benny swallowed hard. He hadn't eaten since the hot dog the night before. He grasped the drumstick in shaking hands. It didn't taste too bad. Not bad at all. He washed it down with water and ate more.

"Mama!" Juice screamed.

Benny jumped, choked, and coughed.

"Jumpy little thing, ain't ya?" Maricela laughed. "*Idiota,* don't yell at me. It's under my bed. Just a little. It's gotta last."

"Just a little."

Juice disappeared.

Maricela pursed lips under the beginnings of a wispy black mustache. Then she started after Juice. At the doorway, she crooked one skinny finger at Benny. Her yellow fingernails were long. "You come with me. Stay where I can keep an eye on you. I don't know what Juice's up to, but you figure in somehow."

Benny tore one last bite of meat from the bone and followed her into the living room. The place reminded him of his mom's apartment. Dirty clothes on the chairs, the springs of the couch showing through ripped fabric, newspapers piled in corners, empty pizza boxes on the coffee table. Smoke hung in the air so thick he coughed again.

"Sit." She pointed at a chair a few feet from a big screen TV that blared MTV.

Juice had his feet up on a coffee table next to a needle and a long piece of rubber. Benny had seen that kind of stuff before. Scary stuff. "In a few hours I'm gonna have my ticket out of this town. You and me, *hijo,* you and me. And don't you be thinking you'll get out of here, go find your buddy, Daniel. *Señor* Daniel is in the hospital. Yep. He's sick. He may be dying. Dying like your

313

momma died. Done died. Done dead."

"No. He ain't. No she ain't!" Benny started to slide from his chair, the muscles in his arms and legs suddenly limp and weak. "You're a liar. He ain't sick. He ain't dead. My mom ain't dead neither. She's in prison."

Juice hopped up and whipped across the room. "You just keep believing that, *m'ijo*." He started moving his hips and jumping around like he was dancing. "Man, I like this music. You like U2, man? How 'bout Mariah Carey? Great stuff. Come on, boy, get up, get up and dance with me, man. I love to dance."

He dragged Benny from the chair. Benny's legs were so bruised, he could barely stand. Juice sneered. "You don't know how to dance, son? Man, that Shawna, what kind of mother was she? Here, I'll show you. A good daddy shows his son how to dance."

Juice hopped around and jumped up and down. Suddenly, he switched to an air guitar, dipping forward and backward, his head thrown back, eyes closed, face screwed up with excitement. "You play the guitar?"

He didn't wait for Benny to answer. "I always wanted to play, never had no money for the guitar or the lessons. But I do a mean air guitar. Maybe when I get the money, I can buy you a guitar. You like that, little man?"

Benny tried to think. He didn't want to make Juice mad. It was nice to offer to buy him a guitar. Nobody ever did that. Juice seemed okay sometimes, like he was really thinking he was Benny's dad. Maybe he was. So where'd he been all this time? Why was he back now?

"Well, would you? Come on, kid. Are you retarded or what? Answer me, man."

When Benny didn't answer, Juice abandoned his fake guitar. His hand smashed into Benny's face. His face on fire, Benny jolted back and landed on his rear end.

"Answer me when I talk to you. That's the respectful thing to do. When a dad asks a question, the son answers. Understand me? Understand?"

"Yes." Benny whispered.

"Yes what?"

"Yes . . . sir?"

"That's better." Juice staggered from the room.

Benny didn't think it was better. And he was sure Juice wasn't his dad.

CHAPTER TWENTY-SEVEN

Alex pounded on the metal trailer door again, harder.

The ride over had given him time to think about his approach. He would confront Chavez straight on. Lay it out for him. No sympathetic lead-in. Either the guy killed his daughter and his wife took the kids and ran because she was afraid, or Clarisse Chavez killed Nina and ran for fear of what her husband would do when he found out. One way or the other, someone was going down for it. And Tómas Chavez was the only person within handcuff range at the moment. If he ever came to the door.

Alex pounded until his fist hurt.

The door jerked open. Chavez's bleary stare, rumpled T-shirt, and jeans suggested he'd either been sleeping or passed out in a drunken haze. His body odor and the stench of cigarette smoke wafted around him. Chavez rubbed at the dark stubble on his cheeks and then scratched his posterior. He hacked and coughed. "You got news?"

"Yeah, I got news."

Chavez moved aside. The smell of alcohol got stronger. Alex stopped at the edge of the tiny living room. Chavez shut the door and shuffled into the kitchen without looking at Alex. "So." The sound of cabinet doors slamming and glass clinking followed the inquiry.

"So, maybe you should have a seat."

Chavez returned to the living room, a glass of amber liquid in one hand. He didn't offer anything to Alex. "It's Nina."

Alex nodded. "Yeah. It's Nina."

Chavez slugged back the liquid in one long, neat swallow and then exhaled noisily. "So what you gonna do about it?"

No facial reaction. No emotion. Maybe a faint challenge in the words.

Alex rocked on the balls of his feet. "First I'll ask you some questions. Then I'll find a killer and put him in jail. Somebody took a blunt object and crushed your daughter's skull five years ago — about the time your wife and children disappeared. I want to know everything you know about their disappearance."

Chavez slapped the empty glass on the coffee table. It teetered on the edge and fell on the carpet. He didn't retrieve it. "I told you before. I came home. They were gone. I figured she took all five of them. I had no reason to think otherwise."

Alex studied the man's face. He could be telling the truth, or he could be an accomplished liar. Nothing in his face gave him away. "Tell me about your wife."

Chavez shrugged. "Nice rack — at least when I met her — but not much upstairs, if you know what I mean."

He grinned a little. Alex didn't smile back. The grin disappeared. "What do you want to know about her?"

"How long had you known her when you married her?"

"Six months, eight months — I dunno — something like that. She was waitressing in a bar on Fredericksburg Road. I liked the way she looked. I guess she liked what she saw, too. It wasn't no big deal, until she came crying to me that she was knocked up. I'm a man. I take care of my obligations. I married her. Ended with twins that time — double the trouble. Then she kept squeezing 'em out like puppies after that."

"Did she ever talk about her life before you got together? Did she say anything about being married before?"

Chavez's eyes narrowed, and his thin lips

turned down. "What are you talking about? She said she'd never been married before."

Alex watched his face closely. No hesitation in the words. Only a sort of belligerent confusion. "She told you that?"

"Yeah, she said the right man never come along. I was it for her."

"So if I said I'd seen a marriage certificate showing she married when she was sixteen years old, you'd say I was crazy."

"*Loco.* Yeah, I'd say you were *loco*. My wife wouldn't lie to me about something like that."

"Your wife wasn't your wife. Maybe you found out, and she ran because she knew what you were capable of doing after she saw what you did to Nina."

The string of curse words that emanated from Chavez would've made Alex's dad proud. The man swiped the glass from the floor, stood, and stomped into the kitchen. More cussing and glass clinking. A few seconds passed and Chavez returned, his glass full to the rim this time. He looked genuinely shocked. Or he was a very good actor. "No way. You saying I was never married to that —"

"Never."

"I don't believe you. How did you find out?"

"The PI you hired."

"Phillips? His partner said he never found her. He retired in the middle of the job. I got my money back."

"He never found her — as far as we know. But he did discover she was married to a guy named Ezra Dodge four years before she married you."

"And she ran back to him." Chavez stood so suddenly he knocked the coffee table over. Alex slapped his hand on his holster and ducked as the glass sailed over his head and shattered against a wall. "Unless you're here to arrest me for something, get out of my house."

"We don't know whether your — whether Clarisse went home, but we'll find out, Mr. Chavez. In the meantime, I have to ask, are you more upset about your wife's past or your daughter's death?"

Chavez advanced toward him. Alex held his ground, his fingers tight on the butt of his weapon. Chavez stopped a foot away. "Both."

The look on his face belied the response. He seemed more upset about the revelation regarding his wife's previous marriage than Nina's death. Maybe because the murder was not a surprise. The marriage was. Alex worked to maintain a relaxed stance as the man moved a step closer. "I'm sorry for your loss, Mr. Chavez. I just want you to know I'll do everything possible to find whoever murdered your daughter. And when I do, I'll lock that sorry excuse for a human being in jail. Do you understand what I'm saying?"

Chavez halted, his face inches away, his dark gaze fierce. "You didn't just threaten a grieving father, did you?"

Alex smiled and strode to the door. He paused, one hand on the doorknob. "I'll be back . . . one way or the other, Mr. Chavez; that you can count on."

CHAPTER TWENTY-EIGHT

Benny shifted on the mattress, trying to get comfortable. Juice had locked him in a bedroom. It smelled musty, like somebody had wet the bed. A cockroach scuttled across the foot of the bed, another followed. At first, they had scared him, but now they almost seemed like company.

Thunder crackled. Rain tapped at the window. He wondered what Marco was doing. Was he eating leftover wedding cake? Did Uncle Ray and Aunt Susana go on the honeymoon? It was a big secret, but Uncle Ray had told him they were going to Spain. They'd fly over the ocean. Benny wanted to fly over the ocean.

He swallowed hard, trying to hold the tears in. Was Mom really dead? Why didn't Mr. Daniel come for him? Was he really sick? Was he dying? That would explain why he hadn't come. Course, Mr. Ray and Mr. Samuel were cops. They wouldn't give up, even if Mr. Daniel couldn't come. He'd send them.

But if Juice kept moving Benny, they'd never find him. They might give up. No, they'd give Juice the money he wanted, and then Juice would give him back. That's the way they did it in the movies. They called it ransom.

What if they didn't want to give Juice the money? Maybe they didn't think Benny was worth it. They might figure he was long gone. He sniffed through tears in the dark. Mr. Daniel would never do that. He knew how much Benny liked those pancakes for breakfast and pepperoni pizza on video night. They still had a bunch of movies to see together. Mr. Daniel had promised.

The door punched open, throwing light on Benny and the mattress. The cockroaches hurried away. Benny rolled into a ball and waited for the blows.

"Just me, kid." Juice sounded like he had marbles in his mouth. "Looking for something. Used to be my room. Long time ago."

He rooted around in a cardboard box in the corner for a few minutes, cussing under his breath. He stank, worse than ever. Benny held his breath.

"Got it." Juice pulled a black stocking cap with holes for eyes and a mouth in it. He stumbled to his feet. "You okay, kid?"

"Yes . . . yes, sir."

Juice laughed. "You learn fast. That's good, *m'ijo.*"

He leaned against a wall and slid down until he squatted next to the mattress. Benny heard the click of a lighter, saw the flame, and then the end of a cigarette glowing in the dark. Juice's breathing got louder. "You 'fraid of the dark?"

Benny thought a minute. "No, sir," he whispered. "Not much. More afraid of what's in it."

Juice laughed, a hog snort. "Good point. Smart kid. Not like me. Must get that from your mama." He shifted until he sat with his long skinny legs sticking out. "What about storms? You scared of thunder?"

"No."

"How come?"

"Cause it's a long way away. The stuff that hurts is usually close to me."

A drag on the cigarette made a hissing sound. The smell of the smoke filled the room. The smoke burned his eyes. It stank like the homeless men who waited at the bus stop by his old apartment.

"You got that right." Juice's words ran together in one big slur now. "When I was a kid I was scared of thunder. My mama cured me. She stuck me in this room and locked the door. Left me here a couple of days. Said she had stuff to do. It stormed bad the first night. Nothing to do but get used to it."

Benny nodded in the dark. He knew about getting used to it. Another long, low rumble of thunder rippled outside the window. "Where was your dad?"

"Don't know. Mama never told me nothing about him." Juice sniffed like he had a runny nose. "She said no point in crying over spilt milk or something like that."

Benny licked his cracked, swollen lips. "Mr. Juice, can I ask you another question?"

"Don't know why not."

"If you're my dad, how come you never came around until now? Where were you?"

"You calling me a liar?"

"No." Benny squeezed down in the corner, trying to make himself small. He should have shut up, just shut up.

"Your mama and me got into it." Juice said it like it was no big deal, the anger gone. "Lots of broken dishes, broken furniture. She tore up my poster of Selena. Then she stabbed me in the leg. She was vicious, your mama, in those days. I can't abide by no woman shanking me. So I left."

Benny had seen fights like that. Sometimes

he had to clean up the mess. "So why'd you come back?"

"Your mama was a terrible girlfriend, but she was a pretty good businesswoman. We did some business. That's all."

"You didn't come to see me?" The words slipped out before Benny could stop them. He knew better. No guy ever came to see him. Mostly, he was in the way when his mom's boyfriends came around. At least, that's what she said.

"N'ombre." Juice got to his feet, dropped the cigarette on the floor next to the mattress and squished it with the heel of his tennis shoe. He turned and opened the door. Benny caught a glimpse of the gun, a glint of metal in the hallway light. It was stuck in Juice's waistband. "It'll be time to go in a while."

The door closed, leaving behind a silence that seemed peaceful. Benny stayed still, waiting for his heart to stop pounding. His eyes adjusted to the dark again. Only, this time it wasn't so dark. Not so dark at all. He shifted on the mattress, then rolled over so he could get up on his knees. Light seeped in around door, more light than before.

Holding his breath, he crawled toward the crack. Juice hadn't closed it completely. It had stuck. Not locked. Benny couldn't breath. He touched the crack. He could open the door. He could get out.

What if Mr. Juice caught him again? What if he hit him with the leather belt again? Benny quivered at the thought. He couldn't stay here. If he could get out, he could get to Mr. Daniel in the hospital. He could go see him, help him get better. If he stayed here, Mr. Juice would kill him.

Daniel opened his eyes. He had a fleece blanket in his mouth and his muscles felt like marshmallows, but his mind seemed clear for the first time in days. The faint memory of someone lifting him from the floor and helping him back into bed swirled. Covering him with a sheet that weighed a thousand pounds. Leaving him in the dark with eyelids too heavy to lift. Now, the hospital room was empty. He had no idea what time it was or even what day. He squirmed until he was upright and reached for a glass of water on the table next to the bed. A couple of swallows and his horrible thirst eased.

This time he'd make it to the door. He had to get out of here. He didn't dare call Samuel first. His brother would sic Susana or Lily on him again. Or worse, Mama. If he just showed up, there wouldn't be a thing they could do about it. He'd go to the apartment first, then PD. No more lying around while Benny was out there in the hands of a drug-dealing ex-con. He slid his legs over the side of the bed and stood. His head swam and the walls wavered for a second, then righted themselves. This time he didn't go down.

Now, to find his clothes. One tottering step. Two. One more and he reached the closet, hanging onto the wall, sweat trickling down his forehead into his eyes. How could he be so weak after only two days in this place? That's what hospitals did to people.

Dressing took three times as long as it normally did, but he managed to pull on his socks and shoes before going through his pockets. His money clip and credit cards were still in his jacket. So was his cell phone, but the battery was dead. Now if he could get down to the lobby without being seen.

Minutes later he eased through the double doors in the lobby out into the cool, wet night air. Breathing deeply, he surveyed the scene. He needed a taxi. A taxi and a cup of coffee. If he was going to find Benny, he had to get back to his car and he needed caffeine.

"What are you doing out here?"

Nicole stood on the sidewalk, blocking his exit.

Daniel stopped. "I could ask you the same question. Where's your new boyfriend?"

"Stop it, Daniel. No more." Her cheeks were pink in the crisp breeze. Raindrops spattered around them. Thunder rolled in the distance. "I was coming to tell you I will stop punishing you if you stop punishing me. Did the doctor approve your discharge? Why isn't someone with you — you're not planning to drive yourself, are you?"

Daniel stuck a hand on the back of a bench to steady himself. "What do you care?"

She smoothed her jacket with both hands. "You've been my husband for a lot of years. I care about you. I couldn't stand you being in here and Benny out there. It's too hard."

Tears trickled down her cheeks. She brushed them away with her fingertips. Daniel teetered and sat on the bench. "I don't have time for this right now. I have to find out what's going on with the investigation."

"I just talked to Ray." Nicole sat next to him. Her tone sounded almost eager. "You need to go back inside and get in bed. Ray and Samuel have it covered."

He shook his head. No deal. "What did

Ray say?"

"They have a lead on the kidnapper. They went to his cousin's house on the west side. When they got there, they found the body of a man named Miguel Suarez. You know the name?"

"Yes, I know the name."

"They found evidence that Morin had been hiding out there, and it's likely he had Benny with him."

Daniel wrapped his arms around his chest and tried to contain his shivering. "What kind of evidence?"

Nicole rubbed a hand on his back. "They found marbles in a closet."

Daniel closed his eyes and focused on the motion of her hand. Why was she doing this? Why was she here? Now wasn't the time to get into it. He had to find Benny. "What are they doing now? Did they find anything else?"

"The kidnapper called."

And he'd missed it. Benny needed him, and he was passed out in a hospital bed. "Who talked to him?"

"Samuel did. He set up a ransom exchange."

"How much?"

"A million."

The amount was like a punch to his gut.

All the air leaked from his lungs. "Where are we getting that kind of money?"

Nicole scooted closer to him. "You're shivering, Danny. You need to go inside."

"No. Where's the money coming from? Did Ray say?"

"He said the DEA's handling it. Drug dealer money."

"When's the drop?"

"Tonight at midnight."

Daniel stood. "I need your help. I need to go there, and I may not be up to driving."

Nicole stared up at him, her face filled with a mixture of compassion and something else — he couldn't be sure what. She sighed. "You had a fever of one hundred and three last night. You haven't eaten in two or three days. You need to lie down."

Daniel started walking. "I'll take a taxi to the church and pick up my car." He stumbled, kept going, not caring if she could hear or was following. "He could already be dead. They could hand over the money and never see him again."

Nicole fell into step next to him. Her hand went to his elbow. "He's not, Danny. He left some marbles in a closet. He's leaving clues."

Daniel stared at the sidewalk, afraid she'd see the fear in his eyes. "We went to Wal-

Mart for some supplies. He never asks for anything. I told him he could pick out one thing. He picked out marbles. I asked him why marbles. He said a lady gave him some marbles once. He thought it might have been his grandmother. He wasn't sure because he never saw her again. But it was the only present he'd ever received. Ever. I don't think he even knows for sure when his birthday is."

Nicole's hand tightened on his arm. "He's had a very hard life, Daniel, no doubt about it, but the time he's spent with you has been good. You've given him some good memories."

Emotion ripped through Daniel. Benny deserved a lot more good memories, and Daniel intended to make sure he had a chance to make them. "He's never had cake and ice cream, never blown out candles, never ripped the paper off a present. Do you understand what I'm saying?"

"I understand." Nicole steered him toward the street. "He doesn't deserve this. No child does. We'll get him back."

"We?"

She nodded. "The car's right here. I'll drive you."

"Just take me to my car at the church."

"No. We're in this together."

"Together?"

"Danny, I don't know what tomorrow will bring, but for tonight, we're in it together."

It wasn't the declaration he needed, but he'd take it. For tonight.

CHAPTER TWENTY-NINE

The Dodge Farm
Dickinson County, Kansas

Esperanza twisted closer to the knot hole in the barn wall so she could hear what the sheriff's deputy said to Uncle Ezra. She squinted through the hole, hoping Uncle Ezra couldn't see her spying on him. She wanted to hear. Maybe the sheriff had come to help them — finally. Too bad Estrella couldn't be out here with her, but her twin sister had to make supper, leaving Esperanza to finish cleaning the stalls. Uncle Ezra looked as if he were mad and trying not to show it. He nodded his head and waved his hands around a lot.

"No, sir. No, sir. What lame-brained idiot called you, anyway?" Uncle Ezra's voice got louder and louder. Esperanza didn't have to strain to hear now. "I take good care of the animals around here."

Sure, he did. Leaving the horses out in a

pasture when a dry fall had caused the grass to shrivel up early. They could only forage so much. Momma said Esperanza should be happy Uncle Ezra took the family in when they had no place to go. Esperanza disagreed. She'd wanted to stay in the station wagon and keep going so far away *Papi* could never find them.

Besides, Uncle Ezra didn't look like Momma's brother. Not at all. Esperanza couldn't see anything about him that seemed familiar. And sometimes at night, when she got up to go to the bathroom, she'd seen Uncle Ezra going into Momma's bedroom. The memory made her stomach do funny things. She tried not to think about it, but she didn't want to think about the sheriff's deputy and Uncle Ezra arguing about the horses, either.

"Sir, I'd like to take a look at those horses, if you don't mind." The sheriff's deputy's voice was real low and deep. Like a preacher's voice. He kept looking around as if he were checking the place out.

Esperanza wished she could talk to him for a few seconds so she could ask him why he was so worried about the horses and never asked how Uncle Ezra and Momma took care of the kids. Esperanza didn't need taking care of any more, but little Frankie did. Nobody asked if they were getting enough to eat. Nobody asked about the things going on in the house. Not even her teachers at school or church. People seemed to care more about animals than kids sometimes.

Uncle Ezra was really getting worked up now. "Yes, I do mind. You got a search warrant, Deputy? Unless you have a legitimate reason to be on my property, I want you to get off. Now."

"Mr. Dodge, I'm just trying to save you a visit from the SPCA people. Once they get wind of this, they'll have you in court lickety-split." The deputy took a package of gum from his pocket, unwrapped a piece, and stuck it in his mouth. "I just wanted to give you fair warning so you can take care of any problems you might be having."

"I told you I haven't got any problems."

Esperanza's brothers, Dom and Frankie, hurtled across the yard, laughing and trying to trip each other. They halted when they saw Uncle Ezra standing there with the stranger.

"What's going on, Uncle Ezra? Why's there a sheriff's car here?" Dom was the one to ask. He was the least afraid. No matter how many times Uncle Ezra whipped him with the belt, he never cried. He said he

336

wouldn't give Uncle Ezra the satisfaction. No sirree. Dom went to bed with his backside black and blue, nasty welts puffed up all over the place. Esperanza could hear him sniffing through the walls. Sometimes she'd slip in and put a cold rag on his back. He'd just sniff and tell her to go to bed before Uncle Ezra decided to whale on her.

"Nothing a child should be concerning himself with. Go inside, boys." The cold steel in Uncle Ezra's voice made Esperanza shiver.

"Hey, boys. What's your names?" The sheriff's deputy held out the pack of gum. They were gonna get gum. A wave of jealousy raced through Esperanza. There was never money for gum or candy or soda. "Have a piece of bubblegum."

"I'm Dom. This here's Frankie." Dom held his hand out.

Uncle Ezra's hand knocked Dom's away. "That's all right, Deputy. They were just going in to supper. Be a waste to give them gum. I said get on in the house, boys."

"Where are your sister's girls?" The deputy glanced around again. Esperanza could've sworn he looked right at her peephole. She jerked back, her heart racing.

"What does that have to do with the animal cruelty complaint?"

"Nothing. Just trying to be neighborly. She's got twins? That's a lot of work, raising four kids."

"Yeah, but she's got me to help her out. Keep them in line."

"I bet you're right, Mr. Dodge. You likely got your hands full. My wife and I were never blessed with children. Not one. Funny, how that works. Well, I best be getting back into town. Sheila gets downright irritated if I'm late for supper." The sheriff's deputy slapped a big cowboy hat on his bald head and moved toward his car. "Like I said, I'll be back to check on those horses."

Esperanza waited until the car was out of sight and the dust settled before she crept from her hiding spot and ran up the porch steps into the house. She eased the screen door open and shut it carefully. Uncle Ezra didn't like it to slam.

She was halfway across the dining room when she heard the whack. Leather against skin. *Whack. Whack.* Uncle Ezra had Dom face down on a dining room chair, his pants down. Uncle Ezra looked up, his face red, beads of sweat trickling from his gray sideburns down his leather-skinned neck. His cold eyes bored into her.

She tore her glance from him to Dom. Her brother's chest heaved, but no tears rolled down his face. Red, angry welts made a bizarre pattern across his back and behind. The pain and humiliation in his eyes told her he didn't want her looking at him, not like this.

She whirled to run to the kitchen.

"Girl, get back here!"

She stopped. Slowly turned to face Uncle Ezra. *Please, God, help us.*

A cruel grin formed on her uncle's face. "Where're you going, girl? You think I don't know you were out there in the barn listening to every word that was said. You think you're allowed to sneak around and eavesdrop on grownup conversations? Sneaky kid. I am so thankful to God that you ain't no kid of mine. None of you. I give you the hospitality of my home even though you ain't even mine. What thanks do I get for feeding and clothing you? Nothing. Not even a thank you. No, sir."

He snapped the belt back and let it fly against Dom's bare skin. Esperanza flinched, gritting her teeth to keep from screaming at him to stop. He shoved Dom from the chair so hard the boy landed on the floor, falling over the pants twisted around his ankles.

"Move, boy. Your sister's next."

CHAPTER THIRTY

Benny tried to run, but it was too late. Mr. Juice had seen him in the hallway. He was gonna kill him, for sure. Benny's legs wouldn't move fast enough. He couldn't get away. Mr. Juice shoved him to the floor in the hallway. Benny cowered, waiting for the blows to fall. Nothing happened. He peeked between his arms. Mr. Juice towered over him, the gun in his hand inches from Benny's face. "Time to go. I told you it was gonna be time to go. You don't listen, do you? Kids just don't listen. Time to get in the car."

Benny flattened himself to the floor and crawled away from the barrel. He didn't want to go anywhere with Mr. Juice. He looked and smelled like Benny's mom at the end of the evening when she'd been sipping on the bottle too long. Mr. Juice's hand closed on the collar of his shirt and jerked him up. "Gotta hurry. It's almost midnight.

Move it!"

Benny scrambled to his feet and scurried forward. They pushed through the screen door and into the backyard. A blast of cool, damp night air hit Benny in the face. Thunder rolled and lightning crackled in the distance. He halted at the back of the car. The oily smells and the darkness of the trunk swirled around him even before Mr. Juice opened it.

"You can ride up front with me." Juice pushed him forward to the driver's side door. He laughed, coughed, then laughed some more. "I'll show you how to drive. Dads should teach their sons to drive. That's what dads do."

His stomach flopping with fear and surprise, Benny crawled across the front seat. Once upright, he pulled on the seat belt and snapped it across his chest. Mr. Daniel said always use a seat belt. It'll save your life. For a second, he felt safer.

"Mr. Juice, where we going?" He figured he had nothing to lose by asking.

Mr. Juice shoved a key in the ignition. The car's engine coughed, sputtered, and died. "We're going to do some business, boy." Business came out *busshhnisss.*

He turned the key again. This time the engine caught, its sound rough and uneven.

"Some business with Mr. Daniel?"

"I told you. Mr. Daniel is out of commission." Mr. Juice slurred the s's in a long hissing sound. He messed with the knobs on the dash. The radio blared. Benny jerked in his seat, startled.

"Oh, yeah, ACDC. All right. The best classic rock in town." Mr. Juice pounded on the steering wheel with one hand. The gun dangled in the other, as he pretended to bang his head. "Wahoo! Wahoo!"

He tossed the gun on the seat next to him and put both hands on the wheel, still singing.

Benny eyed the gun and then Mr. Juice, who cussed under his breath and gunned the engine. The car bolted forward, snapping Benny's head against the seat. They slammed out of the driveway and down a long, pitted dirt road, every hole jolting Benny's entire body.

"Mr. Juice, maybe you should slow down a little." He had to yell to be heard over the music. A new fear invaded his body. Grownups weren't supposed to drink and drive. "You don't look so good."

"I'm fine, boy. I can drive fine." Mr. Juice slammed his foot down on the gas pedal and the car fishtailed, throwing Benny against the passenger-side door. His neck popped, and his head hit the door handle. He held in the sob that wanted to come out of his mouth, keeping his lips stiff and tight. No more crying. He would make Mr. Daniel proud.

Bright lights blinded him. A car was coming. Help, maybe. Somehow. It was huge, whatever it was, and dark-colored. The lights passed. Seconds later screeching and squealing sounds filled the night air. Then the lights were behind him, reflecting off the passenger and rearview mirrors.

Mr. Juice said bad words, a lot of them, real fast until they were a stuttered mess. He stomped on the gas pedal. The car jerked forward. The back windshield exploded. Glass shot at Benny from behind like tiny, jagged missiles. He tried to duck, but his seat belt stuck and held.

Cold air rushed through the car. Popping sounds. Benny squeezed around and peeked over the seat. A Hummer gained on them. A man hung out the window on the passenger side. Muzzle blasts lit up the side of the Hummer. Benny ducked down, all his breath gone for a second. "Why are they shooting at us? Who is it?"

"Barrera. It's gotta be Barrera. He's trying to kill me. I ain't got his stuff." Mr. Juice screamed cusswords. He jerked the car from the uneven dirt road onto a paved road without stopping at a stop sign bent at a crazy angle.

The car jumped forward. They flew through the darkness. Lights coming from the other direction flashed by them, each one faster and faster, making Benny dizzy. He closed his eyes and opened them, hoping it was a bad dream.

"*M'ijo,* get the gun! Shoot back at them!"

Benny wasn't sure he'd heard Mr. Juice right. The gun had slid across the seat so close he could touch it. He slapped his hands on his chest. His heart beat so hard, his chest hurt. "No!"

Mr. Juice fought to keep the car on the road. "Pick it up! You gotta shoot at them, or they're gonna kill us both. Do it. Do it!"

Mr. Juice's eyes were wild. Spit ran down his chin. The smell of pee wafted through the car. Benny gagged. He was gonna puke. Then Mr. Juice would be madder. He let his hand creep toward the gun. He couldn't let the bad guys kill them. And if he had the gun, Mr. Juice couldn't hurt him, either.

His hand closed over the gun. It felt cold. His fingers tightened around it. Heavy. One finger slid into the hole where the trigger was. He'd seen plenty of guns. He knew what they did. He stopped breathing. His hand began the slow slide back toward his body.

"Hurry up! Do it, kid. Turn around. Start shooting. Do it! Hurry!" He lunged toward Benny like he was going to push him. His hands weren't on the wheel anymore. No one was driving the car. Benny flattened himself against the door. He had no place to go.

The car veered side to side, dancing across the road. "Mister, drive, mister!"

"I got it. I got it." Juice righted himself and grabbed at the wheel. Too late. They slid across the median and shot across on-coming lanes as high-pitched horns ripped the blackness.

Benny pitched forward and backward, the seat belt locking him in place. The force bruised his chest and sucked the oxygen from his lungs. They bucked across a ditch and slammed into a field full of trees.

The car sideswiped a tree, bounced, then rocked into another one. The world tilted. The car rolled. Suddenly, Benny hung upside down, suspended in air. Pain swelled in his chest as the seat belt tightened, refusing to give up. He gasped, but the air seemed all gone. The screech of tires and ripping of metal stopped seconds after the car landed on its side.

Silence. The tick, tick sound of a hot engine filled the air.

Benny listened to his own breathing. It still came, in and out, in and out.

His eyes adjusted to the darkness blanketing everything inside the car. He peered around. The windshield was smashed into thousands of tiny pieces. Lines crackled through it, creating a puzzle. Tree branches stuck through it. The driver's side was gone, now a big gaping hole that let in cold air. Air that helped him breathe again. He couldn't see anything outside the car. Only dark.

"Mr. Juice?" His voice sounded really high, like a girl's voice. No answer. Embarrassed, he cleared his throat and tried again. "Mr. Juice, you okay?"

No answer. "I'm sorry. I didn't mean to make us wreck."

Still nothing. To his surprise, he still clutched the gun in his hands. He wanted to drop it, let it go, let it disappear. Fear won. He needed the gun. The men in the Hummer were coming.

His whole body shook. The gun trembled in his hand, and he almost dropped it. "No! No!" He sucked in air and steadied the gun with both hands. Better to put it away. He lifted his body away from the seat and shoved the gun into the waistband of his jeans in the back the way he'd seen Mr. Juice do.

Fumbling, he worked the seat belt buckle. The pressure of his body pressed against the belt made it hard to get the buckle to release. Panic screamed inside him to hurry. He worked harder at it. He had to get out. The men were coming.

Tears blurred his vision. He swiped at his face. The buckle released. Benny fell to the bottom of the front seat. He landed on his side, face smashed against the frame of the door, his feet sticking out where the windshield had once been.

Pain made it hard to think. He groaned and panted through the pain. *Get out. Get out.* He pushed through the window and crawled through glass on his hands and knees until he could slide down the front of the car. He landed on his face in the grass, arms outstretched. One hand touched something warm. His fingers tightened around it — an arm. A warm arm.

"Mr. Juice?"

He rolled up on his knees and shook the arm. Mr. Juice didn't answer. His eyes were open, but they didn't blink. They didn't move. They didn't do anything. He had a lot of blood on his face. It ran from his nose

down the side of his face all the way to his
ears on both sides.

CHAPTER THIRTY-ONE

Headlights blazed in a sudden blinding flood of light. Crouched next to Mr. Juice's body, Benny swiveled. A loud engine growled behind the light. The Hummer bore down on the smashed car. Benny flung himself toward the thick trees at the edge of the clearing. He couldn't let them catch him. He had to get back to Mr. Daniel.

Bushes scratched his face. He stumbled, fell, righted himself, and darted toward a huge pile of stones. It had been some kind of building that had fallen down. Little sobs escaped from his mouth. He ducked and wormed his way in between two walls that teetered, holding each other up. He collapsed in a pile as far back behind the stones as he could get. *Stop breathing. Stop breathing. Stop moving. Disappear. Be invisible.*

Benny peeked around the pile of stones. Two men got down from the Hummer and stomped toward the wreck. "It's Morin.

He's dead." A tall man dressed in green army clothes squatted next to Juice's body. His hands touched the body. He turned his head and spit. "No loss."

"Yeah, it is, *estúpido.* If he's dead, he can't tell us where the stuff is." The second guy, shorter, with a backward cap on his head, disagreed. "Enrique ain't gonna be happy."

"Oh. Yeah." The camouflage man's voice sounded mad now. "Maybe it's in the car."

They jerked on the doors, opened the trunk, and tore things apart. Benny leaned back in his hiding place and tried not to breathe too loudly. His whole body shook. He couldn't stop it. His chest hurt from the seat belt, and blood trickled down his forehead into his eye.

He pulled the gun from his waistband. It felt heavy and solid in his hands. It felt good. He knew how to use it, but he wasn't so sure it would be enough. Those guys had big guns that shot a lot of bullets fast. Faster than this dinky old thing. He was better off hiding from them.

He closed his eyes and tried to think happy thoughts. He tried to remember one good thing. One good thing. Rocky. Mr. Ray's dog. Licking his face while he sprawled on the swing on Mr. Ray's porch. His tongue was scratchy and wet. Mr. Ray said Rocky was kissing him. That had made him giggle. Benny could feel the shaking stop. He would be okay. He just had to sit tight.

"It ain't here. He had the kid with him. Maybe the kid took the stuff." Camouflage man threw trash on the ground from the backseat of Mr. Juice's car.

"He's like eight or something. He ain't big enough to carry it."

"He couldn't have gone very far. We need to look for him."

"*N'ombre,* it's gonna rain cats and dogs any minute."

"We gotta find the kid."

"Whatever. If it makes you happy." Baseball cap man started walking away. "You look. I'm waiting in the Hummer."

"Enrique's gonna ask if we looked around."

"So look. Then we're going to Morin's ma's house. I'm thinking he left the stuff there and that old bag Mari's gonna know where. She'll crack in two seconds. Offer her a hit, she'll crack in one."

Both men laughed, the sound like the wild hyenas Benny had seen on the Discovery Channel.

Camouflage man pulled a huge black gun from the back of his pants. Benny shrank into his hiding place, so afraid his legs and arms went numb. He hugged the gun to his chest, his finger on the trigger, careful to point it away from his shaking body. *Don't move. Don't move. Don't move.*

Scuffing sounds came closer, like feet crunching up leaves, then breathing. The man was close, outside the walls. Benny closed his eyes and pictured Rocky, his tongue hanging out the side of his mouth as he lay on the porch, panting. Benny wanted to go home. Home to Mr. Daniel. He wanted to pet Rocky and ride Mr. Ray's horses Fella and Doc. *Please.*

The footsteps went away.

The seconds tiptoed by. One second. Two seconds. Benny tried counting them. An engine roared. He kept counting. Tires squealed. He kept counting.

The wind blew through the trees. It was quiet now. Cars passed on the highway in the distance, the hum of their engines a comforting sound. He eased down on the ground and rested a minute, listening to his breathing, in and out. It was so tempting to close his eyes and go to sleep. No more bad guys. No more Mr. Juice.

He shoved himself to his feet and started walking. He would go home now. To Mr. Daniel's. No one could get in his way. Get between him and Mr. Daniel.

If they did, he had Mr. Juice's gun.

"It's twelve twenty. He's not going to show." Daniel eased back onto the car seat. Sweat soaked his collar despite the cool night air. It could be a reaction to the shock of being on his feet again or angry letdown because Jorge Morin hadn't shown. Daniel had dragged himself from the hospital, ridden to the station with Nicole, and then fought with Samuel and Ray until they had capitulated and let him come along. Only for this guy to be a no-show. "We have to find him."

Samuel shook his head, his craggy features rigid with anger. He stared out at the other vehicles in the parking lot. Ray was back there with a couple of DEA agents and half a dozen PD officers. "I don't know what kind of game he's playing." Samuel smoothed his mustache in an impatient gesture. "He called this shot. Why would he do this?"

"Maybe Barrera got to him." Daniel shivered again. If Morin was dead, chances were good that Benny was, too.

That speculation warranted no answer. The radio crackled. "Samuel." Ray's voice sounded loud in the night's stillness.

"Yeah."

"We got a report of a one-car rollover on IH-35 south of here. They radioed dispatch after the responding officer recognized the deceased from the APB we put out on Morin."

"Deceased?" Daniel shoved the car door open.

Samuel grabbed the sleeve of his coat and pulled him back. "Wait."

"Just one body." Ray responded. "An adult male. Hispanic. No ID on him. Went through the windshield."

"Give me an exact location."

Daniel longed for lights and siren. Samuel raced to the scene, but he stayed at the speed limit, despite Daniel's comments. He shoved from the pickup before it came to a complete stop and ran to the body.

Jorge Morin was stone cold dead. Lying on his back, his head turned to one side, blood coagulated on his forehead and nose, he stared into the distance with open, unseeing eyes. Officers had already searched the scene. Benny wasn't there. Daniel wanted to shake Morin. He wanted to scream. Where was Benny? What had he done with Benny? Had he been in the car?

"Move back, Danny. Let Sanchez do his thing." Samuel's words were terse, but his tone kind.

The medical examiner investigator gave them a quick, tight smile and went to work. One of the evidence techs joined him. "We looked through the stuff in the backseat, checked the trunk. It's empty. There's some small blood stains. We've got fiber, dirt, sand, hair. Lots of trace evidence. We should be able to tell if the child was in there at some point." The evidence tech used the back of her forearm to push hair out of her face as the wind kicked up, heavy with rain that wouldn't fall. "Oh, and it looks like we weren't the first to toss the car. Someone else had gone through it."

Daniel stared up at his brother, unable to move. Samuel grabbed his arm and pulled him to his feet. "You should be in the hospital, Danny. You're shaking and you look like you're about to pass out."

"Where is he?" Daniel jerked free. "Did someone else get him? Barrera's goons? How will we find him now?" Daniel tried to keep his voice even. The chills didn't help.

He glanced toward the mangled wreck that had been an Impala. The car was too old to have air bags. The collision with the tree had shattered the windshield, flattened the front end. Hubcaps had parted ways with the tires and lay strewn across the ground. It looked like Morin had been ejected through the windshield. How could Benny have survived that horrific impact? Had a seat belt saved him? Daniel doubted Morin had been too concerned about something as mundane as a seat belt. "We need to organize a search party. Maybe he ran into this property and is hiding."

"You're probably right. If Morin really intended to exchange Benny for the ransom money, then Benny was in the car." As the ME knelt next to the body, Samuel took Daniel's arm again and moved him toward his pickup truck, parked on the side of the road. "If he walked away, that means he wasn't badly hurt."

Daniel shivered. San Antonio's October weather typically meandered from warm to cool and back. After dark, the temperature dropped steadily. The predawn hours had brought a cool preview of winter, complete with the prediction of severe thunderstorms. Benny was out there and who knew if he had a coat or had found shelter. He could be hurt. Seriously injured. But ambulatory. "We need to find him before this storm hits."

"We've got skid marks," Alex trotted along the side of the road toward them, Deborah right behind him. "Looks like he was coming from the south. Something happened and he started swerving back and forth, then braked for some reason."

"Deer in the road?" Deborah looked as if she didn't really believe that was the problem. Daniel agreed. It wasn't a deer.

"Struggle in the car?" Samuel said it, but his tone implied he wished he didn't have to.

"Maybe. Maybe he was drunk and was driving too fast —"

"Samuel, Daniel," Ray broke in. He'd been talking on the cell phone. "Jorge Morin's mother lives on some land about five miles from here, off WW White Road. Maybe he left Benny there. Maybe he didn't intend to make the trade."

"If he left Benny there, he left a body." Daniel said the words everyone else was thinking.

"Have faith, Danny." Samuel's face was grim despite the words.

"Let's go," Daniel pulled the car door open. He wanted to get this over with. He couldn't stand the not knowing anymore. *No more, God. Let it end. Give me the strength to accept whatever happens and just let it end.*

"You know what's strange," Samuel started the truck. "No gun. We didn't find a gun or a weapon of any kind in the vehicle or on the body. No way Morin came to meet us without a weapon."

"Maybe it was thrown out with him, and it's on the ground somewhere in the dark."

"Yeah, the guys may still find it. But there's another possibility."

"Well, yeah. Maybe he had a partner."

"His mother?"

"Or another partner. Whoever that person is may have Benny now."

"Yeah. Or there's one other possibility," Daniel said, thinking of Benny's preoccupation with guns and cars. "Benny could have it."

Samuel shook his head. "I know he's precocious in some areas, but do you really think he'd take a gun?"

"In a heartbeat. He lived in a home where guns and drugs and prostitution and violence were staples. Nothing would surprise me."

Samuel was silent, his gaze intent on the road in front of them.

"Samuel?"

"If he's out there, we better be very careful approaching him. The child is traumatized. No telling what he'll do."

The inference hit Daniel. "Benny would never hurt anyone."

"Under normal circumstances." Samuel wheeled the truck out onto the highway.

"We don't know what Jorge Morin has been doing to him for the past two days. He needs to be approached with caution, especially if there's any chance at all he has Morin's gun."

Daniel nodded. Under any other circumstances, he would have agreed with his brother. But this was Benny. Benny would never hurt him.

Never.

CHAPTER THIRTY-TWO

Dodge Farm
Dickinson County, Kansas

Esperanza rolled to her side and stifled the shriek of pain with a hand clapped over her mouth. Maybe if she shifted a little more to the right, her back, behind, and legs wouldn't hurt so much. She rested on top of the sheets. Anything that touched the welts that had sprung up after the belt whipping hurt too much. The pain kept her awake more than Estrella's snores. Her twin so was worn out from mopping and waxing all the floors in the house that even Esperanza's misery couldn't keep her awake.

Esperanza didn't remember much of the beating. After a few rounds, the room swam in front of her, the pain so big she couldn't think or hear. When Uncle Ezra finally stopped, she'd stumbled from the room, climbed the stairs on all fours, and collapsed on the hallway floor in front of the bedroom door. Frankie and Estrella had dragged her in and closed the door behind her. No one had eaten supper, and Momma had never come to look in on them.

Esperanza closed her eyes and whispered, "God, are you coming for us? Or sending someone? If you are really there, please help us."

"Who you talking to?" She opened her eyes. Dom crept toward her.

She rubbed the tears from her face with one hand. "God."

Dom snorted. "Girls." He held up a plastic bread bag filled with ice. "Got ya something."

"You're lucky he didn't hear you." Esperanza fought more tears. "I don't think I can stand to put it on there."

"Come on, I'll do it for you." Her brother's face was white in the moonlight streaming through the open window curtain. During the day, Dom never let anyone see anything in his face. Now, in the night, she could see a lot of stuff there. Dom hurt just like she did. "It'll numb it a little so you can go to sleep."

She turned on her stomach so he could lay the bag on her back. The icy sensation sucked the air from her lungs. She closed her eyes and concentrated on repeating her memory verse for the week — *Keep me safe, O God, for in you I take refuge. Psalm 16* — until the pain subsided enough to talk. "What about you? Where's your ice bag?"

He ducked his head so she couldn't see his face. "I'm okay."

"He's gonna send us help."

"Momma says God helps those who help themselves."

Esperanza had heard that speech, too. She'd rather get her scripture from the preacher at the neighbor's church. He had a kind face. He said God was a God of love, not hate. God was kind, not mean. "Momma doesn't know nothing about God. If she did, she wouldn't stay here with Uncle Ezra."

Dom snorted again. "He ain't our uncle."

"I know."

"Well, I know something, too. We gotta get out of here. Momma ran away from *Papi* once. We can do that, too, even if I have to get a gun and shoot Ezra Dodge to keep him from coming after us."

Dom's voice got a little louder. She glanced toward the closed door. "Shhh! We're just kids." The horrible image of Uncle Ezra, his face bloody, falling and falling until he smashed into the ground danced in her head. She shuddered and grabbed her brother's hand. "Promise me you won't do nothing like that. Let's just run away."

"They'd find us and drag us back, and he'd beat us some more. We gotta find a way to stop him."

Esperanza rolled over. The ice pack fell away, but she ignored it "You can't take on Uncle Ezra. He's too big and too mean. I seen him kill a man once. Snuck up on him from behind and smashed his head in with a baseball bat."

Dom didn't answer for a long time, but she could hear his breathing, loud in her ear. "You're lying. You never told no one."

"I ain't lying." Esperanza sat up, relieved to finally tell someone what she'd seen. They'd only been in Kansas a little while. The tall man in a blue suit had come out to the pasture where Ezra had been fixing a fence. They'd talked. Then they'd gone in the house. She'd see them coming from the kitchen window.

They were in the living room. Then Ezra had gone into the hall closet. She'd heard him. Heard the thud, heard him dragging something. Seen him pulling the body out the back door. "Nothing to tell. He dragged the body out behind the barn and buried it. You was at school. I couldn't go that week on account of that bruise on my face shaped like his hand. He didn't know I saw, but I did. If he can kill a man like that, what kind a chance do you got? You're just a kid. Besides, how would you get your hands on Uncle Ezra's hunting guns? He keeps them all locked up. The key chain is on his belt all the time."

"Don't worry about me. I can take care of myself. You just watch."

He slipped away, as silent as he'd come in. Esperanza grabbed the ice bag and held it against her cheek. It was cold outside but she felt as if a fever were eating her alive. *God, if you don't send someone soon, it's gonna be too late for all of us.*

CHAPTER THIRTY-THREE

Daniel peered at the dark, dirt road ahead, willing Samuel to hurry. A thorough search of the crash site had revealed no Benny and had taken valuable time. Instead of speeding up, his brother slowed the pickup. The deep pit in the rutted road made mincemeat of the underside of the truck. Samuel would need an alignment and new struts. Daniel gritted his teeth. If they didn't hurry, it would be too late for Benny. "Why are you slowing down? We need to hurry."

"Because this road is a mess and —" The radio crackled drowning out the rest of Samuel's response.

"There's a Hummer parked in front of the house." Ray reported. "The windows are tinted. I can't tell if anybody's in it. We're holding back while I run the plates."

A Hummer. Most likely, Enrique Barrera's posse had found Morin's mother's house. Samuel pulled in behind Ray's

Bronco. They were protected by a long stand of trees that hugged the road before it spread out into the front yard of a ramshackle house still several hundred yards away. A couple of floodlights attached to the porch roof illuminated the Hummer. No sign of movement.

"You think Barrera?" Daniel hugged his arms to his chest and tried to keep his teeth from chattering.

"Or somebody he sent."

"Somebody is going to be dead if we don't get in there." Daniel tugged his weapon from inside his jacket and opened his door. "Once Barrera knows Morin isn't there, nobody will be left standing."

Samuel gripped his arm. "The DEA and SWAT are right behind us. Give them a minute."

"Can't wait."

Daniel slid from the truck and darted to Ray's pickup. His brother-in-law crouched next to it. "We need to go in."

"Wait for —"

A scream punctured the silence. A protracted scream.

"Go, go." His weapon drawn, Ray scrambled in front of Daniel, heading toward the Hummer. He paused there, peeked around the edge. Samuel squeezed in next to him, Daniel landed on the other side.

"We gotta get in there now or that woman doesn't stand a chance," Ray whispered.

"Let me get closer. See what we're up against." Daniel started to inch forward. Ray caught his arm and shook his head.

"My turn."

"Susana will kill me, anything happens to you."

Ray moved ahead of him anyway. Daniel stayed close. They eased up on the porch. Ray took one long step and leaned against the wall, angled his head for a quick glance in the front window. He nodded. Daniel followed suit.

Two men in the living room. One woman. They had her tied to a chair. A man in camouflage was waving a lit cigarette in her face. It connected with her cheek. She screamed. The man struck her with the back of his hand, her head snapped to one side and dropped. No more screaming.

"*Idiota!* Did you knock her out?" A guy in a baseball cap got in the other man's face. "She ain't gonna tell us nothing knocked out."

"Keep looking. It's gotta be here somewhere. Juice ain't smart enough to stash it anywhere else." The men drifted away from the woman's inert body slumped in the chair.

"Now." Daniel nodded at Samuel.

The front door wasn't even locked. Daniel smashed through, rolled to his right, Samuel went left. "Police. Freeze! Everybody down on the ground. Down on the ground."

The men didn't listen, of course. They never did.

The spray of gunfire lit up the house. Daniel dove behind the couch. He could hear Samuel's short bursts of angry breathing, but he couldn't see Ray. He stuck his weapon over the top of the couch and took his shots, three in rapid succession.

"DEA. Everybody down on the ground! Freeze! Down on the ground." The firepower this time was much more intense. Camouflage man tried to run for it. A DEA SWAT team member took him out with one shot. The man in the cap flung his weapon on the ground and dropped to his knees, hands in the air. "Don't shoot. Don't shoot."

"On the ground! On the ground, hands behind your back, thumbs up!" Samuel slapped his handcuffs on the man, his knee on the man's back for good measure. "Where's the little boy? Where is he?"

The guy squirmed under Samuel's knee. "What you talking about, man? We ain't got no little boy. He wasn't in the car. He ain't here, neither."

The man in Army fatigues writhed on the floor, blood dripping through his fingers where he pressed his hand to his shoulder. "*Cállate!* Shut up!"

"Where'd he go?" Daniel got in his face, shoved him against the wall, the barrel of his gun smashing the man's nose. "You saw him? Where'd he go?"

The guy struggled against Daniel's grip, but fierce anger gave Daniel more strength. The guy stopped moving, his face stoic. "I seen him in the car. But after it crashed, he wasn't there no more. I looked around. *No estuvo.*"

"Back off, Daniel. Now." Samuel's hand tightened on his shoulder. "You need to back off now."

Daniel eased back a step, whirled, and shoved past Samuel.

"He was in the car," Samuel called after him. "He got away. That's good."

"He's out there alone." Daniel pushed through the front door, letting the screen door slam behind him so hard it rattled. Thunder rolled and lightning cut a jagged pattern across the dark sky. He doubled over, trying to breathe. "Alone."

CHAPTER THIRTY-FOUR

His legs felt heavy. His head pounded. Benny lifted one foot and then the other. Counting the steps to twenty and then starting over. He'd been walking along the highway forever. At first, every time a car passed, he dropped into the ditch and hid. Now he stuck out a thumb. He needed a ride. Otherwise, he'd never get to Mr. Daniel's. The darkness wasn't lifting. Rain wet his face and clothes. A cool wind blew, making him shiver. Or maybe it was the thunder rolling overhead followed by flashes of light that lit the scenery around him. He'd never been outside in a storm before.

He wanted to lie down, curl up, and sleep forever. Every step made his ribs and chest ache more. He stumbled, pitched forward, and caught himself as his knees hit the ground. Pain shot through his body.

A car passed, the first one in a long, long time. He didn't have time to stick out his thumb. He tried not to cry. The car slowed, slowed more, then pulled onto the shoulder of the road and started to creep back toward him.

Benny's hand flew to the gun in his waistband. He'd tucked it in tight, secure, under his T-shirt. A man with little bits of white hair around a shiny, bald head rolled down the car window. "Hi, there. I'm Pastor Henderson. You look like you could use a ride into town. I'm going as far as my church up north of the city, if you care to get in."

Benny looked at the pastor man's face. A pastor worked in a church. Like Pastor James at Greater Good. Daniel said pastors worked for God. It would be okay to get in a car with someone who worked for God, wouldn't it? He wavered. What if the man lied? God would be real mad. The inside of the car looked warm. What could it hurt? Benny could protect himself now. The gun had bullets. He'd checked.

Benny climbed in. The inside of the car smelled like coffee and cough drops. The heater spun waves of warm air that covered him better than a blanket. The radio played a familiar Sunday school song. He sank back into the seat. His eyes wanted to close. He wanted to sleep. His nose ran. He sniffed and wiped with his sleeve.

"Here." The pastor man handed him a box of tissues from the seat. "Got a little cold myself."

Benny nodded and blew. The loud noise embarrassed him.

"What's your name, son?"

Benny shuddered at the word *son,* but managed to keep his gaze on the road in front of him. "Benny," he whispered.

The pastor man flipped the knob on the radio, lowering the volume. "Benny? Benny, how old are you?"

"Old enough, sir." Benny tried to sound older, but his voice came out in a little squeak. His throat hurt.

"How far are you going?"

"Just to my house in San Antonio."

"Somebody home?"

"Yes, sir. My dad." Benny stumbled over the last word. "Mr. Daniel. Mr. Daniel's there."

The pastor's eyes were kind, but they looked worried. Benny could see the question in them. What was he doing out on the road? *Don't ask. Please don't ask.*

"Here." The pastor man took one hand from the wheel and dug into his coat pocket. "Use my cell phone to call him. He must be worried sick about you out here on the side of the road all by yourself."

Ignoring the question in the pastor man's voice, Benny took the phone with a shaking hand. Finally, he could talk to Mr. Daniel. He had to bite the inside of his cheeks to keep from crying. He could make sure Mr. Daniel was okay. Mr. Juice had lied.

His fingers stiff and cold, he punched in the number. Then it rang. And rang. Finally, Mr. Daniel's voice started talking. The recording. Tears formed in Benny's eyes. He knew Mr. Daniel's number by heart. Mr. Daniel said that was very important. Every child had to know his telephone number. But Benny didn't know any other numbers for Uncle Samuel or Aunt Piper or Aunt Susana. Or Uncle Ray. Nobody. He couldn't call the police. They'd know he killed Mr. Juice. They'd put him in jail.

He pushed the off button on the phone.

"No answer?"

Benny shook his head and tried to look sure of himself. "He'll be home soon."

"Good. I don't think you're old enough to be at home alone."

Benny didn't know how to answer that. He didn't remember a time when he hadn't been left at home alone.

The pastor man patted Benny's arm. "I know you don't want to tell me what happened to you, so I'm just gonna be patient

374

until you feel like you can. In the meantime, your clothes are wet, you're shaking, and you're all bruised up. Your lip is split, and your eyes are black and blue. You're a mess, son." The pastor man nodded his head toward the backseat. "I've got a bunch of bags of clothes that I'm taking to the church clothes closet. I can pull over and you can crawl back there and take a look. I'm sure you'll find a nice warm jacket in there and some dry pants. I've got a first aid kit. I can try to fix you up. Or I can take you to the emergency room. That might be best."

"No, please don't stop. Please." The shaking worsened as fear wracked Benny. He tried to bring his voice down, but he wanted to get home so bad. Couldn't the man understand that? "I have to get home. I'm fine, sir."

"Okay, son, it's all right. Just calm down. We'll keep going, if that's what you want."

They rode in silence for a long stretch. Benny relaxed against the seat, fighting the urge to lean his head back and close his eyes. His eyelids were so heavy, and it was warm in the car. He jerked forward and wiggled hard. No sleeping. Not until it was safe.

"You know about Jesus, Benny?"

Startled, Benny nodded at the pastor man.

Nobody but Mr. Daniel and his Sunday School teacher ever talked to him about Jesus. "Yes, sir. My friend Mr. Daniel told me about him."

"Your friend Daniel sounds like a smart guy."

"Yes, sir."

"Sometimes Jesus sends someone to help a person who's in trouble."

Benny thought about this statement for a second. "Like an angel?"

The pastor man chuckled. "If angels are old and bald and have dentures."

That didn't sound like the angels Benny had seen in pictures. "Huh?"

"Nothing. Not always angels. Sometimes ordinary people can help. Like me."

The pastor man wouldn't want to help if he knew Benny had killed a man. A man who might have been his dad. "I don't need help." Benny pressed his lips hard together to keep from crying.

"It's a standing offer. Do you know what that means?"

Benny peeked at the pastor man from the corner of his eye. He looked nice. Benny worked to stifle a sob. It wanted to come out so bad. "No."

"It means the offer is always there, ready when you need it and are ready to accept it.

God made sure of that when his son Jesus died on the cross. It's hard to understand, but just remember. You're never alone."

The pastor was silent for a moment, his eyes on the road. "Never," he added, as if talking to himself. "Remember that."

"Yes, sir."

The pastor glanced at Benny and smiled. "Such good manners. Well, I've got to stop and get gas up here at the Stop n Go. At least let me buy you a hot chocolate, child, before you pass out from exposure."

Benny swallowed hard. He was in an awful hurry to get home. But something hot sounded really good.

The pastor man eased the car toward the exit ramp. Seconds later they were in the parking lot.

"You can wait here while I pump the gas, and we'll go in together." The pastor man opened the door.

"I have to go to the rest room." Benny glanced around the parking lot. No Hummers. No cop cars. It seemed safe enough for a quick visit. "I can't wait."

"Oh. Okay, I'll be right in as soon as I pump the gas. Why don't you wash your face and hands while you're at it, get cleaned up a little?"

Benny staggered into the store and

stumbled through the aisles, trying to find a sign that said rest rooms.

"You gonna buy something, kid?" The guy behind the counter didn't look so friendly.

"I'm with the guy pumping the gas." Benny jerked his head toward the front of the store. The clerk looked out. Benny followed his gaze.

The pastor man was talking on the cell phone, one hand fluttering in the air.

The police. He'd figured out Benny was on the run. He was calling the police. They would arrest him because he delivered crack and killed Mr. Juice. Benny shot out the door and raced toward the highway. He had to get to San Antonio. He had to get to Mr. Daniel.

Panting, his legs like jelly, Benny stumbled and glanced back, sure the pastor man was right behind him. The man still stood by his car, a look of surprise on his face. He dropped the phone on the hood and started across the parking lot.

Benny darted across the highway, a cold rush of air in his face and a blaring horn telling him the bumper of a truck had just missed hitting him. More horns screamed. He ran faster, his legs pumping, arms reaching. Just a little bit farther, a little bit more. His muscles hurt so bad, they burned. He hit the ditch on the other side, fell, rolled, and jumped to his feet. He climbed the other side and ran through a field toward a bunch of huge trees. He could hide in there.

Gasping for breath, he looked back.

The pastor man stood on the edge of the highway, cars and trucks making a speeding, continuous fence between them. He waved his arms. His lips moved, but Benny couldn't hear him. He turned and kept running. The pastor man couldn't be trusted.

No one could.

Without his baseball cap, Pedro Diaz looked much older. His bald head shone in the glare of the fluorescent light in the interview room. He also looked smaller. Not the big man who tortured women with cigarettes. Daniel forced himself to remain still. A constant shiver told him his fever was up again. His legs shook with it. He itched to rip into the man, but this was Samuel's station, his jurisdiction.

Samuel opened the folder on the table that separated them and then leaned back in his chair, an unreadable expression on his face.

"Interesting reading, *Señor* Diaz." Samuel slapped his hand down on the paper and spread his long fingers wide. "Let's see. In and out of juvie starting at age twelve.

Graduated to adult fun at age eighteen. Auto theft, breaking and entering, possession of stolen goods, possession of drugs, possession with intent to sell. A nice progression."

Diaz's gaze flickered from Samuel to Daniel. Daniel kept his face blank. Samuel had to fight to get this interrogation. Narcotics wanted a piece of Diaz and so did the DEA. Daniel wanted to wrap his fingers around the guy's neck and squeeze until his head exploded. But he didn't. He couldn't blow it before they got what they needed.

Narcotics hadn't been able to get anything from the wounded man. He'd lawyered up at the hospital. Samuel leaned in toward Diaz. "You listen to me. This time you're looking at hard time. Aggravated assault on Mari Morin. Possession of illegal firearms. Murder. Kidnapping. Did you know killing someone in the course of committing a felony, such as kidnapping, is capital murder in the state of Texas?"

"Murder? I didn't kill nobody and I didn't kidnap nobody. Morin crashed the car and killed himself. The kid was gone."

Samuel chuckled, a sound without mirth. "You're in a bad way, man. Whose idea was it to kidnap the kid to get Shawna Garza to talk? Yours? Now the kid's missing, maybe dead. I'm sure you can imagine what that lethal drug cocktail flooding your veins will feel like. You don't have the drugs, you don't have the kid, and Morin is dead. You got nothing for Barrera. And when he finds out you've been talking to us, you're a dead man walking. Lethal injection or Barrera's brand of execution, which would you prefer?"

Rivulets of sweat slid down Diaz's forehead. He wiped his face with the back of his sleeve. "No *ese*, you got it all wrong. I'm just the muscle. I don't run the show. I didn't know nothing about snatching the kid until Chavez told Barrera —"

Daniel surged forward, grabbed Diaz's shirt, and jerked him closer. "Chavez? Chavez was in on this?"

Diaz struggled to stand. The uniformed officer was on him in a second. "Huh-uh. Sit."

"Daniel, back off." Samuel's fingers bit into his shoulder, pulling him away. "Back off now or you're out of the room."

He shrugged off the hand and circled the room, trying to control rapid-fire breathing that made him dizzy. Samuel eased back into his chair. "Are you talking about Tómas Chavez? How does he figure into all this?"

Diaz shook his head, his fat jowls quivering. "You want information from me, I want a deal. What're you offering?"

"That's up to the DA." Samuel gave him an appraising stare. Daniel admired his brother's calm. Personally, with each passing moment, the desire to rip the man's head off down to his waist increased threefold. Samuel never even broke a sweat. "Are we talking about Tómas Chavez? Because if we are, I can promise you, I'll work something out. But first you gotta tell me what Chavez's involvement is."

Diaz fingered the thick gold chain around his neck. "He's a *primo* of Barrera. Family. Used to be heavy into the trade. Semiretired now, but he hangs with Barrera some. That's how he knew Juice. He gave Juice some information to help him get the stash back after Shawna refused to tell Suarez where it was. Juice thought it was to help him, but really Chavez was helping Barrera."

"Chavez is a handyman."

"He likes to have a legit job. That's his cover. He said it wasn't smart to live like a gangbanger." Diaz grimaced, pursed his lips like he might spit, and then thought better of it. "Always thought he was better than the rest of us. Living on the north side. Working on ranches like some sort of dude rancher. It was just a smoke screen."

"The information — it was about Shawna's son Benny being at the Spanish Oak Ranch? And the wedding preparations?"

The man shrugged. "Maybe. All I know is Chavez backed off after the police came out to his place and started nosing around. He told *Señor* Barrera he needed to fly under the radar for a while."

Samuel glanced at Daniel and then stood. "We're done."

"What about my deal? Hey, man, you said —"

"Sit tight. We'll get back to you on that." Samuel's grin had a wicked edge. "You aren't in any hurry, are you? I mean, once Barrera and Chavez find out you been talking to us, your life outside these four walls isn't worth squat anyway."

"You —" The man sputtered but Daniel didn't wait to hear what he said. He shoved through the door and into the hallway behind Samuel.

"We need to confer with Cooper. Chavez's place is in the county. Cooper deserves to be able to pick this guy up. We'll get him for Benny and for Nina Chavez." Samuel's long stride challenged Daniel to keep up. "Chavez's been in on this all along." His cell phone chirped, but he slowed only slightly as he slapped it to his ear. "Martinez."

Daniel slowed, waiting, watching his brother's face. There wasn't much point. Nothing ever showed there. "Got it. Daniel's with me. Go talk to the guy and call me as soon as you know anything."

He disconnected, his lips pursed in a thin line, his dark eyes hooded.

"What?"

"They've got a line on Benny."

"Is he —" Daniel couldn't voice the words.

Chapter Thirty-Five

"The pastor said he stopped at this convenience store to get gas. Benny took off from here." Alex eyed the highway that ran in front of the gas station as he spoke. The cars zoomed past at fifty and sixty miles an hour. According to Pastor Henderson, Benny had darted away from this spot and disappeared into the fields on the other side. It was a miracle he hadn't been killed crossing the road. They'd allowed Pastor Henderson to continue into San Antonio with the assurance that they would call him as soon as they found Benny. Which better be soon.

"We need more bodies to work this." Deborah pulled on a black leather jacket and slid from the car's passenger side. Daybreak had brought steadily dropping temperatures. The wind picked up under a gray sky, giving her cheeks a bright pink tinge. Her eyes drooped with fatigue, but her voice sounded strong. "We could call Sarge, and he can ask for the canine unit."

"Benny's been out there for at least an hour, exposed and scared. He's hurt." Alex pictured the kid's sweet face, trying so hard to look tough. It would take at least thirty minutes, maybe more to mobilize a large-scale search party. "We need to find him fast. Let's do a preliminary search. If we can't find him, we ask for additional manpower."

They ran across the highway at the first break in traffic and then walked in silence, their breathing the only sound as they trudged deeper into the wooded area. A light rain turned heavier. Thunder rumbled overhead. The wind kicked up, sending a chill through Alex. If it got any colder, his PD windbreaker wouldn't hack it.

"Lovely." Deborah wiped at her face with the back of her hand. "Just lovely."

Alex agreed. He preferred summer. "Benny must be freezing."

"Yeah, I'm trying to focus on that." Deborah stumbled over a downed tree limb. Alex reached for her, then pulled back. He didn't want to spook her. She pulled herself upright without looking at him and forged ahead. Lightening rippled across the sky, the only light in a day that had faded to dark.

Thunder shook the ground under Alex's feet. He pulled his windbreaker tighter. "I don't like this."

"I thought you were the outdoor type." Deborah grinned and pulled on a pair of black gloves.

"Who told you that? I prefer air-conditioned adventures."

Deborah laughed. "Figures."

Was she making fun of him? "What's that supposed to mean?"

"I don't know. You aren't what you seem. I can't figure you out."

"At least that's something we have in common."

Alex stopped talking. He needed all his concentration to struggle through terrain that had turned slick with mud and wet weeds. Huge rain drops pelted them in a sudden torrent. Water ran through the ravines that had been dry a few minutes earlier. Visibility shrank to a few feet. Another crack of lightning, this time overhead, lit up the sky, and thunder, a long, low ominous rumble, rolled over them.

"We need to find shelter," Alex yelled over the sound of rain that fell in sheets. "Wait this out."

He couldn't hear her response, but she waved in the direction of a dilapidated stone barn. Even on a sunny day it would have looked abandoned. In the pouring rain, it looked in danger of collapse. Alex pushed ahead, searching for a door, hoping it wouldn't be locked.

Lightning so close he had to shut his eyes against the glare struck a tree a few yards away. The crack of sheering branches reverberated around him. "Get in, get in!" He grabbed Deborah's arm and pulled her toward the barn. Together they managed to slide open a long, heavy door that screeched with lack of use.

Darkness and a dank, moldy smell greeted them inside the old building. At least it was semi-dry. And away from the lightning.

His flashlight revealed a wheelbarrow, rusting and covered with cobwebs, shovels, rakes, and other tools that were a mystery to him. Alex peered at the corners and then circled back to Deborah.

"Don't shine that thing in my eyes. Put it out." She shoved wet hair from her face. "It's not that dark in here, just give your eyes a chance to adjust."

"Sorry." Alex killed the light and leaned against one wall for a second, listening to the sound of her breathing. It came light and fast. He could almost hear her shiver. "You want my windbreaker?"

"And what would you wear, Mr. Macho Man?" Deborah wrapped her arms around her chest. "My coat is lined. Yours isn't."

"Body heat would help." He voiced the words without thinking about how they would sound.

Nervous tittering filled the dusky gloom around him. "Excuse me?"

A rush of heat swarmed his face. "I only meant, if you'd come over here next to me, I'd put my arm around you and our body heat would warm us up."

She was silent for so long he didn't think she'd answer. "I don't think so. Sorry."

He stared at his feet. The heat on his neck and face burned. "Don't be. I'll do some jumping jacks or run in place or something."

That got a laugh. Good. She wasn't afraid of him. Not too much, anyway.

The laugh ended closer to him than it started. He looked up. She'd moved so she was standing next to him.

"I admit it. I'm freezing." She slid down so she was sitting on the floor, back against the barn wall. "And you look like an icicle. Come on."

Barely allowing himself to breathe, he slid down next to her. She leaned in and pulled his arm up so she could get underneath it. "Relax. I don't bite."

"I think that's supposed to be my line." He tried to relax, but between the cold and her nearness he couldn't move.

"Alex, I know you don't bite. Don't take it so personally. It's a knee jerk reaction. It's not like I can control it." He felt a shiver run through her. "Man, what I wouldn't give for a cigarette right now."

"It hurts to think you're afraid of me." Alex cringed inwardly. He'd just told her she had the power to hurt him. They hadn't even had a date. Smooth operator, that was him. He dug into his pocket, found a peppermint, and handed it to her.

She took it. The wrapper crinkled, telling him she'd unwrapped it. "It blows my mind to think I have that kind of effect on you. How'd that happen?"

Sitting there in the semi-dark, Deborah close and warm, made it at little easier to talk. He didn't have to look at those blue eyes that had seen too much to trust him. "I wish I knew," he said, allowing himself to enjoy for a second the weight of her body leaning against his. "It just happened. I used to see you places, and I admit, at first I saw a beautiful woman. But then I started studying the person. Did you know you have an expressive face?"

Her body stiffened next to him. "Do not.

I'm very good at the poker face thing."

"You wish."

They were quiet. The wind sounded as if it could tear the walls down around them. Alex tightened his arm around Deborah. She didn't flinch, but she sighed, a deep, almost sad sound. "So did you think about what I said about being a Christian?" she asked.

Here we go. "I did. I actually had a conversation with Ray about it."

"And?"

"Ray thinks we're perfect for each other."

"What?" She laughed. It was nice sound. "You're making that up."

"I'm serious. He says you're like the woman at the well —"

"Who goes to tell the others about the living water." She interrupted, her voice full of tears.

"What's the matter?" He ducked closer to see her face. He'd made her cry. "He meant it in a good way."

"Oh, no. It's good. The idea that God would use me for something. Me. The drunk. The messed up, promiscuous drunk? Don't you see?" She used the back of her wet sleeve to wipe her face. "Here, I was so sure He was angry with me because I —"

"Because you have feelings for Daniel."

391

The second the words were out, he wanted them back.

She shifted away from him. "That's crazy. He's married. What gave you that idea?"

The obvious. "For starters, you smashed an entire jar of mayo on the floor."

She drew her knees up and wrapped her arms around them. "His wife saw me hugging him. I didn't mean for it to happen. He was asleep, and I was trying to wake him up. He had a nightmare, and he thought it was her. He was hugging her, not me."

Wrong place, wrong time. Alex had been there, done that. "And you're afraid they won't get back together because of you. Now who's the one who lacks faith?"

"Touché."

This wasn't the wrong place, wrong time. He had to believe that. They had been thrown together alone in a falling-down barn for a reason. He might never get another opportunity like this. *God, help me.* "You know what I think?"

"Somehow, I'm sure you're going to tell me."

"Well, my theory is you focused on Daniel because he was safe. He's married and in love with someone else. He'll never be a threat to you. You'll never have to put yourself out there for him. Now, somebody like me, I'm a huge threat. I'm right here, right now, and I'm interested. Very interested."

Steady, ominous thunder filled the sudden silence, followed by a crack of lightning so close it lit up the room and Deborah's face. It was full of uncertainty. She was thinking about it. That was a good start. Alex soldiered on. "There's something else you should know."

"You're full of information."

She tried to play it light, but Alex heard the emotion. "Yeah, I prayed."

"You did?"

He couldn't help but smile at the sound of hope in her voice. She cared. If not about him as a man, she cared about him as a person she would like to see find Christ. That was an excellent beginning. "Yes."

"Wow."

She sounded as impressed as he had felt. His heart did a drum roll. "I was pretty impressed with myself. But I think God was wondering why it took me so long."

"He knows why."

"The problem is I'm not sure I can forgive Him."

"Forgive Him?" Her voice crackled with dismay. Maybe he'd made a mistake being honest. "He's done everything for you.

Given everything for you."

The pounding of the rain matched the pounding of Alex's heart. "He didn't save my parents' marriage. He didn't save my sister."

"My parents got divorced, too." The edge in her voice told him they were getting closer to the crux of her problem.

"More than half of all marriages end in divorce." He didn't want to be another statistic.

"Which is why you can't commit in a relationship."

She was a smart woman. "Don't see you doing it either."

"Your sister died?"

She'd switched tracks, but Alex could follow her train of thought. "My mom was a nurse. After the divorce she worked all the time. She wasn't around. Then my sister moved out. To live with her boyfriend. They had a fight. He got drunk and shot her to death." A quick, bare recital worked best. Even after all these years, it was difficult to muster the neutral tone necessary to get through it. "When the police went after him, he killed himself. They were twenty years old."

"The boyfriend killed your sister. Not God. Was she a Christian?"

Emotion he'd smothered for years suddenly had a strangle hold on his throat. He inhaled and exhaled, scrambling to get a grip on it. "I don't know." His voice only cracked a little.

"That's a tough gig, isn't it?" She kept her head down, her wet hair draped across her face, hiding her eyes. He slipped the hair back behind her ear. She looked up at him, the darkness hiding her expression. He'd held on to his anger over his sister's death for a long time. Letting it go would be a relief. He wasn't sure how to do it, but Deborah was right. He knew his sister would want him to be happy.

"Don't let it happen to you." Deborah spoke before he could, emotion making her voice quiver, even as her tone was adamant.

"What do you mean?"

"You're a police officer, Alex. You could get killed tomorrow. Today. Get straight with God before it's too late."

Easier said than done. "How did you do it?"

"Counseling. AA. Friends. Church. Letting go of my anger. Letting go, period. Trusting. It's hard for me to trust people, but Jesus, I can count on. So can you." Her voice broke. "I don't have many friends. If I make it to eternity, I'd like to know you'll be there, too."

Alex closed his eyes, willing the tears to disappear. He hadn't cried since his sister's death. He listened to the wind lash tree branches against the building. It sounded like the barn would be ripped from the foundation. Yet, they were safe. He forced himself to relax. "How long do you think this'll last?"

"Not long. It's too ferocious. It'll blow out of here pretty quick."

"Thank you, Miss Meteorologist."

"You asked."

They both laughed, but Alex still heard the sound.

A rustling sound. It came from the hayloft. There it was again. An animal? It could be a possum or a rat. Or an animal of the two-legged variety. They should have swept the place before making themselves at home. It had such an empty feel to it, he had been sure the barn was abandoned.

Had someone heard their conversation? Anger coursed through him. It had been private — very private. He could see from Deborah's face that she'd heard the sound, too. He lifted his index finger to his lips. She nodded and pulled herself to her feet.

Trying not to make a sound, he stood up next to her. She pulled her gun. Alex grabbed her arm and made her look at him, shaking his head. She jerked away, moving toward a rickety ladder that leaned against the opening to the loft. The sound had stopped.

Alex halted at the ladder, his hand on Deborah's shoulder. He shook his head again. "Wait," he mouthed the word without making a sound.

She shrugged and stopped. No sound, but bits of hay floated down from the opening, landing in her hair. He reached a hand out to brush them away and then stopped. She had a gun in her hand, after all.

Deborah put one foot on the lowest rung, a hand in the middle, and took a step up. The ladder creaked, the noise loud in the silence.

A blast lit up the dark.

CHAPTER THIRTY-SIX

Alex threw himself toward Deborah. He forced her off the ladder. They smashed to the barn floor. She rolled away from him, her Glock still in her hand. He rolled with her, trying to give her cover. He strained to hear, strained to see in the semi-dark. The person in the loft firing at them had the advantage. They had no place to hide.

"Get off me." She meant to whisper, he was sure of it, but the words came out in a scream.

He scrambled to his feet and grabbed her arm to pull her up. She needed to forget being afraid of men and be afraid of getting shot. "Get away from the opening!"

Deborah shrugged away from him. She crouched behind the ladder where she couldn't be seen from above. "Benny, is that you?"

Benny? With a gun? Alex shook his head at her. She nodded hard and whispered,

"Ray said they didn't find a gun at the accident scene. He thought that was odd. Maybe Benny took it and ran. Get Daniel on your cell. Get him over here."

She turned her focus back to the loft. "Benny, please answer me. I just need to know if it's you. It's me, Deborah. I'm a friend of Daniel's. We met at the wedding. He told me to come look for you, find you."

A shot answered. This one smashed into the wheelbarrow. The ricochet made a pinging sound that forced Alex to the ground, Deborah next to him.

"If it's Benny, why is he shooting? He's got to recognize your voice." Alex tried to keep his voice a whisper, but a kid shooting at him didn't sit well.

"The kidnapper probably told him something similar. Your mom sent me. Stupid of me to use that line." The light filtering through the windows had increased. The storm had started to move on. Alex could see the tension in Deborah's face and the frustration. He shook his head at her. Not her fault.

"Get Daniel here, now." She didn't bother to whisper now. "Benny. We'll wait. I know you'd feel better if Daniel were here, so we'll wait for him. Just don't shoot anymore, all right? We promise not to come up there.

We'll wait for Daniel, okay?"

No answer. But no shots, either. Alex squeezed Deborah's shoulder quickly, before she could duck away. He dug his cell phone from his pocket and eased toward the door, careful to stay out of the line of fire. She was right. As ironic as it seemed to him, they did need Daniel.

The good part was that he was easy to reach. And — even though it seemed to take forever in the moment — he was able to get to them, and to Benny, relatively quickly once given directions.

A quick nod at Alex and Deborah, and Daniel slipped across the barn and eased his hands onto the ladder. Nicole was right behind him. She'd been waiting in the lobby at the police station. She insisted on helping him search in the pouring rain. Benny was up there. Alive. Safe. But not home yet. He had a gun. After almost three days in Juice Morin's company, Benny might not be the same child who loved pancakes and pizza and watching movies on Friday night. Daniel gripped a rung on the ladder to the hayloft. "Benny, it's me."

A small sniff. Benny could hear him. Daniel put his foot on the first rung. He wanted to get up there. He wanted to know how badly Benny was hurt. He wanted to take care of him. Now.

Except Benny had a gun.

"What are you doing up there?"

Silence. Then the small, tearful voice. "I don't feel good."

Daniel swallowed. Benny was within reach. Nicole took a deep breath next to him. The relief in her face reflected his own. "One piece, Benny needs you in one piece."

Easy. Take it slow. Benny was an eight-year-old with a gun. Scared beyond belief, he had to be cold and hungry and traumatized. But alive. Daniel could fix those other things. First he had to talk him down. He cleared his throat. "Why are you up there?"

"It smells like Mr. Ray's barn." The voice quivered.

Daniel grasped for understanding. He glanced at Nicole. *Safe.* She framed the word with her lips without a sound. He nodded.

"You feel safe?"

"Yeah." The matter-of-fact response ripped out a piece of Daniel's heart. "Mr. Daniel?"

"Yes."

"I got my church pants dirty. I-I-I'm-m-m sorry. They got a hole in them. I'll work and pay for new ones, okay? Only . . . can you not call the police?"

A retching sob wafted after the words. The rough wood under Daniel's hands bit into his fingers. "Benny, I don't care about the pants. I only care about you. I'm not calling the police. The police were looking for you to bring you back to me, that's all."

"They aren't going to arrest me?"

"No. No!" What was going through his traumatized head? "Why would they arrest you?"

A huge hiccupping sob. "The man — Mr. Juice — my-my-my — he said the presents I took to the guys for my mom — they had crack in them. And then, then I . . . I didn't mean to . . . but I think I killed Mr. Juice."

"Benny, nothing you did was your fault. You're a kid. Your mom and Morin — Mr. Juice, they're responsible for everything. They're the adults."

Another sob. "My mom's really dead?"

Daniel bit his lip so hard he tasted blood, salty and bitter. "Yes, Benny. I'm sorry, but she is."

The silence stretched, taking Daniel's decimated nerves with it. He stuck one foot on the second rung. Nicole's grip on his arm tightened.

"Was Mr. Juice really my dad?" The disbelief and disappointment in Benny's voice tumbled through the air and landed on Daniel's shoulders, heavy.

"We don't know yet. There are some tests they can run to find out."

"Is-is-is he really dead?"

"Yes."

"Mr. Daniel." The boy's voice, filled with anguish, rose. "I didn't mean to kill him."

"Benny, you didn't kill him. The car crash did."

"He was supposed to hold on to the wheel. He wanted me to shoot at the guys in the other car. They were shooting at us. I was too scared. I had the gun, but I couldn't. Mr. Juice was supposed to be driving. He drank a bunch of stuff before we left, and he had needles. I didn't think he should drive. They always say don't drink and drive. I told him I'd do it, but he didn't believe me."

The rush of words ran faster and faster until they ended with hysteria-laden sobs. Daniel searched for words that would bring Benny down — into his arms. "It's not your fault. He was an adult. He should have known better."

"Maybe I killed my dad. I didn't mean it."

"Nobody blames you. I promise. No one."

"What happens to me now?" Sobs fractured the words.

Determination gripped Daniel. This was his child in every way that truly counted. "I'm your foster dad, Benny. I'll fight for you, but first, I have to take you to the hospital."

"No." Outright hostility. Fear.

"Benny, you have to put the gun down so I can come up there and get you. I won't let anything bad happen to you. I want the doctors to look at you to make sure you're all right."

"What then?"

"I'll take you home with me."

"For good?"

A flutter of hope in his voice. Maybe. Daniel couldn't be sure. Hope would be better than the angry defeat of a few moments before. "I can't promise that, not yet, but I do promise I'll do everything humanly possible to make it happen."

Daniel shut his mouth and forced himself to swallow.

More sobs. Daniel gripped the ladder rung harder. Nicole patted his arm. He eased up a little.

"I want you to be my dad."

Daniel closed his eyes and hung his head, dizziness threatening to make the room go dark. "Me, too. But first you have to put the gun down and let me come up. Or you come down. Whichever you want."

Tiny particles of hay fell through the slots in the loft floor. The boards creaked until Daniel saw Benny's dirty face peeking through the trapdoor. Massive purple and green bruises covered his face. Dried blood darkened his lips and nose. His eyes were almost swollen shut. His nose had been flattened. Daniel's stomach heaved. "Benny, where's the gun?"

The boy held it up with two fingers.

"Can you lay it down on the hay for me?"

Benny laid it down. Then he sat on the edge, his scuffed shoes on the top rung of the ladder. His face scrunched up. Tears flowed down his cheeks. He began to rock back and forth.

Daniel pulled himself up the ladder, hands and feet stumbling over each other to get to him. He dropped on the hay next to Benny, folded the boy's thin body into his arms, and felt the trembling blossom into full-scale shaking. "It's over, it's all over."

"I was scared." Benny sniffed. "I'm not a crybaby. I'm not, but I was so scared. He kept hurting me. I made him mad. It was my fault, but I just wanted to come home. I was scared."

He stuck two grimy fists inside Daniel's

jacket and grabbed his shirt in a tight grip. His runny nose, dirt, and tears stained the white shirt. Daniel's throat closed. He struggled to get the words out. "I know. I was scared, too. It's okay to cry."

"You get scared?"

"All the time." Daniel looked over the boy's head at Nicole, standing below, looking up at them, tears on her cheeks. "Sometimes, I even cry."

"The ambulance is on its way," she said, her voice hoarse.

"No." Benny burrowed deeper into Daniel's arms. "Home. I wanna go home. I want to have pizza night and movies."

Daniel ran his hands over the boy's arms and back. "We have to make sure you're okay. Where does it hurt? How bad did he hurt you?"

"I'm okay. You've got me."

Daniel choked on the answer. "Yes, I do."

CHAPTER THIRTY-SEVEN

Alex found Deborah banging on a vending machine outside the hospital's closed cafeteria. She looked as exhausted as he felt. They'd been waiting for more than an hour for some word on Benny's condition. She smacked the machine again. "It took my money and didn't give me the sandwich." She said it like two dollars in quarters had been the last of her earthly treasures.

"You poor thing." He tugged a handful of change from his pocket and began depositing the coins in the slot. A few seconds later he handed her a packaged roast beef sandwich.

She sniffed and took it. "Show-off."

After selecting a ham sandwich for himself, Alex sat down on the closest bench and motioned for her to join him. In the cold light of the hallway, the events in the dusky barn on a stormy night seemed distant and surreal. Had he really had his arm around

407

her? He had. "Do you think this qualifies as a date? I'm buying you dinner after all."

Her hair was wet and plastered to her head, makeup long gone from her face. Her clothes were muddy and wrinkled. She looked beautiful to him — and confused by the question. "Why?"

"People sometimes kiss on a first date." Lame. The words sounded really lame said aloud like that. "Or hug."

She stared at him, the look on her face a mixture of consternation, fear, and pleasure. He was sure there was a little pleasure in there. Embarrassment tinged her brittle laugh. "I don't kiss on first dates. Not anymore, anyway."

"Well, we ate those sandwiches in the car, and then we walked in the woods and survived the storm and Benny shooting at us, I think we're up to maybe even a third date." He unwrapped his sandwich, glancing sideways at her as he did. Their gazes intertwined. He went back to his sandwich. Ham on a soggy bun.

"Then you have a very weird idea of what a date is." She took a bite and chewed slowly. "This bread is really gross."

"What would happen if I kissed you right now?" Happy endings for Benny and Daniel. Alex wanted happy endings, too. He wanted to make a commitment. The *C* word didn't scare him anymore. He laid the sandwich on the bench and swiveled so he faced her.

Her expression was full of trepidation. "I don't know."

"Would you run from me? Or shoot me?"

Her gaze was glued to the sandwich in her hands. She plucked the lettuce from it and dropped it in the plastic wrap. "I wouldn't shoot you. People go to jail for that. I wouldn't run. I'm not a coward. But I might slug you in the nose."

"Fair enough." He touched her chin, making her look up. "Are you afraid to find out?"

"Now?" Her cheeks turned a rosy color that made her even prettier. "Here?"

"Where could be safer than a hospital? And it would only be a *little* kiss. I promise not to scare you." She could never know that he was just as scared as she was. "Let's see if we can trust each other that far."

He took her sandwich and laid it next to his. His hands were shaking, but it was okay. So were hers. He leaned forward, stifling the urge to touch the soft skin of her long neck and then wrap his arms around her in a tight hug. As his face inched toward hers, he looked into those blue eyes. He closed his eyes and let his lips touch hers. They were soft against his. She didn't pull away. Neither did he. It was the sweetest kiss he'd ever experienced.

When he opened his eyes, tears slid down her cheeks. He brushed them away with his fingertips. She sighed but didn't flinch. "All right?"

She ducked her head and picked up her sandwich. "All right."

"Then it's a start."

"There you are. I need you two."

Alex looked up to see Samuel striding toward them. "Get over to Chavez's place. Cooper's meeting you there. This guy has been playing you all along."

Alex stood. "He was in on it."

"Yep. He gave Morin the information that led him to Benny. Go get him."

Alex was already moving, Deborah right behind him. They made the twenty-minute drive to Chavez's trailer in half that. Deborah didn't speak, and Alex was too focused on his anger at Tómas Chavez to attempt small talk. The guy had given Juice Morin the information he needed to use Benny as a pawn in a drug dealer's game. He'd probably murdered his own daughter. And he was still walking around free, enjoying life. That would end now.

Cooper was parked a distance from

Chavez's fence line. He slid into the back-seat. "Let's get this over with," he said as they drove forward.

At the steps to the trailer, Alex slid his gun from his holster and nodded at Cooper. Deborah did the same. Cooper rapped on Chavez's trailer door. With any luck, Chavez wouldn't decide to shoot first, talk later. One shoot-out a day was more than enough.

No answer.

"Again."

Cooper pounded harder. The door opened a crack. A young woman clad in a skimpy, red negligee peered out. "Cut it out, dudes. I'm sleeping in here."

Cooper stuck his foot in the door before she could shut it and flashed his badge. "Is Tómas Chavez here?"

The woman — who looked more like a teenager now that Alex got a good look at her — pushed tangled curls from her face and frowned at him. "No. He ain't. Now go away."

Alex shoved past her through the door "Yes, we'd like to come in, thank you."

Deborah slid in behind him. "Mr. Chavez is the homeowner, right? I guess that would make you a trespasser if he's not here."

"No, he's my . . . my significant other." Her lips turned down in a pout. "You know, that common-law thing. We're married."

"Right." Alex glanced around. Empty beer bottles, overflowing ashtrays, empty pizza boxes. A royal mess in sharp contrast with the day Alex had first come here to tell the man about the remains found on the ranch. Chavez's mental state seemed to be deteriorating rapidly. "So where's hubby now? Are you expecting him soon?"

She snatched a cigarette from the coffee table and then a lighter. The nighty didn't cover much, and she wasn't wearing anything under it.

Alex fixed his gaze on the light fixtures. "Ma'am, we need to know where your . . . where Mr. Chavez is."

She studied the cigarette's glowing tip as smoke curled around her. "I think he's out of town."

Deborah fanned smoke away from her face. "You think?"

"He didn't say exactly where he was going, but he packed a gym bag with some underwear and stuff."

"Look, little girl, Tómas Chavez may have been involved in the death of one of his own children. He definitely helped engineer the kidnapping of a young boy." Cooper's hand went to the cuffs on his belt. "If you know anything about it, you're an accessory. We can take you down and charge you with aggravated kidnapping. Go change into something decent. Now."

"You don't have to be ugly about it." Big turtle tears appeared in the corner of eyes framed by smudges of mascara. She sat on the couch with a thud. "I didn't have nothing to do with no kidnapping. Tómas doesn't tell me anything. He treats me like a kid, but I think he said something about going somewhere. . . . He took the truck so I don't have no way of getting home, and he didn't pay the phone bill so I can't call and the battery of my cell phone is dead and —"

"Going where, Miss . . ."

"Ana. Ana Limon." She stubbed out the cigarette in the overflowing ashtray. The stench of stale ashes billowed from it. She snagged a semi-soggy piece of paper from the table. "I think he mentioned Kansas. See here, it says Kansas City on it."

The curl of her lips and the way her eyebrows shot up told Alex she was flabbergasted at the idea that anyone would want to go to a place like Kansas. He plucked the paper from her fingers. It was an American Airlines ticket confirmation. The reservation had been made online. Tómas Chavez was already on his way. He had a connecting flight in Dallas that would take him to Kansas City.

Deborah started for the door. Alex beat her by a half step.

"You ain't gonna arrest me?" the woman called after them.

"Maybe later." Alex pounded down the steps and across the yard.

"At least give me a ride somewhere!" She stood in the door, hands on her hips. "Come on, don't abandon me, too!"

"We'll call you a taxi." Alex didn't look back. He didn't need any more images of her half-naked body in his head. "I promise."

Alex jammed the key into the unmarked unit's ignition. Deborah slid in on the passenger side and Cooper popped the back door shut at the same time. "You think he's figured out that's where his kids are?"

"I think he figured out his PI's disappearance had nothing to do with retirement. Our messing around in this stuff must have given him the idea to do some investigating of his own." Alex slammed his foot on the gas. "We need to get to Simon Phillips's shop. We'll come back for your car later."

The door of Simon Phillips's detective agency stood open when they arrived ten minutes later. Alex pulled his weapon. He

414

nodded. Deborah stepped inside, Cooper right behind her.

The place had been trashed. Filing cabinets overturned, chairs on their sides, lamps upended. Alex advanced slowly, training the gun from side to side. He veered right, Deborah a close second, toward the back office where the records were kept.

BeBe Hamilton's body sprawled on the floor behind Phillips's desk. Her platinum blond hair tangled around her head. Mascara dried in tear tracks on her still face. Her blue eyes were wide and empty. Anger and mind-numbing fatigue cancelled out the adrenaline of the past few minutes. Alex lowered his Glock with a shaky hand and knelt to touch her neck even though it was obvious she'd been dead for a while. "Chavez was here."

Deborah began to pace. "This guy is really testing my patience. He's an animal. We need to find him and put him a cage."

Alex stood. "That's the plan."

A resigned look on his face, Cooper stuck his weapon in its holster. "We're in PD territory — you want to call it in?"

Alex made the call, and they waited. No one bothered to talk. Nothing to say. They'd led Chavez right to the woman.

It didn't take long before the place was

overrun. According to the ME investigator, it looked like someone had used his bare hands to strangle Hamilton. When Cooper stomped from the building, Alex left Deborah talking to an investigator and followed the sheriff's detective. "So I guess we can assume Chavez knows where in Kansas he needs to go."

"Yep." Cooper tugged his cell phone from his pocket. "Can you handle wrapping things up here?"

"Sure, what are you going to do?"

"I need to call my boss. I'm going to Kansas."

Alex held up a hand, palm out. "Wait. I'm going with you."

Cooper adjusted his Stetson, his lips pursed for a second. "I'd be glad to have the backup. Get someone to handle this, and we'll run by your place on the way to the airport."

"I think Deborah should go, too."

Cooper's shaggy eyebrows rose and fell. "You do, huh? What does she think? What does your boss think? We don't have a lot of time for negotiation here — or time for office romances."

Alex glanced back to see the guys from the ME's office wheeling BeBe Hamilton's body to the coroner's van. "Deborah's an outstanding homicide detective, Coop. You want her on your team when things get hot. And I have a gut feeling they'll get really hot in Kansas."

CHAPTER THIRTY-EIGHT

Deborah stood in the foyer after the ME's crew pushed the gurney through the door. What now? Tómas Chavez was probably on an airplane headed to Kansas where he'd do who knows what to whom. She smacked the wall with her fist.

"Hey, don't take it out on the wall."

Alex walked toward her, an odd look on his face. She studied his expression. He wanted something. Uncomfortable, she crossed her arms. He needed to focus on the job and not her. "This guy is a piece of work, Alex."

"So come to Kansas with us. We'll catch him and put him away."

That was not what she was expecting. "Kansas? You want me to go to Kansas? Why not let the authorities there deal with this guy?"

"It's some little town in the middle of nowhere with no police force. Just a couple of sheriff's deputies. Cooper is going. If he goes, I go. You should come, too."

Deborah caught something in Alex's tone. He wanted her to go. Not because of the case. Yeah, because of the case, but also because of the other thing. The kiss. This was going to complicate things. She couldn't handle complicated. Not right now. "I don't think so."

"Cooper is making the arrangements. I called Sarge. He said to go. He wants Chavez as much as we do. And whether Chavez killed Nina or the wife did it, we need to bring them both in."

"What do you need me for?"

"Don't you want to see this through? Don't you want to get the guy who showed Morin how to get his dirty hands on Benny? And think about that little girl. You saw her bones, dumped in a shallow grave —"

"Stop. Stop it. I get it." She turned her back on him. Tried to breathe. She teetered on changing her mind. If she went, what would that mean? Anything? She wanted to go. The thought surprised her. For the first time in a long time, she could have something she wanted. Alex was offering her a chance. Fear seeped in. What if she couldn't overcome her fears? It wasn't fair to Alex. He would end up hurt. But he was right.

There was Benny. And Nina. "Fine, I'll go. As a fellow officer of the law. Nothing more. And I want my own room."

The look he gave her singed her hair. "I would never . . . don't worry. Two hotel rooms and Cooper as a chaperone. You have nothing to worry about."

Right. Then why did she feel like she'd just agreed to play Russian roulette.

Daniel wandered through the hallway, looking for the vending machines. The doctor had finally sedated Benny so he could put stitches in his forehead. The little guy had become too agitated. His body shook so much it scared Daniel. He wanted to bring him some hot cocoa for when he woke up. And then take him home where he could feel safe. The machines should be around here somewhere. He rounded a corner. Susana stood in front of a coffee machine talking to Nicole. She was still here. For some reason, that surprised him. She'd stood by him through the search and the rescue. How long would that last? Maybe she was through being mad. Maybe they had a chance. He moved forward.

Nicole's gaze met his. She started to say something. Then she stopped. Her gaze skipped over his shoulder.

A tall, athletic looking man strode into the room. He had eyes for Nicole only. "Nicole, you haven't been answering your cell. Your mother said I would find you here. We were supposed to —" He stopped, his gaze going to Susana and Daniel. "I understand they found the child."

Nicole moved toward him. "I'm sorry I didn't call you back. It's been crazy. Daniel needed a ride. Then they found Benny, and it's just been . . . You really shouldn't have come here."

Susana held up a cup of coffee. "I'm just going to take this to Samuel." She scurried through the door like a pack of pit bulls was chasing her.

The man's face flushed a painful brick red all the way to the roots of his blond hair. He stuck his hand out at Daniel. "I'm Joshua Brown. I work with Nicole. We had a . . . we were supposed to . . . I just. . . ."

"You just what?" Daniel ignored the hand. White-hot anger raced through him like an all-consuming fire. He glanced at Nicole. "Is this the boyfriend? You called him, and he came running?"

"He's not my boyfriend, Daniel." Nicole stepped between them. "He was concerned when I didn't answer my phone so he called the house and my mother told him I was here."

Joshua's hand dropped. He stuck it in his pocket. "We had some things we were planning to do this afternoon, and then she didn't show up at the office so I called. I was concerned when I found out she was at the hospital."

Daniel tensed on the balls of his feet, a second away from a fistfight "We? There is no 'we.' Nicole and I — we're the 'we.' "

He brushed past Nicole so he could crowd the other man. Joshua was a foot taller and muscular — for a lawyer — and hadn't recently been hospitalized with the season's worst strain of influenza.

"Daniel. Please don't do this." Nicole inched toward him, her tone placating. "What did the doctors say? Is Benny okay?"

"Morin hit him, threw him around, beat him with a leather belt, subjected him to a car crash. Fixed it so he could watch a man die. Terrorized him. Other than that, he's fine." Daniel couldn't keep the sarcasm caged. It was an ugly animal scratching its way out.

"I'll go. I shouldn't have come. I apologize." Joshua backed toward the door. Daniel recognized the emotions on his face. An agony of confusion and desire for something he wasn't sure he could have. Daniel knew that feeling. "You two will want to talk."

"Wait. I have a question for you." Daniel grabbed the man's arm.

Joshua shrugged Daniel's hand off, but stopped moving. "What?"

"My wife says you're a Christian."

"Yes, I am." Joshua's eyebrows tented. He cocked his head to one side. "But I don't claim to be perfect. Surely you don't either."

"So you're familiar with the Bible's teachings on divorce?"

"I am." His gaze met Daniel's squarely. "I am very aware of what it says. I'm divorced myself. I know what you're going through. Both of you."

"Yet, you chose to make it harder. By getting involved with my wife."

"I'm not — I didn't intend to make it harder." Joshua stuck his hands back in his pockets, his shoulders bowed in dejection. "You of all people should understand where I'm coming from. Nicole is an intelligent, beautiful woman. And she's unhappy in her marriage. I could make her happy. Because I care about her. Like you do."

He stopped, looking as if he expected blows to rain down on him.

"No, not like I do." All the anger drained away. Daniel saw in Joshua's face the powerful emotion that buffeted him day after day. He did understand. The difference was that he was Nicole's husband. Still . . . "Sorry, bud, I've got sixteen years on you. You're too late."

"I believe that's up to the lady." Joshua did an about-face and disappeared through the doorway.

Nicole brushed past Daniel and ran to the door. "Josh, I'm sorry . . . I'm sorry!"

Daniel tugged her back. "Make no mistake, Nikki, you are still my wife. Until the ink is dry on the divorce decree, you're still my wife. Don't disrespect me by bringing this man around me. Do you understand?"

Tears stained her face and her lips quivered, but her chin came up. "I didn't invite him here. He came on his own. Because he cares. He's a caring person."

Daniel let his hands drop. She didn't move away. They were so close he could have kissed her by leaning forward ever so slightly. He was furious with her, yet all he could think about was kissing her.

"Will Benny recover?" She eased away from him a half step, her gaze locked in his.

"They had to put stitches in his lip and his head. He got so frantic they sedated him. I wanted to get a cup of hot chocolate for him when he wakes up. He's got cracked ribs, bruised kidneys, a broken finger and dozens of contusions and abrasions. He couldn't stop shivering. I don't know if he's cold or still scared or in pain."

"I'm so thankful you got him back alive."

He grabbed her hand and hung on to it for a minute. "Thank you. The doctor was talking about keeping him for a day or so, but I convinced them to let me take him home. He needs to be someplace where he feels safe."

"Is he talking about it?"

"No. He's too traumatized. He thinks that 'Juice' guy was his dad."

"Was he?"

"I've asked for DNA testing. For Benny's sake, I hope the answer is no."

"In the long run, it won't matter."

Her voice was curiously soft. He raised his gaze from the floor. "What do you mean? If he's —"

"It won't matter because Benny has you, the best real dad he could ever have."

Daniel swallowed hard. He was too tired to keep the emotion from his voice. It came out in a hoarse whisper. "Nikki, there's nothing you can do here. Go home. Be with the kids. Tell them I miss them."

"What about you? Are they going to re-admit you?"

"No. No way." Like Benny, all he wanted to do was go home, sit in a chair, and watch a movie — preferably a comedy. "I'm fine. I'm past the worst of it."

Nikki's hand, soft and cool, brushed his forehead. "The fever's down. You should ask the doctors if you're contagious . . . you don't want to give . . ."

"I will."

"He could stay with me."

"I'm fine."

"Are you sure?"

No, but what else could he say. "Yes."

"Fine." She ducked her head for a second. "If you . . . need . . . if Benny needs any-thing . . . if you need any help with him . . . let me know."

Daniel stood, head bowed, unsure of the meaning of what he'd heard.

"Nikki?"

She was already gone.

CHAPTER THIRTY-NINE

Daniel pulled the blankets around Benny's shoulders and watched the boy's face for a few seconds. Reluctantly, he turned off the lamp next to his bed. A nightlight on the bedroom wall cast a tepid light that allowed him to make sure Benny's chest rose and fell. His eyes were closed, but Daniel couldn't be sure he slept. Sighing, he trudged to the door.

"Mr. Daniel."

He turned back. "What's the matter?"

"Could you leave the door open, please?"

"No problem, big guy. I'll be right downstairs if you need me. I'll leave the light on in the hallway, too."

Benny's eyes closed again.

Daniel teetered down the stairs, his legs almost too weak to carry him. He picked up the delivery box from the coffee table. Most of the pizza remained untouched. Neither of them had an appetite. Maybe tomorrow.

Benny loved cold pizza.

The hours had bled together, hours at the emergency room, hours of police interrogation. The doctors had added malnourishment and dehydration to the litany of Benny's physical ailments, all of which would heal themselves.

The emotional wounds — that was another story. Benny had clung to Daniel, refusing to be left alone with doctors or police officers. He had answered questions in tight, monosyllabic responses. Not once at the hospital had he cried. When they'd decided that Daniel's illness was abated and what Benny needed was familiar, safe surroundings, they'd finally agreed to let Daniel take him home. His only conversation in the car had been to ask for pizza. Pizza and a movie.

Curled up on the couch, leaning on Daniel, still he hadn't said a word about his captor. Still hadn't talked about the things that had happened to him. Sooner or later they would have to come out. Daniel would ask Susana to work with him when she returned from her honeymoon. For now Benny needed to sleep and eat and just be.

The doorbell rang. Daniel dumped the box in the trashcan in the kitchen but was tempted to ignore the doorbell. It was almost eleven. He had no desire to talk to anyone and the mind-numbing exhaustion made it hard for him to shuffle to the door. The bell rang again, the sound insistent.

"Who is it?"

"It's me. Chris."

"Chris?" He fumbled with the chain and jerked the door open. Chris stood on the doorstep, eyes red and swollen, shivering in a T-shirt and pajama bottoms. "Son, what are you doing here? How did you get here?"

"Can I come in? I'm freezing! Please."

"Of course, you can come in." Daniel grabbed his son and pulled him against his chest, letting the door slam behind him. He took a good look, head to toe — no obvious injuries — before wrapping him in a hug. The boy shook in his arms. Daniel tightened the hug. "What happened? What's wrong? How'd you get here?"

The boy broke away and sank onto the couch. Fresh tears rolled down his cheeks. "I rode my bike."

"Ten miles? Across major roads in the dark? Why? If you wanted to talk to me, why didn't you call?"

"Grandma wouldn't let me. She said you had your hands full with Benny." A half sob made Daniel sink onto the couch and put an arm around his son. "She said you'd call me when you had time. I said that wasn't right. I wanted to see Benny. I wanted to see you guys."

"Where's your mom?"

"I don't know. I think she went to talk to that other guy — the one she — the one I told you about."

Anger burned through Daniel. She couldn't stay away from the guy one night. "How did you get out of the house?"

"I waited until Grandma fell asleep and just went out through the garage. It was easy. She was snoring." His son grinned a little through the tears. "When she snores, that means she's really asleep."

"You could've been hit by a car. You don't even have a light on that bike, and it's a very long way, Christopher."

"Don't be mad, Pop, please don't be mad. I just wanted to see you and Benny, and you know, *be* with you."

Daniel knew he should be furious, but all he could muster was heartsick. "Benny's —"

The phone rang. Nicole had probably already figured it out by now. He grabbed the receiver.

"Daniel, is Christopher —"

"Yeah, he's here."

"Is he all right? I knew he'd go there. My

mother is frantic. I'm on my way —"

Daniel waited for her to take a breath and then broke in. "He's fine. Just cold. Let him stay, please, Nicole, just this once. He wants to see Benny, and he's already asleep. They could spend some time together in the morning, eat breakfast. It'd be good for Benny."

The line crackled with static for a few seconds. "He can stay." An odd note colored his wife's words. "I'd like to come over anyway, if you don't mind. There's something I want to say to you."

He fought to keep his composure. He didn't want to know what she'd been discussing with Joshua. Was she coming to demand the divorce? Surely not tonight. "Something you can't say on the phone?"

"Yes. I need to tell you something."

When the doorbell rang ten minutes later, Daniel forced himself to turn the knob and open the door. The sense of impending doom saturated him. This was it. The final showdown. He'd sent Chris upstairs to take a shower. The boy didn't need to hear this conversation.

Nicole stood in the doorway in a long, black leather coat, her hair swept up in a ponytail, her face anxious. "Can I come in?"

431

"Sorry. Sure." Daniel moved aside, rubbing his hands on the kitchen towel he'd forgotten he still held. She stepped inside. Stopped. So near him he could have touched her face.

"Where's Christopher?"

"In the shower. I told him to get ready for bed. I figured whatever you . . . whatever you came to say, he didn't need to hear."

She nodded and glanced around as if she was looking at his apartment with a new view. "How is Benny?"

"Passed out."

"What about Deborah Smith?"

Daniel straightened. "What? What about Deborah?"

"Are you in love with her?"

Daniel laughed, the sound slightly hysterical in his ears. He couldn't help himself. "You must still love me, Nikki, if you're jealous of Deborah. She's a friend who's trying to get sober and stay sober. I'm trying to be supportive. That's it. I promise."

Nicole slapped her purse on the coffee table and sat down on the couch. "Good. Sit down. Now, let's talk about Benny. Will they let you keep him?"

Nonplussed by the lack of transition, Daniel sat. "At least until we go to a court hearing next week. I'm going to fight for him."

She studied the carpet, then drew a long breath. "Do you want me to go with you?"

She had to know how he would interpret that. What was she really offering? Why?

"Do you want me to go to court with you?"

"That depends."

"On what?"

"I want to adopt Benny. It would be a lot easier to convince them to let me do that if I were —"

"Married?"

"I am married."

"So I should go to court with you?"

She threw the words down like a gauntlet. He stared at her. She stared back, the emotion in her face telling him something, but for the life of him, he couldn't be sure what. "I won't lie to the court, Nicole. If you go with me, that means you're in it for the long haul."

"Fine. Name the time and the place."

"Pardon me?" The words hummed in Daniel's ears.

"Did you mean what you said about quitting your job?"

Everything came into focus, into this one simple question. "It's already done."

"What will you do now?"

He shrugged. "I don't know. I'm out on

the high wire without a net."

Her eyebrows popped up. "That's so un-like you. I'm impressed." She hesitated. "I wonder . . . I wonder if you can forgive me."

Daniel was afraid if he opened his mouth, he would do something incredibly unmanly, like cry.

"I don't want a divorce." She kept talking, saving him from himself. "If you're willing to sacrifice your job for our marriage, I'd be crazy not to love you."

Her hand tightened on his. "Seeing you on the floor in Pastor Wilson's office . . . it was the worst moment of my life. It's one thing to be apart from you because I said so, when I controlled the situation. It's completely another to realize I might never see or talk to you again. Everything was totally beyond my control. I had to give it up to God, knowing only He has control. I realized I need you, I love you, and I'm stuck with you, for as long as He lets me have you. I'm hoping that it's a long time because we have lost so much time; we have so much to make up."

He managed to swallow his emotions long enough to string words together. "You need me?"

"Yes. Do you still need me?"

Daniel opened his mouth and shut it.

After a second, he was able to get the question out. "What about Brown?"

"I went to Joshua's house tonight to tell him — that's where I was when Christopher snuck out. I realized when he kissed me so soon after you did that my feelings for you have been knit together by sixteen years of shared experiences and hopes and dreams. Joshua barely scratched the surface." She sighed, her face lined with sadness. "I feel horrible about what I've done to him. I told him it was a case of temporary insanity. He agreed. But he also conceded that he had told me he would stand aside if I decided to try to make my marriage work. And I've decided. I want it to work."

"How will you and Joshua . . . I mean you're both employed by the same law firm." Daniel tried to imagine that. Could they deal with it? Could he? Anything to have her back. Anything.

"Not for long. That wouldn't be fair to him. None of this is, but there's no way we could continue to work together. I'm thinking about going back to criminal law, maybe even the public defender's office. I need a change. I need to get back to the kind of law that made me become a lawyer to start with."

"You're sure?"

Her look was so sharp he could feel it probing inside him. "The question is are you sure? We can't get back together if you'll resent everything that's happened. You won't hold it over my head and make my life miserable? I need to know now because I couldn't handle that."

"No. I won't do that." He'd have to work at forgetting it. Forgiving would come first; forgetting would take longer. "There's something you have to do for me." He lifted his free hand to her face, touching her soft skin. She didn't move a muscle, her gaze locked in his.

"What?"

"We keep going to the counseling sessions."

She didn't flinch. "That's a given. The things that have happened, the words that have been said, they won't disappear overnight. It'll take some time for us to trust each other."

"The kids need to go, too."

"Absolutely."

They stared at each other.

"How will we do this?"

Daniel's heart resumed beating in the old regular rhythm for the first time in a year and a half. He knew how he wanted to handle it, but he didn't want to scare her away. He wanted his life back, the kids, the house, the family vacations, the Sunday mornings at church, the barbecues in the backyard, the spontaneous basketball games, the late night movies. He wanted it all. "Well, we could start with a hug. I need to know I'm the only guy — besides family — whom you're planning to hug from now on."

She leaned into him. The expression on her face was an open invitation.

A second later, he had her in his arms, his mouth on hers.

"Danny."

It was a few minutes before he could answer. "Yes."

She leaned away from him, her head tilted to one side. "You feel warm. Are you sure you should be sitting here kissing me?"

"Absolutely sure."

She touched his forehead. "What did the doctors say? They tried to keep you and you insisted on bringing Benny home, didn't you?"

"Wrong. They said I suffered from unrequited love and as soon as the love of my life returned the fever would lift."

"Danny, I'm being serious."

He grinned. "Well, they were wrong. The fever is definitely rising, not falling." He kissed her some more. "But it has nothing to do with the flu."

She laughed, a breathless sound, reciprocated for a few seconds, and then pulled away. "I think we should consider getting married."

He pushed back so he could see her face. "We are married."

"Again, I mean."

He shook his head, puzzled. "What?" Tears trickled down her pink cheeks. Her mouth was red from his kisses.

"I think we need to stand before God and put ourselves back together again."

"You want us to renew our vows?" Daniel had a sudden image of wounds being sewn closed.

"Yes."

"And until then."

"It'll be like we're dating again. You could ask me out to lunch. I could cook dinner for you. We could go to the movies."

Daniel stifled a groan even as he saw the beauty of the suggestion. A new beginning. "So when were you thinking we'd have this marriage ceremony?" He pulled her close again so he could bury his face in her hair and inhale her scent.

"Well, I have to buy a dress, and we have to get the church, and there's the cake and the invitations." She pushed his head up. "And vows to write and memorize."

He managed a weak smile. "So two weeks should be plenty of time."

She leaned into him, the jasmine scent making him dizzy, the feel of her skin under his hands so soft he couldn't stop touching her. "I might be able to get it together in ten days."

"How about six?"

They both laughed, an unfamiliar chorus. "In the meantime, I suggest we get reacquainted."

"Danny."

"All engaged couples kiss."

"Fine. But I'm leaving in five minutes."

"Fifteen."

"Ten."

Time was short. He focused on kissing, not talking.

"Hey! Mom? Is that . . . ? Dad?"

Daniel glanced up. Christopher stood at the top of the stairs, a puzzled look on his face. "Go to bed, Son, your mother and I are talking."

A delighted grin danced across his son's face. "That doesn't look like talking to me."

"Do what your father says, Christopher." Nicole laughed softly, her gaze on Daniel's face. "He has five minutes of talking left,

439

and then I'm going because he needs to rest and get his strength back for the big wedding."

Daniel didn't look to see if his son obeyed. He was busy talking.

CHAPTER FORTY

Abilene, Kansas

Alex slammed the cruiser door and leaned back in the seat next to Deborah. She turned away from him and peered out the window as if fascinated by the view of barren trees that dotted the autumn Kansas landscape. She'd been quiet during most of the trip. He'd caught her looking at him a couple of times, her expression confused. It had been late when they'd arrived at the airport in Topeka, so he hadn't tried to talk to her on the drive to Abilene.

The kiss had been too much too soon. That had to be it. He wanted to bang his head against the door. He was always doing that. Charging in instead of using a little finesse.

Detective Boyd Baker had the lined face of a middle-aged man coming up on senior citizenship. He shifted his belt under an ample belly that hung over his uniform

441

pants before putting his hands on the wheel. Cooper sat in the front next to his crony. Baker pulled on to the street and headed out of Abilene. The sign said the road they were on was Old Highway 44.

Baker had the heater blasting, but Alex zipped up his overcoat anyway. He'd been freezing from the second he'd stepped from the airplane. The wind blew across plains, even though Kansas wasn't as flat as he'd imagined it. "So you haven't run across Chavez yet?"

"Not yet, but I've been watching the Dodge place. Like I told Coop, I played it cool when I went out there. Just said I was checking up on their horses. Dodge was his usual arrogant self."

"So you got a good look around?"

"Yeah. The place is falling down around them. Ezra is no farmer. He lived alone for several years. Then all of a sudden about five years ago, this woman shows up, and he introduces her to everyone as his sister. Says her name is Clarisse Dodge, a widow with four kids." Baker swerved to avoid a dog in the road. He didn't miss a beat. "According to Dodge, she never married the guy — that's why she's still a Dodge, he says. I talked to the neighbors on both sides. Also called the high school and the middle school. We got records on twin girls at the high school, Estrella and Esperanza. Got two boys at the middle school, Domingo and Francisco. Funny names, huh? All registered as Dodges."

The names were definitely funny the way Baker pronounced them with that Kansas accent.

"What do the neighbors say about them?"

"Quiet. Keep to themselves. The kids stay close to home. No extracurricular activities. The mom lets the girls go to church with a neighbor sometimes. That's it."

Twenty minutes later they pulled into the yard. The Dodge house needed a coat of paint. A tired-looking pickup truck sat on blocks in the yard, one tire missing. They exited the SUV and an equally tired-looking woman trotted from the house and along the porch, hands tangled up in a dishtowel, a scrawny kid about eleven or twelve trailing behind her. "Detective Baker, you back again so soon?" She wrung the towel in her hands. "Ezra's not here. He shoulda been back an hour ago. I don't know what's keeping him."

"These here law enforcement folks have come all the way from San Antone to talk to you, ma'am." Baker had his cowboy hat between his hands. The sun made his bald head shine. "And then your . . . husband."

Clarisse's face blanched white. Her hand went to the railing on the porch steps. "I ain't got no husband. You best wait until Ezra comes back. I don't want to talk to you."

Alex caught Cooper's glance. The sheriff's detective coughed once, twice. "I'm sorry, ma'am, I seem to have something in my throat. Could I trouble you for a glass of water or maybe a cup of coffee, if you've got a pot on? I'm not used to this cold weather."

She didn't move.

"It'd be the hospitable thing to do." Baker slapped his rotund belly. "Wouldn't want these folks to think we're standoffish here in Kansas, would we?"

Clarisse twisted her hands around the dishtowel. "I . . . okay . . . well, fine. Detective. . . . Detective Cooper was it? I'll bring it out to you."

Cooper coughed some more as he followed her up the steps. "I'll just come in with you, ma'am. Living in Texas has thinned my blood — can't take this cold. My colleagues are younger and a lot tougher."

As soon as they disappeared from sight, Alex turned to the young boy who was doing flips over the porch railing. His shirt and pants were threadbare, and one of his dirty sneakers had a hole in the toe. "What's your name?"

Alex eased into the porch swing. Deborah leaned against the railing, her back to the boy, making a show of watching the road.

The boy stopped flipping and plopped down on the edge of the porch, breathless. "Frankie."

"Hey, Frankie. I'm Alex. You know Deputy Baker, right?"

The boy nodded and shrugged.

"Where are your brother and sisters?" Baker asked, his voice casual.

"Esperanza and Estrella are looking for eggs in the hen house. Dom's slopping the hogs."

"You don't have any chores?"

"I got a fever. Ma says I gotta stay inside until it goes down. 'Course when Uncle Ezra gets back —" The boy stopped. His gaze dropped to the ground.

"What'll happen then, when your uncle gets home?" Baker pulled a pack of bubble gum from his windbreaker pocket, pulled out a piece, unwrapped it, popped it in his mouth. Frankie watching, licked his lips. Baker held out the package to Alex. "Want some?"

Alex took a piece and unwrapped it. Baker offered a piece to Deborah, but she already had a mouth full of whatever her flavor of the day was. After a long moment, Baker swung his arm toward the boy. "I don't suppose you chew bubble gum?"

Frankie snatched a piece from the top. "Well, he don't set much store by this being sick stuff. He says walk it off, work it off. Otherwise, I'm gonna grow up to be soft. That's what he says."

"So what does your dad say?"

"My dad." The boy's features froze. "My dad . . . he don't say . . . he . . . he's dead. Yeah, he's dead." The panic eased a little as if the boy had grasped onto something. "He's dead."

Alex blew a big bubble. It popped. The sticky pink stuff covered his lips and the edge of his nose. The boy laughed, Deborah and Baker with him.

"Frankie, did you have a sister named Nina?" Baker asked the question while Alex picked gum from his face.

Frankie stopped laughing. "I want my sisters . . . I want Estrella. I don't want to talk no more." He got to his feet, the panic back.

Deborah stepped in front of him. "Why don't you stay here with Detective Baker, and I'll bring your sisters to you."

"I'll go with you." Alex stood and started down the steps.

"You've got gum all over your face." The look on her face stopped him dead in his tracks. "Maybe you should go get cleaned up. They're just girls. I can handle them."

She whirled and walked away.

"Fine." Alex ignored the grin on Baker's face. "I'll just check on Coop."

Clarisse's kitchen smelled like rotting bananas and coffee grounds. Alex found Cooper sitting at the kitchen table and Clarisse pouring coffee into two heavy ceramic mugs.

He rapped on the door frame and then moved into the room. Clarisse jumped and sloshed coffee down the side of the mug. It dripped on the cracked, black-and-white-checked linoleum. "What do you want? You got a frog in your throat, too?"

"Just a little bubble gum on my face." Alex kept his tone light. He glanced at Cooper. The detective raised his eyebrows but didn't speak. "Mind if I wash up at the sink there?"

"Don't suppose there's much I can do to stop you." She slammed the mug down in front of Cooper, spilling more of the hot liquid. "What y'all want from me anyway?"

Alex washed his hands and then rubbed

his face a little. Who cared about bubble gum at a time like this? He turned around and leaned on the counter. His gut told him something big was about to break this case wide open. He didn't want to miss it.

Cooper took a sip from the mug. Clarisse started toward the door. Cooper set the mug down, then dropped the question like a stone. "What happened to Nina?"

Clarisse swayed. Alex straightened and took two quick steps forward, thinking he would have to catch her if she fainted. She laughed instead, a high pitched, quivering sound that held no humor.

Alex stopped in the middle of the room, waiting. Finally, maybe someone would tell him how that little girl ended up in a shallow, unmarked grave, all alone, for five years.

"I don't know what you're talking about. Nina who?"

Or maybe not. Forget patience. He plunged in ahead of Cooper, sick of waiting, sick of the disingenuous attitude of the adults who should've been the ones who took care of her and protected her. "Mrs. Chavez. We have the records from the CPS visits, from the school. We have her birth certificate. Do you know where she is? What happened to her? If you do, you better tell us. Now."

"She's not here." Clarisse clasped her hands together as if she were praying and teetered toward the table. Cooper pushed a chair out so she could sit. "You're talking about my youngest, I guess. We called her Marie. That was her middle name. That's why I didn't catch on right away who you were talking about. You mean Marie."

Alex hovered over her, keeping the pressure on. "So we know you have Esperanza and Estrella at the high school and Dom and Frankie at the middle school over in Abilene. Nina — I mean Marie — she'd be ten now. Fifth grade, maybe. No record of her going to school here. Where is she?"

"It was too much for me, too much. I had too many children to take care of so Ezra decided — so we decided to send Marie to live with his sister in California." Her gaze darted to the door every few seconds, her mouth trembling. "Yes, she was a handful. Very difficult child. Unruly. Strong-willed. Tómas — Ezra — we thought it'd be best."

Tears brimmed in her eyes. Alex could see them banking in the corners. Finally, one slid down her cheek. She swiped at it with the back of a red, dishpan hand. He felt no empathy for her. "Mrs. Chavez, I know your husband isn't dead — your second husband, Tómas — because my colleague and I have talked to him. He doesn't know what happened to Nina. He thinks she disappeared with you. And he's looking for you."

"No. No. Did you tell him where to find me?" Fury billowed in the words, a fury nurtured for several years. "If he finds us, he'll kill me. And the kids. Tómas knows what happened to Nina."

"How does he know?"

"Because he did it."

"Did it? He killed her? And you didn't do anything about it?"

She jerked as if he'd slapped her. Another tear joined the first one, trailing quickly to her jaw line. Cooper took another sip of coffee, looking like a spectator watching a tennis match, his gaze bouncing from Alex to Clarisse and back, his lips stretched in a tight line across his mouth.

Clarisse's breath came in short spurts like a cornered animal's. Finally, she spoke. "I was afraid. So afraid of what he'd do to the other kids. If he killed one, he could kill them all. I had to run. I ran."

"So you ran to your ex-husband, a man you'd already left once."

Her head jerked up. "You know?"

"Yes, we know. You were never married to Tómas Chavez because you were already married to Ezra Dodge. Why would a man like Ezra Dodge take you back?"

"To punish me."

He should feel pity for her, but he didn't. He kept seeing the skull peeking out from under the clods of dry earth. The scraps of faded pink material. The plastic barrettes. The bones laid out on the ME's table. So neat and precise. "Chavez could show up here any minute, Clarisse. We know he left San Antonio yesterday to come to Kansas. He's already in the state. He's probably watching, waiting, waiting to pick the perfect moment to swoop down and give you what he figures you deserve. You'd better tell us what happened. Tell us the whole story, and we'll find a way to protect you and the kids."

"How?" Her face turned whiter than the milk she'd left sitting on the counter. "How does he know?"

"He found out a private investigator came up here four and a half years ago looking for you and never came back. You know anything about that?"

"No — no, sir, I don't." Bright red spots in the middle of her cheeks gave her a feverish look. "I don't know nothing about no investigator. He's . . . Tómas is coming here?"

"We think so." Cooper spoke for the first

time, his voice gravelly with the same anger that consumed Alex. "Your husband is involved in one of the most violent gangs in south Texas. He manufactures meth and distributes drugs for a living. He recently was involved in the kidnapping of a little boy on the ranch y'all used to live on. The kidnapper died in a chase with some of your husband's goons. What do you think he'll do when he finds you?"

Her hands went to her throat in a convulsive gesture. "He'll kill me. He'll kill me because I know what —" She swallowed a sob and stopped.

"You know he killed Nina." Alex spoke softly. An eyewitness maybe. Or an accomplice. Either way, her testimony would put Chavez away for a long time.

"He'll kill me and the kids — the girls for sure. You have to help me. You have to hide us. Please." She fell to her knees, her hands on her face, sobbing at his feet. "Please."

Cooper knelt next to her. Alex couldn't bring himself to help her. She was the worst kind of mother. He searched for compassion in his soul and found none. That fact scared him. He *should* care about her.

He started to bend down. A scratching sound stopped him. Startled, he paused, waiting to hear it again. The sound was coming from behind a closed door next to the refrigerator. The door had a padlock on it. "What was that?"

"Nothing. It was nothing." Mrs. Chavez jerked from Cooper's grasp and stumbled to her feet, knocking over a chair in her haste. Her legs banged against the table, and Coop's mug went flying. Coffee spread across the table and dripped onto the floor. "I have to pack. I have to take the kids and get out of here before he finds us."

Alex brushed past her and strode over to the door. "Where does this go?" He jerked on the padlock. "What's in there?"

"It's just a storage room. We keep extra supplies in there." She didn't move from the table. "Just flour and sugar and such."

Alex pounded on the door and rattled the padlock. "Hello, who's in there? Hello!"

"Mommy. Mommy," a small voice called, "I'll be good now."

CHAPTER FORTY-ONE

The high-pitched sound of giggling filtered through the cracks around the chicken house door. Deborah put her hand on the metal bar handle and pulled it open. The door creaked and groaned. She peeked in. Two girls, dark braids to their waists, stood in the middle of the shack, frozen, looks of guilty fear on their matching faces.

"Uncle Ezra, we were just —"

Deborah stepped inside. "Hi. I'm Detective Deborah Smith from the San Antonio Police Department." She left the door open behind her. "You must be Estrella and Esperanza. Frankie said you were out here."

"San Antonio, Texas?" The slightly taller girl spoke first. She tossed her braid over her shoulder. "You don't have any jurisdiction here."

Deborah suppressed a smile. Whatever this girl had been through, it hadn't broken her. She felt the tug of a kindred spirit.

"Whoa. A budding lawyer. Are you Esperanza or Estrella?"

"Estrella. I'm the oldest."

"By two minutes." Esperanza protested, her lower lip stuck out in a pout. Her gaze grazed Deborah's, then sank to the floor. "Did God send you to save us?"

She hesitated. A sense of something big washed over her. "If you need saving, then I think He did." She took a step closer. "Esperanza. That means *hope* in Spanish, doesn't it?"

"Yes." The emotion that suffused the girl's face was so like her pretty name. She slapped a hand on her sister's hand. "I prayed someone would come and help us."

Estrella stuck both hands on her hips. "Well, la-de-dah. My name means *star* in Spanish. And it's prettier. Now what?"

Deborah smiled. "My . . . my partner — he's up at the house, you'll meet him in a few minutes. His name is Alex Luna, and *luna* means moon. So we've got the moon and the stars. And hope. Not a bad combination. Couldn't be a coincidence, could it?"

"Stop trying to snow us." Estrella frowned. "Ain't like Momma's gonna let you just take us away. You ain't got no jurisdiction here. You ain't even wearing a uniform. Uncle

Ezra will eat you for lunch, sure as I'm standing here."

"You're right about jurisdiction, but we're here with Detective Baker from Abilene. This is about making sure you're okay. It's also about your sister, Nina."

Neither girl made a sound, but Deborah saw the simultaneous flinch.

"Momma said they sent Nina to California," Estrella said, her tone fierce.

"California?"

"It was right before we moved here." Estrella's look dared Deborah to contradict her. "She said Nina went to live with *Papi's* sister in California."

"But she didn't." Esperanza glanced at Deborah and then at the ground.

"How do you know?"

Estrella glared at her sister and shook her head. "Esperanza!"

"But —"

"No, you can't. He'll find out. You know he will."

Esperanza gave her sister a mutinous look and went back to hunting for eggs. The ammonia smell of chickens and their waste made Deborah wonder why anyone would be a farmer. "Look, if you know something, it would really help. It's not right if something happened to your sister and no one did anything about it."

Estrella crowded her sister, her back to Deborah. "We don't know anything."

Deborah started to lean against the wall, saw the chicken excrement splattered on it, and thought better of it. "You said she didn't go to California. Tell me how you know. We'll do everything we can to protect you from your dad."

"Is he still alive?"

"Yes. And he's in Kansas. He's looking for you. You have to let us help you. We can protect you."

Estrella's face crumpled. She began to sob. Esperanza put her arm around her sister. They huddled together. "Momma said we didn't have to worry about him coming after us no more. That he couldn't ever find us. She lied. She lied to us, and now you've probably led him right to us. As if Uncle Ezra isn't enough."

"Why? What does Uncle Ezra do to you?"

Esperanza's hands fluttered around her face as if to protect it. "Beats us with a belt buckle. And he . . . he touches us, me and Estrella, but not the boys."

Thick, wooly blackness swooped over Deborah, blocking out the light. A sharp, angry cry came from her own mouth, surprising her. She gripped her hands together hard, focusing on the pressure of her fingers tightened against each other. "We'll get you out of here." Her mouth was dry, making it hard to say the words. "Before Ezra Dodge comes back."

"Where are we going to go? Foster care? We'll get separated." Estrella's voice was level, but her shoulders trembled under the thin material of the faded dress that hung below her knees.

"I'll do everything I can to help you. So will Detective Baker, but you've got to help us. Your sister is dead. We found her remains on the ranch of a friend of ours. She'd been buried there for years with no one knowing. No marker. All alone. Alone! Do you think that's right?"

Esperanza sobbed some more. Estrella hugged her against her skinny chest. "Don't think about it, sis. We agreed. No thinking about it."

Estrella jerked away from her sister and turned to stare up at Deborah. "We saw him do it."

"Who?"

"Papi."

"What did he do?"

"I skinnied up the tree," Esperanza explained. "Estrella was on the ground, catching the pecans when I threw them down. I looked over at the porch. Nina had made drawings on the porch with chalk, and *Papi* was making her clean it off. She started crying. He grabbed the shovel and swung as hard as he could. Hit her in the head. She fell down. She stopped crying."

The matter-of-fact recitation chilled Deborah. Perspiration soaked her blouse despite the frigid north wind that rattled the henhouse. "Why didn't you do anything? Say anything?"

"Because we were afraid he'd do it to us, too." Esperanza sounded angry at having to explain the obvious. "He said he would do it to us."

"Nobody's gonna hurt —"

The door to the henhouse swung open. In the sudden piercing light, Deborah could only make out a shadow. A gangly figure holding something — something with a long barrel.

"Get away from my sisters, or I'll kill you."

CHAPTER FORTY-TWO

Alex whirled and stared at Clarisse Chavez. She cowered behind the kitchen table, her expression wild like a feral cat's. He advanced on her, hand outstretched. "Give me the key!"

"I can't let her out. He'll punish me." She raised her arms in front of her face as if fearing a blow. "You don't know what he'll do to me. She's strong-willed, like her sister. She has to be taught. She has to learn the lesson."

"Give me the key now, or I'll blow the padlock off." Cooper put one hand on the gun on his hip. "Now."

"You better protect me." She rooted around in the pocket of her apron and flung the key at Cooper. "I won't be responsible for what he does."

"No, ma'am, but you are responsible for what you do."

Alex crowded Cooper as he fumbled with

the lock. He threw the padlock on the floor and wrenched open the door. It was a tiny, barren room, meant for storage, just as she'd said. The shelves were empty. A soiled bunk mattress lay on the floor. Next to it was a pail brimming with stinking excrement. No furniture. No toys. Nothing. Just an elfin girl who curled up in a ball in the corner. "I'm sorry, Uncle Ezra, I promise I'll be quiet." The arm she'd thrown over her face muffled her voice.

Alex brushed past Cooper and took two steps into the room. There was hardly space for his frame. He squatted down so he wouldn't tower over her. "Sweetie, I'm Alex Luna. Who are you?"

She dropped her arm. Alex swallowed. She had beautiful green eyes, fair skin, and dark black hair chopped short around her face. She looked about four or five. "I'm Nadia."

"Hi, Nadia. I've come to take you out of here."

He stood and held out his hand. She rolled up on her knees and tried to follow suit. Her legs collapsed under her. He crouched again. "What's the matter, darling?"

"My legs don't work."

Alex glanced back at Clarisse Chavez, who stood half-in, half-out of the room, as if

461

poised for flight. "Cerebral palsy."

He scooped the girl into his arms. She didn't weigh more than thirty-five or forty pounds. She smelled of urine and worse.

He stopped next to where Clarisse stood, staring down at her, baffled until the obvious answer struck him like a physical blow. "He killed Nina, but you were already pregnant with another baby, weren't you?"

She didn't answer.

"Weren't you?"

"Yes!" She screamed the word, her mouth wide in agony. "Only I didn't know it until I got here. And Ezra didn't want nothing to do with some other man's baby. He's made my life a living hell over it. She was another mouth to feed who would never be able to pull her weight. He wanted to kill her, drown her like a baby kitten. I begged him to let me keep her, so he said I could — as long as I kept her out of the way."

She said it as if it all made perfect sense.

"So you punished her for having a disability by locking her in a storage closet."

"No. No. No." Clarisse screamed the word again and again. She rocked back and forth, animal sounds coming from her mouth. "He punished me, not her. I made her with another man, so he punished me."

Alex turned and walked away, hugging

Nadia close to his chest, murmuring comforting words. His gaze caught Cooper's. The man looked a hundred years old. He held out his arms. Alex handed him the child.

Cooper sighed. "Now I know why I don't retire."

Alex nodded. There might be one more Nadia out there who needed rescuing.

"Are you Dom?" Deborah kept her tone casual as she contemplated the space between the rifle and the door to the shed. She couldn't get past it. Not without taking a chance that this kid would accidently blow her brains out and end any chance he had of ever having a real life. The barrel dipped and shimmied in his shaking hands.

"Shut up. I'll ask the questions." He sounded like grown man. He couldn't be more than twelve. "Get your hands in the air."

Deborah held her hands high. "Dom, I'm Detective Deborah Smith, from San Antonio. I've come to help you."

"You're a cop. I knew it right away when I saw you walking out. You got a gun under that jacket. I want it. You best take it out real careful-like with two fingers and lay it on the ground."

"Dom, she wants to help us." Estrella took a step toward her brother. "She's a police officer. She's says *Papi's* coming after us. They're gonna protect us from him. You can't shoot her."

"And you believed her?" Dom's tone said his sister was no more than a stupid girl. "No one will help us. None of them. They're just more adults who'll tell us lies and keep us apart and send us to stupid foster homes until Momma and Ezra get us back and beat us some more."

The despair in his voice, the desolate lack of hope, sounded so familiar to Deborah. Her body hummed with the desire to tell him it would be okay, but she couldn't make that promise. It hadn't been okay for her. Not really. Through high school, college, the academy, she'd pretended it was all right, but it wasn't. The hole inside her had gotten bigger, not smaller.

Maybe that was a defect in her. Maybe these kids still had a chance to get over the despicable things adults had inflicted on them. God was giving them a chance to escape the terrible cycle — through her. "Esperanza and Estrella witnessed the murder of your sister. If they testify, your father will go to prison, and you won't have to worry about him any more. Ezra Dodge, we'll take care of. We can protect you." Deborah tried to put every ounce of persuasion in her voice. "We can protect you."

"You *can't* protect us. You don't even know the half of it. Momma's as bad as *Papi* was. And when Ezra comes back and sees you here, we'll just get another beating. This time I'm gonna fight back. I don't need you to fight my battles, just your gun. Hand it over. Now."

The boy cocked the rifle and took another step toward Deborah. She put her hand on her holster. "You won't shoot me, Dom. Let us take your sisters where he can't hurt them anymore. Let us help you protect them."

"No — the only way is to kill him —"

"They found her. They found Nina's grave." Esperanza's voice dropped to a whisper when she spoke her sister's name.

"Found her — they couldn't — she's —" Dom looked shocked and confused. "She's lying."

Deborah took another step forward. "No, I'm not."

The boy lifted the rifle so the sight was just below his eye. "Move again and I'll blow your head off."

Esperanza began to sob. "Dom, please. Why won't you let them help us?" She dropped to her knees, her hands on her face. "I prayed. I prayed so hard. I asked God to send us help. And he did. He sent us the police. Please, can't you see?"

"If God sent them, why'd it take them so long to get here? Momma and Ezra done almost killed us already."

Deborah opened her mouth and shut it. She was too new at this religion thing. A question like that would keep her up many nights to come — if the boy didn't shoot her first. "I asked that question a lot when I was a kid. My mom's boyfriend hurt me. Like Ezra has been hurting your sisters. Day after day, week after week. No one did anything to help me. Not even my own mother."

It was a relief to say it. To say it to someone who would understand. Someone who wouldn't feel pity. Wouldn't offer platitudes.

Estrella sighed.

Dom nodded, but the rifle didn't move.

Deborah searched for the right words, the words that would keep the boy from doing something he would have to live with for the rest of his life. He needed a chance to start over. She wanted to be the one to give it to him. "It took me years to understand something. A good friend of mine explained it to me. God didn't make evil, He fights it.

466

He wants us to fight it, too. He's here with us, holding on to us, helping us get through it. Without Him, we'd be overwhelmed, we'd drown in it. But we don't, we hang on."

As she talked, she let her gaze trail over his shoulder to the door. She needed to get the rifle from him. Or make enough ruckus to get Baker's attention. A shadow flickered on the open door behind the boy. The snout of Baker's gun came in first, then his arm, followed by his potbelly. No need for a ruckus after all. Deborah didn't move. She focused on Dom. "Please, let us help you."

The boy rested the rifle butt against his shoulder and swiped at his face with the sleeve of his jacket. "No."

"Dom, put the rifle down." Baker had his gun two inches from the back of the kid's head. "Now. Put it down nice and slow."

Dom sobbed, a heartbreaking squeak of a sob, but he laid his weapon on the ground.

"It's okay, son." Baker grabbed it and straightened. "You're gonna be fine now."

The boy crumpled on his hands and knees sobbing. "I want to kill my mom. I want to kill Ezra. And my dad. It's the only way we'll ever be safe. He's coming to get us, and he'll kill us. You can't stop him. He'll kill us."

Deborah got to him first. She threw her arms around him. The physical contact didn't bother her. Not with this kid. He was a walking wound. "Your dad's outnumbered, Dom. He's going to find out what real justice is. Count on it."

"That's right."

Deborah looked up. Alex stood in the doorway. "And so is Ezra Dodge. Wait until you see what we found in the kitchen — who we found."

He put a hand on her arm as if to help her up. She ripped away from him and stumbled back, putting space between them as fast as she could. The look on his face sent an ice pick ripping through her heart. "Hey, I thought —" He backed away, hands in the air. "Sorry."

"Don't touch me, okay? I don't need help."

CHAPTER FORTY-THREE

It only took Alex, with Baker and Cooper's help, about ten minutes to find the makeshift grave where Ezra Dodge had buried private investigator Simon Phillips. Alex squatted next to the gravesite, covered with overgrown weeds and rusted farm implements. He rested his hands on his knees. The sick feeling that had lodged in his gut when he'd seen Nadia lying next to that filthy bedding bloomed, making it hard to breathe. That and the memory of the hard look in Deborah's eyes when she'd rejected his help.

"The cavalry has arrived." Baker pointed a finger toward the line of cars streaming along the dirt road that led to the main house — an evidence unit with equipment for digging, ambulances, more Dickinson County Sheriff's Department vehicles. "Guess I better go direct the show."

Alex stood. "We have to find Ezra Dodge

and Tómas Chavez — now. Those kids haven't got a chance until we make sure neither one can ever get close to them again."

Baker started down the incline. "I've already issued an APB for Chavez and a BOLO for Dodge's pickup, but they're not coming back here. They're probably hiding out until the commotion dies down. The kids are safe for now."

Alex went in search of Deborah. Her about-face had him baffled. And angry. He wouldn't let her get away with it. They'd come too far. He found her mothering the kids, who were gathered around her as if they'd found a solid anchor.

"What are you looking at?" An acerbic tone punctuated the frown when she finally looked in his direction.

Why was she so mad at him? "You. You got a problem with that?"

Deborah patted Estrella's arm and disengaged Frankie's hand from hers. "I'll be right back, guys." She stalked over to where he leaned against the porch railing. "You're giving me the willies, Luna. Go do something constructive, like find Dodge."

"The name's Alex, as you well know. We'll find Dodge as soon as we deal with the issues here." He kept his voice down, not wanting the kids to hear. "I would never do what Ezra Dodge did to those girls. Most men wouldn't, so stop punishing me."

She looked startled, then stricken. "I know. I know, Lu— Alex, I just . . . I can't . . . Never mind. What are they going to do with these kids? They can't stay here. Maybe we can —"

"No, not *never mind.* Why are you doing this? I thought we had made some progress." He let his voice drop to a whisper, cognizant of the dozen or more people milling around the yard. He grabbed her arm, ignoring her attempts to break away, and propelled her around the corner of the house. "I thought you were going to trust me. I kissed you. You kissed me back. You did. I felt it. Now you're treating me like a leper."

She jerked away, but she didn't run. "All right, all right." She rubbed her arm and stood her ground. "You want to know what the problem is? You want to know why I'm so . . . damaged? Because my mother's boyfriend did to me what Ezra Dodge did to these girls. More than that. He raped me. On a regular basis for almost a year. When I was thirteen." She stopped, breathing hard. "Satisfied?"

She tried to brush past him, but Alex

caught her arm again. This time he folded her against his chest in a hug. "Thank you."

"Thank you?" She struggled to break free but there was no fear in her voice, only sadness.

"Yeah, for trusting me enough to tell me." He let go. She might never let him hug her again, but at least he knew now what he was dealing with.

She disappeared around the corner of the house without responding.

He leaned against the wall for a few seconds, trying to get his equilibrium back. So now he knew. Knew what Ray had been trying to tell him. What Deborah had been trying to say. She didn't have relationships with men because men couldn't be trusted. She couldn't believe a man wouldn't use her and throw her away. *Please, God, help me.* It was all the prayer he could muster.

He forced himself to follow her back into the yard. A dusty white passenger van rolled to a stop a few yards away, rocking on the rutted road. The engine died and two women got out. The older one, who carried a clipboard, looked around, spotted the kids, and headed their direction.

"Who are they?" Deborah sounded as if she might know the answer to her own question. Estrella began to cry. Dom and Frankie both jumped to their feet. Alex was caught between corralling them and trying to get Deborah to back off.

He put a hand on her shoulder. She shrugged it off and started toward the woman. Alex tried to intervene. "Detective Baker called Social Services — it's called SRS here. Deborah, they have to have a safe place to stay until this is over."

"No. No, they can't take them." Deborah met the two women halfway. When the woman held out her hand and introduced herself, Deborah refused to take it. "These kids are witnesses in an active police investigation. They have to remain in protective custody for the time being."

"I'm sorry, Detective . . . ? As I said, I'm Jill Davis, Social Rehabilitation Services. We were called out here by the police. We were told these children needed our kind of protective custody. We're accustomed to these situations. We just need to take a few clothes, any paperwork they might have, shot records if they're available —"

"Shot records?" Deborah snorted. "These girls have been molested. They've seen people murdered. They've been beaten with belt buckles. And you want shot records? You people make me crazy. There's no way you can keep them safe."

"We deal with abused children everyday, Detective. That's what we do. Step aside, please."

Alex stepped between Deborah and Davis, afraid of what Deborah might do if he didn't. "I'm sorry, Mrs. Davis, could you give us a minute with the kids. We'll bring them to you, okay? Maybe y'all could go in and gather up their things. The mother is sedated. I doubt there are any records, but you're welcome to look around. Please."

The woman nodded, compassion warming her face, making her look like someone's grandma.

"They aren't the bad guys either." Alex eased in close to Deborah, talking in her ear as he forced her back toward the kids. "Think about how much harder you'll make it for the kids if you fight this. Do the right thing. Make it easier for them. Tell them we'll do everything we can to help them. Assure them."

Deborah inhaled and exhaled hard, her blue eyes smoldering as if they might ignite. She might explode, or she might never talk to him again. He wasn't sure which it would be, but right now, he had to think about these kids.

"If they get placed in some stinking, horrible foster home, it's on your head. I won't forgive you or Cooper or anybody — ever!"

"Has it occurred to you to pray about that?"

She stopped in her tracks. She looked as if he'd struck her. "No." Her voice quivered. "No."

"Well, hurry up because we've got work to do."

A minute later, she sat down at the picnic table, stared Esperanza in the eye, and told her not to worry. "SRS will take you to a safe place and take care of you while we go find Ezra Dodge and put him in jail for a long, long time."

"No, no, please, please, don't make us go. You said it would be all right now. You said we would stay together," Esperanza screamed.

Estrella simply sobbed, a sound Alex would never forget.

Dom didn't wait for Deborah's response. He shot off in a dead run. Frankie immediately followed.

"Come on, guys, don't make me chase you." Alex took off after him, feeling like an old man at thirty-four. Maybe he should take his own advice. *God, how is this a good thing? Show me how. Help them. Help me help them. Something.* Eloquent he wasn't, but it was the best he could do.

Dom stumbled and fell in the furrows of the plowed field. Frankie tried to help his big brother up. Alex slammed to a stop.

"Get away from us, get away!" Dom lifted a dirty tearstained face, his arm tight around his brother's neck. "Why don't you just shoot us and get it over with. Put us out of our misery like stupid dogs no one wants anymore. You could drown us like they do the baby kittens no one wants. Whatever, just do it."

"I know things seem really bad right now, but you can't give up." Panting, Alex inhaled the smell of sweat, dirt, and fear. "Your sisters need you. They need you to look after them. All you guys have is each other. You can't lose sight of that. What will the girls do without you?"

He held out his hand. "Come on. The worst part is over. Foster care will be a piece of cake compared to what you've been through. We'll find your dad and arrest him. And we'll be watching out for you guys. Checking up on you. We're not abandoning you. I promise."

Dom looked at Alex's face, then at his hand. After a few seconds, he took the hand. He didn't say anything as Alex pulled him to his feet, but Frankie did. "Can you get the other guy to give us some more bubble gum?"

Alex felt a chuckle bubble up inside him. Kids had an impossible resilience that faded as they grew older. Frankie still had his. Good for him. "I'll see what I can do, buddy."

When they got back to the yard, Deborah stood next to the open van door, talking softly to Estrella and Esperanza, who were sitting close together in the middle seat. Tears still fell, but the anguished sobs had stopped.

"Okay?" He tried to get Deborah to look at him, but she turned her back and helped Frankie climb in, Dom after him. Fine. He turned away as well. "Detective Baker. Detective Baker!"

The sheriff's detective lumbered over to the van, his face sweating with the effort. "You guys headed out?"

"Frankie was wondering if you might have any more of that bubble gum. I think they could all use a shot before they face whatever comes next."

Baker winked at Alex and nodded. "You betcha." He pulled a stash of gum from his back pocket and started handing it out. Not one of them smiled, but each said thank you. "And don't you all worry. Me and my wife are gonna be out to see y'all real soon. You're gonna like her. She loves children and never got to have any of her own. I gave her a call a minute ago, and she's chomping at the bit to meet y'all."

Deborah's head came up at that statement. She met Alex's gaze, a small smile starting to spread across her face. Detective Baker had already returned to his investigation. "Don't worry about a thing," she said to the children. "We'll let you know how this investigation comes along, every step of the way."

The kids nodded, but Alex only saw resignation in their faces, no hope. They hadn't gotten Detective Baker's message, but they would.

Deborah slammed the door shut and stepped back. Four faces turned to stare out the window as the van disappeared down the road.

Alex couldn't help but feel the stares were accusing. He turned his back on the road and looked at Deborah. "Are you all right?"

Deborah didn't answer. Just started walking away.

"Where are you going?"

"To find a cigarette."

She disappeared into the crowd of technicians and officers working the scene.

He felt curiously flat, like all the oxygen had been sucked from his lungs. She wouldn't take comfort from him — he'd known that — but the fact that she didn't care that he could have used a little comfort from her — that stung.

"She's a tough broad, ain't she?" Baker strode toward him, his admiring gaze following Deborah's exit. "Wouldn't want to cross her."

"Me neither." Alex tore his gaze away from her. Better to focus on work. "We've got to find Dodge. Find Dodge and we'll find Chavez. My theory is Chavez caught up with Dodge first. Maybe he was watching the place, waiting for his moment. He wanted to get Dodge out of the way so Clarisse would be alone and unprotected. Who knows? Then he comes back, sees she's got company, and hightails it out of here."

"Maybe." Cooper joined them. He tossed a cell phone from one hand to the other. "I'm thinking he's still watching. He's gonna go after her first chance he gets. And the kids."

"The location of the children's shelter in Salina is a well-kept secret." Baker leaned against the bumper of his pickup and unrolled another piece of bubble gum. "And we have SPD keeping an eye on this place.

The kids are safe with SRS. Nadia is in the hospital. We've got an officer at her door. The doctors are checking out Clarisse, too, since she went all hysterical on us. The problem we have now is there is no reason for him to come back here. How do we lure him out?"

"He could be anywhere by now." Alex forced back the obscenities. He was getting better at it. "He probably already killed Dodge."

Baker's phone chirped a second later. "Excuse me, folks." He walked away.

The interruption allowed Alex to sneak a glance at the porch. Deborah was back, sitting on the steps of the porch, a lit cigarette between two fingers. She wouldn't smell so good now. So what? He had to admit the sorry truth. He didn't care if she reeked of smoke. She would always smell good to him.

"Let's go. Dispatch got a 911 call from a motorist on Old Highway 77." Baker trotted across the yard in what amounted to a run for the big guy. "Says he stopped on the side of the road to help two hysterical ladies who had been carjacked."

"What's that got to do with us?" Spurred by the urgency in Baker's voice, Alex started after him.

"He says one of them keeps moaning

something about four kids being kidnapped."

CHAPTER FORTY-FOUR

Alex paced on the shoulder of the highway, waiting for the EMT to finish working on Jill Davis. Deborah stood on the other side of the truck, interviewing the farmer who'd stopped to help the SRS caseworkers after seeing the van leaving the scene. Cooper and Baker examined Dodge's pickup truck, complete with Ezra Dodge's body in the back under a blue tarp.

Mrs. Davis's eyes were swollen, and one cheek bore an ugly bruise. She'd burst into tears the minute he approached her. The other caseworker was unconscious, apparently from a blow to the back of her head from the butt of a gun. So far the details were scanty, but they involved a truck stopped in the middle of the road and a man flagging them down. He'd claimed engine trouble and asked to borrow her cell phone.

The paramedic affixed a bandage to the

cut under her eye and patted her shoulder. "We'll take you into Abilene to the hospital so we can get an x-ray of your shoulder. You'll be fine, ma'am."

Mrs. Davis looked up at Alex from her seat on the bumper of the ambulance. "Which is more than I can say for those kids." Fresh tears threatened. "They were so scared. Dom tried to run, and that man grabbed him and wrapped his arm around the child's neck. I thought he'd strangle the poor boy right there in front of me. I should've done something to stop him."

"Ma'am, Chavez had a gun. The most important thing at that moment was to keep anyone from getting killed." Killed like Ezra Dodge or Nina Chavez. "Do you feel up to telling me exactly what happened?"

Davis held an ice pack to her bruised cheek. "It all happened so fast. I saw the truck in the road. He was standing next to it, waving at me with one arm, so I stopped. I shouldn't have stopped, but around here . . ."

Around here, in rural middle America, people still did the neighborly thing. Alex understood that. "Go on."

"As soon as I rolled the window down, he stuck the gun in my face and opened the door. He was grinning like a crazy man. He kept saying something in Spanish. I don't know much, but I did catch *hijas* and the girls' names. He said to get out or he'd kill me." Her voice shook. "I got out. The kids were screaming."

She was crying again. Alex shifted his feet, then stared at the clouds over her head for a few seconds, giving her time to compose herself. "How did you and your coworker get your injuries?"

She sighed. "We were responsible for them. We couldn't just let him take them, even if he had a gun."

She dropped the ice pack onto the floor of the ambulance and buried her face in her hands. Her shoulders shook. Alex sat down next to her and touched her arm. "Mrs. Davis, I'm sure you did everything you could. He's a cold, vicious criminal, and he was armed."

She raised her head. "Dom tried to stand up to him. He jumped from the van like he was going to take the man on. Obviously I couldn't let him do that. When the man lifted the gun as if to hit Dom, I stepped in front of the boy. He hit me. By then Sarah was out of the van and she ran at him, trying to keep him from hurting me. He let her have it with the gun."

"You're lucky he didn't shoot you instead."

"I got the impression he didn't want to do it in front of the kids."

"A little late for a conscience."

"Yes." She wrapped her arms around her middle and shivered in the cold evening air. The sun had retreated behind clouds on the horizon and dusk had begun to gather. Alex zipped up his jacket as he waited for her to find the words to finish. "I'll never forget the looks on those kids' faces when he got in the van and drove away with them. I don't know what I was doing. I guess I was crazy with fear and anger. I ran after the van, and I could see them looking back at me. Crying."

"You aren't to blame for this, Mrs. Davis. You just sit here and relax. I'll be back." He rose and stomped on frozen feet to where Deborah and the Good Samaritan stood.

She glanced at Alex, her face emotionless. "Mr. Whittaker says the van headed south. The description matches Tómas Chavez." She held out her hand. Whittaker shook it. "Thank you, sir. We'll get back to you if we need anything else."

The man's face sank in a rueful frown. "If I'd known what was going on, I'd have gone after him. At least followed him."

"The man is armed and dangerous. It's better that you didn't, sir. Thanks again." Deborah turned her back and started toward the pickup truck.

Alex nodded at Whittaker and took off after her. "Deborah! What?"

"We told those kids we'd keep them safe. And we handed them over to a baby killer." Anger flashed in her eyes. Her mouth tightened. "We might as well have killed them ourselves."

"I don't think he plans to kill them. I think he wants to be their father." It was just a theory, but one that had been growing in his mind. "He missed all those years of being a father because of what he did to Nina. Maybe in some twisted way, he's decided he wants to be a family again. He might've killed Clarisse, but not the kids. Otherwise, he would've killed these two women when they resisted. He must've been watching the farm. When he saw us drive in, he backed off and waited for his chance."

"And we gave it to him on a silver platter."

"He'll try to get to Mexico." Alex grabbed her arm. She jerked away. "This isn't your fault."

"No. It's yours for insisting that we turn them over to SRS or whatever they call it here. They would have been safer with us. We have the firepower to protect them."

"We had no way of knowing —"

"Yeah . . . right!" She snorted and turned her back on him. "What's the deal, Detective Baker?"

Baker pulled back the tarp so they could get a look at the body of Ezra Dodge. He was a middle-aged, balding Anglo, overweight, overalls and dirty work shirt. And with a bullet hole to the back of the head. The man had been executed.

"Cold." Alex stepped back and let Baker's evidence tech get to work. "Chavez got his revenge on Clarisse with one shot."

"Yeah, I'm surprised he would let her get —"

"Detective." A young, skinny deputy whose avid expression said this was his first homicide, marched toward them, flapping a piece of paper in one hand.

Baker snatched the paper, a quizzical look on his face. "What is it?"

"Dispatch just called. An officer outside of Florence saw a van matching the description of the SRS vehicle parked at a convenience store getting gas. He's confirmed there were four kids in the van, two girls and two boys. The license plate number matches. He's keeping them under surveillance. His department is backing him up. They want to approach."

"No." Baker slapped his hat on head. "Tell them to continue surveillance but to wait to approach until we get there. Our friends from Texas know more about these guys than anybody here. It'd be best if they'd do the negotiating."

Alex's hand went to his holster. If negotiating didn't work, he wanted to be the one to convince Tómas Chavez to give himself up — the hard way.

CHAPTER FORTY-FIVE

PD in the small town of Florence had been plenty happy to wait for their arrival. Officer Robert Sampson had done an excellent job keeping tabs on the van. It was now parked at a single unit cottage at a locally-owned Scenic Road Motel that — despite peeling paint, sagging awnings, and cracked, pothole filled parking lot — trumpeted itself on a neon sign as the finest sleeping establishment in the city. Alex leaned against Baker's Explorer and waited while the detective confirmed with the motel owner, who said Chavez had paid cash for one two-bedroom cottage — number eight.

A single streetlight at the entrance illuminated the area closest to the street but didn't reach the last row of cottages. The owner of the place had turned off the neon sign and the lights at the restaurant and the office at their request, leaving only the naked bulbs that hung over the doors of the individual units. Cottage number eight was dark, and there was no sign of movement behind the curtains of a large window at the front of the cottage.

"They're in there. I watched him go in." Officer Sampson looked pleased with himself.

Mid-twenties, smooth shaven, a patch of acne on both cheeks, another guy with no experience. Alex stifled a sigh. "Did all four of the kids seem all right?"

"One of the boys was helping one of the girls. She was leaning on him, but she was walking."

Alex nodded and turned to watch Baker try to calm the owner.

"I don't want no trouble." The guy's frown revealed a set of crooked gray teeth. Mr. Seeley had been reluctant to cooperate, saying he was trying to build on the RV travelers passing though his city going south. The number of 18-wheeler cabs lining the back of the parking lot told the true story. "I just renovated number eight — new seventeen-inch color TV, nice queen, and a coffeemaker."

"Everyone wants this to end peacefully, Mr. Seeley." Baker gave the man an encouraging nod. "Why don't you go on back across the street and wait where it's safe until we decide on a course of action."

Mr. Seeley didn't look happy, but he did what he was told.

"All the units are the same." Baker spread a sketch the owner had made across the hood of his vehicle and shone his flashlight on it. "There's a front door and a back door. The back door is to your right as you face the back side of the structure. There's a living area and kitchen to the front of the structure. To the back are the bedrooms, separated by the bathroom."

"What's the plan?" They couldn't go in with guns blazing, not and guarantee the kids' safety. Still the thought of wiping that ugly smirk from Chavez's face with his Glock gave Alex a momentary flash of satisfaction.

"We could call him to try to negotiate some kind of exchange," Cooper offered. "Safe passage out of the state if he gives up the kids. The owner says the unit has a working phone."

"Thing is, that tips him off that we're here," Baker argued. "We lose any element of surprise."

Alex kicked a rock across the parking lot, then stamped his feet. "What other options do we have — short of breaking the door down?"

"How about a little maid service?" Deborah's tone said she was absolutely serious. "Why don't I offer Mr. Chavez some clean sheets and towels?"

"No way. The guy's crazy — besides he's not going to open the —"

"Shut up, Luna —"

"Both of you, hold your horses." Cooper broke in, his voice sharp. "Just hold on, for a minute. There may be some merit to Detective's Smith's suggestion. If she can distract him at the front door, we can use the key to get in the back. It'll only give us a few seconds head start on him, but it could be enough to pull it off. Baker, you focus on getting the kids out of harm's way. Officer Robertson will be out front on the radio, letting us know if Detective Smith gets in. Alex, you and I will go after Chavez. All you have to do, Detective Smith, is keep his attention on you long enough for us to get inside."

"This is nuts." Alex forced himself to shut his mouth. She was a cop. And he had no right to let personal feelings get in the way of doing the job. "Nuts."

It only took five minutes for Deborah to change into the maid uniform provided by Mr. Seeley. She had taken Cooper's advice about keeping Chavez's attention to an undue extreme. She'd rolled the skirt up so her slim legs were exposed and left a couple of buttons too many unbuttoned on the thin, white blouse under a dark green sweater. Alex wanted to swear at the sight of her hair loose on her shoulders.

"Look, Deborah, please be careful —"

She swept past him and then, as if reconsidering, turned back. She glared at him, but kept her voice down. "The only way any of this will work is if you treat me like you would any other cop. You treat me like a girlfriend, and it's over. *All* over! Do you understand what I'm saying?"

He understood — at least he thought he did. A tiny bit of hope trickled through him. "Right. Just like any other fellow officer, I want you to go home at the end of your shift in one piece. Be careful."

She took off, balancing a stack of towels in one hand and pulling a cart of cleaning supplies that camouflaged her weapon across the pothole-pitted parking lot. Cooper slapped his shoulder lightly, and he was forced to follow the older man. Baker brought up the rear. They crept around the back of the tiny cottage, careful to stay away from two grimy windows. The curtains were drawn. Nothing to see, no hint of what was happening inside.

Silently, Cooper slipped up to the back door and fumbled with a tiny pin flashlight in one hand. He had a radio to his ear. After a second he whispered. "Chavez opened the door. They're talking."

Cooper stuck the radio in his back pocket and slipped the key into the lock. He eased the door open an inch, two inches. He tilted his head and peered inside. He pushed the door wider and motioned for Alex to squeeze inside.

Cooper nodded toward the bedrooms. Baker disappeared into the first one. Alex tiptoed down the short hallway to the front of the cottage. Cooper's soft tread echoed behind him. The light in the living area blinded him for a second.

Then he could make out the two people at the front door. Girls sitting on the couch. The two boys crouched on the floor. Someone was crying.

"Tómas Chavez, you're under arrest for the murder of Nina Chavez, the murder of Ezra Dodge, conspiracy to commit kidnapping and whatever else we can think of. You have the right to remain silent." It took Alex a second to focus on the gun. She'd already pulled her gun. She'd moved too quickly. "If you choose to give up that right —"

Chavez backed up a few steps, still holding the towels Deborah apparently had handed him. Deborah moved forward, into the room. Chavez chuckled, a soft ugly sound. "*Chiquita bonita,* you don't want to mess with me. Pretty lady, come on, we have nice time you and me. Just give me the gun."

"You killed a little girl, Chavez, and an innocent woman. Now you're going to pay for it."

"I don't know what you're talking about, pretty lady. You put down the gun, and I'll show you a real good time."

Wrong tact to take with Deborah. Alex started forward. "Police! Down! Drop the weapon! Hit the floor! Now!"

Chavez did neither. He threw the stack of towels at Deborah, whipped out the weapon stuck in his waistband, and fired in one quick motion. The room lit up with the shot and the smell of gunpowder ballooned in the air.

Deborah returned fire. She went down in a heap on the floor. Alex squeezed the trigger again and again. Time halted. The muscles in his arms and legs felt heavy, so heavy. He was vaguely aware of screaming, of Cooper beside him, gun raised.

Chavez staggered. His arms flopped. His gun dropped to the floor. "I'm hit." He teetered, took one more step, and crumpled into the sofa face down next to the girls.

Esperanza's mouth opened. Her cries cut the air like the wail of a siren. Estrella grabbed her sister's arm and dragged her to the floor. They scrambled on hands and knees toward the door, trying to escape, desperation on their faces that made them look like old women.

Dom crept across the floor toward them, dragging Frankie with him. His mouth gaped open, but no sound came out.

Alex didn't see any blood on any of them. Time rocketed forward. He bolted toward Deborah. She sat on the floor, her back against the doorframe. The walls seemed to squeeze together and fall apart. His heart banged back and forth in his chest, bruising his ribs. "Where'd he hit you?"

"Treat me . . . like . . . any other cop, remember?" She grimaced and gasped. "It's not bad. Not bad. I had to go for it. Frankie was excited to see me. Dom tried to shush him, but he was about to give me away."

"Shut up." Alex lifted the sweater. Blood was already seeping through her blouse. He slid his hand behind her head and gently eased her away from the wall and down to the floor. *God, please. God. Don't take her. The people in my life have always left me. Let her be the one that stays. Please.*

496

He ripped his cell phone from his pocket and jabbed in 911 with one hand, trying to shrug off his jacket at the same time. "Where are we? How do I tell them where we are?" Frantic, he sought Baker's gaze. "Is there a hospital in this town? How long will it take to get an ambulance out here?"

"I'm taking care of it." Baker already had his phone to his ear. He headed toward Cooper, who bent over Chavez lying motionless on the couch. "Is he alive?"

"He's dead."

One of the girls whimpered. Cooper eased down next to her. "It's all right. It's over." He glanced over his shoulder. "How's Detective . . . how's Deborah?"

"Bleeding all over — we need an ambulance." Alex squashed back the panic. He dropped the phone, balled his jacket up, pressed it against her chest. Her blood stained his hands. Bile rose in his throat, choking him. "You're an idiot, Deborah, an idiot."

The *whoop-whoop* of sirens filled the air. The bodies of local PD crowded the room. More guns and more confusion. "Get out, everyone, get out." No one listened to him.

"I love it when you sweet talk me like that." Deborah's words were softer, breathless. "I had to make sure he couldn't hurt

497

those little girls. Everything had to end now. I wanted it to be over. For them. I ended it all."

"Yeah, you ended it." He peeked under her sweater again. More blood than he knew what to do with. He pressed the jacket down harder, trying to staunch the flow. She groaned. Her body trembled. He was hurting her, but he had no choice.

She wanted everything to end. She might get her wish.

CHAPTER FORTY-SIX

"Any news?" Coop strode down the hospital corridor toward Alex, a cup of coffee in each hand.

Alex took the cup and shook his head. "Nothing. They've been in there forever."

"Doctor said he didn't think any vital organs were hit. A lot of bleeding, but it looked worse than it was."

Easy for Coop to say. He didn't have Deborah's blood all over his hands, jacket, and shirt. Alex tried to contain the shudder that ran through him. Deborah's face kept floating to the surface, smiling at him in the hospital waiting room after they'd found Benny. That tentative, scared look when he'd kissed her. The way she ducked her head, embarrassed, when he'd said it was a start. "That's what the doctor said."

So what was taking so long? The surgery, like the wait for the ambulance and the ride into a hospital in some town called Emporia, seemed endless. Deborah had faded in and out of consciousness, worrying about the kids. Where would they end up now? Alex tried to calm her, but she fought him until her strength had faded and she'd shut her eyes and drifted away. He closed his own, trying to get the stillness of her face out of his head.

How many gunshots did the ER staff in this place deal with? Couldn't be many. An occasional hunting accident, maybe. He leaned back in his chair and let his head touch the wall. Looking at the ceiling was a slight respite from staring at the floor.

"Baker called while I was downstairs." Alex heard Coop shift in his chair, squirming like a little kid. "Coroner also says Chavez was hit twice, two bullets to the chest, one in the front, one in the back."

"So Deborah and I both took him down." Together. They'd never know which shot killed the man, so they'd simply share in the guilty relief that he was gone. They would have to ask to be forgiven for taking a life. Alex was new at this stuff, but surely God understood how limited their choices had been.

"Yep. Don't beat yourself up. If I'd been a few years younger and a step or two quicker, I would've joined you."

"I was doing my job. Deborah is the idiot."

Coop laughed a little. "Hits you like that, doesn't it, when you love a hard-headed woman?"

"Who said anything about love?"

Cooper laughed again, this time a big booming laugh. "Son —"

The sound of doors banging open and shut brought Alex's focus down from the ceiling. He surged to his feet. The surgeon trudged toward them.

Alex tried to read his face. "Well, how is she? Is she . . . She's okay, right?"

"Easy, Detective Luna." The doctor frowned. "She made it through. There was a lot more damage than we anticipated. The bullet banged around in there, shattered a rib, collapsed a lung. Much longer without treatment and she wouldn't have made it."

"But she'll recover."

"The good Lord willing."

Alex leaned over and put his hands on his knees, suddenly lightheaded.

"Maybe you should sit down." Coop grabbed his arm as if to make him do it.

"Call Ray. They're all sitting by the phone, waiting." Alex jerked away. "I have to see her. She owes me an apology for blowing it and recklessly endangering all of us."

The doctor held up a hand. "She's in

recovery. She should be awake in about an hour. She'll feel like an eighteen-wheeler ran over her, so you might want to take it easy on her for a while."

"Good, I want her to be awake when I kick her butt." Alex turned his back on the two men and rushed down the hallway. That way they wouldn't see the effort it took for him to hold back the tears.

CHAPTER FORTY-SEVEN

Winter had decided to visit early. The bright November morning sun did nothing to warm Alex as a north wind swept across the ranch. He stood a little apart from the group as Ray read from the book of Mark. "He took a little child and had him stand among them. Taking him in his arms, he said to them, 'Whoever welcomes one of these little children in my name welcomes me; and whoever welcomes me does not welcome me, but the one who sent me.' "

Alex swallowed, guarding against the emotion that rolled over him. Ray had erected a small marker where Nina Chavez's remains had been found. He'd invited his family and friends — mostly those who'd been at the scene the day Nina had been found or who had been involved in the investigation — to share in a memorial service. Only Kim Glover and her husband, the foster parents, had actually met the child. Mrs. Glover's eyes were glazed with tears and her nose red from wiping it with the tissue clutched in her hand.

Ray stood closest to the marker, his head down as he read, his face hidden in the shadow of a huge, black Stetson. Susana hadn't left his side since the service started. They were leaving on their honeymoon in a few hours — only after Daniel and Samuel had convinced them a decision about taking Nadia Chavez into their home could wait ten days. They wanted to care for the little girl until the long-term custody of all the children could be decided.

Clarisse Chavez had been admitted for evaluation to a mental facility in Topeka, Kansas. Nadia was still in the hospital. The remaining four children were staying with Detective Baker and his wife. After their experience with Tómas Chavez, the SRS caseworkers had been happy to bulldoze their way through the red tape to give the kids a shot at a real, loving home.

Alex had no illusions. Adjusting to a normal family life would not be easy. And the Bakers had no experience with that level of dysfunction, but what they could offer might be what those children most needed — love.

Despite his best effort, his gaze traveled to

Deborah. She looked pale and thin and moved like she still hurt. Served her right. Acting like a crazy person. The memory of her still face against the pillow in that hospital room that stank of disinfectant and Betadine assailed him. And with it, the awful out-of-control feeling that his life might slip away if Deborah didn't open her eyes.

He'd waited until she was stronger to let her know he'd changed his mind about her, about them. He wasn't a monster. Nor was he a fool. He couldn't take a chance with someone who was that careless with her own life. Who cared so little about the devastation she'd leave behind. They hadn't spoken since.

"She might not have found love on earth, but we can take solace in the fact that she is greatly loved now." Ray shut his Bible.

Benny and Marco stepped forward. The bruises on Benny's face had faded to horrific shades of yellow and green. Stitches decorated a swollen lower lip. He and his foster cousin read from a scrap of paper in his hand, their voices blending in a high, sweet sound that carried on the wind. "Mark 10, Verses 13 through 16, 'People were bringing little children to Jesus to have him touch them, but the disciples rebuked them. When Jesus saw this, he was indignant. He said to them, "Let the little children come to me, and do not hinder them for the kingdom of heaven belongs to such as these. I tell you the truth, anyone who will not receive the kingdom of God like a little child will never enter it." And he took the children in his arms, put his hands on them and blessed them.' "

Benny laid a bouquet of daisies in front of the marker. Marco added one of pink roses. "These are for you, Nina." He stepped back. Cooper, one hand clasped in Maddy's, was next. Then the others made their way to the marker, showering it with flowers and small stuffed animals, homemade pictures, and brightly colored balloons fastened to the hands of chubby-faced dolls.

They began to leave then, without conversation. The wind whistled through the cracks in the walls of the old tool shed beyond the marker. It was so quiet. Some music would have been nice. Something a five-year-old would have appreciated. Alex couldn't move. He stared down at the marker anchored in the dirt, with the flowers — little pink roses, daisies, baby's breath — bright against it.

The sound of footsteps on the brittle grass made him look up. Deborah wavered a step from him, one hand out as if she might touch his arm.

They stared at each other.

His mouth dry, his heartbeat strangely off kilter, he brushed past her.

"Alex! Wait!"

He kept walking.

Daniel drained his coffee cup and set it on the coffee table. "You ready?"

Nikki stood in the doorway, her coat already on. She'd been very quiet since he'd picked her and the kids up from the house for the memorial service. "That was a beautiful service."

He swiped a quick kiss. "Yes, it was. Are you all right?"

With a slight breathless laugh, she wiggled from his grasp as she grabbed the door. "I'm fine. The kids are already outside. We better go. You're making me crazy."

"Hey, this wait-until-we-renew-our-vows strategy was your idea." He started after her. She pulled the door open. Deborah stood on the other side, her hand up as if she'd been about to grab the knob.

They stared at each other. Nicole spoke first. "Detective Smith, how are you doing?"

"Fine, thank you for asking."

Nicole moved aside and Deborah brushed past her. She came within inches of Daniel but didn't make eye contact. "I wanted to say good-bye to everybody. I have to get back to town."

Daniel started to reach for her, to make her stop. He let his hand drop. Neither woman would appreciate that approach. "What's the hurry? Maddy made hot chocolate and cookies."

Deborah didn't respond. She started down the hallway with an exaggerated saunter that belied the rigid set of her shoulders. Daniel glanced at Nicole. She nodded, her face encouraging. "Go. I'll get the kids together and wait in the car."

He turned toward the hallway. "Deborah, wait."

She kept walking. "Deborah, stop! Now!"

She glanced back at him. "I don't take orders from you. What do you want?"

He matched his stride to hers. "After . . . after that day in the guest bedroom, we never talked."

"Nothing to talk about." Her gaze traveled over his shoulder toward the now closed door. "No harm done, obviously."

"Well, yeah, there was, at the time." Daniel didn't let his mind dwell on those difficult days. They were over for him. He and Nicole would renew their vows in ten days — just as soon as Ray and Susana returned from their honeymoon. "But it wasn't your fault. You didn't do anything wrong."

"I never said I did." Her chin lifted. "I just woke you up, that's all."

"You're acting like you feel guilty. We were friends, Deborah, I'd like for us to still be friends."

Confusion colored her face. "How can we be friends? Nicole hates me and I . . . I . . ."

"She doesn't hate you." The topic had been discussed thoroughly at counseling sessions after their reconciliation. Nicole had let go of her anger. Daniel was still working through his regarding Joshua. "She realizes you were just waking me up."

"She's not stupid. She knows it was more than that."

Not for Daniel. It had never been more than that. "Nicole knows I love her. And that's what counts. And for you, Deborah, it was a reaching out. That's a big thing for you. You don't reach out to very many people. You trusted me enough to care about me. That's a very special thing — a gift. I just wanted to thank you."

Deborah stared at him, biting her lip, her forehead furrowed in confusion. "You're thanking me?" She shook her head. "I caused you so much trouble. I — you know — it was more than just a hug."

"Maybe. At the time. You liked me because I was unavailable. You need someone who has as much love to give you as you have for him." Daniel wanted to reach out to her, but he was afraid she would bolt. "I just want us to be okay."

Deborah met his gaze. "We're okay."

"Good, because from what I've been hearing from Ray, I think I'm seeing a black Altima in your future."

She snorted. "Alex won't give me the time of day. He can't even look at me."

Daniel smiled. He'd tried talking to Alex about Deborah. She was right. The guy was hanging onto his anger and fear for dear life. A good sign he was in over his head when it came to his feelings for Deborah. "That's because he loves you. Men are stupid about that kind of stuff. You got yourself shot. It scared him. Men don't like being scared, so they get mad. Rationally, he knows you did what you had to do under the circumstances. He'll come around."

"If he's going to be such a jerk about stuff, I'm not sure I want him to come around."

They were almost to the kitchen, full of people eating cookies and drinking hot chocolate and letting go of sadness. "Don't be a wimp."

"I'm not a wimp." She turned her back on him.

"Wimpy, wimpy, wimpy!"

She whirled and glared at him. "Quit it! You don't need to worry anymore. We're good. We're fine. You can get on with your life. Let it go."

"Go after him. Right now. Don't wait." He wanted Deborah to have what he had. Love, happiness, a family life. Along with the love of God, those were the best antidotes for loneliness and the ugly ghosts that led back to a bottle.

She shook her head. "I can't."

"Yes, you can." He grabbed her arm to keep her from plunging through the kitchen door. "Don't be a coward! It'll be worth it. I promise."

He let go and she disappeared from sight. He walked back toward the front door, back to the life waiting for him on the other side. Without effort, he picked up speed until he was almost running.

So worth it.

Deborah strode down the dirt road that led from Ray's house to the highway. Alex's black Altima was parked between an SUV and a pickup truck. From the looks of it, he hadn't started the engine. He sat there, not moving.

Maybe he felt as paralyzed as she did. Deborah had tried calling Alex. He never returned her calls. She was still on medical leave, so there was no chance of running into him at work. His apartment . . . as much as she wanted to make things right with him, she couldn't go to his apartment. When she'd had the chance to talk to him at the service, she'd chickened out and let him walk away without saying a word.

She was afraid it would be like his response in the hospital in the physical therapy room. He'd ended their friendship. And then he'd marched away without looking back. The hazy yet seemingly real memory of a hand brushing her hair from her face and lips touching her cheek must have been a dream, just a dream before the drugs had worn off after the surgery. She was sure he'd told her he loved her. He had a seriously strange way of showing it. Like most men in her life, Alex had bailed out when things got rough.

The Altima's engine revved. He'd started the car. Before she could lose her nerve, Deborah marched over to the car and planted herself in front of it.

After a few long seconds, the window rolled down. Alex stuck his head out and stared at her with those opaque brown eyes that seemed to see through her. "Did you need something?"

"Yeah. For you to stop being such a horse's rear end, for starters."

The engine died. He got out and tromped toward her. She instinctively took a step back and stumbled over a large rock. The sudden motion made her catch her breath. The pain in her midsection never seemed to subside completely. She was afraid to take the drugs, afraid of a whole new level of addiction. Alex must have seen the pain on her face. He took her arm, his fingers warm against her skin. "Sorry, I didn't mean to hurt you. Are you all right?"

"You didn't mean to hurt me?" Deborah jerked away from his touch. "So you don't think you're hurting me by being so unforgiving and distant, for bailing out when it got a little rough?"

"A little rough? You took on a murdering gangbanger by yourself when all you had to do was wait a minute or two more and we'd have been there to take him out. It could've ended without gunfire, without a bullet in your gut. You endangered yourself, those kids, Baker, Cooper, and me by trying to act like a one-woman show. Cops back each other up by sticking to the plan. Friends back each other up. You and me . . . we . . . you should've . . ."

"You know Frankie would've given me away." Deborah leaned in a little closer, in his space, but not touching him. She'd come a long way, but not that far. "I couldn't wait. You *know* that."

He breathed hard, panting like he'd been running. "I know. I know. You're right. I'm sorry. It's just . . . there should've been another way."

"But there wasn't." She needed for them to be all right. "Let it go so we can get on with . . . things."

"Deborah." He smoothed back thick windblown hair with two shaking hands. "I can't. Don't you see, I —"

"I do see." Deborah threw her hands up in the air. "You're scared. You're scared of making a commitment. You're scared of giving it a shot and then being left alone. Welcome to the club, Luna."

"Alex." He glowered at her. "And I'm not scared. Just . . . wary. So sue me."

"Scared! Me, too. More than you can imagine, but you're the first guy in my life who's made me want to at least try. I thought you wanted to try, too."

Alex swiped at his face with the back of his hand, his gaze on the ground. Finally, he looked up at her, his eyes black with emotion. "I can't have any more people I love leave me."

That was it, his need and his fear lay bare at Deborah's feet. The raw agony in his voice propelled her another half-step forward. "I can't make any promises. No one can. But I'm willing to depend on God to see us through this, if you are."

Conflicting emotions chased each other across his face. He sighed as if he'd been holding his breath. "You won't freak on me?"

"I can't guarantee I won't freak." Ignoring quivering fear, she forced herself to reach for his hand. "In fact, there's a good chance I will."

His hand met hers halfway. His grip was gentle. "You're going to make me crazy, aren't you?"

"More than usual? Probably."

"This is nuts." He slid his fingers between hers so they were entwined and then kissed her cheek, a feather of a kiss. "God help us both."

Deborah tightened her hold on his hand. "He will."

ABOUT THE AUTHOR

Born in Abilene, Kansas, **Kelly Irvin** moved to the Texas-Mexico border town of Laredo to work as a journalist after graduating from the University of Kansas. A stint in El Paso garnered her the love of her life — photographer Tim Irvin — and more border fodder for her fiction. In 1989, she moved to San Antonio, a city of rich multicultural heritage that she now calls home. In 2010, she published her first novel, *A Deadly Wilderness.* A public relations professional, Kelly is also the mother of two phenomenal young adults. To learn more about Kelly's books, go to www.kellyirvin .com.

The employees of Thorndike Press hope you have enjoyed this Large Print book. All our Thorndike, Wheeler, and Kennebec Large Print titles are designed for easy reading, and all our books are made to last. Other Thorndike Press Large Print books are available at your library, through selected bookstores, or directly from us.

For information about titles, please call:
(800) 223-1244

or visit our Web site at:
http://gale.cengage.com/thorndike

To share your comments, please write:
Publisher
Thorndike Press
10 Water St., Suite 310
Waterville, ME 04901